DEVIOUS MEASURES

MIKAEL CARLSON

WARRINGTON
PUBLISHING

Danbury, Connecticut

Novels by Mikael Carlson:

– The Michael Bennit Series –
The iCandidate
The iCongressman
The iSpeaker
The iAmerican

– Tierra Campos Thrillers –
Justifiable Deceit
Devious Measures
Vital Targets
Revealed Secrets
Decisive Endgame

– Watchtower Thrillers –
The Eyes of Others
The Eyes of Innocents
The Eyes of Victims

– The America, Inc. Saga–
The Black Swan Event
Bounded Rationality
Boiling the Ocean

For Joe Forte

PROLOGUE

"S.O.F."

Nashua, New Hampshire

Of all the surprises he planned to execute before the primary, this is the first and most dangerous. There are a lot of moving pieces and everything needs to go right for this to work. He checks the location of the car on the screen. So far, so good.

"Tell him to pick up the pace a little," Sartre says over the wireless earpiece. "He's cutting it too close."

Marx doesn't bother questioning Sartre's analysis. The two men have been together for a decade and trust each other implicitly. At this stage of the operation, mistrust is likely to lead them to failure.

"Mr. Spencer, you are trying my patience," Marx says into the burner phone. "The Mercedes AMG GT R coupe you're driving goes from zero to sixty in three and a half seconds and has five hundred and seventy-seven horsepower. Its top speed is almost two hundred miles per hour. You're driving it like an old lady."

"I'm not. I, uh…"

"I beg to differ. You understand what happens if you are not precisely where I tell you to be when I tell you to be there, correct?"

"We can talk this through. I have money. I can pay you."

"Rich people crack me up. Money is the only thing you think about. You think it can solve all your problems. It doesn't. In this case, it *caused* yours, Mr. Spencer."

"That's it. I'm not doing it!"

Marx hears brakes squealing through the phone a moment before the roaring engine becomes a purring idle. He shakes his head and sighs before reaching for the radio handset.

"Engels, you're a go. Entry only."

"Roger."

"We don't have time for this, Marx," Sartre says.

"I can see the clock, thank you very much. Do you have eyes on the target, Trot?"

"Roger. He's parked about a hundred meters from the target. It looks like he's crying."

"Yeah, that sounds about right. Sartre, pipe the video feed from Engels to your site."

Marx takes a deep breath. He has one shot at this. He stares at the video feed streaming into his console as Engels breaches the house. The alarm was previously deactivated. So long as nobody gets up for a glass of water, Engels shouldn't run into any issues.

"Mr. Spencer, while you're sitting there whimpering like a spoiled brat, let me remind you of the stakes and assure you that I'm not bluffing. I just texted you a hyperlink to a site with a video feed. You conduct business on the dark web, so I know that you have a Tor browser to view it. Use that to open it."

"At the top of the stairs," Engels reports.

"Hold there."

"He opened the link. His eyes are the size of dinner plates," Trotsky informs him.

"Yes, Mr. Spencer, that is your house. You see what is about to happen. Left or right? Who do you want to die first? Your wife or your children?"

"No, no, no," he says, crying. "Please don't."

"You can still save them. Pull forward onto the tracks."

"One minute," Sartre says. "The gates will come down at any moment."

"If your car isn't moving in five seconds, your family dies one-by-one, and you get to watch. And then you will die anyway. Make your choice."

Marx leans back as he watches the digital timer on his other screen tick off five seconds. What a scumbag. He is so vain that he's willing to sacrifice his own wife and children. They're better off without him either way.

"Time's up. Start with the wife. Then you can take your time with the kids."

The video moves down the hall to the master bedroom. Everything is bathed in the green hue of night vision as Engels slowly creeps to the door.

"Did you know that the human eye can distinguish more shades of green than any other color? It's amazing how much detail these night vision devices capture. Do you want to see how blood shows up in them?"

"No, please don't! I'll do it. I'm moving."

"Car in motion," Trot reports.

"Forty-five seconds out," Sartre adds.

"Leave the car in drive, brakes applied. Do not place it in park. Do you understand, Mr. Spencer?"

"Ye-yes," he says through his tears.

"Crossing gates are coming down."

"Don't hurt my family. Please."

"If you sit there for another thirty seconds, we won't touch your family. You have my word."

Marx watches the timer as it dwindles closer to zero. Each second is another step closer to success. All he needs to do is bear with this insufferable elitist for a few moments longer.

"Why are you doing this? Who are you?"

"I'm just a concerned citizen."

"He's on the target. Point of no return."

"Heavy braking. Decelerating."

Marx smiles at the two reports. Nothing can stop it now.

"Who are you!" Dylan Spencer screams.

"Nobody of consequence. You have done a great service to your nation, Mr. Spencer. Know that your sacrifice will not be in vain."

Marx hears a scream as the video on the phone switches to a long shot of the railroad tracks. The fully loaded twelve-thousand-ton train slams into the three-thousand-seven-hundred-pound supercar, rupturing the vehicle's gas tank and igniting a fireball as it's pushed down the tracks.

He's seen this same picture play out in movies and is surprised how similar the two are. The fireball was smaller here, though. That was disappointing. At least the result wasn't.

"Goodbye, Mr. Spencer," Marx mumbles. "Wrap it up men, our work is done."

Trot terminates his video. Engels leaves his feed enabled as he exits the house, disconnecting it only when he has cleared out of the back yard. Marx can finally allow himself to relax. The men will be back to the safehouse before long, and the authorities will be left with a tragic accident to clean up.

He stops the recording. Everything went according to plan. He reaches over to another phone and types a quick text message to Machiavelli: MISSION ACCOMPLISHED. PHASE ONE COMPLETE.

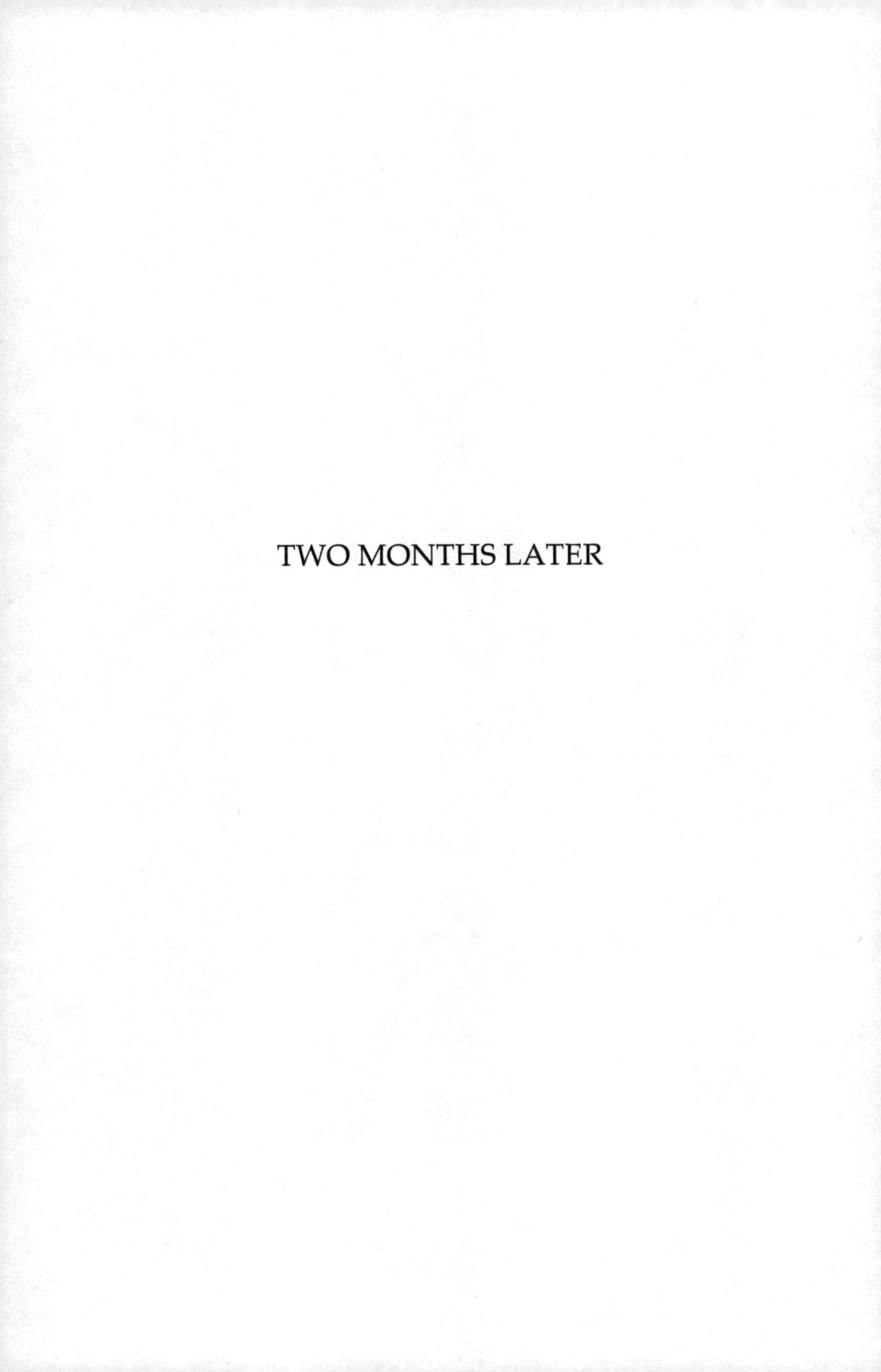

TWO MONTHS LATER

CHAPTER ONE

CAPITOL BEAT

Cable News Studio
Washington, D.C.

9 Days to the New Hampshire Democratic Primary

Tierra likes to close her eyes during the break. It helps her focus on the delivery instead of just reading the words that appear on the teleprompter. The first time she did it, the production staff thought she had fallen asleep. The executive producer panicked and started screaming in her ear to wake up. After a week, they are used to it.

"Welcome back to *Capitol Beat.* The Iowa Caucuses, the first hurdle in the race to the presidential nomination for both parties, will soon be in the rear-view mirror. National attention is turning to the upcoming primaries in New Hampshire, where the races are much closer, and I'm turning my attention to my final thought.

"This election year has started as expected. Both party favorites are ahead in the polls leading up to the Iowa caucuses. Governor Burgess of Illinois is ahead in his back yard in the Democratic contest, and Republican frontrunner Colin Bradford is pulling away in a battle that most thought would be tighter. When the race shifts to New Hampshire, Senator Alicia Standish is expected to stop Burgess's momentum, and Bradford is expected to win his second contest. Everything is going as expected. So why does it feel so wrong?

"The death of megadonor Dylan Spencer in a tragic accident in Nashua two months ago was the first in a series of strange incidents that have cast a dark shadow over this election year. Campaigns in both major parties have been accused of shady tactics, intimidation, and outright fraud. The war of words between candidates has devolved from policy disagreements to hostile personal attacks.

"Desperate campaigns using dirty tricks in American politics is as old as our Republic. The twenty-four-hour news cycle and prolific social media usage have taken the rumors and innuendo from taverns and meeting houses to the devices in our pockets. If our public discourse turns into an old episode of the *Jerry Springer Show*, then we are in for a long nine months."

Tierra changes cameras and gives a slight smile, mimicking a move that the long-time host she is filling in for mastered decades ago. The show was sure to make her first few "final thoughts" segments upbeat and optimistic so that the audience could see her smile. Now they will observe how viewers react to a slightly more depressing synopsis.

"That is my final thought, and it's for the record. Wilson Newman returns tomorrow. Thank you for watching *Capitol Beat*, I'm Tierra Campos. Good night."

The producer calls them out, and the staff gives her a warm applause. From the back of the studio emerges Wilson Newman, beaming like a proud father.

"Wilson? What are you doing here? Your vacation doesn't end until tomorrow."

"Did you think I wasn't going to come to see you live at least once?"

"You own a television, which you should be watching in Aruba."

"I went to Turks and Caicos, but nobody cares. You did a fantastic job this week, Tierra. You're a natural."

She blushes a little. The journalist has never been good at taking compliments. The hardest thing about the notoriety she's earned since Ethan Harrington's arrest for the Brockhampton massacre is accepting the accolades that come with it. The reporting was more of a team effort than is acknowledged, and the praise makes her uncomfortable.

"Thank you, Wilson. You're too kind. It felt like I was forcing it."

"You didn't come across that way at all. You'll get the hang of it."

"I was only filling in for you this week."

"Yeah."

Tierra squints at the tone of that single word. Wilson Newman is one of America's most respected journalists. The constant drumbeat of daily programs and grit of modern politics has worn him down. He needed a vacation, but everyone knows he's looking farther down the road than that.

"What aren't you telling me, Wilson?"

"They're ready for you in the conference room," one of the producers informs him.

"I'll be right there. Walk with me, Tierra. Do you remember our first interview after Ethan Harrington was arrested, and the Safe America Act failed?" Wilson asks as they make their way out of the studio.

"Like it was yesterday."

She could never forget. Her reporting on the motives and coverup in the worst school shooting in American history made her a household name. The articles run by *Front Burner* with her byline set Internet news records. It made her a lock to win a Peabody Award when results are announced in April and is considered a definite favorite for a Pulitzer Prize in online journalism when they make their announcement in May.

Tierra paid the price to get there. There are no physical scars from the home invasion and assault at the hands of two men under the employ of Ryan Baino, the now incarcerated head of the political action committee Action Not Prayers. The psychological wounds have taken longer to heal. The process of restoring her reputation after the identity theft that Ethan Harrington arranged is taking even longer.

"You were my first choice to take over this show before we went to our first commercial break."

"And I told you that I never wanted to see you retire," Tierra says, recalling the conversation.

"There are two things I know as a fact that cannot be stopped: politicians from lying and the steady march of time."

"Not true. Black holes slow time."

Wilson laughs. He loves this young woman. She has an answer for everything, and it's always a good one.

"Fair point, although even a black hole will not stop my retirement."

Tierra stops in the corridor before they reach the main conference room. Wilson turns to see her eyes full of realization and pain.

"I'm retiring this year, Tierra. I want you to take my chair."

"Wilson, I don't know what to say."

"A year ago, you were reporting on the algae growing in the reflecting pools on the National Mall. *Front Burner* showed incredible talent recognition when they rescued you from that, but it's a waste of your talent. You belong here. *Capitol Beat* is the most successful political news program in American history. Say that you will. Otherwise, I'm going to have to give it up to the guy the corporate brass likes."

"Who?"

Wilson frowns and gestures behind her. Tierra turns and is hit in the face with successive waves of horror and nausea. She thought it reeked of ambition and cheap cologne in this corridor. She was right.

"Hello, Tierra. It's great seeing you again."

"Good evening, Carl."

Before she had even heard the name Brockhampton, there were two people Tierra had voodoo dolls of. The first was her sadistic fifth-grade gym teacher who laughed every time she was beaned in the face playing dodgeball. The second was the anchor of WWDC's flagship news program, Carl Brennan.

"What's it been, Tierra, almost a year?" he asks as if they were long-time friends.

"I didn't realize the two of you knew each other," the executive producer says.

"Yes, we had a tussle or two in the office when I was at WWDC. Don't you remember, Carl?"

The smile falls off his face. The last interaction Tierra shared with Carl was when he was manhandling her in a news studio in front of thirty people. It's the last thing he wants to rehash now.

"It was great seeing you again," Carl says, walking with the producers into the conference room.

"Are you kidding me with this?"

"I wish I were," Wilson says. "You are my first pick. Carl Brennan is the backup plan in case you turn us down."

"When is my interview?" she asks, watching Carl kissing the asses of the men dressed in suits on the other side of the conference room table.

"You just finished it ten minutes ago."

Tierra is rocked by a feeling of déjà vu. That was almost exactly how Austin Christos made an offer for her current job. She started her career in television after graduating from college. The move to online journalism for the investigative arm of *Front Burner* was an exciting new direction. She was hoping that filling in for Wilson occasionally would last for a while. The thought of now choosing between the two is unbearable.

"I work for *Front Burner*, Wilson. They've been nothing but great to me since the day I joined."

"I know. I wish I didn't have to put you in this position. I know the decision is going to be agonizing, but you'll have to make one."

"How long do I have?"

"My last broadcast will be Election Night. They are going to want my replacement ready by the party conventions this summer, so a decision needs to be made by June. That gives you about two months to let them know."

Tierra and Wilson say their goodbyes, and she heads to makeup to get hers removed. Her head is swimming, in disbelief that they are even considering Carl Brennan. It would have been easier for her to say no if they weren't. Maybe that was part of their plan and, if it was, it's working. She doesn't know what to do.

CHAPTER TWO

SENATOR ALICIA STANDISH

The Hawkeye Hotel & Conference Center by Imperial
Des Moines, Iowa

Alicia has never understood what makes Iowa's caucus so important. It is a quiet, mostly agricultural state that's over ninety percent white and doesn't represent a diverse cross-section of America. Despite the disaster her party experienced during the 2020 caucuses when the results couldn't be accurately tallied, it still maintains its status as the essential first test of support for candidates. The media proclaims that middle-American Iowan support for a candidate is an accurate barometer of how they will fare with the rest of the nation. Alicia isn't so sure.

"You can't leave before the polls close," Angela says, shooting down the half-hearted proposal that the senator put forth to her team. "You need to get out there tomorrow, show your face and give a speech. We can fly to New Hampshire immediately following that."

"It was just a thought. I'm not going to win here. It's Burgess's back yard."

"Yes, Illinois borders the state, so he has the name recognition and shares the same Midwestern values. He won't lose, but he can underachieve. That's our target."

"Poll numbers back that up," her pollster declares. "You have name recognition, too. If he doesn't meet the margin of victory the media expects, it's as good as a win for you."

"Plus, the more delegates you earn, the closer you are to the promised land," Angela finishes.

Angela Mays has never run a national race. With her impeccable credentials, it was a travesty that Alicia quickly corrected before most other candidates even formed exploratory committees to run for president. Angela has incredible political instincts and is straight with the truth, even when it isn't easy to hear. That's why the senator trusts her.

The fallout from the arrest of her allies Ethan Harrington and Ryan Baino nudged her fledgling campaign to the edge of the abyss. A political disaster of that magnitude would have been terminal for most candidates. History is replete with those who crashed and burned over far less. Angela helped her regain her footing and kept her in the race.

"Plus, we don't want to look too eager to get to New Hampshire," Michael Ross says, staring over his reading glasses. "That's your back yard, and the same applies in reverse."

"All the more reason to get there as soon as possible. I read the polls. I'm winning, but my support there is faltering."

Angela and Michael share a look. Since her legislative failure last summer freed the senator up to focus on her campaign, she has spoken to over fifty thousand people in the Granite State and hosted seventy-five events across all ten counties. Despite the effort at the expense of states like South Carolina, Nevada, and Iowa, her approval numbers there haven't budged. She still holds the lead in the state, but Burgess is coming up fast as other candidates begin to fade.

"It's not faltering, Senator," Michael explains. "It just isn't growing as fast as we'd like."

"It isn't growing at all. We have twenty thousand volunteers in the state. I've raised a small fortune to spend. Explain to me why we're stuck at thirty-seven percent when I used to be at sixty."

"Brockhampton."

Alicia stares at Michael. The failure of the Safe America Act still hurts, and not because of the negative effect on her candidacy. She was days away from getting the most impressive gun control legislation ever proposed passed through a Republican Congress. Had Tierra Campos and that rogue FBI agent not found the truth about Ethan when they did, it would have. She may never forgive them for that. She certainly won't forgive Ethan for lying to her or Ryan Baino for ordering the assassination of her friend and ally, Landon Flynn.

"You said the polling would recover."

"And it will," Angela says, "but during the primary process, not before it. You need a strong second here. That shows America that the party is moving past what happened last summer. Let's skip New Hampshire for a moment. Nevada is a toss-up. A win is a bonus, but you just need to keep it close.

"You're up in South Carolina, but a majority of the population is black, and Burgess can leverage that if he makes the contest about race. If you win there, it gives you the momentum going into Super Tuesday. Thirteen states and American Samoa go to the polls, with California and Texas being the prizes."

"Our internal polling indicates that whoever leads the polls going into those two races is likely to have the edge," Michael adds. "If you win Texas and California and take at least five other races, you are the clear frontrunner and have the easiest path to the nomination. The party will coalesce around you, and we can shift our focus onto whomever the GOP ends up supporting."

Alicia leans back in her chair. Her top advisors aren't telling her anything she doesn't already know. The difference is, the senator had already mentally chalked New Hampshire in the win column. She can drive there from her Cambridge home in less than an hour. Losing that state, even after failing to pass the Safe America Act, is inconceivable.

"And you think New Hampshire is the key to all of it?"

"I do," Angela says. "You have to win New Hampshire to have a chance. If you underperform, the road gets rockier. If you lose, it's game over. You'll be on the stump trying to unite the party behind Governor Burgess this fall."

"And the others?"

"The third-tier pretenders will all be out after Iowa or New Hampshire, and the second-tier longshots will fold after Super Tuesday," Michael concludes. "The financial well is already drying up for many of them. They won't have the resources to run a national race, and that's what Super Tuesday is all about."

"We finish strong here and then move on to Manchester," Angela says.

"There's one more thing," Michael says, easing up on his seat on the couch and leaning forward, his hands clasped in front of him. "You have to bring your A-game, Senator. There is no room for error. Mistakes are fatal at this point."

"Thanks for the tip," Alicia sneers, not appreciating the lecture about the obvious.

"And Brian Cooper can't make any mistakes either."

Alicia knows where this is coming from. Angela wasn't thrilled with the decision to make him the New Hampshire for Standish campaign chairman. There were good reasons to do it, especially considering his political contacts in the state. After the *Front Burner* articles and FBI clearing her of any responsibility for Ethan and Ryan's deceit and crimes surrounding the massacre and its aftermath, she decided to give him one last shot.

"You run the campaign, Angela. Talk to him."

"I have. It needs to come from you."

"Fine. If there's nothing else, then I'll see you tomorrow."

Alicia rises from the couch, causing her staff to do the same. It's going to be a long day tomorrow, and she needs to get her rest. The challenge will be turning her brain off so that she can sleep. Her mind is racing. After months of campaigning, the first test is finally here.

CHAPTER THREE

SPECIAL AGENT VICTORIA LARSEN

New England Regional Computer Forensics Laboratory
Chelsea, Massachusetts

8 Days to the New Hampshire Democratic Primary

Victoria doesn't spend much time in this part of the building. The New England Regional Computer Forensics Laboratory exists to assist federal, state, and local agencies in enforcing criminal laws related to computer crimes. The technicians here can examine and extract data from digital media ranging from computers to mobile devices. It's the latter she's interested in.

"Attention on deck! We have FBI nobility in the room!" Miranda exclaims before bowing at the waist as Victoria shakes her head, smiling at the effort.

"You're mixing U.S. Navy and British royal family protocol again."

"It's to be expected. I don't know a damn thing about either."

"Your email said you had something for me?"

"I do. I know you're the queen bee around the Bureau now, but you must have pulled some serious strings for this. This was a New Hampshire State Police request."

Computer Forensic Examiners work in one of the sixteen FBI Regional Computer Forensics Laboratories. The Chelsea office Victoria has called home since her graduation from Quantico is one of them. The lab assists other law enforcement when requested. The evidence and information from those investigations are often not shared with the FBI.

"The Massachusetts State Police helped arrange it. They owe me a favor or two."

"That's true," Miranda says. "You saved their bacon on the Brockhampton case if you'll pardon the politically incorrect pun."

"What do you have?" Victoria asks, ignoring the accolades. She still isn't used to them in the wake of her investigation up there.

Miranda grins. "His phone was thrown from the car upon impact. It wouldn't have survived an impact with a steel locomotive if it hadn't been. The model was an iPhone 11 Pro Max."

"I don't care about the device, Miranda. I want to know what was on it."

"Patience, Queen V. I'm getting to it. The phone was beaten up, but I pulled some data from it. It's all in this report."

Victoria begins leafing through the report. Nothing looks out of the ordinary. Mostly just business discussions and news and financial app usage.

"What are you looking for?"

"I don't know yet. Anything that sticks out."

"Well, you're not helpful, so I'll tell you what wasn't on there: porn, dirty pictures of his wife, or anything that links him to the commission of a crime. By all accounts, Dylan Spencer was a stand-up guy. Impressive, considering he was a multi-billionaire. It's a shame about the car."

Victoria purses her lips and shakes her head. He was wealthy beyond imagination and a political power broker who funded a boatload of cash to Democratic political action committees and campaigns. She would bet her salary that he has skeletons stashed in a closet somewhere.

"There was nothing unusual in his text messages?"

"It was all bad yogurt," Miranda says, waving a hand and earning a confused look from Victoria. "Plain vanilla. SMS messages were sent to business contacts and family members. Nothing out of the ordinary. Your turn, Queen V. Why the interest?"

Victoria continues paging through the report. "I checked his phone records. Dylan Spencer was on a call when the train hit."

"Okay, that's odd for a suicide. Who was he talking to?"

"That's the question, isn't it? I don't know. It wasn't family or a close friend. Here's the catch – the call was inbound and made from an untraceable pre-paid cellular phone. Wait, what's this last text he received?"

"It's a hyperlink to a dark net address. We checked it and got nothing but a blank page. I asked some of the team to track it down, but don't expect much. It's called the dark web for a reason. Is it important?"

Victoria sighs. "I'm not sure, but it was sent less than a minute before he drove on the tracks and waited for death. Let me know if they find anything. Thanks for this, Miranda."

"Anything for you, your Highness," she says with another awkward bow and a smile.

Victoria is lost in thought as she returns to her floor and crashes into the chair at her desk. She stares at the framed picture of her and Tierra. It was taken a couple of months after the arrests of Ethan Harrington, Ryan Baino, and the Mayfields.

The reward for her persistence earned her accolades, but only after she was stalked by the state police, shot at by thugs, and arrested for attempted murder. That harrowing journey began with a tingle at the back of her neck that something wasn't right. It was a once-in-a-lifetime thing, or so she thought.

"The last time I saw that look on your face, you ended up with a state warrant for your arrest," Special Agent Takara Nishimoto says, taking it upon himself to sit on the corner of her desk. "Is this about the Spencer suicide?"

"I don't call it that, but yes."

Takara shakes his head. "You love delving into cases not assigned to you, don't you?"

"Call it a hobby. Needlepoint didn't work out for me."

"Aren't you working on the Alvarez case?"

"Takara, you aren't my boss, and sure as hell aren't my mother."

He holds his hands up in surrender. "I'm just looking out for you. When you decided to stay in the FBI, I made that my mission."

Victoria's eyes settle on a spot on the floor. She wasn't coming back. When she left the range after her reinstatement to the Bureau, she wasn't sure if it was for the last time. After not being able to justify the actions of law enforcement to the families of the students who lost their lives that day, she decided that she was done. She only changed her mind when she realized that without her, they never would have gotten the answers they deserved.

"Don't fret. The boy wonder is all over Alvarez."

"Aren't you lucky?"

Special Agent Ian Drucker is fresh out of Quantico and about as eager as they come. She was the same way when she first arrived here. Sleep was optional, and there was no stone she wasn't willing to leave unturned. Ambition is a better drug than anything you can buy on the street.

"Hey, you've worked some strange cases in the past."

"To say the least," Takara moans.

"How many of them were suicides where the subject was on the phone at the time of his death? A nineteen-minute call not to a parent, spouse, family member, or friend, but received from a burner phone that only ended when a freight train ran him over."

"I've seen plenty of things that don't make sense, Vic. Sometimes they don't."

"And sometimes a school shooting victim knew it was going to happen and could have stopped it. I don't know if this is that, but I'll only call it a suicide after I know who he was talking to."

Victoria's unauthorized investigation into Ethan Harrington helped Tierra Campos and *Front Burner* expose a fraud that may be unmatched in American history outside of the Watergate break-in during the Nixon administration. Victoria knows that Takara is right: things don't always add up, but it doesn't mean you don't do the math.

"Okay, I'll play your game. Let's assume it wasn't a suicide. There's nothing I've seen about Spencer's dealings that justifies murder. He wasn't having an affair, and his business dealings are legitimate and on the level. He had enemies, like just about anyone loaded and politically active, but none that would want him dead. Unless you know something that I don't?"

"No. It just doesn't feel right," Victoria says, rubbing the bridge of her nose.

"I've learned the hard way not to question your instincts. Just be careful this time. Despite your rock star status, there's a limit to the latitude Fuller will give you."

Takara eases himself off her desk and gives her a pat on the shoulder before moving off. He's right. She has some leeway, but that won't be enough to let her chase white rabbits down dark holes. Fuller isn't going to let her run with this unless she can find something concrete. She stares at the link Dylan Spencer received in his last text. That's the only thread she has found to pull.

CHAPTER FOUR

ANDREW LI

The Prairie Rose Hotel
Des Moines, Iowa

Governor Luther Burgess lays his overcoat and suit jacket over the back of the couch before finding the softest cushion he can settle into. Andrew and Isiah opt for the sofa and one of the high-backed chairs. The rest of the staff stays standing for this meeting.

"Are we really going to do this now?" the governor asks, rubbing his eyes from the lack of sleep. "We have three more rallies today and another five thousand hands to shake in the freezing cold."

"Running for president is an epic journey designed to separate the contenders from the pretenders," Andrew says.

"Could that journey have run through Florida in January instead of Iowa?"

Andrew smiles. He is a national campaign veteran, this being the third one he's been a part of. He's never wanted to be a campaign manager, despite the early successes getting congressmen elected in races they were losing. He likes the strategy side of things, and consulting pays much better.

"We need to talk about New Hampshire," Isiah Burgess interjects.

"Aren't we still in Iowa, son?"

"You're going to win Iowa, Pops."

Luther looks at Andrew, who nods. "So long as you don't do anything dumb in the next twenty-four hours."

"By how much?"

"Not enough for my tastes," Isiah mumbles.

Isiah Burgess, the headstrong son of a career politician who spent his entire life preparing for this moment, will never be satisfied with where they are. The seven-point lead in Iowa needs to be ten, and they need to be winning big in South Carolina, given the demographics. Andrew has a plan for all that, but Isiah lacks patience.

"You're going to meet expectations here," Andrew says. "You'll split the delegates and take a small lead into New Hampshire. That's what Isiah wants to talk about."

"Standish is expected to win in a landslide there. Most of New Hampshire's population is close enough to Massachusetts to shop for groceries there. She has the name recognition and the Northeastern pedigree to be unbeatable."

"Like us here. I get it. What are you saying?" the elder Burgess asks, sitting up a little straighter on the couch.

"We can win the nomination with a win in New Hampshire," Isiah says.

The governor shifts his stare to Andrew, who looks at him impassively. The consultant has already briefed the candidate on this, so it's old news. What he doesn't know is what the campaign manager has in mind.

"Okay, are there any other miracles you need me to order up, Isiah?"

"Pops, we don't need a miracle. Alicia Standish is damaged goods. She blew the Safe America Act and compounded that failure by allying herself with the Harrington kid and the psycho running Action Not Prayers. She should be winning the state in a landslide, but she isn't. She's vulnerable."

"Your son is right on that account, sir. Standish's lead has been slowly dwindling for months there. Despite spending more time in New Hampshire than a Massachusetts resident should have, she's losing support. All she's managed to do is remind voters that she couldn't get her signature legislation across the finish line, and make them question her decision-making skills."

"I assume you have some grand plan to squeeze out a win there?"

"Can you all excuse us for a few moments?" Isiah asks the gathered staffers. "Thank you. You can stay, Andrew."

The staff leaves the suite, and Isiah waits until the door is closed.

"Was that necessary? I trust every one of them."

"Not for this. If you want to beat Standish, you need to be willing to hit her hard, repeatedly, and where it hurts most."

"Isiah, I know you pay closer attention to what I say than that. I've challenged her on a host of issues: Medicare for All, free tuition, increased taxes on high-wage earners… I stopped just short of calling her a Republican at the Iowa debate because of her weak stances."

"That's not good enough, Pops. The party knows where you both stand on the issues. The establishment will choose her over you every time. They've proven that again and again. You need to win big to secure the nomination. That starts with trouncing Alicia Standish."

Luther rises from the couch and heads to the bar to pour himself a soda. He quit drinking years ago and vowed never to touch alcohol again. Cola, with a squeeze of lime, is his poison now. Unfortunately, his doctor and his waistline both object. He doesn't like the sugar-free stuff.

"You want me to go negative. That's a bold move, son. What do you think, Andrew?" the governor asks.

"Negative advertising suppresses voter turnout, particularly for Independents who can vote in the open primary. That's an advantage for us since they favor Standish by fifteen points, but it will hurt us in the rest of the primaries and the general election. It's an enormous risk."

"'Never was anything great achieved without danger,'" Isiah says. "It won't matter for the primaries after we win New Hampshire. Voters have a short attention span. They won't remember the attacks by the time we reach the convention."

Luther sits back down on the couch and takes a sip from his Coke before setting it on the end table. He strokes his chin in thought. Isiah taps his foot impatiently but remains silent.

"When I was running to become an alderman in Chicago, I was approached by an older woman in a bar. I had a bad day and didn't really want to talk to anyone, but that wasn't about to stop her. She pulled up a stool and sat next to me. I asked if I could help her and she said, 'You're a fool. Do you want to know why? You're trying to be something you're not. That's why you're so bad at this.'

"She patted me on the shoulder and left. I thought she was talking about being a politician. She wasn't. She was talking about me attacking my opponent."

"Pops, I—"

"She was right. I focused on my message and won. Love trumps hate, and optimism beats pessimism every time. I have spent my entire political career trying to build a better world. I have no interest in changing that now."

"Andrew, if we lose New Hampshire, Nevada, and South Carolina, what happens?" Isiah asks.

"The two big prizes on Super Tuesday are California and Texas. The winner of the previous races controls the outcome, and Standish will have won three of four."

"And if she wins Texas and California?"

"Depending on the size of the victory, it would be difficult to gain enough delegates to beat her in the remaining races. She would be the presumptive nominee. The pressure to drop out to prepare for the general election would be enormous."

"So, if we lose the next three races, is there a way to win without going negative?"

Andrew shifts uncomfortably. As a political consultant, he's had to answer difficult questions for candidates before. This is no different. He knows where Isiah is leading him but won't lie to avoid following him there. His job is to provide insight and strategies, not insist on getting his way.

"No."

"Pops, 'the wise man does at once what the fool does finally.' It's your campaign and your choice. I just don't want you running into another old woman six months from now who asks why you weren't willing to do what you needed to make a difference in her life."

Isiah gets up and lets the staff back into the room on his way out of the suite. Andrew watches as the aging governor takes another sip from his soda. This is his one and only shot at the presidency. A decision like this will make or break his chances.

"What do you want me to do, sir?"

"Give me a day to think about it. Let's just get through today."

CHAPTER FIVE

"S.O.F."

Granite State University
Durham, New Hampshire

Marx hates college campuses. He's the kind of man who values intellect but not higher learning. In his experience, the more prestigious and expensive the school, the worse the education. He got his intelligence by reading every book that he could get his hands on, and through learning the hard lessons that life often provides.

"I'm in place," Trot says through the tiny earpiece fitted inside Marx's ear.

"Roger. Classes are adjourning. Make contact and execute," Marx whispers into the microphone concealed in his sleeve as he carefully scratches the false nose he's wearing.

Anonymity is a warm blanket, but not always practical for missions. This one requires close personal contact, and neither Trot nor he can afford being identified. That required them to don a believable disguise created by a professional makeup artist who could keep her mouth shut.

"Contact," Trot says, stalking his quarry on the other side of the campus.

Marx looks around as students begin pouring out of the classroom building. He hopes he picked the right exit. It's the one that is closest to her dorm, so it's the safest bet. That assumption is validated as she exits the building and starts down the long sidewalk.

Marx falls in behind her, making up the ground between them as they walk. She lights a cigarette and plants herself on a park bench to smoke it. Thank God for designated smoking areas. Once he learned about her habit, he knew he would get an opportunity.

"Hi there," he says, sitting on the bench next to her, careful to stay far enough away as not to appear too sketchy.

"Hey."

"You're a big Burgess supporter," Marx says, nodding at all the campaign paraphernalia adorning her jacket and bag.

"What gave it away?" she says, turning her head away from him to show disinterest.

"It was in the file I read about you, Leila."

That gets her attention. Her head snaps back to face him so fast that he thought it may career off her shoulders.

"How do you know my name?" she asks.

"Didn't you tell me?"

"No, I didn't."

"I suppose you didn't tell me that you were just in Introduction to Philosophy class or have Modern Political Thought in an hour and a half. I think your class schedule is a little too heavy in liberal arts. You should think about taking a science class or two to round it out."

"I don't know who you are, creep, but I'm done with this."

"Fine," he says, as she begins to walk away. "I'll continue this conversation with Wanda and your stepfather, Marco. I know they're both at work at the hair studio and auto shop now, but they should be home on Holman Street in Laconia after work. Or maybe I can speak to your little brother following his band practice after school."

"How do you know about my family?"

"Sit."

She looks around, unsure of what to do. Marx gives her a moment to decide before running out of patience.

"It wasn't a suggestion, Leila. Sit."

"Who are you? What do you want?"

"I'm a concerned citizen. What I want is for you to rethink your support for Luther Burgess."

"Why would I do that?" Leila asks, contempt dripping from her mouth.

Marx takes measure of the young woman. She's a fanatic. She dresses like one, speaks like one, and has the attitude of one. He could spend the next three months on this bench arguing with her and not cause her political needle to quiver. She's that dedicated.

"You're the president of the school group mustering support for Luther Burgess."

"And I'm proud to support him. You won't change that."

Marx smiles. "I have no doubt."

"Are we done?" she demands, standing again.

"Almost. You have a rally planned for this weekend ahead of Tuesday's primary and are leading a grassroots "get out the vote" effort to encourage students to cast ballots. You're going to cancel both."

"Why would I do that?"

Marx stands, and the pleasant smile he's forced since the beginning of this conversation disappears. She needs to know he's serious.

"Because if you don't, I will kill your entire family."

"What?" she asks, her eyes filling with fear. Leila's legs tremble as she takes a step back.

"You heard me. Home invasions are common in America today. If the rally happens as planned on Saturday, there will be at least one more. Can you live with that on your conscience?"

"How do I know this isn't some sort of ploy?" she asks, her voice quivering.

He rattled her, just as he knew he would. Her default attitude of defiance has been replaced with a much stronger emotion: fear. He nods back at the bench. She sits, her posture tight and guarded.

"Look me in the eyes and ask yourself if I look like the kind of man who doesn't make good on his word. If that's the conclusion you come to, then you have three funerals in your immediate future."

"And…and if the rally is canceled?" Leila asks, her voice cracking.

"Then you will all live your lives as God intended."

Marx rises from the bench and stares down at the terrified girl. She raises her head at him, tears forming in her eyes.

"I don't know if I can cancel it. If I try, my partner will pick up where I left off."

"*Gatsby*," Trot says in his ear. The code word lets Marx know that his counterpart's mission was successful.

"Travis has been dealt with," Marx says, smiling at the timing as shock registers on the girl's face. "We'll be watching, Leila."

"What if one of the other students in our group tries to hold the rally?"

Marx turns his head back as he continues walking. "Then I suggest you find a way to stop them."

He takes an erratic, although not circuitous route through campus to the rally point with Trot. He removes his hat and coat. There is no reason to be obvious in case Leila has reported the incident to campus security. One down, three more to go. This is going to be a long day.

CHAPTER SIX

TIERRA CAMPOS

Front Burner Washington Office
Washington, D.C.

My return to the *Front Burner* office was a frosty one. I got congratulations from the rank and file reporters on the floor but was shunned by half of my own team. Olivia and Tyler were quick to ask me about the experience and were wondering what television is like. Their enthusiasm wasn't shared by the rest of the team.

Logan and Madison were almost hostile to me, not returning my greeting and going out of their way to avoid eye contact. Jerome was only slightly warmer, and Janey showed her usual indifference. The worst was Austin. He often swings by first thing just to chat. Today, he didn't emerge until lunchtime and breezed right past me. He's been locked in there with Tyler and Logan since his return. Only at a quarter to five when everyone else is about to leave does he emerge with them.

"We have an assignment," he says, without preamble.

"Please tell me it's alien abductions in Jamaica or a pickpocketing crisis on the French Riviera," Jerome says. He hates the cold weather more than I do.

"Think more north."

"I was afraid you were going to say that."

"There have been some developments in the Democratic race in New Hampshire. Logan?"

Logan connects his laptop to the office's large screen television. The team gathers around, pulling up chairs or sitting on desks. I stay seated at mine.

"Around noon today, the Burgess for America website was hacked. The text was changed from his policy issues to those of one of his opponents."

"Which one?" Madison asks.

Logan calls up jpegs of the site, and it's unmistakable. Pro-Standish propaganda is all over the page, including quotes of Burgess praising her and explaining how she would make a great president. I wonder if they're all attributable to him. I bet they are.

"How does a campaign allow this to happen?" Olivia asks. "It's an obvious target."

"Which is why they all take extraordinary measures to protect their sites. Somebody has incredible hacking skills."

"Okay, I get it, but is this our assignment?"

"Madison is right, boss. This kind of stuff isn't unique," Tyler adds.

"It's only the appetizer. I have a source in New Hampshire who told me that police reports were filed on college campuses for harassment of Burgess supporters."

"Okay…"

"To be specific, seven incidents on four different campuses happening within hours of each other. The five students who filed police reports all said the same thing: the men knew everything about them and their families…and he threatened to kill them if they didn't comply with their demands."

"Whoever did this had a lot of information on these kids," Logan offers. "They knew exactly where to find each of them. It takes time and resources to compile that kind of intelligence. That level of planning means they're organized and financed."

The group stays silent. They all think the same thing: it wasn't random targeting. Harassment and intimidation are not uncommon in election years, but rarely does it happen with a degree of military precision.

"They aren't ordinary students. Each is setting up rallies this weekend for Luther Burgess and involved in mustering the youth vote for him," Logan adds.

"The men were described in detail. They were wearing the same clothes and had the same facial features. A single incident is expected, but four different schools? That sounds like a coordinated effort."

"Coordinated by the campaign or another group?"

"I don't know, and that's what we need to find out. Tierra, Tyler, and Olivia will go up to investigate, assuming Tierra can pull herself away from her extracurricular activities at *Capitol Beat*. Find out what you can. You leave in the morning for Manchester. Arrangements will be made for you. Contact us once you get up there."

I'm so hot with anger right now that I could steam broccoli. The comment about *Capitol Beat* was not only unnecessary, but it was also petty and immature. The rest of the team noticed it, too. Half of them grinned with approval, and the other half look like they wanted to throw something at Austin. I'm not about to take it. I don't care if he's my boss.

"What the hell was that?" I ask, storming into his office.

"What was what?" he asks, shuffling some papers while standing behind his desk.

"Don't play games, Austin. It's childish, and you're better than that. I don't need you making snarky comments about *Capitol Beat*, especially in front of my colleagues."

"If you weren't doing the show, it wouldn't be a problem, would it?"

"Is that what this is about? I take a week of my personal vacation time to host, and you're bent out of shape about it?"

"I'm not bent out of shape about anything. If you want to moonlight on your own time, do it. It's not a problem until it becomes one. Then I'll solve it."

One of the most significant adjustments I needed to make going from television news at WWDC to print journalism is the inability to use tone. Natural voice inflections convey a message as effectively as words do. When writing an article, I present it much differently than I do on camera. I recognize that Austin's words were matter-of-fact, but his tone conveyed a much different message.

"What do you mean by that? I have a good imagination, and none of what comes to mind is particularly pleasant."

"It's exactly what it sounded like. Your job is with *Front Burner*. The moment your other career interferes with that, one of them will have to go. This job is demanding, and this team needs all its members to function. The moment that isn't the case, I have to act."

"What makes you think—"

"I know they offered you a position."

I'm stunned even though I shouldn't be. Washington is a big city with a small town's gossip network. Information travels fast here.

"I haven't made any decisions," I say, reflexively.

"Did you tell them 'no?' Because if you didn't, then you already have. You just haven't told me yet."

"I…I don't know what to say to that."

"You don't have to say anything. Get some rest before you leave for New England. We're going to keep you busy up there. Pull the door closed on your way out," Austin commands.

I'm not a petulant child, but I storm out of his office like one. It beats the alternative of picking up a chair and throwing it at him. I joined *Front Burner* because they were unique. It was a refreshing change from my experiences at WWDC television. Now I'm not so sure it's different after all, so I grab my stuff and get the hell out of this office before I explode.

CHAPTER SEVEN

CAPITOL BEAT

Cable News Studio
Washington, D.C.

Wilson feels like he's seen it all. He's been in journalism longer than most of his audience has been alive. Over that time, he's covered wars, historic events, and presidential and midterm elections going back to Ronald Reagan. He's watched the nature of campaigns change with the growing chasm dividing the electorate. They get nastier and nastier.

"Good Evening," he says, on cue from his set producer. "It is Monday, January thirty-first; I am Wilson Newman, and this…is…*Capitol Beat.*"

The short opening graphics roll, and the music plays. For Wilson, it's the parting of the curtain or the first pitch of a ballgame. The next hour is his time with America, and when this ride is over, it's what he'll miss most.

"On tonight's show, we have reports from the major campaigns of both parties. Our expert panel will discuss the Iowa Caucuses and what it means to the race for the Republican and Democratic nomination. We will also have the latest poll numbers from around the country, and a special report from the White House.

"But first, shady and malicious campaign tactics are as old as our Republic. During what was called the 'Brooks Brothers riot' during the Bush-Gore recount in 2000, hundreds of paid GOP operatives caused a disturbance outside a counting room in Miami-Dade County. Their actions forced the canvassing board to shut down the count.

"Fast forward to 2010. A Republican political operative recruited homeless people to run for various offices in Arizona on the Green Party ticket in the hopes that they would split the liberal vote in the state. But if you think that campaign shenanigans are limited to just the GOP, you'd be mistaken.

"In John F. Kennedy's first run for Congress in 1946, his father decided to bolster his son's chances in the primary. Joe Kennedy allegedly paid a man named Joseph Russo to run for the seat at the expense of the other Joseph Russo, who was already running in the primary.

"In the 2000 presidential race, false rumors were spread in South Carolina that John McCain's adopted Bangladeshi daughter was his illegitimate offspring. On the eve of the election, the Republican National Committee's website was hacked to display an anti-Bush message and a link to Al Gore's campaign website. It seems that history has repeated itself.

"Today, on the eve of the critically important Iowa Caucuses, the campaign website of Governor Luther Burgess of Illinois was hacked, and propaganda from one of his competitors was posted on it. As campaigns become more digital to keep pace with the Information Age, these kinds of unsavory tactics are becoming commonplace. Governor Luther Burgess is leading in the polls in Iowa, and that makes him a prime target, but nobody is immune."

Wilson changes his view over to camera two when the red light glowing above the one facing him clicks off. He takes a breath without making it evident to the viewers at home as he picks up where he left off on the teleprompter.

"The campaign is scrambling to figure out how their defenses were breached to ensure it doesn't happen again. There is little doubt that candidates of both political parties have their staffs working to ensure they don't meet the same fate. The reaction on social media was predictable. Senator Alicia Standish's supporters cheered the defacing while Burgess's own supporters lashed out at the tactic. They have a right to be upset.

"There is nothing more patriotic than the free exchange of ideas. There is nothing more American than our elections. Despicable actions like this are neither patriotic nor American. They're childish and foolhardy."

"*Easy, Wilson, don't ad-lib on this,*" his executive producer whispers into his earpiece. His EP knows he's angry and is trying to reel him in. Wilson fights off a scowl. He's too old to take orders from a Millennial.

"There is no evidence that links the intrusion to the Standish campaign, but they have yet to condemn the cyberattack on their opponent. Requests for comment from the campaign have gone unanswered. That's unacceptable in a Twitter world where reactions are often instantaneous, and we are continuing to reach out to the campaign for comment.

"Iowans go to the polls in twelve hours. Will this attack help sway their decision one way or the other? We will pose that question to our expert panel when we return from the break."

CHAPTER EIGHT

SENATOR ALICIA STANDISH

Gas 'N Go
Cedar Rapids, Iowa

The cold air hits her like a sledgehammer when she gets out of the car. A resident of Massachusetts has a natural defense against winter temperatures, but Alicia never developed that immunity. It's freezing out here.

Cedar Rapids is a two-hour drive from Des Moines, and despite standing for four hours before and after the rally, Alicia wants to stretch her legs before settling into the back seat for the drive back to the hotel. She seizes the stop for gas to make a long-overdue call to her New Hampshire campaign chairman.

'Good evening, Senator. How was the rally?" Brian Cooper asks after the call connects.

"It was okay. I had to cut short the meeting with the press when I found out someone hacked Burgess's website."

"I heard about that. It's terrible timing."

"And their campaign has been quick to blame us for the intrusion."

"Based on what evidence?"

"They didn't offer any."

"Naturally."

Alicia walks farther from the car to get out of the earshot of Michael and Angela. This conversation is at their request, but that doesn't mean they have to be privy to what is said.

"I'm going to lose in Iowa. Any chance I had disappeared when someone decided to deface the website. Middle Americans don't like that kind of thing. That makes New Hampshire critical."

"Yes, ma'am. We're working hard for you here," Brian ensures her.

"I'm sure you are, but that might not be enough."

"What do you mean?"

Alicia inhales a lungful of the cold Great Plains air. "You were my chief of staff. We have a long history, some of it good, some of it…not. What happened last summer…some think I took a big gamble by making you chairman up there."

"By *some people*, you mean Angela and Michael. That's why you're calling from outside your car instead of inside it where it's warm."

"How did you know I was outside?"

"Your teeth are chattering."

Alicia grins. Brian Cooper was a capable chief of staff who always gave her solid advice, even if she didn't heed it. He crossed a line on their walk down the National Mall that day, and that's why she dismissed him. Despite the loss of his position, he stayed loyal to her and supportive of her campaign. She's counting on that loyalty and wise counsel to win the New Hampshire Primary.

"I didn't accept this position to get back into your good graces, Senator. I took it because I have the contacts up here to deliver you a win in this state."

"My poll numbers are slipping."

"Yes, they are. New Hampshire is retail politics, and people don't like the merchandise they see in the window. You have likability issues and a trust deficit that you haven't overcome. Your advertisements aren't hitting those notes."

"Don't sugarcoat it for me or anything, Brian."

"I can paint you pictures of unicorns and rainbows if you want me to, but that won't help you win the presidency. You need to talk to Michael Ross about your messaging."

"I have."

"I'm sure he told you to talk to me, and that's why you called. Senator, I'm doing my part. I've set up the largest and most organized ground game in New Hampshire's primary history. The poll numbers don't matter right now. Who shows up to cast a ballot does. The energy around a campaign or a candidate is the difference between victory and defeat in this state. I've taken all the measures I can, and then some."

Alicia looks back at the car to see Angela and Michael looking in her direction. She knows they are as eager as she is to get back to Des Moines, but they can wait. She has another minute or two before she loses feeling in her fingers.

"They painted a gloomy picture of my chances if you fail. New Hampshire has always been our firewall. I didn't realize how critical it was until yesterday."

"You're from Boston, so you took it for granted. It's your Achilles' heel."

The comment bites. Alicia took Daniel Wetzel's cloture vote for granted when the Safe America Act was on the Senate floor, and it ultimately cost her passage of the bill. She wants to avoid that mistake again.

"I'm not now. What do I need to do?"

"Focus on finishing up in Iowa," Brian says. "Give a kick-ass concession speech when it's over and remain positive. Don't let Dr. Doom and Debbie Downer talk you into giving Burgess more credit than he deserves. He was supposed to win there. We can talk about the next steps when you get here. I have some surprises in store for Luther."

"Okay. I'll talk to you after we land on Wednesday morning."

"Until then, Senator."

Brian hangs up, and Alicia stashes her phone in her coat pocket, keeping her hands in there to warm them up. She walks back to the car, where her consultant and campaign manager have already retreated inside, and hopefully, cranked up the heat.

She's uneasy about Brian, but he said all the right things. She questioned her advisors weeks ago about the tenor of her advertising in the early states. They answered with polling that showed their effectiveness. It hasn't panned out. New Hampshire isn't the only place she's faltering, and Brian Cooper can't be made a scapegoat over what's happening in South Carolina and Nevada. If he says he's taking extraordinary measures for her, he is. Brian Cooper may be a lot of things, but he isn't a liar.

Nothing she says will pacify Angela or Michael. They will spend the next two hours pressing her for details, but she won't feel compelled to offer any. Alicia knows she's going to have to trust her former subordinate, even if they don't. With Iowa a lost cause, she has no viable alternative.

CHAPTER NINE

"S.O.F."

Burgess for America Campaign Office
Manchester, New Hampshire

7 Days to the New Hampshire Democratic Primary

The term "campaign office" is a misnomer. It more closely resembles an Apple store with campaign branding everywhere. People mill about doing whatever tasks they are assigned. What you don't find is the staple seen in most offices: desks.

The Burgess for America Manchester headquarters is located on a block of small shops just north of city hall. It's a retail space, once operating an ice cream shop or some other endeavor in keeping with its hair salon and tanning spa neighbors. The point of the location is to maximize exposure to foot traffic while not costing too many precious campaign dollars. They want as much visibility as their budget can afford.

They couldn't have picked a worse spot. Marx knows many of the shops and buildings on this street have cameras. City hall most certainly does, and all of those need to be avoided. He parks his car in an area that he knows isn't covered by video and angles the mirror to see his target. Everything is ready. All he needs to do is wait for the lone staffer inside to leave.

He peels his eyes off the door, checks his watch, and curses under his breath. The timing of this operation is everything. He can't sit here and wait for this clown to call it a night. This mission is easy to execute but challenging to complete without getting caught. This guy's presence is making that even more complicated. Marx frowns as he checks up and down dimly lit Elm Street. He knows what needs to be done.

Marx pops the trunk and removes the black nylon bag, slinging it over his shoulder as he crosses the street between streetlights. Paranoia comes with his line of work. He spent a month casing this street and documenting everything. Still, he pulls his hat down and the collar of his jacket up as he approaches. He's not going to get pinched because he missed a single webcam that someone stuck in a store window.

When he reaches the closed nail salon, he places his kit down behind a small snowbank between the building and the sidewalk. He edges closer to the window and peeks inside to find the man paying no attention to what's happening outside. Marx takes a deep breath. He's going to need to make a show of this, and it's going to hurt.

He takes a couple of bold steps into view of the window and forces his foot to slip on the icy sidewalk. The loss of traction was more than he expected, making his scream more authentic. He lands hard on the concrete and lies there prone, writhing in pain. The door unlocks, and the man comes rushing to his side without a coat on.

"Hey, are you okay?"

"Uh, no, I think I broke my ankle. It hurts like hell."

"Let's get you off the ground and inside where it's warm so we can look at it. If it's broken, I'll call for an ambulance."

The man is strong. He hefts Marx upright, who is careful not to put any weight on his leg. They hobble into the office, where the man eases him down into a chair.

"I'm such an idiot. Thank you for this. I'm glad you were here. There's no telling how long I'd be on that sidewalk if you weren't."

The man pulls a folding chair over and elevates Marx's leg. "This area is a ghost town at night, and most of the businesses here don't open until eight. Our staff won't be here until the governor gets in from Iowa sometime mid-morning. Unless a cop drove by, it might have been a while."

"Why are you here?"

"I'm a workaholic, I guess. You?"

"Same deal. My wife says my job will kill me someday."

The guy looks away as he laughs, giving Marx time to lower his leg off the chair and retrieve his knife. He moves like lightning, plunging the steel blade into the man's left eye as he turns toward him. He feels the knife slice through to the brain stem. With a couple of quick flicks of his wrist, the deed is done. Marx withdraws the blade. It was quick. The good Samaritan never knew what hit him.

Marx hustles outside and retrieves the black bag. Unzipping it, he pulls out a plastic can and douses the inside of the office and the man's body in gasoline. He looks around the room. There are piles of placards and reams of paper here. That should suffice to get the fire hot enough to start the inferno he needs. He lights a match and retreats to the door before tossing it into a puddle of gasoline. The fire spreads across the floor and climbs up the walls in seconds.

The clock is ticking. Marx stashes the gasoline container in the bag and pulls out a can of white spray paint, writing "SOF" in capital letters on the sidewalk. It was the part of the plan he liked least. Machiavelli had better know what he's doing.

With no time to waste, he hurries back to the car and drives off, heading north up Elm Street, opposite the direction of the nearby firehouse. After traveling a couple of miles, he parks and opens his door. The distant wails of fire engines pierce the quiet New England night. Even if they manage to douse the flames before the fire spreads, his mission is accomplished.

Marx checks his phone. Sartre has already checked in with "*Invisible Man*," meaning he was successful. There's nothing from Trot. He rechecks his watch—no reason to panic yet.

He types "*Of Mice and Men*" into their group chat, the code that lets the others know there was a development. Murders command attention, and the team will steer clear of the safehouse until given the all-clear. It will take them days to comb through the video, but he can't be sure there wasn't a pedestrian who spotted him leaving the scene.

A message pops up from Trot: *INVISIBLE MAN*. Marx exhales and then tosses the phone onto the passenger seat. He stares out the windshield for a long moment before slamming his hands on the steering wheel.

Weeks of meticulous planning was undone by one hard-charging volunteer who decided to work late. The man was in the wrong place at the wrong time. Life is sometimes like that, not that Machiavelli will understand. He isn't going to be happy.

CHAPTER TEN

ANDREW LI

Burgess Campaign Event
Des Moines, Iowa

Andrew stares out at the brave group of hearty Iowans who assembled in the freezing temperatures to listen to a politician speak. Antipathy exists in modern society, but not here. It was one of the highlights of the original speech he drafted for this rally. Too bad it got shredded the moment the news from New Hampshire found its way to his smartphone and into his candidate's ear.

The priority changed, and he immediately went to work on a new message. It had to drive home a point without reeking of political opportunism. It was a tough thing to balance, and he failed. Governor Burgess read about a third of the first page before handing the speech back to him, explaining that he knew what he wanted to say and didn't need a script.

"Do you know what your father will say?" he asks Isiah, as they stand off to the side of the platform.

"Not a clue. Pops didn't want to talk about it. He didn't want to talk, period. The news of the man's death hit him hard."

"This is an important moment, Isiah. He'll be judged by America based on what he says on this stage."

"He knows that."

"You're not worried?"

Isiah allows himself to grin. "My father has worked for this his whole life. If I have faith in anyone to rise to this occasion, it's him."

Luther Burgess is announced onto the stage to the deafening sound of cheering supporters. Andrew is surprised people's voices still work in these temperatures, and he's thankful they do.

"Thank you, thank you," he says, patiently waiting for the raucous applause to die down. "Iowans caucus tonight in the nation's first step towards picking their candidates for the presidency. I wanted to speak this morning about my vision for America and how it differs from the other candidates. Unfortunately, I can't do that."

The governor hangs his head and lets the silence speak to the crowd. It's great theater, except there's nothing fake about it. Luther Burgess is nothing if not an emotional man with a big heart. He's choosing to let it show.

"I want to talk about Frederick Lamm. He grew up as an average kid who went to an ordinary school in an average town. He studied hard and graduated from high school in the top quarter of his class. His parents worked hard to send him to college, but they couldn't overcome the rising cost of education in this country. Fred chose a different path than his peers and immediately began an apprenticeship as a plumber.

"He worked long hours but still found time to marry and father three children. He built a loving, stable household. He wanted to spend more time with his family but offered to work for our campaign because he believed in what we're doing. Fred understood and embraced our vision of economic fairness. He was a fixture in our Manchester operation and often worked long after everyone else left for the day.

"Father. Husband. Self-made man. Hard worker. That was who Fred Lamm was, and he died last night in the fire that destroyed one of our campaign offices. The circumstances are still under investigation, but any way you portray it, he was murdered for the sin of supporting me. Fred didn't deserve that. It shouldn't have happened."

Luther lets the weight of the words settle onto the crowd. You could hear a pin drop. There are no coughs, sneezes, or fidgeting. The people are hanging on his every word and feeling the pain that he is sharing with them. In the back, cameras from the countless news outlets capture it too.

"I would love to stand up here and tell you that I received heartfelt condolences from Alicia Standish over his loss. I wish I could pass on to Fred's wife and children that the senator called and asked me to relay her thoughts and prayers to them. I can't. We never received any message."

The crowd erupts into a cauldron of hearty boos. There are no cue cards at political rallies. If there were, the laughable scene would become the butt of jokes by every late-night comedian. If a candidate wants a reaction from his or her supporters, it must be earned. Words, and the passion behind them, are the cue cards here. The governor just landed a verbal hard-left cross square on Alicia's jaw.

"Instead, if you can believe it, her campaign sent out a tweet — an impersonal, cold, unfeeling digital message intended to avoid appearing callous. The Digital Age is a lot of things, many of them great. Twitter is not an effective way to deliver heartfelt sympathy. Unless, of course, you have none.

"I was asked by a reporter this morning if I thought Senator Standish's supporters were behind this heinous attack on my campaign. Yes, I do. I believe the blame is laid at her feet. I believe in my heart that the still-smoldering ruins of our office were set aflame by her supporters. The blood of Frederick Lamm is on her hands.

"I call on Senator Standish to set aside our political differences and do the right thing: condemn, in the strongest possible words, the actions of those who trivialize our democratic process. Decry those who seek to turn our great nation into a third-world banana republic. Say anything that discourages hatred and vitriol in our political discourse. Rebuke anyone who believes the path to victory includes intimidation, voter suppression, and violence against each other. Say those words. Say anything."

The clapping begins sporadically and slowly builds. The governor doesn't attempt to hype it up. He waits patiently at the microphone until it subsides. Visuals are everything in modern politics. Burgess is doing everything right with both his words and his actions. Andrew is happy that he discarded the speech. This is far better.

"New Hampshire is better than this. America is better than this, and I'm going to prove it. I will continue this journey undaunted because the cause for economic equality cannot be stalled over a charred office. I will continue to fight for the rights of all Americans to an education, adequate healthcare, and to free themselves from the scourge of economic disparity. I will press on to the White House to be a voice for all of you. I will fight on in the memory of Frederick Lamm."

By the time everyone thinks it's appropriate to join the cheering, the sound is thunderous. A gracious and stoic governor full of resolve stares back at them. He isn't hamming it up as he often does. He's a man on a mission, and the people know it. With every passing moment, they grow louder and more determined to hand him the most delegates from the great state of Iowa.

CHAPTER ELEVEN

SPECIAL AGENT VICTORIA LARSEN

Burgess for America Campaign Office
Manchester, New Hampshire

The three agents climb out of the car as the Chevy Suburban pulls up behind them. Additional agents pour out of that vehicle, representing the vanguard of the FBI response to the firebombing of Luther Burgess's Manchester campaign office. The same scene is repeating itself at the other arson sites in Portsmouth, Nashua, and Concord.

"What a mess," Takara says, surveying the scene.

Victoria studies the burnt-out shell of the makeshift campaign office and adjoining buildings. This fire moved fast. Firefighters were rolling within a minute of the report of flames but had no chance to save the building.

"You have to feel for the owners of Josie's Hair Salon and Summer Sun Tanning. They lost everything."

"Business owners across the country will be paying higher insurance premiums every time an agent finds out that a campaign moved in next door," Ian grumbles. Victoria can't argue with that.

"We're glad you're here," a burly man says after striding over to them. "I'm Detective Diego Velez, New Hampshire State Police."

"We wish we were here under better circumstances, Detective," Takara says as they all shake hands.

"What can you tell us?" Victoria asks as the FBI forensics team walks over to talk to their counterparts.

"Four campaign offices, four arsons. It appears all of them used gasoline as an accelerant. No ignition source has been found at any of the scenes, but we assume it was either a paper or a wooden match. Nothing sophisticated."

Victoria isn't so sure about that. The fires might not have been set using a Rube Goldberg machine, but the tactics behind them are another story.

"There was only one victim in the attacks: Frederick Lamm, thirty-five, from Manchester. His next of kin was notified."

"Smoke inhalation or something else?" Takara asks.

The detective grinds his teeth. "Unknown at this time, but I personally don't think it was an accident."

"Why not?"

"The only reason for him to have been in there was to fight the fire, but the extinguishers were untouched. He had plenty of time to escape unless he had been incapacitated or..."

"Killed ahead of time," Victoria says, finishing the sentence. She came to that conclusion the moment she was briefed on what happened.

"Forensics will confirm if there was any smoke in his lungs at the time of death," Diego continues. "That will tell the tale. We're keeping that out of the press for now."

"For as much good as that will do," Ian offers. "Luther Burgess's speech this morning in Iowa set social media on fire. It took all of five seconds for the blue-check mafia to leap to that conclusion on Twitter."

"They don't know about this. There's something you should see."

Diego walks them across the street and has a pair of officers remove a blue tarpaulin covering the sidewalk. Victoria expected to see a bloodstain or something the arsonist dropped that they wanted to preserve. Instead, she sees the large letters SOF scrawled in white spray paint.

"I assume this wasn't here ahead of time," Victoria says.

"Nope. It's fresh paint and wasn't on the sidewalk when the campaign staff left yesterday. Any idea what it means?"

"Special Operations Forces? Soldier of Fortune?" Victoria offers.

"Statement of Fact? Save our Future?" Takara adds.

"Songs of Freedom?" Ian says with a smirk. The trio looks at him. "Sorry, I'm a big Bob Marley and the Wailers fan. It was the name of their box set."

"Did you find the spray can?" Takara asks, getting back to business.

"Nope. We didn't find the gas can either, at least, not yet. It could be a plastic blob in there, but there's no sign of it."

"Were these letters sprayed at all four sites?"

Diego nods at Victoria. "All right out front so they wouldn't be missed, even with firefighters stomping all over it."

Victoria runs her hand through her hair and walks around the tarp the officers just recovered the graffiti with. She stares at the front of the building and then looks up and down the street.

"What is it, Vic?" Takara asks.

"They took everything with them and still left this as a calling card. Why?"

"Fingerprints and DNA can be traced if the evidence isn't incinerated. Finding the meaning of three letters is like searching for a needle in a stack of needles."

"Maybe that's the idea," Ian says. Takara nods in agreement.

"There's something else," Diego interjects. "The door to this office was found unlocked. The ones in Nashua, Portsmouth, and Concord had windows broken or a back door shattered."

"Did the offices have alarms?" Ian asks.

"You're going to love this. They all did except the one with the break-in through the back. The Portsmouth office alarm was out of service. Before you ask, none of the locations had cameras. We're checking if any local businesses had something we can use."

"Detective," a female trooper interrupts after walking over. "Can you come and take a look at this?"

"Excuse me," he says before walking away with her.

"Thoughts?"

"All four attacks within minutes of each other shows a high level of coordination," Victoria says.

"They were professionals."

"Then why leave the letters? They took great pains to stay anonymous, and then they left that clue. It makes no sense."

Ian shrugs. "It could be a decoy. Something to throw us off the trail or lead us down the wrong one."

"Or it could be significant. Ian, call Bedford and have them run it through the database," Takara orders. "I want to see if a hate group or militia pops up."

"Will do."

Ian heads back under the police tape and across the street to the vehicles. Victoria turns to watch the state police and FBI forensics team scurry about their work. The windbreaker-clad army has a lot to process at this scene. She imagines it's no different at the other offices.

"Think Ian will find anything?" Takara asks, taking in the scene before them for himself.

"No. I don't think whoever is doing this is trying to be that obvious. Something else is bothering me. The arsonists broke into the office whose alarm was out of order. The other two were hit through the front window. Do you know what you need for that? Research and surveillance."

"You think they were cased?"

"That or they have someone on the inside."

"Frederick Lamm?"

Victoria presses her lips together. "Could be, but why bother eliminating him? He'd be more valuable as a source of intel. We need to run a check on him and find out if the governor's words of praise earlier today reflect reality."

"Yeah. Let's assume Lamm wasn't involved. Did they plan to take him out, or was he in the wrong place at the wrong time?"

"I'm betting the latter, but Diego can confirm that for us. If he wasn't supposed to be here, then whoever hit this office adapted to the situation. You know who's good at that?"

"The United States military."

Victoria nods. "This has the characteristics of a special operations mission."

The two agents subconsciously look down at the blue tarp covering the SOF. "Special Operations Forces" fits, maybe too well. Still, it's a lead they should check. Victoria is uncomfortable thinking that soldiers who swear an oath to uphold the constitution are capable of such a flagrant act against it. There is nothing more sacred than democracy in action.

"I can get a list of veterans who live in a fifty-mile radius and see if anything abnormal pops up," Takara says.

"It will be a long list. Takara, we need to do it quietly. I don't think the Bureau should advertise that there may be a military connection to this."

He nods and heads off to join Ian at the vehicle. Victoria waits for Diego to return so she can give him their contact information. She shakes her head. Something is wrong about all this.

With a week until the New Hampshire Primary, there is an obvious political connection. She shudders, unable to shake the thought that this could hamper a political candidate's outreach efforts before a crucial election. Someone wanted to hurt Burgess before people go to the polls. The list of his potential enemies is long and answering who and why isn't enough. She needs to find out if they're done and stop them if they aren't.

CHAPTER TWELVE

TIERRA CAMPOS

Granite State University
Durham, New Hampshire

I park the car and head off with Olivia on the trek across campus to the student union, where we agreed to have the interview. Two things don't mix well: cold air and wind. I zip my coat up to the top and pull down my hat as I pick up the pace to encourage Olivia to walk faster. I prefer the warmer weather of Arizona and don't know how anyone deals with these temperatures in New England.

"This reminds me a lot of where I went to school," Olivia says, enjoying the brisk walk in the frigid weather.

"All universities look the same to me," I say, trying to stop my teeth from chattering.

"Maybe. The vibe is different here. Are you leaving for *Capitol Beat?*"

That came out of nowhere, but at least it has me thinking about something other than frostbite.

"I don't know yet. I feel like I'm the only one who doesn't."

"What do you mean?" she asks.

"Madison and Logan barely spoke to me before we left. Jerome looked at me like I kicked his dog when he wasn't watching. Austin…well, he threatened to fire me. It felt like I was back at WWDC."

My time at the preeminent Washington news station was anything but pleasant. I spent years there telling myself it would get better. It never did. My colleagues only became more conniving, backstabbing, and ruthless. Carl Brennan was among the worst of them. That's what makes his interview with *Capitol Beat* so troubling.

"That explains why Tyler and I are up here," Olivia says.

"Why is that?"

"We're solidly on team Tierra. I don't want to see you go, but you earned the right to make whatever choice you feel is best. I love *Front Burner*, but it's changing and not for the better."

"Yeah, we're losing our objectivity."

"*Front Burner* is a victim of its own success. The dollars came in like an avalanche after Brockhampton. The brass celebrated that breakthrough by betraying every principle we hold dear. If you think you can do for television news what you did for online journalism when you broke that story, I think you should consider taking Wilson's chair at *Capitol Beat.*"

"You hold the minority opinion."

Olivia sighs. "Austin doesn't want to lose you. The same for Logan, Madison, and Jerome. They've been with him since the beginning, and their loyalty is unquestioned."

We arrive at the student union, and I'm happy to feel warmth again. I open my coat and pull off gloves that are more decorative than capable of keeping feeling in my fingers. I rub my hands, trying to massage blood back into them.

"My goal isn't to rip the team apart," I say, trying to avoid any misunderstanding.

"I know. Let's go to work."

Dozens of college students are hanging out and killing time while waiting for their next class. The guys look at us like a fat kid eyeing a Twinkie as we walk past the tables and chairs set against the windows. Olivia can be nostalgic all she wants. I don't miss college life. Fortunately, we find who we're looking for quickly.

"Leila? I'm Tierra—"

"Everyone knows who you are."

I nod. "This is Olivia. She's one of my colleagues at *Front Burner*."

"It's nice to meet you, Leila."

I notice her backpack sitting on the chair next to her as we sit. Most politically active college students adorn their stuff with all sorts of campaign swag to show their support. Hers is naked. If she had anything on it before she filed the intimidation report, it's gone now.

"Thank you for agreeing to speak to us," Olivia opens. "Have you done any interviews about what happened to you?"

"No. I didn't want it to be national news in the first place. I was terrified that day. My family is still scared because it made the national news. We have a cop sitting in front of our house all day. I never would have filed the report with campus police if I had known it'd get leaked."

"Then why did you agree to speak with us?" I ask, confused about why she's here if she wants to stay anonymous.

Leila looks directly at me. "Because you found out the truth behind Brockhampton. I want you to find it about this."

The investigation into the Brockhampton shooting fundamentally changed my life, for better and worse. One of the positives is the door it opens for people to trust me without my having to earn it first. It's something I never want to take for granted.

"You aren't scared?" Olivia asks.

"Yeah, I am. I met his conditions. He never said I couldn't talk to anyone."

"The man approached you after one of your classes?" I ask, confirming the information in the police report.

"Yeah. I sat on a bench outside the building to have a smoke. He sat down next to me."

"What happened next?"

Leila walks us through the encounter, detailing how he compelled her to stay seated, and what he said to intimidate her. She finished with the ultimatum, and what the price would be for failing to meet it. It sends a shiver down my spine.

"You canceled the rally?"

"Yeah," she says, hanging her head. "We had no choice. Our families' lives were at stake."

"We?" Olivia asks.

"My friend Travis. He was threatened, too."

"After or before you?"

Leila shakes her head. "At the same time. I was literally calling him when my cell rang. He was as scared as I was when he told me what happened."

"Wait," I say, making sure I understand. "Are you saying you were both approached at the same time?"

"Yeah, by different guys. The man who threatened him had all his personal info, too. They used the same method."

I share a look with Olivia before leaning back in my seat. That's an interesting wrinkle. If what she's saying is accurate, two men were working simultaneously on this campus. The intimidation was even better planned than we thought.

"And then you both decided to file a report with the campus police?" Olivia asks.

"We didn't know if we were the only two and wanted it documented. If I could do it again, I would have kept my mouth shut. Now reporters won't leave us alone. Some of them are accusing us of making it up."

The pain of that accusation is evident in her eyes. I've been sitting with her for five minutes, and I know she isn't lying about this. Reporters are often cheerleaders for their favorite candidates, and maybe that is driving the questioning of her story. That would be slightly more palatable than using it as a ploy to get an interview and a juicy story.

"Leila, did you tell your parents before you filed the report?"

She nods quickly, fighting back the tears. "Yeah. I wanted them to be safe. They notified our local police. They are watching the house."

"I'm so sorry this happened to you. I can't imagine how terrifying that must have been. Where do you go from here? Are you still going to vote on Tuesday?"

Leila breaks eye contact, staring out the window for a long time. I don't push her for an answer. It was a very personal question that she may not have even considered until I asked.

"No. I don't want anything to do with the election now."

I nod. The reaction is understandable. Olivia collects some more background information from her and issues a promise that this interview is on deep background. Leila thanks us and then heads off to her dorm. We stay seated, watching groups of students walk back and forth in the freezing temperatures on the sidewalk outside the student union.

"What's up?" Olivia asks.

"I don't know. Something."

"Do you think they were Standish supporters trying to suppress the youth vote going for Burgess?"

"Maybe. If it were only a single creepy guy making passing threats or someone on the other side of a keyboard, I'd say yes. Two men, both who know everything about her and her friend's family and strike at the same time? It feels bigger than that."

"Don't forget about the leak," Olivia adds. "It's too convenient. Austin got a confidential tip from a reliable source, yet this was in the wild before we even got on the plane. Even if a reporter has a source in one campus police department, what are the odds of having one in all four of them?"

"It's not impossible. Austin doesn't live up here and still cultivated a source. I had dozens of them on campuses around Washington, and I reported on human interest topics."

"Good point. Do you want to go see the reporter who broke the story?"

I shake my head. "It's a waste of time. We're still the competition. He won't betray his sources, assuming he talks to us at all."

"Tierra, Austin is going to want to run with this interview."

"People in hell want ice water," I snap. "We promised we wouldn't. That's the end of the discussion."

"I know, I'm just preparing you. I'm not sure where Austin's head is right now, but we shouldn't show him the notes from this interview."

"Agreed."

"It seems like someone went through a lot of trouble to get a few rallies canceled," Olivia says, as we head for the exit.

"Yeah, they did, but the tactic worked. Leila is terrified."

We bundle back up inside the student union and venture out for the walk back to the car. I've never missed Arizona so much in my life. My thoughts wander back to Leila and her story. I've watched countless newscasts about intimidation and threats to all manner of people. This didn't sound like a couple of thugs scaring some kids. It was different, and a political angle that nobody is talking about in New Hampshire.

CHAPTER THIRTEEN

SENATOR ALICIA STANDISH

Standish for President Campaign Office
Des Moines, Iowa

Like most of her campaign locations, Alicia's Des Moines headquarters is an old retail shop with a small office in the back that was once for a manager or an accountant to do the books. She leans forward in her rickety swivel chair and stares at the television in the corner. An expert panel of talking heads on cable news is destroying her. The "it will pass" strategy that Michael Ross is pushing isn't going to work.

The events in New Hampshire are terrible timing. The Iowa Caucus is more than an early litmus test for presidential contenders. The campaign for the presidency is a marathon that is only memorable for how it begins and ends. With an entire week before the New Hampshire Primary, the winner will own seven news cycles as the frontrunner. It's a huge psychological advantage.

"Thank you! Thank you so much for being here," she says, entering the main room to cheers and enthusiastic applause.

"Standish! Standish! Standish!" the group shouts in unison, getting fired up.

This is what the ground game looks like. Campaigns spend countless hours and millions of dollars organizing a network of volunteers willing to help get people to the polls. It starts here in Iowa and ends with all fifty states and the District of Columbia on Election Day.

After a pep talk and some pictures with the candidate, these people will take to the streets to distribute information on caucus locations, ask for support, and offer rides if necessary. In the small state of New Hampshire, she will attend multiple kickoffs. She's limited to just a couple of ground launch events here.

"I'm asked why I think I will win in Iowa. The answer is simple. It's because of people like you," she says, prompting another round of cheers.

"You have sacrificed your time and effort to push us over the finish line. I want to carry that momentum to every state in our great union. This is not about my wanting to be president. It is about the future of our nation. We have many challenges, but we will face them together. That starts right here today with all of you.

"I am a candidate of ideas, and today you are my voice. I'm counting on you. Thank you, and I look forward to seeing you out there!"

Alicia's full-time campaign staff begins to get the volunteers organized as she makes her way over to the media, who are capturing the moment for posterity. There are a hundred things they could ask her. There is little doubt in her mind what the first question will be.

"Senator Standish, what do you know about the arsons in New Hampshire?"

"All I know is whatever has been reported on it," she says, moving on to the next reporter.

"What about Governor Burgess's insinuation that your campaign may have been involved?"

Alicia's face changes. "It's sick, twisted, and a cheap ploy by a governor who should know better than to use a tragic death to score political points. He should be ashamed of himself. Voters should see his posturing for what it is."

"So, your campaign wasn't involved?"

"I resent that question," Alicia says, losing the grip on her temper.

"The Burgess campaign says it was done to inhibit his ability to get voters to the polls because you're scared of losing," another reporter shouts.

"That's an interesting theory, considering I'm winning in New Hampshire."

"Your numbers are dropping."

"Yes, but I'm still winning. There are a lot of undecided voters remaining there, and a lot of work to be done. I have no doubt that, after comparing our policy initiatives side-by-side, they will join our camp."

"Why haven't you condemned your supporters for the arsons?"

"Because there is no proof that they are behind it."

"Yeah, but—"

"But what? Do you know something I don't? I haven't heard anything that proves my supporters were involved at all. It could have been someone supporting another candidate. It could have been the Republicans. It could have been teenage hooligans. It could have been little green men from Alpha Centauri. We'll know when authorities catch them, and they will be caught."

"You won't condemn the attacks?"

Alicia forces herself to breathe. She hates the media. They are useful idiots when they support you, like with the Safe America Act, which was universally praised by left-leaning journalists. That honeymoon ended. Now they're searching for a soundbite that will get them clicks and retweets. They don't want the truth. They want a scandal.

"I've denounced political violence here and around the world since long before I even became a senator. I didn't explicitly decry these incidents because I don't want to give the perpetrators the attention they crave. The authorities will catch whoever was behind this. New Hampshire is filled with capable law enforcement—"

"Did you know that the FBI is involved as well?"

Alicia didn't appreciate the interruption but knows she can't say anything. "No, but that isn't surprising, and with federal assistance, justice will be brought even faster."

"Why didn't you send condolences to Frederick Lamm's family?"

Michael Ross made that decision. The senator disagreed with it, but he made a compelling argument. Since she's the candidate, she has the prerogative to take matters into her own hands and did just that. A slight smile creases her lips as she stares them all in the face.

"I did. I sent my condolences to the family in a letter. They should receive it tomorrow."

"Why a letter?" a reporter asks, breaking the stunned silence.

"Because their loss was personal. My condolences should be as well. I've experienced great pain in my own life. A politician sending a tweet or issuing a press release with condolences is hollow. It's also exploitive. They don't need that right now."

"Do you think Governor Burgess was exploiting them at the rally today?"

"I think the good people of Iowa and New Hampshire can determine that for themselves."

"Last question," Angela announces.

Alicia glances at her campaign manager. There is work that needs to be done, but that's not why she's cutting this short. This has become the media's focus, and they have a caucus to win tonight.

"Do you think the arsons will have a lasting impact on your campaign? Will you be able to beat him if he wins Iowa and New Hampshire?"

"This is a battle of ideas. We will defeat the governor in that arena because ours are better. Thank you, all."

Campaign staff swarms the reporters to review the rest of the day's schedule with them. Michael Ross walks over to Angela and stands behind her before leaning over to whisper in her ear.

"This is taking on a life of its own. We need to get ahead of it."

"You're the one who wanted to ignore it in the hopes it went away," she sneers, not agreeing with his guidance in the first place.

"Yeah, well, it's not going to."

"No kidding. Do you have ideas?"

"Yeah," he says, before shaking his head, "but I don't think the senator will go for it."

"Why not?"

"It involves using her parents' deaths."

"Good luck with that," she scoffs. "Make sure I'm not in the building when you approach her with that gem."

Angela moves deeper into the bowels of the office to retrieve her purse. She doesn't like the nonchalant way that Michael handled this. He swung and missed on a pitch down the middle with his garbage advice. An arson with a death involved is a tragedy. Four arsons at the same time are going to have the conspiracy theorists going nuts and will feed the media cycle for weeks. A fourth-grader could have figured that out.

CHAPTER FOURTEEN

TIERRA CAMPOS

Burgess for America Campaign Office
Manchester, New Hampshire

It feels like I stepped onto the set of NCIS. Yellow police tape, cops, agents in windbreakers, gawking bystanders, and national media doing remotes from the sidewalk complete the scene. It's an image Americans see on television but thankfully don't often see in real life.

"This is a mess."

"You should have been in Brockhampton for the riot, Olivia. This is nothing."

"Thanks, but I was happy to pass on that. Is that Victoria?"

I crane my neck to see a tall blond woman striding toward a police vehicle when she spots us and changes direction. Olivia must have the eyes of a hawk. I spent weeks with the woman and didn't recognize her from that distance.

"Victoria?"

"Tierra?"

We share a hug, happy to see each other again. I've missed her. Despite talking every now and again following her reinstatement to the FBI, we haven't seen each other since the day we found Elizabeth Schwarzer's journals. In an odd display of emotion, she even hugs Olivia and Tyler. Victoria is not typically the warm, fuzzy type.

"What are you guys doing here?" she asks.

"The circus is coming to town. Journalists like to follow the clowns. What about you?"

"Someone targeting a high-profile presidential campaign gets national visibility. Authorities asked our Bedford district office for assistance, and they called us in from the mothership."

"Aren't you lucky? Have you found anything interesting?"

Victoria looks around at the crowd and back at her colleagues. "Let's get off the street. There are too many eyes here, and I'm hungry."

We walk away from the mayhem and order lunch at a sandwich shop. The time is spent with small talk about our lives and lack of dating prospects. Tyler politely doesn't interject any snarky comments.

"Are you here by yourself?"

"Takara and Ian are with me, plus a forensics team that tailgated us all the way up here."

"I remember Takara," I say. "Ian?"

"New guy. He's okay. They went to the Bedford office to start tracking some things down. I'm holding back here in case forensics uncovers something."

"Do you think they will?" Tyler asks.

"Nope."

"Do you know anything you can tell us?" Olivia follows up.

Victoria leans back and sighs. "Am I talking to friends or journalists from *Front Burner*?"

Technically we're both, but I know why she asked. "Friends. Always friends."

"We have some leads. Between you and me, I feel like something is wrong about this."

"If you're on the fence about something being off, let me share what we've learned."

I launch into a recap of our interview with Leila Estabrook, with Olivia filling in the details I miss. There was one key point I needed to drive home.

"Military precision?"

"Vic, these intimidations were timed and executed perfectly. Not just at Granite State but the other colleges as well. It sounded more like the SEAL mission to take down Bin Laden than some crusty New Englanders scaring a few college kids."

"Okay, that's interesting. Here's something not for public consumption: the techs working the scenes told me that these four arsons were timed down to the minute."

"Coincidence?" Tyler asks, after a long moment of silence passes.

"You know how I feel about that, Ty. I'm going to tell you guys something else, but it has to be off the record, and you need to confirm it."

"Vic, you know where I stand on that."

Our first conversation after we met at the wine bar was about using her as a source. We came to an agreement that she would be attributed as someone close to the investigation. It doesn't sound like that would fly this time.

"Yes, I do. I can't play that game this time. This is an active investigation."

"Okay." I have no choice but to agree. Tyler and Olivia both nod in agreement.

"The arsonists left a calling card. They spray-painted 'SOF' in big white letters on the sidewalk."

"We didn't see it," Tyler says.

"Did you see the blue tarp in front? It's under that. Does that mean anything to you?"

I look at Tyler and Olivia, and we all shake our heads. Victoria grimaces.

"It could mean anything," I say, "but 'special operations forces' makes the most sense given what we know."

"It does, and that's what concerns me," Victoria admits.

"Because it's too obvious," Olivia concludes. "Calling cards are usually puzzles, not signposts pointing authorities in a specific direction."

"Unless it's a red herring meant to do that," Tyler argues.

"That's one of the things we're considering. Keep that quiet. Don't even tell Austin. Nobody outside of the investigators on the case knows about it. We need to keep it that way."

"That won't be an issue," Olivia mumbles.

Victoria stares at her and then at me.

"It's a long story. We'll keep it between us. I promise."

"There's one more thing. I'm busy here. Can you track something down for me?"

She reaches into the pocket of her windbreaker and pulls out a small sheet of notebook paper folded in half. She hands it to Tyler, who opens it and scrunches his face in confusion.

"What's this?"

"The last thing texted to Dylan Spencer before he drove up on the tracks in front of a cargo train and met his maker."

"What is it, other than a site on the dark web?"

"That's what I need you to find out," Victoria says with a smile, resisting the urge to shame Tyler for asking the obvious.

"How are we supposed to track this down if the FBI can't?"

"You have a good imagination, Tierra. You'll figure it out. We'll catch up later since we're all in town."

Victoria leaves and walks back up the street. The three of us dive back into our lunches, incapable of eating at the speed at which Victoria inhaled hers. I get the unsettling feeling as I sip my Coke that we are going to be spending more time with Victoria than just catching up.

CHAPTER FIFTEEN

CAPITOL BEAT

Cable News Studio
Washington, D.C.

Unlike his producers who embrace drama, Wilson hates political theater. He can't stand it when politicos just want to fiddle while the world burns. Modern problems require bold leaders to solve them. After decades of hosting this show, he knows most Americans feel the same way. The political class either doesn't recognize that or, more likely, doesn't care.

"It is Tuesday, February first, I am Wilson Newman and this…is…*Capitol Beat*."

The brief opening credits roll, and he takes a deep breath. Election years used to be something he looked forward to as a newsman. Now he loathes them.

"The Iowa caucuses are underway, and America has officially taken the first steps on the journey of electing our next president. For the Democrats, Governor Luther Burgess of Illinois and Senator Alicia Standish are expected to take home the largest share of delegates in the state. The Republican field is wide open. GOP frontrunners Colin Bradshaw and Krysti Hylton lead the pack, but several middle-tier candidates have made late charges in the national polls. They could make things interesting in their caucus.

"We will break down last night's poll numbers to explain what it means for the campaigns and the race for the White House. Our expert panel will also analyze some key policy differences and speculate how they might affect the outcome of the Iowa Caucuses. Our field reporters on the ground in New Hampshire, Nevada, and South Carolina will check in with details on those upcoming races. We will finish with the latest on the arsons at the campaign offices of Luther Burgess in New Hampshire.

"We start off our coverage tonight with the Republican Caucuses. With us in the studio is Republican National Committee chairwoman Monica Stengel. Thank you for joining us this evening."

"Thank you for having me," she says, flashing a warm smile.

"The caucuses are underway. What are your thoughts as the people of Iowa make their choices?"

"That they have a difficult one to make. We have a strong field of candidates and a lot of energy behind these campaigns. I think it's going to be a great night for Republicans."

"Any forecasts about tonight?"

"I left my crystal ball at home, Wilson, but I'd expect the two frontrunners to perform well. The story will be who comes in behind them and at what percentages."

Caucuses are a complicated way of selecting delegates because everyone shows up at once instead of throughout the day. It's one of the reasons the format is less popular among the states. Democrats shift people to different corners of the room during each round of the caucus, but Republicans select their candidate via a simple secret ballot. They also eschew the fifteen percent support requirement and mathematical formula Democrats use to determine delegates awarded at each site. It's a much simpler approach, and more effective in Wilson's opinion.

"Do you expect any surprises?" Wilson asks.

"They happen in tight races like this. The one surprise I don't expect is the tabulation disaster the Democrats experienced in 2020."

Wilson suppresses a grimace. The debacle was an embarrassment for the Democrats and easy fodder for the Republicans to capitalize on. She didn't need to bring it up here. Not that a Democrat wouldn't have if the roles were reversed.

"There has been some infighting among Republicans in the lead up to today. Things got a little testy between some of the candidates on the Iowa debate stage."

"Campaigns are stressful," Monica argues, "and there are some strong personalities on stage all competing to be the nominee."

"You don't think that the Republicans are fractured?"

"Candidates have disagreements on policy, but we aren't bombing campaign offices if that's what you mean."

"You might as well run with it now," the producer says in his ear.

Wilson presses his lips together. More political theater. He didn't want to go there with the chairwoman of the RNC, but it was inevitable. It doesn't mean he can't qualify the question.

"I'm afraid to ask you about the arsons in New Hampshire without you politicizing it, Monica. You've had a lot to say on Twitter about it."

"I did, and I do," she says, undaunted. "I'm not politicizing it. What happened in New Hampshire is a Democrat problem, and one I'm thankful I don't have to deal with."

Wilson leans forward slightly. "There are some in the media speculating that the GOP could be behind those fires."

"That's all the media does now. They don't investigate or report. They speculate to earn advertising dollars from those clickbait headlines. Show me a single shred of evidence that any Republican campaign or group was behind it. The media must have something, or the claim would be empty rhetoric. Have you seen anything, Wilson?"

"I have not, and I think blaming anybody for this is irresponsible until authorities tell us otherwise. Are you worried that similar things could happen within the Republican Party?"

"There is always a concern. We live in a polarized, hyper-partisan world. I wouldn't expect our party to devolve into what we are seeing on the Democrat side. The GOP has a big tent, and we don't always see eye to eye, but we respect each other's supporters and candidates enough not to target them."

"Do you think that your party will rally around whoever earns the nomination, or could a bitter fight lead to resentment within the GOP?"

"I believe the Democrats have a much wider policy difference than we do. Standish and Burgess are light years apart on the vision for the country, but both are extreme. Senator Standish tried to go into our homes and remove our firearms in clear violation of the Second Amendment. Her policy views are radical and unpopular. Governor Burgess's policies are un-American. There is a clear choice for our party and a growing number of independents in November, no matter who the Republican nominee is."

Despite being partisan by design, it was also a cogent analysis from a policy perspective. There is a wide gap within the ranks of Democrats, and he could see a moderate sneaking in there if the two frontrunners start eating each other. It's something he will address during his final thought at the end of the broadcast.

"We'll have to leave it at that. Monica Stengel, chairwoman of the RNC, thank you for joining us. We'll be right back with the latest from the Iowa Caucuses."

CHAPTER SIXTEEN

ANDREW LI

Fox & Hound Pub
Manchester, New Hampshire

Andrew didn't have a need to stick around in Iowa. The result is a foregone conclusion, and Luther has plenty of practice giving victory speeches. The only thing left unanswered is the margin of victory and the number of delegates they'll earn. New Hampshire is where the next action will be and where he'll need to prove himself.

There are few breaks for anyone involved in a campaign for president to catch their breath. The first debates began last summer on crowded stages across the country. Getting out, meeting people, and shaking hands occupied much of the fall. By the time the focus centered on Iowa, most of the staff was exhausted. The pace won't let up until the last candidate standing earns enough delegates to claim the nomination. Once both parties host their conventions and officially select their nominees, the real fun begins.

"Can I get a Speedway stout?" Andrew asks the bartender as he sits on a stool at the oak bar.

"Bottle or tap?" she asks, already knowing the answer.

"Tap, please."

Andrew researched the local beers ahead of time. It's how campaigns avoid pitfalls like failing to fold a pizza slice in New York City or eating fried chicken with a fork in South Carolina.

He glances up at the television, where the results from Iowa are getting tabulated. So far, so good. He smirks as he takes a long pull from his glass.

"You visiting from out of town?" the man two stools over from him asks.

"Yeah, I'm here on business."

"For one of those campaigns?" There was a nasty edge to the question.

"No, I'm a consultant. I have a client with an office in Manchester," Andrew responds, not outright lying.

"What kind of consultant?"

"Information technology." Andrew suppresses a grin. Okay, now he lied.

"I can't even check my email."

"Consider yourself lucky. Most of the people I work with would give their left testicle not to have to check theirs."

The man laughs. "I'm Brett. New Hampshire born and raised."

"Andrew. I'm a Californian. It's nice to meet you," he says, reaching over to shake the man's hand.

"It's a lousy time for you to come up here. This place is going to be crawling with politicians and press soon. Damn irritating."

"It's good for business, so stop whining, Brett," the bartender says.

"You don't like it?" Andrew asks.

"It's lousy for traffic and a steep price to pay for a bunch of liars."

"The media or the politicians?"

"Both."

The bartender doesn't argue with him. It's like a tourist trap anywhere in the world; the locals might like the money that they bring, but hate the people spending it.

"I can't argue with you," Andrew says, struggling to sound apathetic. "You don't like any of the candidates?"

"Do you?"

"Not really. Standish is okay, I guess." That tasted worse coming out of his mouth than he thought it would.

"Yeah, she's about the only one. Or so I thought," Brett grumbles.

"You changed your mind?"

"Did you hear about the arsons?"

Andrew sips his stout, formulating how he wants to answer the question. Would a businessman coming into town know that? He figures the answer is yes, considering the coverage it's garnered.

"Yeah, I saw it on the news. Do you think that Standish was behind it?"

"No doubt about it," another guy on the opposite side of Andrew says from the far edge of the bar. "She's been up here a lot."

"I met her three times myself," Brett informs them. "She was shifty."

"She's always been shifty. It got worse when she tried to pass that gun bill. Thank God that failed."

"Shut up, Don. You're a Republican anyway."

"Damn straight, I am. Live free or die," the man says, reciting the state motto.

"They all suck," the bartender adds, cleaning a glass with a rag in what feels like the most cliché thing possible for her to do. "It'd be nice to get a candidate I could get excited about."

"Burgess doesn't do it for you?" Andrew asks, putting the accent in a place that leads others to believe he isn't much of a fan.

"He's a damn communist," Brett sneers.

"Hell, he wins, and I'll move to Canada."

"The thought of Don moving might be enough to get me to vote for him," the bartender quips.

"Burgess will bankrupt the whole damned country. Everybody knows it except him."

"Standish is attacking her opposition, and Burgess is politicizing it. Those are our two best options," the bartender laments. "The rest of the candidates are either crazy or incompetent."

"All the more reason to vote Republican."

"Shut your pie hole, Don. Those scoundrels are no better, and you know it."

Don and Brett start trading barbs across the bar. It's playful banter more than nasty. The two men come from opposite sides of the ideological spectrum, but there is still a friendly camaraderie between them.

"I hope an independent jumps into the race," the bartender says, leaning across the bar. "Maybe then I'll feel like voting."

There is a comfort in anonymity. People don't speak truth to power but will to a perfect stranger. So long as they don't discover that he's the primary political advisor to Luther Burgess for America, he can obtain all manner of information.

This talk was enlightening. Andrew was just stopping in for a quick drink but may order a second, as long as the two men keep talking. This is research at its best and most accurate. It may be only two men in a Manchester bar, but he's willing to bet they have their fingers on the pulse of New Hampshire.

CHAPTER SEVENTEEN

"S.O.F."

Safehouse
South Hooksett, New Hampshire

6 Days to the New Hampshire Democratic Primary

Marx lifts his eyes from his novel and surveys the small living room of their safehouse. Sartre has his headphones on as he pecks away at his keyboard at the corner desk. Trotsky unwinds on the couch with a first-person shooter on his game console. Everyone has their preferred method of escapism, and that's theirs. Marx doesn't have a use for either of those devices.

To him, computers are a necessary evil in society, and video games are a colossal waste of time. He chooses to lose himself in the fictional worlds and the riveting stories that the authors write for him. He sets down his copy of *Fahrenheit 451* when he hears his burner phone chime.

"Yeah?"

"I don't have much time to talk," Machiavelli says on the other end of the line.

"I can't imagine why."

"The FBI arrived in Manchester today."

"Yeah, we know. The feds were tough to miss," Marx says, retreating from the living room to one of the bedrooms to escape the automatic gunfire coming from the television as Trotsky tries to storm a compound.

"Burgess got a briefing from the Bureau. Do you know who went up there with them?"

"Mulder and Scully?"

"Special Agent Victoria Larsen," Machiavelli says, annoyed at Marx's sarcastic sense of humor. He must not have watched the *X-Files* growing up. That's a shocker.

"So what? Engels can control the FBI."

"Nobody controls *her*."

Marx shakes his head. "You're underestimating Engels. Don't make that mistake."

He has a long history with Engels. Of all the soldiers Marx met during his military service, he was the most impressive. That includes the two men in the other room. They are capable, but Engels is a master manipulator who may even give Machiavelli a run for his money.

"And don't make the mistake of underestimating Victoria Larsen. It could be fatal."

"Okay, now you're insulting me."

"I don't care. I followed the Brockhampton case closely. She's a maverick with instincts you can't learn at Quantico. She will figure out what's happening before long and is capable of doing something about it."

"Fine. Do you want me to eliminate her before she becomes a problem?"

"No. That'll bring unwanted attention. She has a weakness I intend to exploit to push her out of play."

Marx smirks and shakes his head as he stares out the kitchen window. Obviously, he has a plan. He has one for everything.

"What do you need me to do?"

"Is Sartre on his computer?" Machiavelli asks.

"Don't ask dumb questions."

"Tell him to check the drafts folder in our email. I have instructions for him."

In a digital world, the first thing governments sought to do was intercept data traveling over wires. The workaround is a simple, yet elegant solution: don't send anything. By having an email address and sharing a password, a message can be drafted and saved without sending it. The group can then log on, read the draft, and then delete it when done. Nothing can be intercepted or read by the NSA, FBI, or any other three-letter agency.

"And me?"

"We're accelerating the plan. Prepare for another mission, too. Victoria Larsen isn't the only problem we may need to solve moving forward."

The call terminates. Marx shakes his head and stuffs the phone into a pocket before returning to the living room. Preparing for another mission is frustratingly vague. He goes to the corner and stands over Sartre. There had better be details in that email draft.

"Check the account," he says, tapping on the hacker's shoulder to get him to remove his headphones.

Trotsky joins them after pausing the game. "What's up?"

"New tasking from Machiavelli."

Sartre pulls it up, and the three men read. The instructions are long and highly detailed. They bring a smile to Marx's face.

"Do you think he came up with all this ahead of time or spent two hours typing it last night?" Trotsky asks. It was a rhetorical question.

"Can you do it, Sartre?"

"Easy, peasy, boss man."

"Get to it. Trot, when you're done with your game, load the truck and prep for tonight. Triple check everything. We can't afford any missteps."

"Wilco."

Trot turns off the gaming system and goes straight to work. Sartre has a new sense of purpose at his keyboard, leaving Marx free to return to his book. He has a little time to finish his own version of escapism before the real fun begins.

CHAPTER EIGHTEEN

SENATOR ALICIA STANDISH

Standish for President Campaign Office
Nashua, New Hampshire

Alicia drops her stuff and heads toward the rear of the building. Much like her office in Des Moines, her office here is an old retail location repurposed to act as a coordination center. Located on a busy Nashua street, it also serves as a billboard for her campaign. Volunteers and staff use the large open area in front to coordinate activities while the back has been converted into work areas for her permanent staff.

The results in Iowa put her in a foul mood despite her knowing what they would be. She's trying to take it in stride and is failing miserably. Nobody likes getting crushed in any contest. When it's in front of the nation and world, it's even more painful.

"Welcome back, Senator," Brian says, looking up from the laptop on his desk in the small room that once housed the store's manager.

"Thanks. It's good to be back in the Northeast after the ass-kicking I got on the Great Plains."

"What happened?"

Brian gets the "are you kidding" look. "We lost, that's what."

"I know. Winning there was a long shot, but losing by double digits—"

"Is someone running around New Hampshire intimidating college kids?" Alicia asks, not wanting to rehash the beating she took.

"Apparently, but nobody knows anything outside of the campus police reports."

"What about the arsons?"

"Ditto. State police investigators haven't told us anything. Now the FBI is here."

"Please don't tell me that means Victoria Larsen came with them."

Brian has spent a couple of years giving her bad news. It's what ultimately got him fired as her chief of staff during the Safe America Act debacle. Those who don't learn from history are doomed to repeat it. Although he doesn't have any reliable information regarding the FBI personnel on the ground, it's not a stretch to think that they would send their best and brightest.

"I don't know."

"The media is blaming us," the senator says, pivoting away from discussing one of her nemeses.

"We have the most to gain by hurting Luther Burgess. It doesn't take any strenuous mental gymnastics to reach that conclusion."

"Are we doing it?" Alicia asks, using an accusatory tone instead of an inquisitive one.

"Of course not. It's hurting us, not him."

"Who is, then?"

Brian shrugs slightly. "It's a long list, up to and including Burgess's own supporters."

"Why would they attack their own office?"

"What has happened to our poll numbers since the arsons?"

"They've dropped."

He cocks his head and smirks. "Exactly."

"I hope you're not going around telling the media that."

"And see pictures of me with tin foil photoshopped on my head circulating around social media? No thanks. It's just a pet theory."

Alicia relaxes. She felt a pang of guilt over the momentary thought that Brian could have been behind it. His firing was traumatic, and a part of her wondered if he arranged this to get back at her. No political operative is that stupid. It'd be career suicide. He'd never work in politics again, and that has been his life.

"Any others?"

"Lots of them, but I have a better question: why didn't you respond to the arsons? That isn't like you."

"Michael Ross, that's why. He thought there was a better strategy."

"That was a miscalculation. Our silence left a crack in the door, and Luther drove a snowplow through it."

"Yeah, he sure did," Alicia sighs, appreciating Brian's restraint. She knows he hates Michael and could've engaged in some old-fashioned character assassination.

"I'm getting advice from a lot of people now. Staff, pundits, colleagues…how do you think I can stop my poll numbers from dropping?"

Brian rubs his chin. When an incumbent politician runs for reelection, the challenger needs to make the race a referendum on that person's time in office. If the strategy works, the incumbent often loses. This situation is different as there is no incumbent, so the dynamic changes. Old-school mudslinging has its place, but the best tactic is to increase the enthusiasm gap. There is only one meaningful way to do that.

"Prove to the country that you're the best for the job."

"You don't think I'm doing that?"

"You need to give people stronger reasons to support you. Burgess is giving them plenty of reasons not to. He's changed the narrative to make you an incumbent that he can beat before you ever hold the office."

"How do I stop him?" Alicia asks, seeing some logic behind his conclusion that she hadn't thought of.

"You don't. Let Burgess make it about you. When he shines a spotlight on you, embrace it. Then show the nation that you have better credentials, more experience, better policies, and the best chance to beat the Republicans in November because sensible people know that he can't. Not with his agenda."

Brian lifts himself out of his chair, prompting a puzzled look from Alicia. He's not used to her being this chatty with him.

"Where are you going?" she asks.

"You'll have to excuse me, Senator. I have rally planning meetings. We have a busy week ahead of us, and you entrusted me to ensure they go smoothly."

"Brian, if you were running my campaign, where would you start fixing this?"

"By changing your messaging," he says immediately.

"Our messaging is effective."

"The polls say otherwise. You know as well as I do that the hardest part about winning an election is all the course changes needed. To make them, you need to be honest with yourself when things aren't working."

"Michael Ross says the opposite," Alicia argues. "I asked him a similar question. He says to stay the course."

"Like I said, you're getting bad advice. Ross hates deviating from the plan, and that's why you're losing."

Brian gives her a respectful nod and departs, leaving her with a lot to think about. She knows the rivalry between the two men is toxic, and they have far different approaches to the problem. Which path she chooses may make the difference between winning and losing. The responsibility of the decision and the consequences is hers, and hers alone.

CHAPTER NINETEEN

TIERRA CAMPOS

Autumn Bluff Suites
Manchester, New Hampshire

It shouldn't be this hard. Austin created an investigative unit modeled on *The Boston Globe*'s Spotlight team and adapted it to the digital era. He was my knight in shining armor when he showed up at Josh's apartment and recruited me after I got fired from WWDC TV and doxxed by hackers.

It's been nearly eight months since that day. The people I've met at *Front Burner* here have become almost family. At least, that's how it used to feel. Now we're the Hatfields and McCoys, and I can't help but feel betrayed by Austin's attitude.

"What is this?" Austin asks over the videoconference during the early morning check-in after I send a scan of the slip of paper Victoria passed me.

"It's the dark web address texted to Dylan Spencer before his quote-unquote suicide."

"Why do we have it?"

"Victoria asked us to see if we could track down the site's owner."

"Why? Are all the FBI's computers broken?"

"She didn't say why."

Austin frowns and leans back from the webcam, folding his arms across his chest. Jerome is standing behind him, also unimpressed.

"We can't exactly do an RDAP or WHOIS lookup. It's not our job to do the FBI's job for them. We have other things to focus on."

"Austin, you know Victoria. She wouldn't ask if it wasn't important."

"She would if she didn't want us poking around the arson investigation."

Victoria owes her career to *Front Burner*. After being arrested on some bogus charges related to the riot in Brockhampton, we led the charge to get them dropped. Between the public pressure we mustered and the FBI's own insistence, prosecutors dropped the charges, and she was reinstated as an agent. I would never take advantage of that, but Victoria wouldn't purposefully deceive us either.

"You can't believe that Victoria would do that to us considering our history? What if the Spencer death is somehow linked to the arsons?"

"What if the moon is made of cheese? This is no time to lose focus, Tierra. What else did she tell you?"

I feel my jaw clench in anger. What the hell is wrong with him?

"Not much."

"Not much? You guys met up over lunch, right? She must have said something. Unless the four of you just met to catch up on *The Bachelor.*"

"I don't watch that show," Tyler argues, being funny and serious at the same time.

"Whatever. Write up what Victoria said and send it to me within the hour."

It is something in his tone. I glance up over the laptop and see Olivia shaking her head. I don't dare risk looking at Tyler and having Austin see me checking with the team here. This is between him and me. I don't want them involved in this.

"I can't. It was off the record."

That gets his attention. Austin's face contorts, and he leans in to his camera. "What do you mean it was off the record?"

"I mean just that. It's an active invest—"

"It's always an active investigation," he says exasperated. "Victoria's a source."

"She's a friend."

"Not right then, she wasn't. This wasn't over a glass of wine. It was steps away from an active crime scene that she was actively working. You never promise to be off the record with a source when you work for me, including her. You know that."

"She wouldn't have given us anything if I hadn't."

"I thought you said she didn't say much? If you can't get information out of her, then you're not particularly good at your job."

I take the comment personally. Austin said that in front of Jerome, and I'm sure Logan and Madison are with him. He knows Tyler and Olivia are here. Not only is it a dressing down in front of my colleagues, but it also hurts on a personal level. I can't believe he really thinks that. Tears that I fight to stop relentlessly form in the corners of my eyes.

"I want the details. Summarize them and send them to me."

With that, he ends the videoconference. There was no apology, hint of remorse, or guilt.

"That was tense," Olivia says. "Are you okay?"

"No, not really."

"He was way out of line," Tyler concludes. "You're the last person he should be saying isn't good at her job."

"Thanks, Ty."

"What are you going to do?"

I look at Olivia. "I'm going to summarize the conversation just as he asked."

"What about the SOF spray-painted on the sidewalk?"

"I don't recall her saying anything about that, do you, Tyler?"

The corner of his mouth curls up. I don't like the idea of having to do this. I'm not about to betray a close friend to satisfy a bitter editor who I once considered to be one.

CHAPTER TWENTY

SPECIAL AGENT VICTORIA LARSEN

Federal Bureau of Investigation Field Office
Bedford, New Hampshire

Victoria pours another cup of coffee from the carafe. Her hands shake from being overcaffeinated, and she needs a hot shower. It was a long night in the cozy confines of the Bedford office that would have been worth the hours invested had they found anything useful. Their fortunes haven't changed so far this morning.

"How about this guy?" Ian says, far too excited about this wild goose chase.

She looks at the picture and scans the file. She commits the critical information to memory and inputs it into the National Data Exchange that's running on her own laptop. The N-DEx is an information-sharing system that enables criminal justice agencies across the country to search, analyze, and share records. It complements other FBI systems like the National Crime Information Center and Interstate Identification Index in providing critical information to law enforcement agencies.

"Completely clean," she says, for about the five-hundredth time tonight.

"I would have put money on that one. This guy just looks shady."

"The one thing you learn when you do this job long enough, Agent Drucker, is that the worst criminals usually look like they work on Wall Street."

"Many of them do," he grouses.

He returns to his search as Victoria leans back in her chair and rubs her eyes. They're combing through the National Personnel Records Center database containing the official personnel records of the millions of discharged and deceased veterans of all branches from the 20th century to today. By cross-referencing that information with the Defense Eligibility Enrollment Reporting System, a portal for veteran health and medical benefits, the two agents are trying to identify possible SOF members. The targets are veterans with special forces training who live within a fifty-mile radius of Manchester and have a police record. Few of them do.

"This is a dead end, Ian."

"I'm not willing to give up that easily. We can expand the search."

"There is no evidence that the arsonists are native to the area. They could be from anywhere."

"Okay, then I have a radical idea that may speed things up," Ian says, spinning his chair around.

"I'm all ears."

"We should cross it with Standish's donor list."

"Please tell me you're kidding."

"I'm dead serious."

"Ian, think about what you are saying. If that ever got out, the media would accuse us of targeting a campaign."

"It won't get out, and if it does, who cares? It's what everyone thinks anyway."

"We are the Federal Bureau of Investigation, Ian. That's not how we operate."

"You just said this is a dead end. You're right, so if we change our approach, we need to start somewhere. It's the logical first step. We've profiled everyone in the area and came up empty."

"It's targeting a campaign."

"Whether we start with hers or someone else's, looking for someone who is either involved in the campaign or a staunch supporter of one of the candidates is just common sense."

Victoria hangs her head. He's not entirely wrong. The problem is, "not entirely wrong" doesn't make it right. It would be basing investigative action on an assumption, and that has gotten the FBI in trouble on more than one occasion.

"We can defend it, Vic," Ian continues to plead. "It's not a stretch to think that either her campaign or her supporters are behind this."

She's uneasy with that conclusion. "I don't think there's any evidence at all that supports that. Don't limit it to Standish. Get the donor lists for every campaign, both Republican and Democrat, from the FEC and run it against N-DEx and NCIC. Take those and check for military backgrounds. See if anything interesting pops up."

Ian frowns and shakes his head. "Okay."

Searching all political contributors to all the campaigns will take ten times as long, and Ian's not happy about that. Victoria couldn't care less about how he feels. Walking into a minefield is risky. Stepping on one on purpose is plain stupid.

A chyron below a news report playing on a television in the corner of the room catches Victoria's eye. She uses the remote to turn up the volume.

"The three letters were sprayed in white paint, likely right before or after they were set ablaze. Neither the New Hampshire State Police nor federal investigators are commenting on this calling card left at the entrances of these four offices. Until they do, America is being left to hypothesize what SOF means and who wrote it."

"Shit."

Victoria doesn't hear the reporter sign off and throw it back to the anchor desk. Her mind is racing ahead, gauging the intensity of the coming storm. Someone let the genie out of the bottle. It will send the media into a frenzy speculating on the meaning. They haven't even had breakfast yet, and she already knows this is going to be a long day.

CHAPTER TWENTY-ONE

TIERRA CAMPOS

Autumn Bluff Suites
Manchester, New Hampshire

My cell phone rings within minutes of the reporter ending his on-site broadcast. Tyler and Olivia both stare at the phone in silence before turning their eyes toward me. I exhale sharply, knowing this isn't going to be a pleasant conversation.

"Hi, Austin," I croak after answering.

"Did you catch the breaking news?"

"We're watching it now."

"Tell me Victoria never mentioned it," Austin says, a smooth calm in his voice. "Tell me you didn't know about the SOF."

I close my eyes. We submitted the summary ten minutes ago and didn't include that information. I'm not willing to push our luck any further.

"She told us."

Tyler rubs the back of his neck, and Olivia closes her eyes. The silence on the line is deafening. I stare at my cell. The meltdown is coming in three, two, one…

"What the hell were you thinking?" Austin shouts. "Did you think that information wasn't critical enough to tell your editor? Because of all the incompetent, grossly negligent things I've seen journalists do, you just shot into the top five. Why didn't you tell me?"

"Would you have run with it?" I ask, fighting my own rising anger.

"It's a huge story. We could have scooped everybody."

"I told you that the information was relayed to us in confidence and off the record. Would you still have run with it?"

There are times when silence conveys a stronger message than words do. Austin doesn't answer the question, and his lack of response speaks volumes. I know he would have. Maybe not six months ago, but definitely now.

"I thought so. That's why I didn't tell you, Austin. Off the record is off the record."

"You don't get to unilaterally make the decision about what goes on our site."

"No, I don't. And you don't get to ruin my relationship with sources by violating a time-honored tradition of commenting off the record. Who would ever trust me again if that ever came out?"

"Your obligation is to *Front Burner*," he sneers. "Or is it?"

I'm about to erupt. If there was any doubt over the origins of Austin's hostility, he just put an end to it. He's making what I thought would be an impossible decision much easier.

"My obligation is to professional journalism and accurately conveying information, regardless of whom I'm employed by."

"Your obligation is to do the job we pay you for. Off the record means different things. You could have not attributed it."

"Victoria was crystal clear what off the record meant, and it was agreed to ahead of time. I was not going to violate that. Not for you. Not for anybody."

"I see. Your friendship with her means more to you than your job. I get it."

"No, I don't think you get it at all, Austin."

The comment hangs in the air for what feels like an eternity. I use the silence to calm myself down. I'm one stupid comment from telling my boss to go to hell and take this job with him.

"You lied to me in that summary," he says, his tone calmer yet still edgy.

"I omitted it from the summary because I knew that you would publish it. You've lost your way. I don't know what's happening here, but you're compromising your journalistic integrity."

"And you're letting Brockhampton go to your head. I'm drafting a reprimand and placing it into your personnel file. Tyler and Olivia are just as culpable, so I will have one for them, too. The three of you have twelve hours to respond after I send it. If this happens again, you're all fired," he says, ending the call.

"I think that went well," Tyler says, his attempt at humor earning a glare from Olivia.

"I'm sorry, guys. You shouldn't be caught up in this. It's about Austin and me."

"We chose our side. Austin's wrong, and we're right. It's that simple," Olivia says.

"I can get the reprimands removed."

"It might not matter, Ty. Regardless of how this plays out, I think my days at *Front Burner* are numbered."

CHAPTER TWENTY-TWO

ANDREW LI

Manchester-Boston Regional Airport
Manchester, New Hampshire

Andrew enlisted a campaign staff member to drive the car to the airport. The governor's connecting flight is late getting in, so Andrew sent him off to the cell phone waiting lot. With one eye on the arrivals board, he read the news on his smartphone. Waiting at airports is one of the downsides of working for a candidate who insists on flying commercial.

"Congratulations on your win in Iowa, Governor," Andrew says, meeting Luther and his son at the baggage carousel once their flight arrives.

"Thank you. You were a big part of that and deserve a lot of credit."

"I'm happy to help execute Isiah's vision for your campaign. I'll phone John and have him pick us up."

"Let's get some coffee first and then take a walk."

The luggage is retrieved, the governor insisting on dragging his own through the claim area. He loves to play the part of the everyman, and it works for him. Andrew sees at least three people snap pictures with their phones. If an intrepid reporter contrasts that with Standish getting off her private plane, it's worth a few hundred more votes.

"Pops, we have a full day today. We really don't have time for this."

"What good is living a long life if you don't take a moment to enjoy the small things?"

"It's an airport."

"Did I teach you nothing, boy? Airports make for the best people-watching on the planet. You see the best and worst of humanity meandering through a complex system that requires all the pieces to work together in harmony."

"And yet it takes longer to get through security than to your destination," Isiah grumbles.

"It's all part of the journey."

"Right now, our journey needs to take us to the Lamm family home and then to what's left of our campaign office."

"I'm not doing that second part, so we have plenty of time," the governor decrees.

The governor stops to take a picture with a young couple. Isiah looks at Andrew, who urges the campaign manager on with a couple of nods when the short photo shoot is over.

"We need to go to the office," Isiah insists, earning a hard look from his father.

"Why? Son, there's nothing there except investigators and media. Unless that's what you want. The photo op."

"You need to show your concern."

"I'm already visiting the family. There's not going to be press there. That's the way I want it," the governor insists.

"Pops, I—"

"I don't want to make this tragedy the issue. I've said what I needed to about it. Anything more will only serve to feed the media trolls."

"I agree," Andrew says, earning a surprised look from Isiah. "You did say what you needed to, and it was brilliant. I don't want you to say anything at the office, other than thank the investigators for their work. Just visit it."

"What good is that supposed to do?"

"You don't want to be blamed for using the arsons for political gain, and I agree with you. Isiah wants the imagery of you visiting your office, and so do I. Let the media fill in the narrative. Turn their overzealous reporting into a strength."

Luther shakes his head. "It will still look like I'm exploiting it."

"You'll look concerned and caring, and that's what people want. Let the media do the dirty work of making it political. Then pivot back to your policies at a moment where everyone is listening."

The governor turns to Isiah. He nods.

"You may be the smartest man my son ever hired. You're absolutely one of the most convincing ones. All right. Let's go."

The governor takes the lead out of the terminal, stopping twice for pictures and a few times to shake hands. This is the part of campaigning he enjoys. Most politicians fake it. His joy is authentic.

"Nice work," Isiah whispers to Andrew as they walk into the car loading area.

"Policy discussions aren't going to be enough to win here. You know that, right?"

"I know how to deliver New Hampshire to him."

"You had better hope to God it's a good plan," Andrew says, not liking the idea that he's being kept in the dark.

Isiah smiles. "'God is not willing to do everything, and thus take away our free will and that share of glory which belongs to us.'"

CHAPTER TWENTY-THREE

SPECIAL AGENT VICTORIA LARSEN

Federal Bureau of Investigation Boston Field Office
Chelsea, Massachusetts

The word came down from Lance Fuller to report back in person once the spread of the SOF story hit terminal velocity. The man running the Boston field office is known for a lot of things, but his patience isn't one of them. On a career trajectory that will take him to the highest ranks of the Bureau someday, he demanded Takara, Victoria, and Ian be there within the hour. They practically broke the sound barrier driving down Interstate 93 to even make it close to the appointed time.

The executive assistant outside the door waves them past. Victoria knows this is going to be bad. That never happens. The head of the Boston FBI is a busy man, and when he isn't in a meeting, he's on the phone.

"Do any of you care to explain this?" Fuller asks as the three agents stand in front of his desk. This isn't a meeting for them to sit comfortably through.

"I don't know who leaked it to the media," Takara says, fielding the first question in the inquisition after Fuller shows them the story on his computer monitor.

"Me neither, sir," Victoria offers as Fuller's eyes drift to her before settling on Ian.

"I don't either, sir."

He looks unconvinced. "That's convenient."

"There were dozens of local and state police working at that site. Why are you assuming it was one of us?"

He straightens up and stares at his desk for a moment. "Did you meet with *Front Burner* while working the Manchester arson?"

Victoria tenses up. So that's what this is about. Someone saw her talking with Tierra, Tyler, and Olivia. Somehow it made its way back here. That left Fuller to make the connection quickly.

"Yes, I did."

"Were you with her, Agent Drucker?"

"No, sir. I was in Bedford with Agent Nishimoto."

Takara nods when Fuller looks for confirmation. All three pairs of eyes focus back on Victoria.

"You met with three journalists alone, and you're wondering why you're here?"

"*Front Burner* didn't break the news."

"You're right, Agent Larsen. As usual, you're right. They didn't break it. It aired on *Capitol Beat*'s network, and Tierra Campos is in the running to take over after Wilson Newman's retirement. She even hosted for him last week."

"Wait a minute," Victoria says, her voice rising. "You think I gave it to her, and she turned it over to them instead of *Front Burner*? That's ridiculous."

"Is it?" Lance asks, leaning back in his chair.

"Sir, I think we need to give Agent Larsen the benefit of the doubt on this one," Takara argues. "I think that she—"

"If you're going to bring up Brockhampton, don't. I've spent the last six months cutting her slack, and she's withdrawn all the currency she banked following that mess."

"There's still a balance left," Victoria argues, knowing they haven't come close to making amends for what they put her through.

"Don't get cute, Agent Larsen. I went to bat for you in a big way with the state police. Don't forget that."

Victoria could argue for hours with him about that. He did push for the charges to be dropped following the shooting at the Brockhampton riot in the wake of Governor Flynn's assassination. Whether the result was Fuller backing one of his agents or a response to the immense public pressure from *Front Burner* is subject to debate.

"The leak could have come from anywhere, sir," Takara argues. "Did Agent Larsen have a lapse of judgment meeting with them? Yes, but they're friends who haven't seen each other for a long time. If she were planning on leaking information, it wouldn't be done in plain sight of dozens of other law enforcement officers and federal agents."

Lance is frustrated. He sees the validity of Takara's point. Victoria chooses to remain silent. She did give them information and doesn't want to lie about it, regardless of whether *Front Burner* printed it. She wants to believe that Tierra didn't give it to *Capitol Beat* or anyone else. Tyler and Olivia never would have let her if she did. Still, the possibility exists, and that bothers her more than getting dressed down by Fuller ever could.

"Thank you for your wise assessment, Agent Nishimoto. You're on a track to run your own office someday, and when you do, you can make the call. So long as I am running this one, my word is what matters. Understood?"

"Yes, sir."

Lance's eyes lock onto Victoria. "Despite your colleague's attempt to whitewash this, meeting with *Front Burner* was more than a lapse of judgment. It was plain stupid. I don't care whether it was Campos who leaked it or the damn tooth fairy. This is your final warning, Agent Larsen. I won't tolerate your maverick behavior anymore. If you step out of line again, in this investigation or any other, I will refer you to the OIG."

"I think we've been down that road before, haven't we?"

Her rogue work on the true story behind the Brockhampton shooting almost got her drummed out of the Bureau. In Fuller's defense, he was under immense pressure from the Department of Justice and the Hoover Building. If she had been wrong about Ethan Harrington, she'd be working as a barista in a coffee shop right now.

"Yes, the OIG is exceedingly familiar with you. It would be in your best interest to stay out of their line of sight. From this point forward, none of you are to have any contact with the media at all, including Tierra Campos. I'm sure the two of you can find time to catch up when this is over. Am I clear?"

"Yes, sir."

"Good. Then get back to work."

The three agents make for the door and hurry out of his office. They stride toward the elevator, eager to get out of the building as quickly as possible.

"Thanks for backing me up in there," Victoria whispers to Takara as Ian forges ahead of them.

"It was stupid to meet with *Front Burner.*"

"How would I know that the information would get leaked to the media and that I'd get blamed for it?"

"Did Tierra screw you over?"

Victoria shakes her head. "I hope not."

"It's my turn to go rogue. I'm going to poke around up there to see if I can find out," Takara says, falling silent as they reach Ian, who is holding the elevator.

Another pit is forming in Victoria's stomach. Everything is wrong about this, starting with Dylan Spencer's suicide. Now they have intimidations, arsons, and the SOF calling card. She can add the leak to the list.

CHAPTER TWENTY-FOUR

SENATOR ALICIA STANDISH

Standish for President Campaign Office
Nashua, New Hampshire

Alicia is sick to her stomach. How could she be kept out of the loop like this? What may have once been a genius plan to help deliver votes in New Hampshire has turned into an albatross around her neck. This could sink her campaign for good, like the last torpedo into the side of a battleship.

"Did you know about this?" she manages to ask, at a near whisper.

"I had no idea what he was up to," Angela admits. "He only told me when the news of the SOF painted outside the offices broke."

Of all the dumb things about this, that is the worst. Angela is the campaign manager and in charge of all activities and staff. How could she not have known? Why would he leave her in the dark unless he had a reason?

"Where is Brian now?"

"Portsmouth. We have a rally planned for you there. He needed to meet with law enforcement and city officials."

"When is he due back?"

"Later today."

"Fire him. I don't want him within fifty miles of this office."

"Will do," Angela says, not daring to go against her candidate's wishes. She knows part of this falls on her.

"I don't think that's the best course of action."

Both women turn and glare at Michael. To his credit, he doesn't retreat or get defensive. He stands his ground, maintaining eye contact with them.

"You don't get to make the decision," Angela snaps.

"No, I don't. This is one hundred percent your call. However, I think you need to take a step back and view this from a wider perspective."

"A wider perspective?" Alicia asks, not believing he just said that.

"You don't think we're doing that?" Angela piles on.

"No, I think you're both rightfully angry and jumping to try to undo something that cannot be undone."

"I didn't think you liked Brian."

"I don't," Michael concedes.

"Then why are you defending him?" Alicia asks.

"I'm defending your campaign. Brian hasn't been accused of anything directly. If you fire him, the media will be all over it. It will look like an admission of guilt before anyone understands the charges. It gives the appearance of your involvement."

"We're taking a proactive stance—"

"Unfortunately, he's right, Angela," the senator sighs, leaning back in her chair and taking a moment to collect her thoughts. "If we fire him, we risk opening ourselves up to even more questions less than a week before the primary."

"Senator, you're not going to like what I'm about to say, but here it goes. If you don't do this and Brian is involved, it's Harrington and Baino all over again."

Alicia lowers her eyes to the floor. Angela is also right. Not taking Brian's advice and cutting Ethan and Ryan loose before they were implicated in the shooting and cover-up cost her greatly. She's afraid of making the same mistake twice. It's a "damned if you do and damned if you don't" scenario. In those situations, she usually does. There's typically less downside to acting.

"There's a third option," Ryan interjects, angering Angela but commanding the senator's attention. "Marginalize him. Keep Brian with the campaign but remove him as chairman. Say it's for health reasons or something like that if anyone asks."

"That's stupid," Angela decrees.

"It will raise far fewer questions than a firing would, and it keeps him close. If you fire him, he can do and say whatever he wants."

"We could force him to sign a fresh NDA on the way out."

"Would you sign a non-disclosure agreement if you were him? This isn't about money. It's about reputation."

"Why should we listen to you, Michael? Your last advice didn't exactly pan out."

Angela's comment stings. Michael became a top-notch political operative by giving advice to candidates that won them their elections. He knows he isn't off to a good start with this one.

"Yeah, I screwed that up. I own that mistake and am grateful that the senator was savvy enough to rectify it on her own. You pay me for my counsel. That is my advice. The choice of direction is yours."

There's nothing more to be gained for him by pleading his case. He rises from his chair and leaves the small office, pulling the door closed behind him.

"Angela, I know you don't like Brian. I chose you to run my campaign and the staff working on it, so it's your decision. All I'm asking is for you to take your personal feelings out of it. Is Michael right?"

She sighs. "He has a valid point, yes. Firing Brian will draw a lot of unwanted attention in the short term."

"Enough attention to lose the primary in New Hampshire?"

"Possibly."

"And nothing has changed with the outcomes of this race if we lose here?"

"No. It's as close to a must-win as you can get."

The campaign manager knows where her boss is going with this. To her credit, the answers she gave are direct and honest.

"I think you should listen to him and demote Brian but keep him working in New Hampshire. We can reevaluate once the primary is over."

"Okay, Senator, under one condition: if he so much as crosses a street outside a crosswalk, I'll ask him to tender his resignation. If you don't accept it, you'll be getting mine."

The blunt terms dictated by her most trusted advisor catch her off guard. Alicia stares blankly at the wall after Angela departs, leaving her alone in the office to think. Americans wonder why politicians make such dumb decisions. The answer is simple: at this level, they're always under siege. The smart ones realize a universal truth when it comes to power: you can't really trust anybody.

CHAPTER TWENTY-FIVE

TIERRA CAMPOS

Prescott Park
Portsmouth, New Hampshire

Portsmouth is located about forty miles from Manchester. Tucked into the southeast corner of the state, it is New Hampshire's oldest settlement, its first capital, and only seaport. Prescott Park comprises over ten waterfront acres along the Piscataqua River and is best known by residents for hosting outdoor productions of Broadway plays during the summer.

I sit on a bench across from the American flag near the entrance of the park, trying not to freeze my ass off. The park is entirely devoid of people on this frigid day, except for the idiot journalist from Arizona who agreed to meet at this moronic location.

"For almost the entire 20th century, Portsmouth built and repaired U.S. Navy submarines," Brian says, standing behind me. Where did he come from?

"Mister Cooper, it's freezing out here. I'm in no mood for a history lesson today."

He watches his breath condense into a cloud as it escapes his mouth into the frigid temperatures. "Yeah, a park probably wasn't the best choice for this meeting."

"Ya think?"

"I bet it's beautiful here in the summer."

"It's not summer. It's the dead of winter in New England. You asked me to come down here, so what do you want? And make it quick."

"Come on, I know a quaint coffee shop nearby that we can talk in."

Unless it is built in an ice cave, I'm not going to argue. We walk a couple of blocks away from the river and settle into a cute little shop. Brian brings over a pair of coffees in large porcelain mugs as I massage blood back into my fingers.

"We could have just met here, you know. I have maps on my phone."

"I wanted to make sure you weren't being followed. This entire conversation is off the record. I know you've had issues with that lately."

I can't hide my surprise, and he's amused by my attempt to stifle it. How could he know that? I want to ask but won't give him the satisfaction.

"This isn't Brockhampton, Mister Cooper."

"No, it's bigger. I'm being set up."

"I'm not following."

"I'm going to explain, but first, some backstory. After Brockhampton, I went and saw Alicia Standish. The Safe America Act had just gone down in flames, and she was angry. I explained that I was protecting her and that you would be fair in your stories about what happened."

"Which I was," I say, a little too defensively.

"Yes, you were. Even the senator would agree. We buried the hatchet, and she asked me to join her campaign as the chairman in New Hampshire. I accepted."

"How is any of this relevant?"

"I'm getting to that. The ground game is going to be everything in this election. Television advertising is expensive and ineffective as more people are watching streaming services. Social media is a cluttered mess of lies and deceit, and nobody likes to read stuff online."

"Gee, thanks," I moan.

"No offense, of course, but this is a campaign. I needed a mechanism to bring the senator's message directly to the people in a very personal way. To that end, I enlisted a group of ardent supporters who were willing to pound the pavement in every neighborhood, shopping mall, and gathering place in New Hampshire. They were my messengers who spoke directly to the people, and they were good at it. I came to rely on them heavily. You could say they were a special operations unit of sorts."

A shiver runs down my spine, and it isn't because of the drafty coffee shop. "Mister Cooper, are you telling me—"

"I called them the Standish Operations Forces. S-O-F."

My eyes grow wide in surprise, and my mouth hangs open. I can't believe what I'm hearing. I start to say something before pausing to take a deep breath.

"Does the senator know?"

Brian frowns, staring down at his coffee. "She does now. I told our campaign manager before the news of it broke. Then I left to come here."

"Did she fire you?"

"Not yet, but it's likely once I get back to Manchester. The senator is politically exposed. Michael Ross will convince her to do something."

"Was it the SOF that torched Burgess's offices?"

"No."

"How do you know?"

"Because I do. It's not a military or paramilitary outfit. I just thought it was a clever name, and they embraced it. They are nothing more than a group of supporters willing to do outreach. That's it. There is no way they were involved in arsons. It was just made to look that way."

I think back to what Austin told me before I met Brian on the U.S.S. Constitution. He's a shrewd political operative and professional liar, and I need to watch out for him. He was on the level about what happened with Ethan and Ryan in Brockhampton, but that doesn't mean he is now.

"Why should I believe you?"

"Because if I ordered them to torch buildings, they wouldn't have spray-painted a roadmap to my office door on the sidewalk. I wouldn't have gotten caught at all."

I can't argue with that logic. "Who did it?"

"I don't know."

"Who else knew about the SOF?"

"Not a ton of people, but enough of them where it wasn't a state secret either."

"Can you give me the list of the members?"

Brian digs through the pocket of his heavy wool overcoat and pulls out a thumb drive. He holds it up before handing it over to me. This could be the motherlode.

"Every computer file ever opened for the SOF is on that."

A thought pops into my head. It's not the first time I've had it, but I've never given it much credence until now.

"Could it be someone out to hurt Alicia Standish?"

Brian smirks. "Outstanding, Miss Campos. That was my guess the moment I heard about it on the news. Someone sprawled SOF on the ground, knowing that it would leak to the media and eventually point back at us. I just have no way to prove it."

I frown and sip my coffee. I'm doing Cooper's dirty work for him again. I would protest, but an election may be riding on this. It's also another huge story that I don't trust anyone else to tell.

"If you think someone is behind this, why are you so worried about losing your job?"

"Politics, Miss Campos. The office kind. I have a complicated history with Senator Standish. There's no reason for people to believe it isn't me looking for some payback after getting fired as her chief of staff."

"She gave you another role, right?"

Brian drains the rest of his coffee and stands. "There is a stark difference between what I was doing then and what I am now. Get to the bottom of this, Tierra. I'm counting on you. My whole career may depend on it. Enjoy your coffee and stay warm while you're up here."

I plan on doing exactly that, at least for the next fifteen minutes. The coffee is hot, the shop is warm, and the temperature outside is neither. I pull out the thumb drive and stare at it. Nobody understands the value of trust until they work in national politics. Brian Cooper is a master at political tradecraft. I spent much of last summer worrying about that, and it looks like history is about to repeat itself.

CHAPTER TWENTY-SIX

CAPITOL BEAT

Cable News Studio
Washington, D.C.

Wilson takes one last look at his written notes as the producer counts down. If he ever thought that the final nine-month stretch of his job was going to be uneventful, he was mistaken. The primary season has barely started, and events are already spiraling out of control.

"Good Evening. It is Wednesday, February second; I am Wilson Newman, and this…is…*Capitol Beat*.

"The Iowa Caucuses are in the books and the race for the White House is officially underway," he says after the show's opening music ceases. "The results were as predicted; the frontrunner won for both parties. Democrat Governor Luther Burgess earned twenty of the forty-one delegates up for grabs, and Republican Governor Colin Bradford earned sixteen of forty.

"Surprise GOP contender Kristi Hylton, the popular mayor of Nashville, Tennessee, had a good showing and will build momentum heading into New Hampshire. The same cannot be said of Senator Alicia Standish. Iowa's proximity to Luther Burgess's home state of Illinois was always going to make this a tough race for her. Additionally, leading up to the caucus, news broke of a series of unfortunate incidents in New Hampshire. Voters in Iowa made their opinions known on the subject, awarding the senator with a disappointing eleven delegates for the convention.

"The Standish campaign has denied any involvement in the arsons and intimidation while vehemently arguing that their supporters were not involved. Authorities have been silent on the matter, but *Capitol Beat* has learned that the Federal Bureau of Investigation is actively investigating the Standish campaign. A source close to the investigation believes that the arsonists who destroyed four campaign offices, and the men who intimidated Burgess supporters at local college campuses, were directly associated with the Standish campaign.

"We have also just learned that New Hampshire campaign chair for Standish for President, Brian Cooper, has been reassigned to other duties within the campaign. Whether this reshuffling is related to the attacks on the Burgess campaign or a reaction to the drop in Alicia Standish's sagging numbers is subject to debate. We did reach out to the Standish campaign and received no response to our inquiries."

Wilson changes cameras as he prepares to summarize ahead of the next segment. His producers insisted on that breaking news being included in tonight's broadcast despite the lack of details. Without context, the actions of the Standish campaign are subject to a wide range of interpretations. Wilson would have preferred to wait until they had a statement from them.

"The results in Iowa and the events in New Hampshire are sure to dominate the roundtable discussion with our panel of experts coming up next. We will also have reports on the reaction in Iowa, events in Manchester and Nashua, and what the White House is saying about this. We will conclude with an exclusive interview with two commissioners sitting on the Federal Election Commission and my final thoughts.

"*Capitol Beat* will continue with our expert panel when we return from these short messages."

CHAPTER TWENTY-SEVEN

"S.O.F."

Second Garage Self-Storage
Manchester, New Hampshire

Storage facilities are designed to appear as impregnable as the gold repository at Fort Knox. There are high perimeter fences, cameras everywhere, access controls on the gate, and padlocks on each unit. The measures are meant to provide patrons with a sense that their belongings are safeguarded. The reality is entirely different. All that security is obscenely easy to defeat for a determined professional.

"Ready?" Marx asks as he sits in the passenger seat of their black Dodge Ram pickup down the street from the facility.

"Let's do this," Trot says, slamming the truck into drive.

The high-pitched whine of turbofan engines overhead causes Marx to look out the top of the windshield. He spots the plane on approach to Manchester-Boston Regional Airport as Trot pulls up to the gate.

He rolls down the window and taps the reader with the card they procured for their own small unit. The light flashes green, and the gate begins its slow roll open. They waste no time navigating to their storage unit. Marx is thrilled that this place offers twenty-four-hour access. It made this job far simpler.

Trot parks and the men jump out. Marx keys open the padlock and raises the flimsy rolling gate. He shines a flashlight on the half-dozen cardboard boxes. Thus far, they've done nothing illegal or even suspicious. That's about to change.

"You have the replacement lock?" Marx asks as Trot retrieves the bolt cutters from the bed of the truck.

"In my pocket."

"All right. Do it."

He pops the lock on the target unit and lifts the door. The storage unit still has plenty of space, which is what he was counting on. Their added containers will blend in nicely with the boxes of pamphlets and yard signs.

"Load it up. Keep everything toward the back," Marx commands.

The two men make quick work of the transfer, tossing in the four nylon bags before closing the rolling door. Trot compares the broken lock to the new one to confirm for one final time that they're the same model. He slaps it on the unit. The owner's key won't work anymore, but they won't likely ever get the chance to use it anyway.

Trot wipes the lock with a rag. The men are wearing gloves, but you can't ever be too careful. One print is all it would take to undo months of hard work.

"You know what to do."

Marx sets off for the main office while Trot repositions the truck and prepares for exfiltration. The lock on the back door to the small building is quickly defeated, and the alarm system disabled. He closes the door behind him and skulks through the dark office to the main desk. The sound of the computer's fan fills the silent room as he powers up the machine and locates the video surveillance system cabinet while it boots up.

"Ok, Sartre, you had better be right about this," Marx mumbles to himself as he pecks at the keyboard. He enters the username and password the hacker provided and hovers his finger over the enter key. He presses it and the application comes to life, causing him to smile. Bingo.

There are two ways to do this. The hard one will take longer and is fraught with problems. The easy one will make this a breeze.

He selects the folder for today's video and inserts a thumb drive into the computer's USB port. He opens it and launches the executable file for an encryption program. Five seconds later, it's complete. Data missing or deleted from the drive will raise suspicions. When encrypted, the video data is present and intact but is utterly unreadable without the key that only Sartre possesses. Even the NSA would need a billion eons to crack it.

With the video now taken care of, Marx navigates over to the access reader information and deletes the log entry for his card information. There's no point in leaving a trail back to them when it's this easy to erase. Finally, he finds the archive that has the backup data and deletes it. Nobody will notice its absence.

The mission completed, he pulls the thumb drive out of the computer and powers the system down.

"*We've got company*," Trot says over the radio. "*One vehicle at the entrance.*"

Marx can hear the clunky metal gate slide open and sees the headlights pull right up to the front of the building. A woman gets out, using the interior light of her car to find the right key to the door. It must be the owner.

"Shit."

He doesn't have time to exit the building without being seen. After a quick scan of the room, he hides along the wall in the kitchenette and pulls out his knife. A clean operation is about to get messy. He races through possible scenarios in his mind. Few of them end well for the woman.

The front door opens, a chain of jingle bells announcing the presence of the visitor. It's terrible timing. He hears the tone of the alarm buttons before she stops.

"Dipshit forgot to arm it. Typical. Damn stupid moron," the woman mutters, turning on the lights before moving around the counter.

Marx hazards a peek around the corner. She has her back to him. He hears a key entering a lock and a file cabinet being opened. The woman digs through it before removing a zipper pouch. Someone must have forgotten to make the deposit at the bank. Storage units still do a lot of transactions in cash or checks.

"Good for nothing worthless husband of mine…"

The office falls still. What is the hell is she doing? Finally, the drawer is slammed shut.

Marx closes his eyes and prepares himself to move. Deep breaths. Quiet calm. Slow is smooth, smooth is fast. He listens for any clues that she knows he's here.

"What a slob," the woman says, followed by the sound of a metal can getting scraped against the counter.

He brings the knife up to his chest, ready to pounce if she walks into the kitchenette. The recycling container is five feet away from him, and her back will be toward him. It's his one chance to make this quick.

The can flies past him in an arc. He watches it clank off the front of the bin. It bounces off the wall and rattles around before falling in. He loosens the death grip on his knife ever so slightly.

"Three points! Not on his best day would he hit from here."

The office light clicks off, and the alarm buttons give off their tone as she resets it. The thirty-second warning sound blares as the door closes, the door handle jiggling to ensure it's secured. Marx lets himself relax. The woman's basketball skills saved her life tonight.

"*Car moving out,*" Trot advises over the radio.

"Wait for five."

He moves out of the range of the lone motion sensor near the back door. The wait is excruciating. He checks his watch every fifteen seconds as time seems to slow to a crawl. He needs to make sure that the lady is gone for good before he exits the gate with Trot.

"*Four minutes until the systems open new files.*"

"Close enough. Move, Trot."

Marx disarms the alarm again and hits the gate open button at the counter. He stares out the window as it clangs to life before he exits out the back, reactivating the alarm system before he leaves. He meets up with the truck as Trot pulls it around the corner. It doesn't need to stop as Marx jumps in.

"Go."

Trot slams on the gas and guides the burly pickup through the gate before it starts to close. They pull onto the street as Marx's watch clicks to midnight. That was cutting it close.

Trot steers toward the safehouse as Marx types a note to the team: EYE OF THE NEEDLE. He grins. He has always liked Ken Follett and was hoping he could use that code. The text message to Machiavelli is a far simpler one: MISSION ACCOMPLISHED.

CHAPTER TWENTY-EIGHT

SPECIAL AGENT VICTORIA LARSEN

Federal Bureau of Investigation Boston Field Office
Chelsea, Massachusetts

5 Days to the New Hampshire Democratic Primary

Victoria has spent way too much time in this office. While she isn't the least bit intimidated by Lance Fuller, it feels much like a high school student visiting the principal. Whether you are in trouble or not, everyone knows you were in there.

"How did you find out about this?" Lance asks, scanning the file.

"I contacted some of the veterans that Agent Larsen came across when we were evaluating profiles of possible perpetrators."

"You just picked up the phone and called them? Why?"

"We weren't getting anywhere," Ian says, "so I thought I would seize the initiative."

"How many calls did you make?"

"I don't know, five or ten."

Victoria catches his side-eye glance at her. She shakes her head. It's the investigative equivalent of cold-calling grandmothers to buy penny stocks and landing Gordon Gekko from the movie *Wall Street*. The odds are almost that infinitesimally small.

"You're telling me that in ten calls or so, you found this guy?"

"I was lucky, sir."

"I'll say. He's a member of this Standish Operations Force?" Takara asks, standing off to the side.

"A proud one. He said it was created to mobilize the senator's strongest supporters in New Hampshire for an outreach and voter registration program."

"S-O-F," Fuller mutters, shaking his head. "Did he admit that they're violent?"

"He said no. He called himself a preacher who spreads the gospel according to Standish to the population."

"How cute."

"Other members of the group could be," Takara says. Victoria rolls her eyes.

"Who ran this group for the Standish campaign?"

"Brian Cooper. He's the New Hampshire chairman," Ian says, with far too much confidence for Victoria's tastes.

"Agent Larsen? You don't look impressed. Thoughts?"

"Well, sir, it makes a lot of sense, but I have two big problems with it. The first is the spray paint outside the offices. Why be so careful about removing physical evidence and then leave an obvious calling card that leads right back to the Standish campaign?"

"You think it's a setup?"

"I think we have to leave room for that possibility, yes."

"And the second?" Takara asks.

"Brian Cooper isn't an idiot. He's one of the brightest political minds in the business. He wouldn't have embarked on something more likely to hurt his own campaign than an opponent's."

"Unless he was trying to sabotage Alicia Standish," Takara says.

Victoria knows that he's buying into this more and more by the minute. "There's no evidence of that."

"Yet."

"She did fire him, Agent Larsen," Fuller posits.

"And the only reason she's even in a position to run for president is what he did for her following Brockhampton."

He nods. "I think the motive is one of the questions we need to answer. Right now, I believe we have reason to request a warrant. Put the paperwork together, Ian. Give me a minute with Agents Nishimoto and Larsen. Good work."

"Thank you, sir."

Ian gives her a sly glance on the way out. It was a strange thing to get from a fellow agent. The Bureau is political and competitive, but that look was different.

Lance stands and looks out the window. Victoria doesn't say anything, opting to wait for him to lob the first grenade. She knows one is coming.

"Did you know Agent Drucker was calling veterans you were helping identify?"

"No, sir, I didn't."

"Did anybody else know what you were working on?"

"Why are you asking *me* these questions and not all three of us?"

He turns and looks at her. "*Capitol Beat's* report last night."

"I was in this building the whole time."

"You don't need to meet someone in person to tell them that the FBI is investigating a campaign, Agent Larsen. The DOJ is screaming right now."

"I didn't leak anything," she says through clenched teeth.

"We'll be checking your phone records. You had better hope that we don't find anything."

"You won't."

"I'm sure. Agent Larsen, I think you are too close to this investigation. You know Senator Standish and Brian Cooper. You're friends with Tierra Campos and *Front Burner*. There's too much conflict of interest."

"Don't pull me off this case, sir."

"I have no choice. You're off the team. It's not up for discussion. Focus on your current caseload. Agents Drucker and Nishimoto will take it from here. That's all."

There's no point in arguing. Fuller's mind is made up, and his decision is rendered. Victoria leaves the office without a word, Takara following right behind her. When they are an appropriate distance from Fuller's office, she pulls him aside.

"Now's not the time for the third degree," he says, cutting her off before she can even speak.

Victoria hates that expression. The origin of the term is a little fuzzy. It may have been coined by nineteenth-century New York City Police detective Thomas F. Byrnes in the nineteenth century as a pun using his name, as in third-degree burns. It could also date back to the Spanish Inquisition as one of the progressive degrees of torture used to extract confessions. Either way, she loathes it.

"C'mon, Takara…none of that was suspicious to you?"

"It was great investigative work. You have to hand it to the Boy Wonder."

"You really think he could put all that together in one night?"

"He did. What are you implying?"

Victoria knows she needs to be careful. Takara is a fellow agent, but not a friend she can confide in. He's the light version of Lance Fuller.

"Something is wrong here."

"He's one of us, Vic. This isn't the CIA. He's not a double agent or anything. Look, you need to get a grip on your emotions before you say or do something stupid. You're done on the case. Get back to work and let this one go. It will all be okay, I promise."

He moves off, leaving Victoria standing in the corridor. "It will all be okay." She's sure that Custer said something to that effect at Little Big Horn. Unfortunately, like Custer's men, she's not convinced of that at all.

CHAPTER TWENTY-NINE

ANDREW LI

Chicken or the Egg Restaurant
Manchester, New Hampshire

Andrew's stomach is doing cartwheels in his abdomen. He didn't think there was anything outside of a roller coaster that could make him this nauseated. Everything about this place, right down to the smell, is repulsive. His system doesn't respond well to greasy food. He doesn't even like the sight of it.

"How can you eat that?" he asks, trying not to gag.

Governor Burgess licks his fingers. "What? You have a problem with a black man eating fried chicken?"

"I feel like I'm living the stereotype."

"Pops, let's see if they have any watermelon just to really freak him out," Isiah says, causing the two men to snicker.

"Andrew, do you like rice? I know you do," Luther says.

"It's different."

"That's right. Asians can't drive and are good at math, white men can't jump, Jews are greedy, the French are good lovers—"

"I don't buy that one," Isiah interrupts.

"Every culture has a stereotype, and generally, each of them has a degree of truth. The real problem with stereotypes occurs when society applies them as universally to a culture, especially out of malice. I have friends who hate fried chicken. My lieutenant governor's son is a white boy who could beat Michael Jordan in a slam dunk contest. You suck at math. You see where I'm going with this?"

Andrew shakes his head slowly. "Are you sure you're a Democrat?"

"I'm a democratic socialist who is running for president as a Democrat. There's a difference."

"That leads me to something I want to discuss with you, Governor," Isiah says, changing the subject.

"Governor? Oh, boy, this must be serious."

"I want to release Vision 2030 while we're in New Hampshire."

Andrew leans back into the pleather bench. This was Isiah's grand plan? He was expecting something profound, not profoundly stupid.

"I thought we were saving that for the general," the governor says, wiping his mouth.

"We'll save the details for the general election. The Republicans will spend months hyperventilating about how we'll pay for the programs, and we can smack them in the head with the how. I want the nation to see our vision now, while the Standish campaign is in too much turmoil to respond."

"Andrew?" Luther asks, his hands steepled in front of his face.

"A massive collection of policies and initiatives that will fundamentally restructure American society will dominate the news cycle…for a day or two. The media will pivot off it once the shock wears off. The Standish controversy is too juicy. It won't get the traction Isiah thinks it will."

"It's bold and visionary. Standish's policies are reactive and regressive. She has nothing like what we're offering."

"No, she certainly doesn't," Andrew says, folding his paper napkin and laying it on the table. "This is an open primary. Independents will hate it, and so will conservatives. It may hurt us more than help. She spent months just talking about gun control. Most people don't know where she stands on issues."

"Which will make it easier to change her stance depending on the reaction?" Luther asks. Andrew nods.

"It won't matter," Isiah argues. "We can suck all of the oxygen out of the room right up to Monday night. When people go to the polls on Tuesday, we'll look like the only contender that can take on the Republicans."

The governor listens to the back and forth between the two men. He doesn't say anything for a long time as he mulls over the decision. When he leans back, both men await the verdict.

"It's not ready yet."

Isiah is shocked. He didn't expect a firm response that quickly.

"Pops, you've been working on it for years."

"I've seen it all, Isiah. I've watched how the system chooses the winners and losers like some demented lottery. I've watched good men thrown out on the streets while the people who condemned them to a life of misery sail their yachts on Lake Michigan and dine in five-star restaurants. When the time comes to articulate what I want a future America to look like, I will do so. Until then, we wait. We're not ready."

"Pops, I—"

"If you'll excuse me, I have to use the men's room."

The governor hefts himself out of the booth and heads toward the back of the restaurant. Andrew waits until the governor is out of earshot before leaning across the table.

"Isiah, do you want me to leak a taste of this to the media to gauge public reaction?"

"No. He'd know it came from us. Nobody else has a draft. Besides, he's right. It's not ready."

"Okay, then why are you pushing for it?"

"He's so close, Andrew. I just want to win New Hampshire to end this thing and the stress that comes with it. Two months ago, I wouldn't have thought we had a prayer. Now, with the attacks on us, it's ours for the taking."

"You just need to get your father to step up."

"'The first method for estimating the intelligence of a ruler is to look at the men he has around him.' With your help, we can get him to do what he needs to and win this thing right now."

"Whatever you need. Just say the word."

Andrew leans back in his chair. Isiah has a complicated relationship with his father, but if anyone can get him to commit to taking down Alicia Standish, it's him.

CHAPTER THIRTY

"S.O.F."

Safehouse
South Hooksett, New Hampshire

Sartre is a digital animal. With enough energy drinks and cigarettes, he doesn't need sleep or food. He becomes a machine in the figurative and literal sense of the word, with his mind thinking in binary as his fingers become an extension of the keyboard. Marx is a veteran of countless PowerPoint presentations and Excel spreadsheets but only visits the *Matrix* out of necessity. The hacker lives there.

"Find it yet? You've been poking around Burgess's network for months."

"I'm not checking my email here," Sartre says, annoyed at the interruption. "Searching for vulnerabilities is time-consuming. Things like tracking trains and burning down offices tend to slow me down."

"They also pay the bills. You know, those pesky things your creditors send you?"

"I just hack into their systems and mark mine as paid. They write off the accounting error."

Marx shakes his head. He has no idea if he's kidding or not.

"I could have built a computer by now. I thought you were the best."

"Burgess has decent firewalls protecting his campaign network. The IT team they hired aren't complete idiots. I can get in no sweat, but that leads to our second problem: the files are encrypted. Even when I get them, we won't be able to read anything."

"Can't you break it?"

"Sure. It's only secured with 128-bit encryption. Just give me a supercomputer to do a brute force attack and a billion-billion years to do it in. Of course, we'll be long dead, along with a few million of our great-grandkids."

"You have a plan, right?"

Marx closes his eyes and shakes his head. It was a dumb question. When it comes to the digital battleground, he always has a plan.

"It's a matter of finding the right devices and installing malware on them to forward documents when they aren't encrypted."

"Did you find one?"

"You didn't bring me along on this journey for my looks. See for yourself. Try not to laugh."

Marx looks at the screen when a name pops out at him. Marx can't hide his amusement. The only thing better than the material they can obtain is the symbolism of who they steal it from.

"Andrew Li? As in the campaign's chief political consultant?"

"The very one. He sits at the center of the inner circle."

"What did you find?"

"The Magna Carta of political documents in this election cycle. It's called Vision 2030. It was still getting edited as of a couple of days ago."

"They're not done with it yet."

"What do you want me to do with it?"

"Exactly what Machiavelli said to if we find something juicy. Send it to Public Knowledge."

Nobody knew who Wikileaks was until they released U.S. diplomatic cables in 2010. Six years later, they became a household name during the 2016 presidential election when they released emails and other documents from the Democratic National Committee. Public Knowledge does much of the same thing, only better and faster.

"How long will it take them to publish it?"

"Not long. It's not a document dump that Public Knowledge would need to index to make it searchable. They'll take a couple of hours to authenticate it, so three hours, tops."

"Upload it."

Sartre nods and goes to work. It will only take him a few moments to accomplish the task. Marx moves back to the corner, sits in his chair, and closes his eyes. His work here is almost done. He can't wait to see what the reaction is when they share Luther Burgess's vision with the world.

CHAPTER THIRTY-ONE

TIERRA CAMPOS

Tranquility Hotel & Suites
Manchester, New Hampshire

There is a striking difference between this hotel and the one Austin arranged for our stay. The Autumn Suites is a nice, mid-priced place, but nothing you take pictures of to post on Instagram. The Tranquility Hotel, on the other hand, is where movie stars would stay. I would love to think that it was a cost-reduction measure, but it wasn't. Austin did it out of spite.

I'd be angrier about that if I didn't have bigger things to worry about. Austin's surprise trip up here caught me off-guard and ill-prepared. As he reviews my interview notes with Leila, he knows it too.

"We had an exclusive with her, and this was all we managed to get?"

"Leila was traumatized. She didn't want to talk about what happened, and I can relate to that. I'm surprised she said that much."

He grimaces and leans away from the computer. "Are you sure you didn't leave anything out?"

I don't appreciate the question, even if he was justified in asking it. Austin's tone was hostile and sarcastic, and the tension in the room amps up because of it. The team is expecting another round in the Tierra Campos vs. Austin Christos grudge match. He has two in his corner, and I have two in mine.

"Yes, I'm sure."

"Well, I can't run with any of this. I expected more from you. Work to get a follow-up interview with Leila and drag it out of her. There must be more to the story than what she said here."

"Is that why you're here? You're unhappy that a young woman whose family was threatened with death because she supports one candidate over another didn't give you any breaking news?"

"The serial targeting of a campaign by a sitting senator and candidate for president is a huge story. That's why I'm here. I'm not going to make the same mistake I made in Boston."

Austin didn't rush up to Brockhampton when that investigation started spinning out of control. There was enough drama happening in Washington, and I really didn't want him up there anyway. He's admitted that he regrets not coming up there sooner. It's a lesson I wish he hadn't learned.

I squint at him. "You're assuming Standish is behind it."

"Aren't you?"

"I'm not sure yet. There's no hard evidence to support that conclusion."

I fiddle with the thumb drive in the pocket of my sweater. I haven't even had the chance to clue Tyler and Olivia in on its existence. There are a thousand reasons I should tell the entire team about the meeting with Brian Cooper. There are also several good reasons I shouldn't.

"How about common sense? The intimidation and the arsons were coordinated efforts that have Brian Cooper and his SOF literally written all over them."

"If that's true, the tactics are backfiring. Senator Standish is dropping in the polls like an anchor. She's getting hurt by these incidents far more than they're helping," Olivia offers, demonstrating I'm not in this alone.

"Not everything works like you want it to," Jerome argues. "He miscalculated the blowback."

"That doesn't sound like Brian Cooper at all, does it?"

Austin's face reddens, and his jaw stiffens. "Get Leila Estabrook to sit with you again. I want more. See if she can link the man that intimidated her to someone in the Standish Operations Forces, or whatever they call themselves."

I glance over at Tyler and Olivia, who are standing with their arms folded across their chests. They're in no mood to cooperate either. I let go of the thumb drive. Austin doesn't deserve to see what's on this before we do.

"Anything else?" I ask.

"Have you seen Victoria?"

"No, not yet."

"What are you waiting for? Find her and see if she knows anything."

"I doubt she'll tell me."

Austin levels yet another harsh glare at me. "All evidence to the contrary."

"What will you be doing?" Tyler asks, sensing that this is about to get ugly.

"Working some sources and doing your job for you. Report back this evening with your progress."

The three of us leave without so much as a goodbye to Madison and Jerome. The greetings we received when we got here were cold and forced. I don't expect either of them to be in my fan club, but a little professionalism would have been a serviceable substitute for the camaraderie we once shared.

"What do we do now?" Olivia asks after we make our way down to the lobby and out to the car.

"We're going to go back to the hotel."

"What about trying to get a meeting with Victoria?" Tyler asks, opening the driver's side door.

"She's already on her way there to meet us."

"Seriously, Tierra, you're spooky sometimes."

"And conniving. I love it," Olivia adds, grinning.

"While I could use a nap, what are we going to do there?"

"We're going to stick this into a computer," I say, showing them the thumb drive. "This is all the information on the Standish Operations Forces. At least all that Brian Cooper was willing to share with us."

Their eyes light up. For the first time today, they have something to get excited about. I know the car ride to the hotel will be about my not telling Austin we have that. Somehow, I don't think it's a decision they'll argue with.

CHAPTER THIRTY-TWO

SPECIAL AGENT VICTORIA LARSEN

Autumn Bluff Suites
Manchester, New Hampshire

There's far more on this thumb drive than anyone expected. Policies, spreadsheets with membership information, financial information, logistics, and action plans are divvied up for review among the three of them, with Victoria looking over Tierra's shoulder. It's a lot to sort through.

"Either Cooper had a great secretary, or he was the ideal kid to cheat off in high school. He logged everything the group did in meticulous detail," Tyler says from the couch.

"The financials are impeccable, too. Documented right down to the last penny. Too bad I don't have access to their campaign expenditures to compare against," Olivia adds.

Tierra scrolls through a folder filled with hundreds of profiles. Every big-money liberal political donor has a dossier with detailed information about their political interests and previous donations. It's an impressive accumulation of data.

"Did this guy ever sleep?" Tyler asks.

"He didn't do all this work himself. Brian is resourceful. He likely acquired it from someone else or multiple people and groups."

"Which means someone else had a full dossier on Dylan Spencer," Victoria says, pointing at the file on the laptop Tierra is using.

"That's creepy," Tyler muses.

Tierra clicks on it, and the two women read through it. It's all standard stuff, much like the others. There's no hint of any operation to eliminate him. Victoria is a little dejected, despite knowing Cooper would never hand over incriminating information.

"None of this proves these SOF members weren't involved in the arsons or the intimidations. Even if targeting Burgess wasn't planned by Brian Cooper, they could have gone rogue thinking they were helping the cause."

"Do you believe that, Vic?"

"I don't know what to believe. I can tell you what my colleagues think, though."

"Should we be sitting down for this?" Tyler asks.

Victoria launches into a synopsis of her bouts with Lance Fuller, issues with new guy Ian, and perception of what's happening at the FBI. Her concerns got her removed from the case, and she's bitter about it.

"If you're not working the case, why are you here?"

"That's an easy one, Olivia. I can't shake the feeling that something is wrong. It started with the Spencer suicide and has gotten worse ever since. Every scandal chips away at America's belief in the system. If someone is messing with the electoral process, our faith in a fair election process is at stake. I'm not letting my peers mail this one in."

"How did you manage to convince them to let you come back to Manchester?" Tyler asks.

"I didn't convince anyone. I have a heroin case I'm working on. So far as the FBI knows, the trail led me up here."

"Well, at least I'm not the only one breaking rules."

Tierra launches into her own description of the problems with Austin and the other half of the *Front Burner* team. Tyler and Olivia both have their own choice words about what's happening. Victoria remembers how well that team worked together. It's amazing how fast things can change in six months.

"It looks like we're in this together again," she says, as Tierra tries to disguise wiping a tear from her eye.

"We are. At least the authorities aren't chasing you this time."

"Tomorrow is a new day."

"Uh, Tierra," Tyler says, interrupting the two women as they laugh. "There's a folder on this thing with your name on it."

"What? I didn't see one."

They all gather around Tyler, who sets his laptop on the coffee table. He stops when he realizes how close the women are to him. Tierra shakes her head.

"Open it before you say something stupid that causes me to hurt you," Victoria orders.

"Yeah, okay, there's a single document in here," he says, opening it.

Tierra scans the simple text document and closes her eyes. That man is full of surprises. Worse for her, she never sees them coming.

"Is this what I think it is?" Olivia asks.

"It's the names, addresses, ages, and personal information for the three hackers that doxxed me last summer."

"You've got to be kidding me. How the hell did he find this when the FBI's Cyber Crimes Division couldn't?"

"He's resourceful, you have to give him that," Olivia says in admiration.

"I need to share this with them."

"Actually, Vic, I have a better idea."

"If you say we're jumping on planes to go kick their asses, I'm in," Tyler says.

"That won't be necessary. We just need to get in contact with them online."

"I like my idea better," he grumbles.

"Not that you need to be told this, hon, but they're hackers. Being anonymous is sorta their thing. Pun intended."

The activist group Anonymous is a decentralized group of international hackers to whom are attributed high-profile digital attacks on governments, religious groups, corporations, and financial institutions. Olivia doesn't know if the hackers who tormented Tierra belong to them, but she couldn't resist.

"Olivia is right. They're impossible to find."

"Maybe not. We just need the key to the lock. Tyler, can you reach out to Velocity for me and set a meeting for today?"

"Do you need representation after you accept your Peabody?"

"Something like that. Find out if Tamara and Xavier are available."

"What does this have to do with the SOF?" Olivia asks.

Tierra pulls out the slip of paper Victoria gave her. "Maybe nothing. Maybe something. Let's go fishing and find out what we catch."

CHAPTER THIRTY-THREE

SENATOR ALICIA STANDISH

Campaign Rally
Nashua, New Hampshire

The week before the general election is a sprint. The month before is a 5k race. The campaigning after the conventions is a marathon. That makes campaigning during the primaries an ultra-marathon. There are emotional highs and lows, good and bad days, and candidates must find the strength to endure all of it. As Alicia stands before the lukewarm crowd of undecided voters she is trying to sway, she knows this is one of those moments.

"Thank you. Thank you for coming," the senator says, taking the stage to half-hearted, perfunctory applause by the people in the half-filled hotel ballroom. "I know you have an important choice to make in a few days, and I appreciate your spending part of your day with me."

Not many people made that choice. The divider in this ballroom has portioned off a third of it. This is how her professor must have felt teaching an eight a.m. economics class to a half-full lecture hall of bored college freshmen. This room is devoid of energy and enthusiasm. That dynamic must change for her to have any chance at the election in the fall.

"This election is more than about who the next president of the United States will be. It's about who we are and who we want to represent us. It's about the kind of country we want to live in and what we value as a society.

"America has faced and overcome many challenges. We have always had the leaders we needed to guide us through those tough times. We need a leader with the vision to bring us forward."

"Like Vision 2030?" someone shouts from the back of the room.

Alicia watches the audience in front perk up. It's not a good sign.

"I'm afraid I don't know much about it."

"It's Governor Burgess's plan for America. Do you have a plan?"

"Thank you for the question. My positions on a variety of issues are already well-known."

"So, you don't have a vision," the man insists.

Light applause starts and then grows louder before fading. Alicia maintains her composure. This rally is going south fast.

"I have a bold vision for America. I have spent my time in the Senate trying to bring it to—"

"His campaign says you hacked their computers and stole it to embarrass him."

"He's embarrassed by his own plan. Is it that bad?" Alicia asks, trying to play it off as a joke. It doesn't work.

"Did you steal it?" a woman asks.

"I honestly have no idea what you're talking about."

"Look at Twitter!" several people shout.

The room erupts with snickers and disgruntled conversations. Alicia looks off to the side of the platform and sees Angela and Michael digging into their cell phones. This stage is the last place she wants to be right now, but with the media in the back of the room, she can't bail now.

"It's on Public Knowledge!"

"Did you hack his systems?"

"Shady bitch."

"You know you stole them!" a man in front of her shouts, drowning out the others.

The crowd turns nasty as questions and accusations are hurled at the senator from all four corners of the room. She seizes on the comment shouted by the man to try to regain control of the crowd and salvage this. It's a long shot at best.

"My campaign does not engage in those kinds of activities. Period."

"What about arsons? Or intimidation?" The questions are echoed throughout the crowd.

"Again, my campaign is not behind it."

"The FBI thinks you are," the first woman replies.

"We're cooperating fully with the authorities."

"Stop lying. They're investigating *you*."

Alicia is thrown by the accusation. She's taking it personally in a business where having a thin skin is the kiss of death. The crowd is flustered because she doesn't have good answers to their questions. She has no answers at all.

"I understand you have questions. I do, as well. Those questions are going to get answered, but this election is about policy and—"

"Like the Safe America Act? You blew it!"

"What happened with my gun control bill wasn't my fault!" Alicia shouts.

She regrets the words as soon as they leave her mouth. The uproar drowns out the speakers as the people start to shout her down. Some of them leave the room. If the participants of this rally hadn't been vetted by the campaign, she would have thought it was full of Burgess supporters. Or Republicans.

"Please, listen… please, if you'll just let me finish," the senator says, desperate to clean up the mistake. It's too late.

"No more lies! No more lies! No more lies!"

The chant starts and becomes deafening. With no other recourse left, Alicia steps off the platform to loud booing. She exits through the back door, absolutely humiliated. Footage of the event will circle the globe in the next fifteen minutes. It's the type of thing that campaigns don't recover from.

CHAPTER THIRTY-FOUR

ANDREW LI

Campaign Rally
Concord, New Hampshire

Andrew surveys the audience after the candidate takes the stage. This place is packed to the rafters and has an energy that tingles every nerve. The media likes to use tight angles to make a crowd look bigger or smaller, depending on which candidate they support. Luther Burgess will never top a list of Democratic favorites, but there is no hiding the size or enthusiasm of his supporters.

"Burgess! Burgess!"

The chant is full-throated and hard to stop, despite the governor's best effort to begin his remarks. He's at least enjoying the moment.

"A few hours ago… A few hours ago, I had a vision for America that Twitter claims was stolen from me. It describes how I will ensure all Americans can get access to quality healthcare. The vision discusses my plans for providing everybody with a good education, reducing the income disparity between the haves and have nots, and increasing the quality of life for all Americans. Ladies and gentlemen, it's true that the document was stolen from me, but the vision belongs to all of us."

The crowd goes berserk. The sound of their roar shakes the platform and feels like it's growing louder. Andrew glances up to see if the ceiling tiles start falling.

"You wrote that line, didn't you?" Isiah asks, leaning in to the ear of their chief political advisor.

"It was your father's idea. I helped him craft it into something impactful."

"It worked. Do you think we're going to have any issue with voter enthusiasm?"

Andrew presses his lips together. He doesn't like jinxing a run of good fortune.

"It's early, but I like the looks of it so far."

"It will make for an interesting contrast on the evening news. Alicia Standish got booed off stage in Nashua about an hour ago. Videos of it were posted online. It was brutal."

"Did you pack her hotel with our supporters?"

Isiah smiles. "I didn't need to. Everything is breaking our way."

"Yes, it is."

"Then why do you look like your dog just died?"

Andrew is taken aback slightly. He's uncomfortable with this but didn't think it showed. There are other priorities right now.

"We shouldn't be doing rallies today. The senator needs to be in debate boot camp."

"You worry more than an expectant mother. My father knows his stuff."

"I know he does," Andrew says. "But debates are like stage plays. It's not just about delivering your lines on cue. How you do it wins over the audience and makes it a great show."

"He's been fine during debates."

"The Governor hasn't been declared the winner of one yet, including Iowa, where he had home-field advantage. He doesn't put his opponents away like he should. He needs to nail this one."

"I don't think I share your pessimism. Standish is imploding. She has more to lose than we do."

"Which means she's going to bring the thunder on that stage. She's desperate. Cornered animals fight for their lives. She's wanted to be president forever, and this is her shot just like it's your father's. She won't cower and wait for this to blow over. She's coming out with guns blazing."

Isiah smirks. "That's an interesting analogy to use with her, given her history. He'll be ready for it. My father has plenty of talking points, and she can't come out strong against him under the circumstances."

"Talking points like Vision 2030?"

Andrew gives him the side-eye following the question. Isiah didn't like the insinuation one bit.

"You think I was behind it. I wasn't. You know that we were hacked."

"I know that's what you're saying. We just had this discussion, Isiah. You argued with your father to release it. You could have just as easily leaked it yourself."

"I didn't."

Andrew continues staring out at the audience. It's not the time or place to challenge Isiah further.

"What's done is done. It's inconvenient timing, though. You're the campaign manager, so I know you understand that."

"Understand what?" he asks, with an edge to his voice.

"The governor is going to be on that stage tomorrow defending Vision 2030 when he should be going after Alicia Standish for her policies and the actions of her supporters."

"He can still do that."

"Yes, but the time will be divided. I told you that this would only own the news cycle for a day. I absolutely didn't want that to be the day of the debate. It shifts the focus away from where it needs to be."

There is no arguing that point, and Isiah knows it. He also knows he didn't leak the document. Nothing he says will convince Andrew of that, but he doesn't really need to. Political consultants work for him, not vice-versa.

"Maybe that's what Standish was counting on."

"Maybe. You need to convince your father to go for her jugular on that stage. If that's her game, it's up to him to make it backfire."

With nothing more to say on the matter, Andrew retreats through the back door into the hotel. He has work to do. It will be up to Isiah to turn Luther Burgess from a pussycat into a tiger in the next thirty hours.

CHAPTER THIRTY-FIVE

TIERRA CAMPOS

Velocity Public Relations Corporate Offices
Boston, Massachusetts

I was surprised we landed this meeting. Tyler was honest about wanting to meet with the two public relations specialists if they were available. An assistant took our information with a promise to get back in touch. I wasn't holding my breath when his phone rang with a call from Tamara ten minutes later to meet at their offices in Boston.

Tyler and I made the hour-long trek to the city and parked in the underground garage across the street from the building housing Velocity's offices. After checking in with reception, we were immediately shown into a conference room. The two PR reps were waiting for us. After a round of greetings and introductions, we all take our seats.

"Is this off the record?" Tamara asks, starting things off.

"It's not an interview," I say, "so I suppose it is."

"Good. Then let me start by thanking you for taking that little shit down."

I smile. Ethan's fallout with Tamara and Xavier was not well-publicized after his arrest. I know the story, but few others do. I also know how much they despised working with him, especially at the end.

"Not a fan of Ethan Harrington, I take it?" Tyler asks.

"Nope."

"Ethan lied to us from the moment we first met him," Xavier says, realizing that I never told my colleagues of our conversation either. "We take that kind of thing personally in this business."

"In the interest of full disclosure, my aim was never to take Ethan down. I just wanted the truth. I never imagined where it would lead."

"We agreed to this meeting because of that," Tamara says, "but we also wanted to know something. Why did you keep Velocity's name out of it? You could have found a lot of fault in how we represented him."

"You mean the interviews."

"Yeah."

"Honestly, I don't think it's a unique story. I've come to learn that a lot of questions are off-limits by journalists who land interviews with public figures. Was it you who changed the questions before my interview at WWDC?"

Tamara nods. That moment sent me on a collision course with Ethan Harrington. It genuinely changed my life. It brought me to *Front Burner*, and now to here.

"What did you want to talk to us about?" Xavier asks. "I assume you aren't here to trade notes on Ethan."

"It's about the hackers who doxxed me."

"You know I can't give you their names," he says, defensive and withstanding Tamara's withering glare. She doesn't like the fact that he's mixed up with them.

"I'm not asking you to." I take a deep breath, not believing I'm about to say this. "I already have them."

Xavier leans back. He didn't expect that either.

"You know who they are?"

"And where they live. What I do need is for you to set up a meeting with them for me."

"Okay, that's just weird," Tamara says. Xavier just stares at me with a confused expression on his face.

"I can't do that."

"Xavier, for what it's worth, that's not a big ask under the circumstances."

"It's bigger than you think, Tamara. We have a complicated relationship."

"It's not something I would ask unless it was important," I say, trying to edge him closer to an agreement.

"I don't suppose you're going to tell us what this is about?" Tamara asks.

"It's best if you don't know."

Xavier fidgets and shifts in his seat. He stares blankly down at his hands. "I don't control who they talk to, and I won't lie to them. I don't think they'll agree to the meeting."

"I think they will."

"How do you know?"

"You make a living by convincing people to think and do things they don't want to."

"She has a point there," Tamara says.

"Why should I agree to this? Are you going to drag us through the mud about Ethan Harrington if I don't?"

I sigh, probably more loudly than I intended. "I'm not that kind of journalist, Xavier. This is a request, and that's all. If you say no, I'll have to live with that. However, there's something big going on that I think they can help with. If I'm wrong, so be it. If I'm right, we're stopping a major injustice. There's only an upside for you."

He shakes his head. "They'll think it's a trap."

"If they're that good, what are they afraid of?" Tyler asks, making it sound like a challenge.

Xavier looks at Tamara, who shrugs. "They're your friends. It's up to you."

He closes his eyes and rubs his forehead. All we can do is wait for his answer. It feels like an eternity for him to make the decision, and it's not exactly what I was hoping to hear.

CHAPTER THIRTY-SIX

"S.O.F."

Velocity Public Relations Corporate Offices
Boston, Massachusetts

Boston is an easy city to blend into during the summer. It gets about twenty-two million visitors a year and is densely packed with tourist attractions along the Freedom Trail, which winds through the downtown. It's a little harder in the winter to look inconspicuous. Most people don't hang around outside a park in below-freezing temperatures.

After trailing them out of the parking garage and watching them cross Congress Street, Marx watches the duo walk into the building adjacent to Norman B. Leventhal Park. He has no idea what brought them here, and it isn't the destination that he expected.

He stays close to the building's entrance to avoid missing their exit while taking measures to avoid drawing attention to his loitering. It works to his advantage. A half-hour later, the two emerge from the building and hustle across the street toward the garage.

Marx falls in behind them at a respectful distance. He knows what floor they parked on, and his vehicle is only a couple dozen spots away. They enter the glass building and start the escalator ride down to the first level. He opens the door to the stairwell and double-times it down six flights of stairs.

The structure is impeccably clean for a subterranean metropolitan garage. It's also well-lit on the parking decks, except for this one. It was a stroke of luck that Marx thanked his stars for. Other than the dim emergency lighting, it's dark enough to obscure movement and trigger a vehicle's automatic headlights to warn him of any traffic entering or leaving.

Now it's the matter of picking the right spot between their car and the elevator. He stoops behind a vehicle near the vestibule when he hears the chime. His heart starts pumping adrenaline. He loves the tingle and heightened sense of awareness it causes. He's missed the thrill of the hunt. He hasn't had the chance to do it in a long time.

The pair enter the garage, still talking to each other as if they didn't have a care in the world. One thing Marx has always despised about civilians is their lack of situational awareness. Most of them meander through life with earbuds in, oblivious to the world around them or the dangers associated with it. They think they're safe. How wrong they are.

Marx slides out from around the vehicle, pulling the blade from its sheath. He has never been a fan of the Ka-Bar, instead preferring the seven-inch Yarborough knife available for purchase by U.S. Army Special Forces Q-course graduates. He's not a Green Beret but is better at poker than the men who are.

Slow is smooth, smooth is fast. Slow is smooth, smooth is fast. Marx repeats the phrase in his head on a continuous loop. He is light on his feet as he approaches Tierra and Tyler from behind, the rubber of his soles absorbing the sound of his footfalls in this echo chamber. Every movement he makes has a purpose; every breath has intent.

They don't see or hear him as he closes the distance. Fifteen feet. Ten feet. Five feet. He comes up right behind Tierra, tightening his hand around the handle of the blade.

He veers off into the line of cars, sheathing the blade and tucking it back into the small of his back. He watches them take a few more steps before he deactivates his car alarm with the telltale chirp and a quick flash of his lights. He shifts his head away from the pair so as not to appear to be paying them any attention.

The sound makes them both jump and turn their heads, but they continue to their vehicle, oblivious to how close death came to taking them. It would have been too easy, even in a monitored parking garage in the heart of Boston.

Marx starts the car and waits. Tierra Campos gets to live another day only because he chose to spare her life. This mission didn't require her to die. The next time their paths cross, she may not be so lucky.

Some people measure power through their ability to influence. For others, it's money, fame, or the ability to control people's actions. There is an element of truth in that, but they are half measures. The ability to take and spare lives at any moment is the real power in this world. It's final, and it's intoxicating.

Tyler pulls the car out and points it at the Pearl Street exit. Marx follows him in the truck, still tingling from the adrenaline. If she starts to get too close to the truth, he's hoping that Machiavelli gives the order to finish them before this mission is over.

CHAPTER THIRTY-SEVEN

SPECIAL AGENT VICTORIA LARSEN

Second Garage Self-Storage
Manchester, New Hampshire

Some requests are meant to be followed without question. When Victoria got word from Takara to come to an ordinary, run-of-the-mill storage facility, the last thing she expected to see was FBI and police vehicles parked everywhere. She pulls her car up outside the yellow tape. A fellow agent walks her over to where her colleague is directing activities.

"How did you know that I was here in Manchester?" she asks, coming up alongside Takara, who's decked out in a matching blue windbreaker.

"Because you're you, and I'm not an idiot. How's Tierra?"

Victoria doesn't answer. She hates the idea of being that predictable.

"What's all this, other than the obvious?"

"We got a warrant to search a unit belonging to Standish's New Hampshire campaign operation."

"A little heavy on the manpower for a simple storage unit, don't you think?"

"We didn't know what we would find, and given the sensitivity of this, I wanted to be prepared."

She can't argue with that logic. "Okay. What did you find?"

He nods his head to the left. She walks with him down a row of drive-up units where agents are hard at work. They have emptied one of them and are cataloging its contents. Cardboard boxes have been tagged and laid out in neat rows on blue tarps covering the asphalt.

"It's political propaganda, mostly. Pamphlets and yard signs."

"That doesn't sound unusual for a campaign."

"No, it's what we thought we'd find. Then we opened those black bags," Takara says, pointing to a separate tarp.

Victoria sees what's laid out on it. The blood drains from her face. Among other items in the arson kit, there are four gas cans and four cans of white spray paint.

"The containers have a residual amount of gasoline in them. None of them has a nozzle for fueling up a tank. All four cans of spray paint were used. We're processing for prints now."

She squats and looks at the materials, careful not to touch any of them. They won't have prints on them. The perpetrators would have used gloves. The fact that they were stashing in this unit is damning enough.

"The Standish Operations Forces, or whatever the hell they're called, committed the arsons. Brian Cooper is our lead suspect as the mastermind."

"Takara, you still have to link these to the arsons. There's no evidence that they were used in them."

"There's also no reason for them to be here. There's one more thing. We found these boxes stashed in the back of the unit."

Takara puts on a set of rubber gloves. He pulls back the flap of another square brown cardboard box. She squats again for a closer look and closes her eyes as she shakes her head. It's stacked to the top with sheets of paper.

New Hampshire voters cast paper ballots, either marked by hand or indirectly using touchscreen voting machines. Election officials working at the polling stations then run both kinds through scanning machines that count and record the votes. The results are then rechecked and transmitted to the central election office in Concord. This box, and presumably the four next to it, are filled with ballots.

"They're perfect copies. Brian Cooper was planning on rigging the election. There are absentee ballots there, too. The SOF may have already compromised the primary using dead people or casting ballots for the homeless."

"How would he pull this off? The voting process is secure in New Hampshire."

"You said that Cooper is crafty. He must think that voter fraud is the way to deliver a win. We'll find out how he planned on doing it after we arrest him."

"Arrest him?"

"The pressure to solve these arsons is enormous, Vic. It's almost worse than Brockhampton. The evidence here would compel any federal judge to issue a warrant."

"When?"

"The request is being made now, so as soon as it gets issued. Tomorrow, probably."

"You can't do that, Takara."

"Why not?" he snaps. No hotshot agent likes being told how to run an investigation.

"Because this is all wrong. Think about it. Why keep cans of spray paint and gas cans? They're incriminating, so you decide to stash them in a storage unit that leads right back to you?"

Takara folds his arms. "Maybe Cooper is too smart for his own good and never thought he'd get caught."

"Seriously? Then why write the initials of the SOF in the first place? And then keep ballots on hand here? If you are doing something shady, why keep them in a unit that the campaign procured?"

"I can't answer any of that. Maybe the thugs in the SOF were supposed to and didn't. Who knows? All I know is that the lock wasn't tampered with. We have footage of people loading and unloading stuff in it before and after the arson."

"It feels like a setup to me. You need to answer those questions before you arrest Brian Cooper."

"No, I don't. My job is to investigate and execute federal warrants. A judge decides that."

"Bring him in for questioning before you get the warrant. Get the answers before it's too late to alter this path."

"Why do you care so much?" Takara asks.

Victoria takes a deep breath. "I've wanted to be an FBI agent for as long as I can remember. I grew up watching police procedurals and imagining myself as one of the good guys. Imagine my surprise when I graduated Quantico and learned that not everybody takes their duties as seriously as I do.

"Someone is messing with the New Hampshire primary…and our democracy. If we don't find out who and stop them, who will? We should be investigating this with every agent we have, not settling for the convenient scapegoat. If it turns out to be Cooper, so be it. But we owe it to the American people to be sure and not react solely out of political expediency."

"This is a done deal, Vic," Takara says as if he didn't hear a word she said. "I'm following Fuller's orders. That's the end of it."

"Yeah? We'll see about that."

Victoria strides back to her car. She doesn't know if Cooper is behind this or not. There is enough evidence in that locker to question his story, but not enough to convince her of his guilt. They can't be wrong about this. The FBI would never recover. She needs to talk some sense into Lance Fuller or get fired trying.

CHAPTER THIRTY-EIGHT

CAPITOL BEAT

Cable News Studio
Washington, D.C.

Wilson swivels slightly and turns to a different camera after the last segment ends. For most of his career, he's tried to keep the ending of his show upbeat. Events like 9/11, the Iraq war, and the shooting at Sandy Hook Elementary School made that impossible. Tonight's remarks aren't nearly as depressing as those were, but they're not something viewers will find uplifting either.

"Now for tonight's final thoughts. Campaign espionage is as old as campaigns themselves. Candidates pour their hearts and souls into crossing the finish line with the most votes to reach the prize at the end. The overzealous ones cheat. Sometimes, it's a staffer who takes matters into his or her own hands. Other times, it's the candidate himself or herself.

"Watergate is the perfect exemplar. The June 1972 break-in at the headquarters of the Democratic National Committee led to an abuse of power investigation into the Nixon administration and subsequent resignation of the president.

"In the digital age, the days of men rummaging around an office with flashlights are gone. The messy 2016 election saw the controversial Spygate scandal and the leak of documents and emails stolen off a Democratic National Committee server. The new front in the war between political opponents is in cyberspace, and, as we heard tonight, it may have happened again.

"The DNC hack ushered in a tactic of using digital espionage to embarrass another campaign or political party. Hackers compromising his campaign network and stealing a critical document authored by Governor Luther Burgess is the latest example. There's one twist to the story that media are taking notice of: instead of decrying the theft and leak of his Vision 2030 plan, the governor is embracing its sudden release.

"It's a smart tactic. While the Burgess campaign struggles to secure their systems to prevent further intrusions, they are not running from the fallout of a vision that some have retitled 'American Socialism.' It's controversial and divisive, but he's standing by his words. The defense has prompted some media outlets to question whether the campaign leaked it themselves.

"Only they didn't, according to security experts at the firm Digital Fortress. Technicians have confirmed for us tonight that the Burgess campaign's systems were compromised, and the document was stolen from a laptop. We will continue to report developments on this new case of political espionage, but the event has heralded in a terrifying new chapter in American politics.

"The machinery that drives national campaigns and elections is large, complex, and ultimately, digital. Cyberwarfare could further erode the electoral process. If that gets shattered, so will America's faith in our system of government.

"Today, it is only the private data of campaigns getting tampered with. As we move closer to an era when paper ballots are replaced with electronic voting, should we be concerned about vulnerabilities with that as well? Candidates elected to political offices often say no. However, those words ring hollow when they can't even secure their own networks and data storage devices. It will be up to America to decide whether the transition into the digital world spells the end of trust in our elections. Those are my final thoughts, and they're for the record."

Wilson switches his gaze to a different camera. He sees the words on the teleprompter but doesn't need to read them. He knows how to sign off a show better than anyone in the business.

"We'll be back tomorrow broadcasting from Granite State University for the New Hampshire Republican and Democratic debates and the primary results next Tuesday. For *Capitol Beat*, I'm Wilson Newman. Good night."

CHAPTER THIRTY-NINE

TIERRA CAMPOS

Autumn Bluff Suites
Manchester, New Hampshire

4 Days to the New Hampshire Democratic Primary

It's after midnight, and I'm still staring at the ceiling of our mid-priced hotel. The suite has two bedrooms for the three of us. It's another reason I think Austin put us here out of spite. I took one, and Tyler, in a rare act of chivalry, gave Olivia the other. He opted for the couch.

Tired of tossing and turning, I don a sweatshirt and walk out of my room to get a drink from the refrigerator. I ease it open, trying to be as quiet as possible to avoid waking anyone. I reach my arm in and pull out a bottle of water, trying to keep as little light as possible from spilling out.

"You don't need to sneak around. I'm not sleeping," Tyler says from the couch, sitting up.

"You neither, eh?"

"Wide awake and exhausted at the same time."

"What's keeping you up?"

"Everything. You?"

"Same. Mostly the thing with Austin."

Tyler sighs deeply, switching on the light on the end table. His eyes are puffy and swollen from a lack of sleep.

"I didn't know it was bothering you. You're not letting on."

"What can I say? I'm good at burying my feelings. I learned that after Summerville."

The memory of that day comes rushing back. The moment when the kid shot my teacher…the feeling of getting pulled off the floor by Josh…waiting to die in that cramped supply closet…the barrel of the rifle coming through the door. I've managed to suppress all of that, except for the times when I can't.

"What are you guys yammering about out here?" Olivia asks, emerging from her room and rubbing her eyes.

"Did we wake you? I'm sorry."

"No, I can't sleep either."

Tyler grabs the remote from the coffee table. "We might as well see what's on television."

"Anything but the news, please."

My phone vibrates in the hip pocket of my pajamas. I fight to retrieve it, earning a confused look from my roommates.

"Who's texting you this late?"

I stare at the screen. "I don't know. There's no number."

"What does it say?"

"Nothing. It's ones and zeros, separated into groups of eight."

Tyler perks up. "Read them to me."

He opens his computer and perches it on his lap. I recite the long string of numbers, careful to do it correctly. He inputs it into a site he brought up in his browser and hits the convert button.

"It's binary code that converts into more numbers: 764001125."

My heart skips a beat. There is no way that's a coincidence.

"It's my social security number."

"Okay, that's creepy," Olivia says.

Another text arrives with a link. Tyler types it into his laptop browser and hovers his finger over the enter key.

"It could be malware or spam."

"No, it's the hackers. Xavier came through."

"An email would have been easier."

The link directs us to a site that leads us to another one, and then another. We're then provided with instructions to activate our VPN to mask our location. A key is provided to decrypt a link to a secure chat room. The whole exercise takes almost fifteen minutes.

Tyler signs in with a username he picks for me. Olivia slugs him for me when she sees it. They hand me the laptop just as three handles pop into the chat.

```
>CyberOreo: What do you want?
>TierraDelFuego: What, no leet speak?
>AnarchyBooster: we did that to annoy Ethan
>DialPirate: you must have been convincing to get X to reach out
>AnarchyBooster: yeah, spill
>CyberOreo: she must want an apology
```

"Not for nothing, you should ask for one while you're at it," Tyler muses. I just shake my head. If I do that, this will be a short conversation.

```
>TierraDelFuego: No, what's done is done
>AnarchyBooster: yeah it is
>CyberOreo: our boy is in prison
>DialPirate: don't care about that.
>CyberOreo: I do
>TierraDelFuego: I need your help
```

Nothing happens for a long time after I type those words. I wonder for a second if I've been disconnected, but the chat is still live.

"I guess they don't know how to answer that," Olivia says.

```
>AnarchyBooster: why should we help you?
>TierraDelFuego: It's in your best interest.
>DialPirate: joke
>TierraDelFuego: Not a joke, Brian.
>CyberOreo: who is brian?
>TierraDelFuego: DialPirate is, Lucas.
>AnarchyBooster: what the hell?
>TierraDelFuego: Be cool, Nikolas.
>DialPirate: how do you know those names?
>TierraDelFuego: I know your last names, too. I know everything
about you. How's the weather in Chicago, Brian?
```

"That's savage," Tyler says, almost giggling.

"It should get your point across," Olivia adds.

```
>CyberOreo: we're done here
>TierraDelFuego: Don't go until you hear me out.
>AnarchyBooster: or else you'll rat us out? give our names to FBI
Cyber? get your revenge?
>TierraDelFuego: I don't want it to come to that. If I did, you'd
be getting swarmed by black helicopters and men with windbreakers
right now
>CyberOreo: what do you want?
>TierraDelFuego: Information on a dark web site
>AnarchyBooster: which one?
>TierraDelFuego: http://hss3uro555xfogfq.onion/
>CyberOreo: what do u want to know?
>TierraDelFuego: who owns it
```

There is a long pause. The three of us exchange glances with each other in silence. It's a moment of truth, and words wouldn't add anything to it.

We stare at the screen in anticipation. Time is relative, and right now, it's dragging. We stare at the answer when it finally pops up in chat.

```
>DialPirate: why?
>TierraDelFuego: not your concern. Find out the info and your
personal information stays with me. Don't, and you'll have an
uncomfortable conversation with the feds. your choice.
>AnarchyBooster: give us a day
```

The hackers disconnect from the chat. Tyler and Olivia don't say anything. It won't take them a day to track that down, but at least we are getting what we wanted. It will be very disappointing if this ends up being a dead end. It feels like the only progress we've made up here.

CHAPTER FORTY

SENATOR ALICIA STANDISH

Standish for President Campaign Office
Nashua, New Hampshire

The location may change, but the morning ritual stays the same. Alicia wakes up, brushes her teeth, showers, pours herself a strong cup of coffee, and checks the news for any overnight developments in the world once she arrives at the office. Today is no different, except that she was hoping for some good news. There isn't any.

"Knock, knock," her husband says, standing in the doorway. "You're here awfully early."

"My work is never done," Alicia says, standing to give Brendan a kiss and hug. "I didn't expect you until later."

"I didn't want to sit in rush hour traffic. I come bearing reinforcements," he says, holding up a garment bag and a small suitcase.

She smiles. She went light on the luggage from Iowa, knowing she has a closet full of clothing down in Cambridge. She didn't expect her husband to hand-deliver it, but she appreciates him always doing whatever he can to support her.

"Thank you."

"You look like hell, honey. You have bags under your eyes that I could put groceries in."

"And thank you for that as well. It's what every wife wants to hear."

"I'm sorry. It's the truth."

"Are the kids coming?" she asks, trying to change the subject.

"They have classes, but they'll be here for the debate. I've never seen a campaign take this much of a toll on you."

"It's the first time I've ever had to do it outside Massachusetts."

"That has nothing to do with what's going on up here. Have you learned anything?"

Alicia gives her husband the quick version of what she knows and what it means for the campaign. She then tells him what Brian Cooper said, what her advisors have told her, and what her campaign manager believes. They all have different opinions on the situation.

"Do you think Brian Cooper is sabotaging you?" Brendan asks. The analytical mind that has served him well as one of Boston's best financial gurus is hard at work.

"I don't know what to think."

"That doesn't sound like you. The woman I married would have come to a decision within five milliseconds and then kicked his teeth in."

"The stakes are too high to be rash."

"They're also too high to do nothing. Is this about the Safe America Act?"

"Some pep talk this is turning into," Alicia moans. "You really know how to cheer a girl up."

"You think you made the wrong move with that bill. You didn't. You stuck with what you believe, and people admire that about you."

"Not enough of them. It's all falling apart. I don't know what to do to stop it."

Brendan nods and plants his elbows on his knees with his fingers clasped in front of his face.

"Remember your first Senate race? You were the new girl, and the Republican was making all sorts of waves down in Washington. He was in the news every day. It was annoying. The pundits thought he was unbeatable because of his name recognition and massive war chest."

"That was different."

"It was, but the solution may be the same. You knew you'd either be loved or hated, but you were determined not to be ignored. You were savage about getting out there and meeting people and convincing them that you should be the one to represent them in Washington."

"Yeah, that worked well yesterday. Unless you've missed the videos with millions of hits on YouTube documenting my humiliation."

"People are confused, Alicia. You're not you. You're trying too hard not to make a mistake instead of working to earn their vote."

"You make it sound so easy."

"And you're making it sound hard. You have a debate tonight that could change everything. There's nobody better on stage than you. Be yourself and show them."

"No pressure," Alicia says with a sigh, not finding his words particularly helpful.

"You can handle the pressure. I'm not your campaign advisor, but if I were, I'd tell you not to lose sight of who you are. Nothing else matters."

"This is my chance, Brendan. What would my mother think if I fall flat on my face tonight?"

"She would be proud either way. I'm here. The kids are here to support you. No matter what happens on that stage or in this campaign, we are proud, too."

Brendan gets up and gives her a kiss on the head, leaving her in the small office to continue her morning routine. That was what she really needed to hear. She closes the laptop. No more looking at the news and reading predictions. She needs to focus on what she must do and stop listening to pundits angling to convince people that they can peer into the future using their crystal balls. They don't know what will happen because the outcome isn't determined until the American people make their choice. Brendan is right. It's time to show the people who she really is and what she's made of.

CHAPTER FORTY-ONE

ANDREW LI

Burgess Temporary Campaign Headquarters
Manchester, New Hampshire

With the destruction of the campaign offices around the state, Isiah ordered the campaign to work out of temporary spaces. In Manchester, the ballroom reserved for the victory speech has been turned into a makeshift command center. Movable dividers have partitioned off slices of it to perform different functions. This one is reserved for the governor to meet and plan with senior advisors. It's not a perfect solution, but they can find space to run the operation in New Hampshire once the nomination is secured.

Andrew is the last to arrive at this emergency meeting and enters the room to find the usual suspects gathered around one of the hotel's folding tables. An FBI agent in a suit stands and shakes hands with him. He's on the younger side but has sharp eyes with drive and confidence behind them.

"I'm Special Agent Ian Drucker. I work out of the Boston District Office."

"It's nice to meet you."

"What brings you here, Special Agent?" the governor asks, getting the meeting started.

"I was asked to update you on our investigation into the arsons and the murder of Frederick Lamm."

"Is providing us an update considered usual procedure in cases like this?"

"Given the circumstances, sir, I think we can all agree that nothing about this case is 'usual.'"

"Fair enough. Please continue."

"We have recovered items we believe were used in the arsons."

"What? Where?" Andrew asks, surprised they have made any progress in such a short time.

"I'm afraid I can't give you that information, sir. We also have suspects that we're looking at closely."

"Who?" Isiah asks.

"Unfortunately, I can't tell you more than that."

"What can you tell us, Special Agent Drucker?" the governor asks, displeased with the lack of information sharing.

"That we want you to know the FBI is working hard on this. We also figured that you would want to keep the man's family informed."

"Is it the Standish campaign?" Isiah asks, frustrated at the non-answer.

"I'm not at liberty to say at this time. Things are moving quickly."

"You understand that the Democratic debate is tonight," he argues. "The primary is in four days. Are you planning on wrapping up the investigation by then?"

"I can't give you an estimate," the agent says, on the defensive.

"Except that you're working hard on it," Andrew says sarcastically.

"If it's the Standish campaign and you wait until after the primary, people will accuse the FBI of playing favorites."

Agent Drucker shifts uncomfortably in his chair. "I understand, sir. I've been given a pledge by my boss that we will move on any warrant the moment it's issued."

Isiah frowns, but Andrew is content to weigh the implications of the agent's words. There's more meaning to them than the others realize.

"All right," Governor Burgess says, rising from his chair and shaking the man's hand. "Thank you for your time, Special Agent Drucker. I'm sure you have a lot to do."

"Thank you, sir. Please know that we will continue to investigate until justice is served."

Andrew and Isiah both shake his hand. The agent nods to the rest of the group and leaves the room. The staffers follow him out, leaving only the governor's two closest advisors to decipher the meeting.

"That was pointless," Isiah says, crashing back into a chair.

"It was a political gesture," Luther says. "The FBI is more worried about a scandal than solving a crime. I don't think they have anything. If they were serious, they wouldn't have sent a kid to brief a candidate for president."

"Then why come at all?"

"Alicia Standish is friends with Conrad Williams. He's the Deputy Attorney General at Justice. He could have had the DOJ instruct the FBI to do this to avoid the appearance of favoritism."

"Then why did you let him off the hook?" Isiah asks.

"He's a junior agent sent here as an errand boy. It's not his fault that Standish is using the FBI and DOJ to manipulate me. That's their mistake, not his."

"I think we should use this to our advantage."

"How?"

"I know you don't like social media, but there's a time and place for it, and what we need to say is stronger if it comes from you and not the campaign."

Isiah looks at his father, who grimaces. "What do you have in mind?"

"Two things: pressure the FBI by citing their lack of progress on the case and the ridiculous briefing we just endured. Let the media fill their airtime by trying them in the court of public opinion."

"And the second thing?"

"When you get on that debate stage tonight, expose her for the world to see."

CHAPTER FORTY-TWO

"S.O.F."

Standish for President Campaign Office
Nashua, New Hampshire

The scene outside the window hasn't changed. People are going about their daily business as they usually would. Marx takes a bite of his breakfast sandwich and checks the time on his phone. They're late. The text said they would arrive by ten a.m.

He shouldn't be surprised. The government never does anything quickly. They expect us to pay our taxes promptly but are never in a rush to give you money back when they owe a return. Inefficiency rules the day in every bureaucracy. This is no exception.

Marx finishes his meal as the first in a convoy of black Chevy Suburbans pulls up in front of the Standish campaign office. He knows he shouldn't be here watching this. The smart move would be not being within ten miles of this place, but he needs to see it for himself.

"Thank you," he says, politely waving to the girls working behind the counter as he tosses his trash.

"Bye, thank you."

Careful to avoid being obvious, he joins the growing crowd as they watch the drama play out like an old episode of *Criminal Minds*. They brought a lot of firepower for someone likely unarmed and not a threat. Cooper doesn't commit violence. Marx does.

They enter the building with guns drawn and at the low ready. They don't want to be seen pointing semi-automatic rifles directly at campaign workers. Once they are inside, he knows the show is over. So is his mission in New Hampshire.

He takes a sip of his coffee to fight against the bitterly cold air. This spells the end of an operational phase. Instructions will no longer come, not that he ever needed them. He knew what had to be done without the guiding hand of Machiavelli to show him the way. He didn't like having his strings pulled like he was a marionette. He's dealt with that enough in his life.

For the first time in a long time, it felt like he was making a difference. America has lost its way. After World War II, the nation evolved into a superpower. It wasn't just because the economies of Europe and Asia were in ruin as some revisionist historians like to lead the people to believe. From the moment Lord General Cornwallis surrendered at Yorktown, Americans were heading down the road to greatness.

That path has taken a detour, resulting in complacency among our fat and lazy population. Americans have lost the meaning of sacrifice and service. Americans are infatuated with the almighty dollar, and the comforts society pampers them with. Gone is the meaning behind a hard day's work and value for those who provide it.

Marx walks back to his vehicle. He settles into the driver's seat and pulls out his phone. The text he concocts to his team is the one with the most meaning: ALAS, BABYLON.

The codeword was taken from a 1959 novel by Pat Frank, which was one of the first apocalyptic novels of the nuclear age and one of Marx's favorites. The narration follows Randy Bragg, whose older brother serves as an intelligence officer in the U.S. Air Force. The two men have a coded warning of imminent disaster drawn from a preacher they once listened to. A telegram is sent with those words not long before the Soviet Union attacks the United States with a full-scale nuclear strike and bears the brunt of the massive retaliation.

The effect on the SOF is not as dramatic, but it seems fitting. They all knew this was a likely outcome. It's also a warning to start buttoning up operations at the safehouse. The FBI has made their first big move. They need to be ready for the next one.

Marx tucks his cell phone away. He pulls out of his parking space and heads up the Everett Turnpike toward Manchester. From there, it will be a quick drive across the Merrimack River up to South Hooksett.

They are almost finished. Marx's thoughts linger on the team's reaction. Sartre is as dedicated to seeing this through as he is. Engels has no choice but to stay the course that Machiavelli plotted for them. Trot is the problem. He's in this for the money and will want to leave.

It's no time to get complacent this close to the finish line. He has witnessed firsthand how that can ruin even the best-planned operations. The situation needs to be monitored, and action taken if necessary. The primary begins in about ninety-two hours. That's the amount of time his team needs to remain in the shadows before disappearing for good.

CHAPTER FORTY-THREE

SENATOR ALICIA STANDISH

Standish for President Campaign Office
Nashua, New Hampshire

Brian stares at Alicia from across the desk. He isn't happy with his new role. She can't blame him and expected the blowback from him to be harsher than it has been. He accepted the news yesterday without argument. The quiet resentment Alicia knows he's harboring is more disturbing than if he had just blown up at her.

"I get that you're not happy with this demotion," the senator says, trying to be as sympathetic as possible.

"That's one way to put it, Senator. I expected to get fired, despite not doing anything to deserve either."

"Understand it from my position, Brian. You set up this SOF group behind my back and without my approval."

"You asked me to mobilize supporters for an outreach and voter enlistment program. That's all it is. I executed the plan you directed me to."

"People that I respect and listen to feel differently."

"That's because they see the polls and need someone to blame, Michael Ross included."

"Leave Michael out of this," Alicia warns him.

"I can't. He is a part of it. So is Angela, and now, so are you. We've been through this once before. I thought we could get past the mistrust. I guess I was mistaken."

"What do you want me to think, Brian? You kept the creation of the SOF from both me and Angela. The FBI wouldn't be investigating it without cause."

"Did Conrad Williams tell you that?"

Alicia purses her lips. She didn't like the insinuation. She cooperated with the deputy attorney general during the Brockhampton fiasco, but that is the extent of their relationship. There is nothing improper, despite what Brian Cooper is digging for.

"I haven't spoken to him."

"Who's lying to who now?"

"Look, the campaign needs to take measures to protect itself, and so do I. It was the same thing you advised after—"

"Brockhampton?" He shakes his head. "Wow."

"I'm sorry, Brian. This is the way it has to be."

"Yeah, I guess so."

A tense silence blankets the office before it's shattered by a commotion in the central area. People are shouting, and others are yelling back. It sounds heated.

"Did another Burgess supporter show up?" Alicia asks.

Brian shrugs. It has happened several times a day since the arsons. Whether they are paid by the campaign, one of the groups supporting it, or just people looking to make trouble, it's a constant irritation. The campaign has filed countless restraining orders to keep the troublemakers away.

Alicia exits the office with Brian following her out. She stops in her tracks when she gets to the end of the short hallway. Men with guns are swarming through the door, herding her volunteers and staffers to the side of the room. Agents with windbreakers emblazoned with FBI in gold block letters follow the men clad in body armor in.

Volunteers and staff pull out their cell phones and live-stream the video to social media sites. The men aren't being overly aggressive and seem undeterred by the filming. The team quiets when Alicia approaches the agent giving the orders.

"What is this all about?" she demands.

"We're looking for Brian Cooper. We know he's here."

"I asked you a question, agent…"

"Special Agent Takara Nishimoto, Senator. We have a federal arrest warrant for Brian Cooper. I'm going to ask you again, ma'am. Where is he?"

"I'm right here," Brian says, emerging from the hallway. He's not about to run, not that he has a reason to or would get far if he did.

"This is unbelievable," Angela shouts. "You're going to barge into the campaign office of someone running for president and make an arrest?"

"Ma'am, I have a warrant signed by a federal judge. I have been instructed to execute that warrant. That is the end of any discussion."

Agent Nishimoto nods to one of his colleagues, who approaches Brian. The two men size each other up. In a fight, it wouldn't be much of a match.

"Mister Cooper, place your hands against the wall and spread your feet apart." Brian complies. "Do you have anything on you that will stick me?"

"No."

"Brian Cooper, you are under arrest for arson, conspiracy to commit arson, conspiracy to interfere with an election, voter intimidation, and conspiracy to commit murder," Special Agent Nishimoto says.

"Are you kidding me with this?" Brian asks over his shoulder.

The agent finishes frisking him and pulls his arms behind his back, slapping cuffs on in front of the entire staff. He turns Brian to face the other agents, and by default, Senator Standish and her campaign volunteers. They all stare at him with a mix of shock and disgust.

"You have the right to remain silent. Anything you say or do can be used against you in a court of law. You have the right to an attorney. If you cannot afford an attorney, one will be provided for you. Do you understand these rights as I have read them to you?"

"Yes."

"I hope you paid close attention to the lawyer part, Mister Cooper. You're going to need a good one."

"You're making a big mistake, Special Agent Nishimoto."

Takara lets out a little laugh and takes a step closer. He loves it when he arrests people who want to lecture him on his mistakes. It happens more than people think it does.

"Do you have a storage unit in the Second Garage facility near the airport that you use for activities by a group you formed called the Standish Operations Forces?"

Brian knows he shouldn't answer, but why wouldn't he? "Yeah, we keep our campaign materials there. Why?"

"The gas cans and spray paint your men used in the arsons were there, amongst other incriminating materials."

"What? Spray paint and gas? What are you talking about?" Brian asks.

"You'll see," Takara says, grinning. "I strongly suggest you remain silent from here on out."

Brian is walked past the senator, the staff, and out the front door to a waiting vehicle. It wouldn't take a genius to know that the crowd gathering outside the office is recording this as well. In less than an hour, millions of people will have seen this arrest without any context as to why.

"Special Agent Nishimoto? Was it necessary to execute the warrant this way?" the senator asks.

"For an arson, no. For a murder? I'm not going to place my agents in harm's way, Senator Standish. I'm sure you understand that and feel the same way."

"You could have asked him to turn himself in."

"Mister Cooper was deemed a flight risk, ma'am," he says, handing over the warrant for her to read. "We couldn't take the chance. I apologize for the intrusion."

He waves his finger in a circle over his head to signal the agents to wrap it up. They begin to file out of the office. Everyone watches in stunned silence as the agents leave.

"Any thoughts?" Alicia asks Angela when she comes up next to her.

"Only that we're in big trouble. Do you want me to confiscate the staff's phones? Some of them caught this whole thing on video."

"No. It's going to leak out anyway. That will only make it worse. Contact Michael and figure out how I should address this at tonight's debate. It's sure to come up, and I need a great response."

"Will do."

Angela gets everyone back to work as Alicia retreats to the office. The television already has breaking news of Brian's arrest. She turns it off and checks her watch. The debate is ten hours from now. The fate of her campaign hinges on how well she tap dances around this latest fiasco.

CHAPTER FORTY-FOUR

SPECIAL AGENT VICTORIA LARSEN

Federal Bureau of Investigation Boston Field Office
Chelsea, Massachusetts

Victoria straightens her suit jacket as she takes long strides down the corridor. If you're going to commit career suicide to make a point, you need to be willing to go all the way with it. She made that choice once. She never thought she'd have to do it again, much less eight months later.

"He's on the phone, Agent Larsen," the admin says as she walks past her desk in the outer office.

"I don't care."

"Agent Larsen, you can't go in there!"

Victoria barges into Fuller's office, completely ignoring the assistant's protests. The door slams hard against the wall, jostling the pictures of him posing with dignitaries adorning it.

"Do you have any idea what the hell you just did?" Victoria barks from the center of the room.

Fuller glares at her with a phone handset nestled in the crook of his neck. His surprise is changing to anger, and it's a slow burn on the fuse.

"I'm going to have to call you right back," he says, cradling the phone. "Have you lost your mind, Victoria?"

"Maybe, but I'm in good company. You sabotaged an election today with that stunt you pulled in Nashua."

"I don't remember you even being reassigned to the Cooper case."

"That's because you didn't want anyone challenging your boneheaded decisions."

"Excuse me!" he says, planting his hands on his desk and standing from his chair. "What the hell were you thinking?"

"I ordered my agents to execute a warrant!"

"One that shouldn't have been asked for, let alone issued on the day of a primary debate. The media is going to shred the FBI for interference."

"You have some nerve barging in here. I did my job and made a tough call. I thought you would be happy that a murderer is being held accountable."

"That's done in a court of law, last I recall. Or were my instructors at Quantico wrong?"

Lance is beyond angry. He's a rumbling volcano mere seconds away from erupting.

"You don't get to walk into my office to lecture me," he says through clenched teeth.

"Someone needs to. Takara is busy kissing your ass, and you're taking everything a kid fresh out of Quantico is telling you at face value without any due diligence."

"What the hell gives you the right to question him? Or Takara? Or me, for that matter? You may think that you're hot shit, but everybody in this building knows the truth. You got lucky with Brockhampton, and it went to your head."

"No, Lance, it went to yours. You took all the credit, remember?"

Fuller's anger ratchets up from volcanic to atomic levels when Victoria uses his first name like that. "I went out on a limb to keep you in the FBI after that, *Special Agent* Larsen!"

"You helped me beat charges trumped up by a crooked state cop. Gee, thanks."

"Understand something," he says, pointing a finger at her. "I don't justify decisions to my subordinates. My instructions come from the Hoover Building, and you don't get to question them. You are—"

"Then maybe you should grow a pair of balls and start questioning them."

"I am speaking, Agent Larsen. Don't you dare interrupt me!"

"Yeah, you're speaking, but all I hear are empty words. You talked about what the people in this building think about me? Let me clue you in on what they think about you: you're a yes man who only cares about his next promotion."

"You had better stop there," he warns.

"Not this time. You're blind if you think the case against Brian Cooper is open and shut. You are jeopardizing a political—"

"You're done here, Agent Larsen. This building, the FBI…it's time for you to move on. You need to resign."

"Not a chance."

"Fine. We'll do it the hard way. I'm going to start a DIO on you for misconduct and insubordination. Then we'll move onto your other transgressions."

Victoria takes a deep breath, trying to regain her composure while giving Fuller a moment to cool off. Delegated Investigation Only inquiries involve allegations of mid-level misconduct matters, such as insubordination. They are examined by supervisory special agents in the field or headquarters division, where the employee who allegedly committed the transgression is assigned. In this case, here in Boston.

The report is sent to the Internal Investigations Section, which reviews and approves the completed inquiry before forwarding it to the FBI OPR. The personnel there conduct the adjudication, including administering the appropriate disciplinary action. Victoria is already a bright blip on their radar.

"You do what you need to. I'm going to do what I have to."

"Agent Larsen, you will not return to New Hampshire under any circumstances. That is a direct order. Do you understand me?"

She takes a step closer to his desk and leans forward. The two lock eyes, and both see nothing but burning anger.

"Stop me."

Victoria turns and exits the office, brushing past the assistant as Fuller protests with all the vocal clarity of Charlie Brown's teacher. It will be another bullet for her referral report. Whether she is right or wrong about Brian Cooper at this point is irrelevant for her career. She just ended her service with the FBI. They don't take insubordination lightly, and in a few months, she'll be shown the door. It's time for her to get the most out of this gold badge before she loses it forever.

CHAPTER FORTY-FIVE

TIERRA CAMPOS

Autumn Bluff Suites
Manchester, New Hampshire

I know Victoria is upset about the showdown with Lance Fuller, but she's filled with a steely resolve that I admire. She thinks she did the right thing, and that's all that matters. Not only did she disobey his order to not come to New Hampshire, but her first stop was a hotel room filled with journalists. That's a mortal sin in the law enforcement community.

My smartphone chimes, and I see another text with digits. I don't bother asking Tyler to decode this one. Instead, I call him, Olivia, and Victoria over and head to the secure chat room after double-checking to ensure the VPN is connected.

"This is still a bad idea. These guys should get arrested."

"Yeah, probably, but this is bigger. If these hackers can help us, I'll take the trade, won't you?"

Victoria doesn't say anything. The FBI is always concerned with snagging the biggest fish that they can. They don't want the dealers or suppliers. They want the kingpin. In the search for better headlines, they make all kinds of deals. Victoria knows that better than anyone.

"Here we go."

```
>AnarchyBooster: we have your information
>DialPirate: first, you working with the FBI?
>TierraDelFuego: Special Agent Larsen is sitting right next to me.
```

"I can't believe you just wrote that," Victoria says.

"This coming from the woman who walked into her boss's office and told him he makes boneheaded decisions?"

"Touché."

"I have no reason to lie to them, Vic. They could have hacked this hotel's surveillance and known you were here. They could be tracking you for all we know."

"That's reassuring."

```
>DialPirate: did you give her our information?
>TierraDelFuego: no, I told you I wouldn't
>AnarchyBooster: how do we know?
>TierraDelFuego: you don't. But I'm sure there is a steep price to
pay for lying to you
```

"Yeah, like doxxing all of us," Tyler says from over her shoulder.

"Nobody wants your identity, Ty," Olivia chides.

```
>AnarchyBooster: fair enough go ahead DP
>Dial Pirate: ring ring
```

"What does that mean?"

The words barely escape Olivia's lips when my cell phone rings with a blocked caller ID. They stare at it like it's possessed.

"That's creepy."

I answer the call and switch the output to the speaker. "Yeah?"

"Is this it, or will you reach out again?" the disembodied voice says.

"I don't know. I have no intention of blackmailing any of you or applying it as leverage. I also can't say that I won't reach out to you again if I need your help."

"We'd rather you didn't."

"I'd rather you hadn't doxxed me. We don't always get what we want."

"Okay."

"Are the others on this call?" I ask, curious why DialPirate is the only one talking.

"They don't like the idea of this and have more to lose than I do. I can disappear tomorrow if needed."

"You won't need to. At least not because of me."

There is a long pause on the line. I watch Victoria eye the phone like she expects it to disconnect. It doesn't.

"The dark web site is owned by a hacker who goes by the name Sartre. Whatever was on it is gone. It may have been streamed or saved to a remote site somewhere."

"Who is Sartre?"

"I don't know his real name. He's mobile and is never in one place for long. He may also be German."

"Why do you say that?"

"He's elite and is a great self-promoter. He liked to sign some of his posts with 'Wille des Volkes.'"

"It means will of the people," Tyler clarifies. "What kind of posts did he write?"

"A hacker is only as good as what he takes credit for. Sartre laid claim to a load of hacks and exploits whose authenticity wasn't challenged. He has a good track record and is well-respected in these circles."

"Can you name some?"

DialPirate launches into a list of his hacks and their impact. Victoria is clenching her hands, almost dying to take notes. The number of companies and government groups he claims to have infiltrated is impressive, and most of them didn't even make the news. It makes me wonder just how much people cover up.

"He likes the political targets," the hacker continues. "Usually Republican politicians in the United States, but not always."

"Is there any way to track him?" Victoria asks.

"No chance. He's good, which means he's careful. How did you all get mixed up with this guy?"

"Did you see the Brian Cooper arrest?"

"I'm watching the coverage of it right now. Gestapo stuff."

Victoria looks like she wants to hit the phone with a frying pan. I think she agrees, which makes her even angrier.

"Does Sartre work for Brian Cooper?"

The belly laugh that erupts catches us off-guard. I wasn't trying to be funny. For whatever reason, DialPirate thought it was hysterical.

"No. Not a chance."

"How do you know?" Tyler asks.

"Sartre explained on a chat board why he took that handle. He admires Jean-Paul Sartre. Are you familiar with him?"

"The French political philosopher," I say.

"And Marxist." We all turn to face Olivia. "I minored in philosophy."

"She's right. Sartre would never work for Brian Cooper or Alicia Standish because he's a devout communist."

That piece of information rattles me to the core. The team shares incredulous looks as the meaning of those words sinks in. We sign off the call with DialPirate and remain silent. I have no doubt that we share the same thought: the need to rethink everything we thought we knew about what's happening in New Hampshire.

CHAPTER FORTY-SIX

CAPITOL BEAT

Granite State University Remote Set
Durham, New Hampshire

Capitol Beat rarely goes on the road. Washington, D.C. is the political arena where the action is, so there is rarely a need to pack up the cameras and crew and leave the city. Primary election season is the rare exception. The Iowa Caucuses and New Hampshire Primaries command the attention of the American people. Every candidate for president is here, so they are, too.

Granite State University in Durham is the site of the Democratic debate. The Republicans will joust at another institution not far away. The school was kind enough to allow *Capitol Beat* to broadcast from their facilities throughout the primaries. It's a logistical nightmare to set up but makes for great television.

"I have a feeling I'm not going to like this," Wilson says, sitting down in a metal folding chair in front of the set.

"You're not," his executive producer admits. The two associate producers nod.

The rift has been growing for years between Wilson and his staff. They maintain a good working relationship but have different ideas about the direction of the show that is seen by millions of Americans every night. He is old-school and still believes *Capitol Beat* is integral to keeping the public informed. Everyone else wants to make it sensational, controversial, and to a degree, more partisan and ideological.

"We want to give Carl Brennan the chair while we're in New Hampshire. He deserves an audition."

"Please tell me you're joking."

"We're not."

"Whose moronic idea is that?"

"Mine," his EP says. "The news director agrees. Miss Campos had her shot when you took your much-needed vacation. Carl should be afforded the same opportunity. He would host the show following both New Hampshire debates. You would resume to wrap them both up on Sunday, preview the primaries on Monday, and deliver the results Tuesday."

"No way."

"You're not giving up your chair for the two days?"

"First, there's no reason to bring him all the way up here when he already works in Washington. Second, I'd rather see Vladimir Putin host than him. I have no interest in him succeeding me."

"Wilson, Carl Brennan is a known quantity," one of the associates says.

"Maybe in Washington, he is."

"He's also an excellent anchor. He has a great resume and a ton of experience. Tierra Campos doesn't have either and isn't the only possible replacement for you."

"She's the only suitable one," Wilson argues. "Brennan is a horse's ass."

"He has high likability in our target demographic."

"That's only because people have never met him in person."

"Well, that might be true, but he's an anchor, not a politician out pressing hands and kissing babies," the associate producer argues.

"He's on board with our vision."

"What vision is that? Divide the people? Take sides? Do what every other network is doing?" Wilson asks his EP, disgusted at the direction of this conversation.

"No, to pay the bills. This is the world we live in now. We don't have to like it, but we do have to play by the rules to survive."

"It isn't journalism."

"The greatest newsmen in television history took sides on a myriad of policy issues. Even you take sides."

"I ask hard questions and relay uncomfortable facts. The party or ideology doesn't matter."

"It's a dying model," the other associate producer concludes.

"My ratings say otherwise."

"It's irrelevant, Wilson. It's not your call."

"Is that so? Last I looked, it's my show."

"After the election, it won't be."

The words hit Wilson like a hammer. They're right. He's looking at the next nine months, but they are worried about the years beyond. It took him a decade to earn his reputation for non-partisanship. What are the odds of finding someone who can replace that? Tierra Campos is his only hope.

"Nobody is going to miss you more than me," Wilson's EP says. "Normally, I would agree that you have absolutely earned the right to name your replacement. Unfortunately, you can't replace the irreplaceable. I like Tierra a lot. We don't know what she's going to do, which means we need alternatives, and that starts tonight. We're trying Carl. You get a couple of nights off, so enjoy it."

The producers all get up and disappear through the door. There's nothing he can do, his show or not. He won't be able to enjoy his time off knowing that a stuffed shirt is sitting in his chair.

CHAPTER FORTY-SEVEN

"S.O.F."

The four men comprising the SOF are different people with varying degrees of dedication to their mission. They have also been friends for a long time. Despite believing that their actions are what's best for the country, each has a personal motivation. Trot makes no effort to hide where his loyalties lie, making the mood in the room tense.

"The money hit our account, right?" Trot says, pausing his video game.

"That's not the point," Marx counters.

"I'm making it a point. Is it there or not?"

"It's there."

Trot sets down his game controller and pops off the couch like he suddenly remembered that he has someplace to be. Sartre removes his headphone and spins his chair around to watch.

"Pay me my share. We're done here."

"We're done when the mission is accomplished," Marx says, the evenness of his voice standing in stark contrast to Trot's excitability.

"The Benjamins say otherwise. Nobody pays in full for a job that isn't complete."

Marx clenches his teeth. He does have a point about that. This is contract work before it's anything else. Payment is never rendered in these situations until the terms of the deal are satisfied.

"We agreed to stay local until the day of the primary. Are you reneging on that?"

"Are you serious? The FBI just raided a political campaign in broad daylight four days before a primary. What do you think will happen if they manage to figure out it was us? It's time to go before we get caught up in the maelstrom."

"Sartre?" Marx asks, turning to look at the hacker over his shoulder.

"My work isn't done, and you pledged to protect me until it is. But Trot is right. I don't think it's smart to stay here a moment longer than we need to."

"You're done tonight, right?"

"Other than some mop-up tasks to cover our tracks, yeah. I can do that from the road, though."

Trot crosses his arms and waits impatiently. He can keep waiting. The finish line is too close for them to waver now, and Marx is in no mood to deal with his theatrics.

"If you want to go, go. You'll get paid when the primary is over," Marx says, an edge to his voice.

"I'll get paid now."

"It's not up for discussion. It's the way it's going to be. Deal with it."

"Sir, yes, sir," Trot says, uncrossing his arms to execute a limp salute. He knows as much as any of them the proper way to perform that courtesy, so he did it out of spite. That can't be tolerated.

Marx turns his hips as he draws his right arm back and thrusts it forward with lightning speed. His fist lands hard on Trot's jaw, causing him to stumble backward and trip over Marx's ottoman before crashing to the ground. He stays there, rubbing his jaw as he recovers from the blindside hit.

"I don't abide insubordination. Drop the attitude, or I'll drop you again."

Trot scoffs as he struggles to his feet, keeping an arm anchored on the back of the couch to steady himself. He cracks his neck and then glares at his friend.

"You're going to get us all caught."

"No, I'm not. We're insulated from the FBI, and nobody else will put it together in time to find us."

"What about Tierra Campos and *Front Burner*?"

"She's not on our trail," Marx says, dismissing the question.

"She wasn't on Ryan Baino's trail either, remember? How'd that turn out for him?"

As much as Marx doesn't want to admit it, Trot brings up a good point. Victoria Larsen and Tierra Campos received all manner of accolades for their investigative skills last summer. By contrast, he has always thought that they stumbled into the revelations about Action Not Prayers and Ethan Harrington. Sometimes it's better to be lucky than good.

"Fine, we can neutralize her."

"I'm not killing a high-profile journalist," Trot protests.

"She doesn't need to die. We'll sideline her, much like Machiavelli arranged for Victoria Larsen. We only need to buy a few days."

"How do you plan on accomplishing that?"

Marx grins. "Everybody has a weakness."

It's a lesson he learned a long time ago. Spies exploit the weaknesses of their targets to turn patriots into sources. They leverage women, financial problems, addictions, or embarrassing information to flip them. If you get to know anyone, you can find out what hurts them the most. If that doesn't work, you just hurt them.

"You're gambling with our lives. Are you going to say anything, Sartre?"

"Keep me out of this."

"Look, after Tuesday, we're gone," Marx says. "If you have a problem with that, there's the door. I'll wire you your cash. But I'm in this until the election, and so is Sartre. Engels would say the same, and he has more to lose than any of us. You make your own choice."

Trot knows there is no point in arguing further. He leaves the room in a huff and slams the door when he goes outside. Marx isn't sure what he's planning, but at least he didn't head to his room to pack. He's still on the team, at least for now.

"You ready for tonight?" Marx asks, turning to the hacker.

"All set."

"Good. Find out everything you can about Tierra Campos. I need to know where she is staying and what she is doing. We have one more mission to execute before we get the hell out of here."

"You got it."

Marx eases himself into his chair and goes back to his book. He just started *Catch-22* by Joseph Heller. It's a novel about a problem whose only solution is denied by a circumstance of that problem and is thus unsolvable. He hopes reading that book isn't a bad omen.

CHAPTER FORTY-EIGHT

ANDREW LI

Jittery Jack Coffee House
Manchester, New Hampshire

Only a handful of Americans understand the stresses that come with running a national campaign. It's a constant grind of eighteen-hour days with no such thing as a weekend. Andrew knows his tank is starting to empty, and there's still a critical debate and three full days of campaigning before they find out if the effort has paid dividends. He's done his part. All he can do now is watch and wait.

The governor is undergoing his final preparations for tonight. Isiah is putting him through the wringer, having staff stand in as the other candidates on stage. He's capable of working with his father on delivering the required message, giving Andrew much-needed time to make a couple of moves. Things aren't happening fast enough, so it's time to speed up the process.

"Hi Marv," he says to the man standing in front of the counter of the quaint coffee house, ready to order.

"Well, well, if it isn't Andrew Li. Is your phone broken? I've been trying to get information out of you for five days."

"I've been busy. How's life at the AP?"

"Let's just say we're being kept on our toes this year. You want something?"

"Uh," he says, scanning the massive chalkboards hanging on the wall. "I needed something better than hotel coffee. Whatever's good. I know you practically live here, so you choose."

Marv smirks before ordering two coffees and paying with his smartphone. The two men go to the counter as the barista goes to work concocting their caffeine fix.

"It's the best coffee in New Hampshire. While you're here, do you mind answering a few questions?"

"Answering questions is not a part of my job description. We have media people for that."

He scoffs. "Please. Luther Burgess wants to be the most transparent president in history and is running the opaquest campaign ever run to get there. None of you talk to the media, and that's becoming the story. Come on, give me something."

"Is there an 'or else' attached to that?"

"The media can be on your side or against it."

"Yeah, that's got me shaking," Andrew says. "I'm sure Governor Burgess is terrified that the AP is going to side with the Republicans in the general election. You have no leverage here, but I can help you out anyway."

They grab their drinks, and Marv nods over at the far corner of the coffeehouse. The place is almost empty. There's nothing illegal about this meeting, but neither man is pining to be seen with the other. Some things are best kept out of the public eye as much as possible.

"This is on deep background only. Don't even think of attributing it to me. If you do, neither you nor the AP will end up with a White House press pass when we get there."

"If you get there. Standish may be slipping in the polls, but she hasn't lost yet."

"All true. Deep background only," Andrew says, his eyes conveying the warning.

"Yeah, okay."

Andrew leans in. "Standish may be in deeper trouble than you think. Some of her staff reached out to me about any open positions in our campaign."

"That's hardly a surprise," Marv says, waving a dismissive hand.

"It is when the people asking come from her inner circle."

That got his attention. "Okay, I'll bite. Are we talking about Angela Mays or other members of the senior staff?"

"I'm not naming names. The individuals in question told me that she's going to fold her campaign."

"Why would they tell you that?"

"Because they have bills to pay and need jobs. They're not going to approach Isiah, so they came through me because the betting money is on Burgess being the nominee. It's over for her, Marv. Do your homework, and you'll get the story first."

"I need names, Andrew. This doesn't work otherwise."

"You're not getting them."

He folds his arms across his chest and scowls. "Then it's the lead political advisor from one campaign shoveling dirt about his opposition. I can't run with that, even in this political climate."

"Does anyone really think we need to shovel anything to win right now? Look at the polls."

Marv looks down at his coffee and takes a long sip. Andrew isn't wrong. In a tight contest, he would have every reason to spread disinformation about a collapsing campaign four days before the polls open. That's not what this is.

He has long applied Occam's Razor to his journalistic work. Named for William of Ockham, it's a scientific and philosophical rule dictating that entities shouldn't be multiplied unnecessarily. Simply put, it means that the simplest answer with the fewest assumptions is often the correct one. In this case, it is more likely that Angela Mays did contact Andrew than that he would conjure up the story while his candidate is winning.

"Does anyone else have this?"

"I went out for coffee, not to talk to the press," Andrew says. "What do you think?"

"All right. Give me a name, and it runs immediately."

Andrew leans back and thinks it over. Journalists are a gullible bunch. It's like playing a game of Hungry Hungry Hippos: press down their levers, and they gobble up whatever marbles are still on the board. He sighs and nods like he's been defeated. This was almost too easy.

"Angela Mays and most of Standish's financial team."

"Will she confirm it?"

"Seriously, Marv? Would you confirm it if you worked there? Oh, and if you ask her, you burn *me*. She made the call in private and only spoke to me. They'll know the source."

"All right, I won't ask her. Here's a question for you, though: why would she call you and ask if she knew you could leak it?"

"Because it won't matter in a couple of days. If single-sourcing this story isn't enough, ask your moles in the other campaigns if they got a similar call. We may not have been the only one Angela Mays took the temperature of."

Marv gives him a knowing look as he gets up from the table.

"I won't forget this," he says, before walking away.

Andrew smiles and sips his coffee. "I won't either, Marv."

CHAPTER FORTY-NINE

SPECIAL AGENT VICTORIA LARSEN

New England Regional Computer Forensics Laboratory
Chelsea, Massachusetts

Miranda is at her desk as usual when Victoria storms up the aisle. She notices the angry gait and grins as Victoria approaches. The woman is a machine with boundless energy whenever she's powered on. The rest of her colleagues tune in, hoping for some fireworks to liven up their ordinary day.

"What's up, Wonder Woman? You look like you're gonna rip someone's head off."

"I've been making enough trips back and forth to Manchester that my car can drive itself there. I'm tired."

"Sorry, girl, that ain't your road rage face."

"I just told Lance Fuller off this morning."

Miranda grins. "That's more like it. Good for you, girl. He's a pompous ass."

"I'm not so sure it will be good for me. Fuller is going to run me out of the FBI for insubordination."

Miranda leans back in her chair. "No, he won't. You're his best agent in this building, and he knows it. What brings you to the Island of Misfit Toys?"

"I need some help."

"Name it."

Victoria checks around the office to see if anyone is intently listening in. They aren't, but she leans in close to Miranda anyway.

"Is there anyone you know in Cyber who can do something on the DL for me?"

"That would be Harley."

"You trust him?"

"Her, and yeah, she's my kind of people. Why are you asking?"

"Because I need some information for a case that isn't a case."

"That's excitingly cryptic. Could Harley get in trouble for this?"

Victoria makes a face and shrugs. She doesn't think so, but who knows how Fuller would react if he found out and what he would say to Harley's supervisor.

"Good. It will be right up her alley then. Let's go."

The walk to the FBI Cyber Division is a short one. The group's primary mission is to conduct federal investigations into computer systems or networks that are exploited by terrorist organizations, foreign governments, or criminal activity. In today's ultra-digital and connected world, they stay busy.

Harley isn't what Victoria expected; namely, she doesn't resemble Harley Quinn, the Joker's love interest in Batman. Instead, she's nerdy cute with an impressive disregard for authority and rules. No wonder Miranda is friends with her.

"I don't usually have field agents drop by my desk. If Mir is involved, it must be something juicy."

"It is, and time-sensitive. What do you know about a hacker named Sartre?"

"Oh, that's a sore spot around here."

"You know him, then?"

"He's what we call a unicorn. Some hackers we know a lot about. They like to take public credit for high-visibility cybercrimes. Others, like Sartre, stay in the shadows. He may boast somewhere on the dark web but doesn't advertise it outside of the hacker community."

"So, you don't know anything," Victoria says with a sigh.

"He's suspected of being behind an impressive number of hacks."

"Yeah, I've heard."

"From where?" Harley asks, perking up.

"It's not important. Do you know anything else? Anything at all?"

"Yeah, we think he spent time in the Army."

Victoria's mind races. Given who he's collaborating with up in Manchester, that makes sense. The arsons were conducted with a level of precision timed down to the minute. The intimidations were well-coordinated efforts. And they call themselves the S.O.F. If Sartre was military, maybe the connection to the group is more substantial than being a hacker for hire.

"Why do you say that?"

"We did find an old chat board he used to post to on the darknet. He likes to taunt other hackers with his exploits, and some of his phraseology screamed military, specifically the Army."

"Okay. Do you have any idea where Sartre is?"

Harley laughs. "Nope. He's a ghost. He could move around, or he could have his own fortress of solitude. When I say that he's a unicorn, I mean it. Outside of the assumption about military service, we only know that he targets anything that's a challenge."

"Yeah, like a political campaign."

"He's targeting a campaign?" Harley asks, her voice rising.

"It's only a working theory. Does Sartre have any known associates?"

"None that we've identified. If you find any, let us know. That dude's been on our radar for a long time and is elusive as hell. It'd be a huge win for us, and we could use one right now."

"Count on it. Thanks for your help, Harley."

"Anytime, Special Agent Larsen."

"You gonna go kick some ass, boss lady?" Miranda asks as they walk out of Cyber.

"Yeah, I just have to find his ass first."

CHAPTER FIFTY

SENATOR ALICIA STANDISH

Standish for President Campaign Office
Nashua, New Hampshire

The tension in the room is thick enough that a jackhammer couldn't dent it. Alicia's rant was impromptu, but her rage was genuine. It wasn't received well. The senior advisors stare back at her with anger in their eyes, and that's too bad. She feels the same way.

"Can I have the room, please?" Angela asks quietly.

Nobody is about to argue. They all file out of the room without a word. Only Michael Ross and Alicia's husband Brendan remain behind. After the last person departs, Angela's face turns red.

"What the hell was that?"

"You read the article," Alicia says.

"I did. It's bullshit, and you know it."

"Do I? Are you leaving the campaign, Angela?"

Angela closes her eyes as she smooths her hair back to the tight bun. Her face scrunches as she clenches her teeth. She stretches her neck side to side before returning to stare at Alicia.

"I've been involved in a dozen campaigns in my life. I don't think I've ever had my integrity questioned like that, Senator. Here's your answer: I don't know where Marvin or the AP got that crap from."

"You and the financial staff never reached out to the Burgess campaign?"

"We didn't reach out to anybody, and if we had, it wouldn't have been them. We've been nothing but loyal to you, and this is how you treat us?"

"Can you blame me? Look around, Angela. Volunteers are abandoning us in droves. It's a sinking ship, and everyone knows it. Why wouldn't you and the others leave? All I ask is that you tell me and not go behind my back."

"When I told my parents that running campaigns was what I wanted to do with my life, they screamed at me. They said I could never earn a living and would never amount to anything. I wasn't smart enough, good enough, or well-connected. I've spent my entire adult life trying to prove them wrong. You gave me a chance when nobody else would. I've been loyal to you, Senator, and always will be. It's only moments like this when I question why."

Angela doesn't wait for a response. She leaves the room without looking at Alicia or anyone else. Michael follows her out, content to stay out of this battle. He's a consultant. He can be fired and replaced tomorrow.

"You handled that well."

"Not now, Brendan," Alicia says, sitting down and propping her elbows on her desk to rub her temples.

"Then when? After you've alienated all the people that you need to win? There may still be a few floating around that you missed."

"I don't trust them," she grumbles.

"You don't trust anyone anymore."

"Because I can't!"

Brendan sighs and takes a seat across from her. He folds his hands between his knees and stares at the floor, biting his upper lip.

"Is this about Brian Cooper?"

"Or Ethan, Ryan, the president, his chief of staff Roger Ackerman… The list of everyone who's betrayed me reads like *War and Peace*."

"You can't win this by yourself, Alicia. You're going to try anyway, but you can't."

She pretends not to hear him, mindlessly shuffling papers around her desk. Two kids and decades of marriage have taught Brendan how she responds when he's getting through to her. Alicia's pretending to tune him out is one of the ways.

"Have you talked to Brian?"

"I have nothing to say to him."

"Then listen and get his side of the story."

"I don't need to hear it."

"Then you already think he's guilty. That's strange because I remember when the kids were little, and they fought, you would always get both sides of the story before one of them got reprimanded. I think you need a break. Take some time to—"

"I can't take time. Don't you get it, Brendan? I'm running a national campaign for the presidency. What do you want me to do? Go to Cambridge and lounge in my pajamas eating ice cream all day?"

"If you'd let me finish my sentence before jumping down my throat, I was saying that I want you to take a moment and think about what you're doing."

Alicia slaps her hand down on her desk. "I know what I'm doing."

"Do you?"

"This is my time! I've worked for years to get to this point to watch it all slip away! I should be up by twenty points, not groveling for votes on the street like some damn pauper."

Brendan shakes his head. "I guess we've found your problem, Alicia. You think you're entitled to the Oval Office. You've forgotten that the presidency is a position that's earned, not inherited."

Alicia closes her eyes and takes a deep breath. Her head throbs and grinding her teeth together for the last hour isn't helping to alleviate it. She rubs her forehead, before finding a spot on the desk to blankly stare at. He's right.

"I need to be alone for a while."

"Okay."

Brendan has always known how to keep her grounded. He can be as frustrating as any man ever put on this Earth, but she couldn't even imagine being married to anyone else. She's a handful, and he's always been able to deal with that in ways nobody else could.

Her husband closes the door behind him, leaving her alone in the room. She stares at the picture of her parents on her desk. She lost her father to suicide and her mother to a murderer. Since those fateful days, she has dedicated her life to fulfilling the lost promise of theirs.

She knew this would be a hard road to travel. Nobody would have guessed how hard. She's tired, and the fight has only begun. It's more than she can handle right now, as she folds her arms on her desk and buries her head in them, hiding the tears and pain that come spilling out.

CHAPTER FIFTY-ONE

TIERRA CAMPOS

Autumn Bluff Suites
Manchester, New Hampshire

I fill in the whiteboard, just like I watched Austin do in Boston when we were working on the Brockhampton investigation. It's slow going, and I spend more time with the marker pressed against the board than I do moving it. He made this look easy. It isn't.

"That board is still ugly," Tyler says, returning to the suite with a pair of pizzas.

"You can't put lipstick on this pig."

Olivia walks over to retrieve a slice. "There's still too much we don't know. We have plenty of pieces, but none of them fit."

"Cooper is still the best choice."

"Yeah, that's why the FBI picked up him, I'm sure. They have a pile of evidence pointing to him but can't provide a motive."

"I can. Brian wanted to sabotage Standish. Payback is a dish best served cold…at the beginning of the primary season."

"I don't think so," I say, capping the marker and pressing it against my lips.

"Do you think you know him that well, Tierra?" Tyler asks, taking a bite out of a slice of pepperoni.

"Or for that matter, trust him at all? He's a political mastermind."

"I can't explain it, Olivia. This kind of revenge doesn't fit his persona. He would have ensured someone else would have taken the fall if the plot were exposed."

Tyler nods. That makes sense to him. Olivia looks less convinced but is more interested in the pizza than in arguing.

"Let's take a few steps back," Tyler says. "What if Cooper's cooperation with us last summer was meant to defeat the bill and embarrass her?"

"It could have been, but why then push me to write a story that exonerates the senator from knowing anything about it?"

"To get back into her good graces and destroy her ambitions for the presidency?"

"That's cold-hearted if it's true," Olivia says between bites.

"Cooper told me that if he were doing it, nobody would catch him. A big part of me believes that. There were too many rookie mistakes. He doesn't make those. This is bothering me."

I tap the dry erase marker against the board where "communist" is written in red below Sartre's name. Both of my colleagues take a break from their chewing to watch me.

"As in, why would a mysterious hacker go after a campaign that he shares ideological beliefs with?"

"Yeah, exactly."

"That doesn't make sense, unless…" Tyler says, trailing off. "We've been focused on the Standish campaign. How much do we know about the other side?"

"Do you mean the Burgess campaign? Why would they sabotage themselves?"

"Well, Burgess or any of the other candidates. There are lower-tier campaigns that would benefit from the two top dogs getting bloody."

"That's true, it could be any of them. The Burgess campaign really wouldn't be sabotaging themselves, would they? At least, not really. Standish is cratering. He's leading in the polls now."

"I think you should put on the tin foil hat now, Tierra."

I smile. It wouldn't be the first time this year I was accused of concocting conspiracy theories. It's far-fetched but worth exploring.

"Humor me for a second. What do we know? Let's start with Burgess."

"I don't know him. I do know his son, Isiah. I did a *Front Burner* spotlight profile on him when there was talk of his father running."

"What do you think? Is he capable of this?"

Tyler shrugs. "Isiah's a good planner. He's well-read, street smart, and has a nose for knowing what to do in a crisis."

"Good enough to plan something like this?" I ask.

"Maybe, but there's a catch. Regardless of what people think about his politics, Luther Burgess is a straight shooter. That's saying something coming from a city like Chicago. His father would disown Isiah if he ever engaged in hacking, intimidation, arson, and murder to win an election."

I don't know much about Luther Burgess outside of what I've read. The first rule in the media is to believe nothing that you read and only half of what you see. Reporters with agendas can make anyone look like Jesus or Satan, depending on their perspective. Despite that, Luther has been characterized as aboveboard.

"We'll see."

"What about his other staff?"

"None of them have the power or access to the finances in that campaign. It's a father-son affair," Tyler says.

"Let's expand on the idea," Olivia says. "What about an outside group or political action committee?"

"There are hundreds of them," Tyler says.

"Thousands."

"We need to start somewhere."

"I wonder who would have won," Tyler says, falling into the couch with another slice.

"Won what?"

"A straight-up contest between Burgess and Standish with Isiah and Brian Cooper steering the campaigns. No shenanigans. Just political moves and countermoves. That would have been a primary race worth watching."

"Well, Ty, it doesn't look like we're going to ever find out."

Olivia's phone dings and she retrieves it from the counter. "Oh, shit. It's from Austin. He wants to meet down in Nashua."

"All of us?"

"No. Just me."

I share a knowing look with Tyler. Whatever this is, it can't be good.

CHAPTER FIFTY-TWO

"S.O.F."

The Queen City Shopping Mall is like every other in New England. It has two stories, a large footprint with anchor stores at each end, and a central walk with cutouts open to below. Marx is glad he dressed in casual attire today. Anything else would make it impossible for him to blend in. He is going to need to be average and forgettable to pull this off.

He nods at a mall security guard passing by, and the man reciprocates the gesture without a second thought. Extremes are the enemy of anonymity. The more standoffishly or obnoxiously you behave, the more you're noticed. It may be why celebrities act the way they do; it's the easiest way to get the paparazzi's attention.

His phone chirps, and he taps his Bluetooth earpiece to activate it. This is not the preferred method of communicating, but this mission is time-sensitive, and text messages are easy to miss when you're mobile.

"Yeah."

"A girl with dark hair getting into her car. I can't confirm it's Campos, though."

"It must be. Proceed as planned." Marx doesn't bother telling him to be careful. Trot knows he needs to be.

"Where are you?"

"The mall, believe it or not."

"You should get a massage while you're there. You're a little tense."

The comment doesn't sit well with Marx. "Don't screw this up, Trot."

"I got this. Your mission sounds trickier. There are a lot of cameras there."

"I know how to avoid them. I like the challenge. Confirm when complete."

Marx taps the earpiece again to disconnect the call. This mission is a critical last step in finishing their work here. To guarantee success, the team built in some redundancy. Only one of these operations needs to succeed, but he's hoping both do.

His target walks into a men's store, and he stops at an adjacent shop to browse the shelves. Tailing anyone through a mall sucks. He hates shopping when it's a necessity, let alone when he needed to tail someone who happens to wander here.

"Can I help you?" an attractive employee asks, approaching him with a helpful attitude and beaming smile.

"I'm just looking, thank you," Marx says with his warmest smile.

"Let me know if you need any help," she says, moving off to a new victim.

He checks the store's offerings while looking out of the corner of his eye. Marx sees his target leave the men's boutique with a bag and sighs. He exits the store he's in and follows along the far side of the upper level. The crowd is thinner here, and that's problematic.

Marx scans the walls and roof with his eyes for cameras. He doesn't see any other than the obvious ones they want people to see, but he knows they're there. Shopping malls are second only to casinos in the surveillance department.

He tugs at his hat, pulling it down far enough to hide him from the cameras above without drawing suspicion. His target stops and leans against the railing. This could be his chance, but it doesn't feel right. He wants to finish this but forces himself to be patient. The man clearly isn't in a rush to leave, and he knows he'll get his opportunity.

CHAPTER FIFTY-THREE

SPECIAL AGENT VICTORIA LARSEN

Boston Common
Boston, Massachusetts

Boston Common is America's oldest public park. Puritan colonists purchased the land rights to the forty-four acres in 1634 for thirty pounds. The equivalent today wouldn't buy a sweatshirt from one of the street vendors that line its perimeter.

The pasture then became known as the "common land' and was used for grazing livestock and meting out punishments at whipping posts, pillories, and the stocks. A large elm tree that is long gone once served as gallows for pirates, murderers, and witches. It also served as a British camp before the Colonials took the city, and the embarkation point on their fateful march to Lexington and Concord that ignited a revolution. It has since served as a place for countless rallies and protests, and now this meeting.

"Aren't you cold?" Seth asks, standing in front of her dressed in a wool overcoat and black watch cap.

"I've lived in New England for a while now."

"Yeah, me too, but it's still freezing out here."

Victoria stands and hugs Seth. She's seen the Massachusetts State Police detective more than she has Tierra and the gang from *Front Burner*, but not nearly as much as she'd like. She likes his company and friendship but doesn't want his wife thinking something is going on between them. Victoria has enough problems connecting with people without being labeled a homewrecker.

"I'd like to think this is a social call, but I know it isn't."

"I needed to talk to you. It's not as easy as it once was when you were always a hundred feet behind me."

"Sorry, other hardened criminals need my attention. What's up?"

"I need your help with something."

"Name it."

"You should really hear why first."

"I don't have to, Vic. If you're here asking me in sub-freezing weather, it's important."

"Okay. Walk with me."

Victoria and Seth wander the sidewalks that crisscross the park, and she gives him the story. She explains her suspicions about Dylan Spencer, interactions with *Front*

Burner, and the details of the Cooper investigation. She finishes with barging into Lance Fuller's office and what she learned from Harley.

"You've been busy. What do you need me to do?"

"For now, have my back. I don't know where this is going, but these guys have intimidated college kids, burned offices to the ground, hacked a national campaign, and killed someone. I don't know what else they're capable of."

"Don't you have any colleagues that can help? They must be good for something when they aren't trying to get rid of you."

"Unfortunately, they're still trying."

"Idiots," he grumbles. "I have some flexibility with my schedule for the next couple of weeks, so your timing is fortunate. What's first?"

"We take a drive up to New Hampshire."

"That's out of my jurisdiction."

"I know."

"Okay, to make it at least semi-legit, we'll need some more help. I have a few friends up there that may be able to provide it. Ironically, you already know one of them."

"Who?"

"And spoil the surprise?" Seth asks, grinning.

Victoria smiles as they change directions and head for her car. First Tierra, Tyler, and Olivia, and now Seth. She's getting the band back together. For the first time since she started looking into the Spencer suicide, she feels like progress is being made towards solving this.

CHAPTER FIFTY-FOUR

"S.O.F."

Now Marx is getting impatient. He has tailed his target around this mall for two hours, like Dante following the poet Virgil down through the seven circles of hell in the *Divine Comedy*. As much as he's trying to contain his frustration, it's a losing battle. He's eager to make his move and end this.

The one thing he's learned by walking around here is that there is no perfect place. He could just as easily break into the man's hotel room, but he needs this to look like an accident. The best way to avoid having people ask any questions is to do this in public. It's a risk, but they haven't gotten this far by being afraid to take a few.

He had his chance on the second floor, but it didn't feel right. There were too many people, and there are more cameras up there than down here. With all the kiosks manned by pushy vendors peddling goods and, ironically, shiatsu massages, the lower level of the mall isn't without its own set of difficulties.

When the man walks toward the escalator at the far end of the mall, Marx sees his chance. He takes a breath. This needs to be subtle. He runs over the scenario in his head, planning the various outcomes. The key is that his reaction needs to be one of surprise and the appearance of trying to help. It's the only way he walks out of here without cuffs on.

He closes the distance behind his target and climbs onto the escalator after him. Slow is smooth, smooth is fast. He climbs a step, then another, and another. He rides it for a little longer and reaches for the back of the man's jacket and pulls when they are three-quarters of the way up.

His target loses his balance, falling backward in what feels like slow motion. Marx reaches out to catch him, flailing and missing on purpose. The visual is perfect.

The man hits his head hard and slides down the escalator on his back as the stairs move beneath him on their constant upward climb. Marx shouts, and a woman screams from the bottom. Someone rushes up to help, trying to heft the unconscious man's body off the machine. He only makes matters worse.

Marx rushes to the top, taking two stairs at a time. He looks down as he fumbles for the emergency stop button. The man's face is bloody, and he's not moving at all. That will do. He presses the button, stopping the escalator, and rushes back down.

"What happened?" the man who responded first asks.

"He just collapsed. Call 9-1-1."

Someone is already on the phone speaking to a dispatcher when the same mall cop Marx passed earlier comes racing to the scene.

"What happened?"

"He fainted or something. Right in front of me. I tried to catch him but missed."

"He hit the stop button," the good Samaritan explains, satisfying the mall cop.

"Good call. We need an ambulance here for a senior citizen who collapsed on the south escalator. He's unconscious and bleeding."

The security guard checks his neck for a pulse. Marx watches him struggle to find one. He should start by placing his fingers on the carotid artery and not an inch to the left, but Marx doesn't correct the man. There's no reason for anyone to assume he would know how to do it, and he wants to keep it that way.

"Should we move him?" the man asks.

"No, he could have a spinal injury. Stand back, sir. Ma'am? Ma'am? I need you to stand back."

"Oh my God," she says, covering her mouth. "Is that Wilson Newman?"

A crowd gathers at the bottom of the escalator as the mall cop waits for paramedics. Marx descends and joins them, allowing himself to be ushered backward through it. The paramedics arrive and the crowd parts to let them through. He uses the distraction to peel off from the crowd and walks off toward the exit.

He glances up to see if he can spot the cameras when he's fifty feet from the doors. There must be one or more at the entrance. He pulls his hat down lower and leaves the mall. He grins as he walks past the ambulance and pulls his phone out.

The success code for his mission is one of his favorite books. It's a John Knowles novel wherein a boy jounces a tree branch, causing a friend to lose his balance and fall. The boy becomes permanently crippled after shattering his leg. That's more fitting given the circumstances than he thought it would be.

He types out a simple text message to inform the others: A SEPARATE PEACE.

CHAPTER FIFTY-FIVE

TIERRA CAMPOS

Southern New Hampshire Hospital (SNHH)
Manchester, New Hampshire

I got the call and raced over to the hospital in a rideshare that I paid double the price for to get me here more quickly. The executive producer knew that Wilson would want to see a friendly face. With no wife and his grown kids spread across the country, his job at *Capitol Beat* is all he has.

I'm a part of that world.

I brace myself when I enter his room, not sure what I'll see. It's bad. Wilson is lying inclined and is covered in a cheap hospital blanket that I straighten. He opens his eyes and smiles at me.

The cuts on his face and bruised eye sockets make it look like he was on the losing end of an MMA fight. The monitor shows that his EKG is normal, along with his blood pressure and blood oxygenation. I have no idea what the rest of the data means.

"You look like hell."

"That's what every man wants to hear from a young woman. They called you?"

I nod and offer a weak smile.

"Did they ask you to host before or after they told you about what happened?"

"The sentence after, if I remember correctly. Your executive producer didn't want Carl Brennan to have his tryout under these circumstances. Why didn't you tell me they were bringing him up here?"

"You have other things to worry about. Did you agree to host?"

I smirk. "Are you okay?"

"Not really, but I'm sure it looks worse than it is." I give him a disapproving look. "I will be, eventually. As you might imagine, people my age don't respond well to falls."

"People my age don't either, especially on a moving escalator. You're lucky you didn't break something."

"I'm too stubborn to break anything."

"What happened?"

"The doctors think I passed out from overexertion or something. As if strolling around a mall is that taxing. They're running tests to figure out why."

I don't have much more than a working knowledge of medicine. I do know that countless things could make a person black out, and none of them are good. I sit down at his bedside and hold his hand.

"Don't look at me like that, Tierra. They won't find anything."

"How do you know? You could have had a seizure or a mini-stroke or…"

Wilson cranes his neck to check the door to see if any doctors or nurses are hovering there. I stop talking and glance over my shoulder, wondering what is so secretive that he needs to go all cloak and dagger on me.

"I didn't black out. I was pulled down."

My face scrunches up. "What are you talking about?"

"Someone pulled me from behind on the escalator and caused me to fall."

"How do you know?"

"I'm old, not stupid. All I remember was my arms flailing as I fell backward. It was like a picture that got seared into my memory. If I had passed out, I wouldn't have it."

"Did you tell the doctors or the police?"

"No."

I want to hit him. "Why not?"

"Because I don't want whoever did this to know my suspicions. It wasn't an accident. It was deliberate, and if whoever did this knew I was talking, I might not be fortunate enough to walk away if they try again."

"You're really not telling anyone?"

"I'm telling someone right now."

He forces a smile, and I pull out my cell. The drama surrounding the Cooper investigation can wait a few hours. I want to know what happened to Wilson at that mall and need someone with a badge to find out.

"Vic, call me when you get this."

"That was very authoritative, considering you're leaving a message for an FBI agent that could gun you down from a hundred feet away."

I give him a kiss on the forehead. "You heal up and don't harass the nurses."

"Okay. If I'd known you'd race out of here, I would have told you after I finished my Jell-O."

"But you didn't wait. I'll be back to visit when I can."

"Where are you going?"

"To see if you're right."

CHAPTER FIFTY-SIX

ANDREW LI

Burgess Temporary Campaign Headquarters
Manchester, New Hampshire

Isiah is watching television in the corner of the makeshift office with a couple of volunteers beside him. The episode at the Queen City Mall is making national news. Even a tumble down an escalator is worthy of breaking into regular programming when the man is a media icon. That's how prominent Wilson Newman is.

Andrew nods at the volunteers, who move off, leaving him alone with the campaign manager.

"Do they know what happened?"

"They're just reporting that he collapsed and was rushed to the hospital. Most of the witnesses they've interviewed only caught the aftermath."

"A heart attack or stroke, maybe?"

"It doesn't sound like it, but who knows? Since when are initial media reports ever accurate?"

If twenty-four-hour media had been around in November of 1963, the first reports of Kennedy's death would have been that he was killed by a drunk driver. When it comes to news broadcasts, only meteorologists are statistically more wrong than on-scene reporters.

"You don't sound broken up about it."

"I'm sorry to hear that Wilson was injured, but I've never been a fan," Isiah says, still glued to the television.

"Don't ever let a reporter hear you say that. You know, there's an opportunity here for us if you want to take it."

Isiah cocks his head. "What are you talking about?"

"This is big news. People are going to tune in to the *Capitol Beat* special after the debate simply to see who they replace Wilson with. We should be on it."

"An interview?"

"The governor has never appeared on the show, and every other major candidate has. That's appealing from a ratings perspective and makes it hard for them to say no. Have they named a host yet?"

"Not that I've heard."

"My money is on the Campos woman from *Front Burner*. She just did the show recently and is in town for the primaries."

Isiah looks at him like he's speaking in tongues. "You don't really want her to interview my father, do you? She ripped Ethan apart last summer and was tough on everyone during the week she filled in."

Andrew smiles. "We can work with her. The governor likes challenging questions, remember? Ethan Harrington was a liar, and she knew it. Everyone she interviewed last week either wouldn't give her a straight answer or tried to hide from her questions. The governor won't do either."

"What if it isn't her hosting?"

Andrew frowns. It's hard to imagine why it wouldn't be. The producers will try to pull her in, and the editors at *Front Burner* will pull back harder not to let her go. He doesn't know who wins that tug-of-war for the future Pulitzer Prize winner. His money is on the ratings draw of *Capitol Beat* over the readership of an online news organization.

"If it's not her, then we get to face off against a rookie. First-timers are nervous, and your father will eat them for lunch. There's no downside for us. The upside is enormous."

"Okay. Make the call and see what they say."

Andrew doesn't wait around for his boss to change his mind. Once you get the answer you want, vanish. He does precisely that and calls the show. It's routed from the switchboard in Washington to a producer in Manchester. After some small talk about Wilson and his health, they get down to business.

"We are offering you an exclusive with Governor Burgess after the debate tonight."

The man laughs. "Your media representatives said that we were more likely to see the seventh angel pouring…something than seeing Luther Burgess on our set. I assume that was some sort of biblical reference."

"It was. The seventh angel poured out his bowl into the air, and out of the temple came a loud voice from the throne, saying, 'It is done!' It's from the Book of Revelation and signifies the end of God's judgments. Basically, the end of the world."

"I didn't peg you for a Bible scholar."

"I'm not. The last candidate I worked for was a reverend. You pick up some things."

"How did we go from Armageddon to Luther Burgess appearing on our show following the debate?"

"Things change."

"Yeah, namely our host being in the hospital."

"We can do a separate interview with Wilson after he recovers from whatever happened, if that would appease you. We know that whoever you have host will need a good draw for the show. The current Democratic frontrunner for the nomination is it. Who is filling in?"

"It's undetermined at this time."

There was a long pause on the line before he answered. That's code for he doesn't want to say who it is in case we change our mind. That must mean Tierra Campos.

"Okay. The choice is yours. Let us know, but post-debate interview requests are coming in from all over, and we're going to pick something in the next half an hour."

"Let's do it."

The corner of Andrew's mouth curls up. *That didn't take long.*

"Okay, get things organized on your end and let us know the details. We can walk right over to your set as soon as the debate is over."

"Sounds good. We're looking forward to seeing the governor."

Andrew disconnects the call and tucks his phone into his pocket. A matchup between Tierra Campos and Luther Burgess is a moment made for television.

CHAPTER FIFTY-SEVEN

"S.O.F."

Everett Turnpike
Merrimack, New Hampshire

This mission was a stupid idea to begin with. It's unnecessary to eliminate someone who isn't even a threat. Marx doesn't see it that way, and that makes him a reckless moron. Why invite more investigations by conducting an operation in broad daylight, on a busy road, and in a populated place? Where he should be is boarding a plane for a tropical island right now.

Trot tailed his target down to Nashua. She stayed for about an hour before heading to a coffee shop to meet someone he presumes is a source. Following that long meeting, she got in her car for the drive back to Manchester.

If she's heading back to the hotel, there are precious few opportunities on the route back to do this. He learned that on the way down here. It's a tricky road to pull something like this off without being seen.

The Everett Turnpike would never be confused for an Interstate highway. It's a four-lane controlled access road, but it has a country feel to it. Large trees line the sides of the stretch between Nashua and Manchester, partially obscuring it from the commercial and residential areas nearby. In the summer, with the leaves on the trees, he imagines this is a pretty road to travel on.

That's the good part. The bad part is that this segment is heavily traveled in both directions. Trot needs to make this plausibly look like a tragic accident. Running the bitch off the road in front of witnesses isn't going to get it done.

His Dodge Ram truck keeps up with her little four-cylinder rental with ease. Trot's eyes cycle between checking the mirrors and scanning the southbound side of the road for traffic. He needs to be ready to pounce at a moment's notice. He's about to make his move when he spots a pair of cars coming in the opposite direction. He shakes his head and lets off on the gas.

"Stupid."

This is never going to work. Trot exhales and regrips the wheel tighter when another promising opening appears. His phone vibrates. He checks the text and sees the words "A Separate Peace." That relieves the pressure, and he sinks deeper into his seat as he relaxes. He never thought he'd be happy to see one of Marx's ridiculous success codes. Only one of their missions needed to be successful. With him finished, this one is only gravy.

Trot starts to enjoy the drive when the traffic lightens again. The car following a hundred yards behind him pulls off at an exit. He checks the on-ramp for vehicles entering the highway. There are none. He presses down on the gas, closing the distance to the little gray Corolla. He slides into the left lane, still maintaining a safe distance from the vehicle to avoid looking alarming.

An oncoming car passes him, and then another. He waits a second. Two. Three. No other vehicles appear. He checks his mirror. The only one heading northbound is way back in the distance. This is it.

He floors it, causing the Hemi V8 under the hood to roar as it translates its power to the wheels. The truck accelerates, now coming even with the back bumper of the Corolla. He eases off the gas, allowing the momentum of the truck to carry him past her car. Two car lengths ahead, his foot presses down on the gas gently, staying ahead of her vehicle while allowing it to edge closer. He grins.

A quick jerk of the wheel at this speed does the trick. The truck lurches into the right lane. The back part of the truck's bed clips the front quarter panel of the Corolla, bumping the little car toward the edge of the road.

She jerks the wheel, causing her car to hit the curb. The girl yanks the wheel back hard, making the vehicle unstable and sending it careening across the northbound lanes. She plows into the center divider almost head-on. The Toyota bounces off the concrete k-rail and spins, causing the wheels to dig in. The car flips several times before jumping over the divider and coming to a rest on its roof in the southbound lanes.

Trot rechecks the mirror. The car behind them was too far back for the driver to know what caused the crash. He checks ahead and sees a vehicle. Damn. Did he see what happened?

He floors it, eager to put distance between himself and the wreck. When the truck reaches the top of the rise and descends downhill, the crash disappears from his view. Trot remembers to breathe. It wasn't as clean as he'd like, but it won't matter in a few days. He'll be on a beach in St. Kitts with a new identity and a hefty sum in his bank account.

He steers the truck off the road at the next exit and pulls into the parking lot of a small strip mall, sure to stay away from the storefronts where there might be cameras. He pulls out his cell and opens the group text.

"What the hell was it?" he mumbles.

Trot finds this whole code thing irritating. Marx likes feeling superior by basing them on novels that most kids refuse to read in high school. He could have at least used more sci-fi.

He types in what he thinks is his success code: THE SOUND AND THE FURY.

He stashes the phone in the center console and stares out the windshield. He needs to get moving again, and it will take double the time via the backroads to South Hooksett. It can wait a few moments longer. He wonders how the beaches are on St. Kitts. Hopefully, they are sandy, with turquoise blue waters and someone bringing him drinks with umbrellas in them. It's a nice thought. He can't wait to find out if he's right.

CHAPTER FIFTY-EIGHT

SPECIAL AGENT VICTORIA LARSEN

Queen City Shopping Mall Security Office
Manchester, New Hampshire

Victoria, Tyler, and Tierra are on a mission. The security office is located off a short hallway leading to the food court restrooms. The medical emergency today was no doubt the talk of their small office. That gossip may be replaced by their interaction with these two angry women.

"Do you have a warrant?" the head guard asks.

"Do I really need one?"

He looks at Victoria, unamused. "I understand you are with the FBI, but this is private prop—"

"I'm telling you that a crime may have been committed on your property. That crime may have involved one of America's leading news personalities."

"When that comes out, and trust me, it will, you're going to want to get ahead of it," Tierra says, picking up the argument.

"That starts with us right now."

"Because the words you want to hear in every news report are 'mall security is doing everything they can to help authorities with their investigation.'"

"Which you're not doing right now."

"In which case, it will read something like 'mall security would not assist in the investigation, leaving authorities to speculate whether Mr. Newman suffered a medical incident or was the victim of a crime in what was once one of Manchester's safest shopping areas.'"

Tyler watches the man's head swivel back and forth like he's seated center court at the U.S. Open. If there are two women in the world that Tyler doesn't ever want to be pissed off at him, it's the ones he's standing behind. The guard is lucky; they're going easy on him right now.

"Are they always like this?" the man asks Tyler.

"They're just getting warmed up. This can last for hours. Trust me, nobody has the stamina to endure it. I speak from experience."

"Sir, we don't want to take physical possession of the tapes," Victoria says, extending an olive branch. "We only want to see what's on them. If we find something, and you agree, you can turn them in yourself."

"You'd be a hero. I can see the article in *Front Burner* now: Eagle-eyed mall security spots possible attack on prominent newsman."

Tierra and Victoria wear the same impish smiles. The man glances back at Tyler, who offers a little shrug. Surrender is the only option.

"You make a very compelling case, ladies. Come on."

He walks them back to the monitoring room that's not much bigger than the bathroom in their hotel suite. Whatever money the managers of this mall devote to security, it isn't spent on their physical infrastructure.

"All our camera feeds are recorded and backed up to the cloud. We can view playback and watch in real-time here."

"Can you bring up any camera with a view of the escalator?"

"We have three. This one is pointing at it from the north," he says, typing in the approximate time of the incident and hitting enter.

"Here we go," Tierra says. "There's Wilson."

"Check out the man behind him," Tyler says, pointing.

"Did you get any details on this guy?"

"No. ma'am. The responding guard reported that he tried to stop the fall and then raced up to hit the emergency stop. He didn't stick around for a statement and left no contact information."

"Why not?" Victoria asks.

"I don't know. We didn't take statements until well after the paramedics arrived. Maybe he had someplace he needed to be."

"Keep playing. Let's see what happened."

The entire incident plays out, the four people studying every movement. When it's done, the man leans back, and the two women look at each other. Tyler shakes his head.

"I didn't see anything," the security guard says.

"I didn't either," Tyler says, as Tierra purses her lips in frustration.

"You didn't know what you were looking for," Victoria interjects. "Play it again. This time watch the man's right hand and Wilson's jacket."

The man rewinds the recording, and they all watch the video again. This time, they see it. The action is subtle, but it was there. Wilson was right.

"Damn, there it is."

"Look, and there's the arm flailing. Wilson was pulled backward."

"We never would have seen it," the guard admits, sounding a little guilty.

"Don't worry about it. We wouldn't have either without knowing to look for it. The guy was smooth. Can we figure out where he went?"

"Absolutely." Now the supervisor is angry. "Okay, here we go. He hangs back for a while and, ah, walks this way."

This guard knows how to work his equipment. He changes video feeds deftly, following the mysterious suspect as he makes his way toward the exit. He switches cameras one more time. The guy is walking, keeping his head down.

"Don't tell me that we're not going to see this guy's face," Tierra moans.

"What part of the mall is this?" Victoria asks.

"It leads to the west exit."

"Damn."

They watch longer. "There! Stop and rewind, frame by frame."

"How did you see that?" Tyler asks.

"Hours of practice. Billy Badass here looked up to check for cameras. Can you zoom in?"

"I can do one better. We just installed this camera two months ago. It's high-resolution and may have a better angle."

The guard opens the feed and enters the timestamp. Sure enough, the picture almost looks like the guy took a selfie. He sends the still frame to the printer.

"Please send me a digital copy,' Victoria says, jotting down an email address.

"Will do. I'm going to track this guy through the mall to see how long he tailed Mr. Newman. Then I'll turn all this over to the state police."

"Thank you. Contact Diego Velez at the Bedford Barracks. Give him my name. He'll take the case."

The three of them file out and stop at a table at the food court. None are hungry, but they are mentally drained.

"You think this guy is SOF, don't you?" Tierra asks.

"It takes skill to make an attack look like an accident. Yeah, I do."

"Why would the SOF go after Wilson Newman?"

"That's the million-dollar question. I'm going to the Bedford office to ID this guy. Once we know who it is, I'm going to ask him and find out."

Victoria hopes that Seth is making some progress enlisting help. She has a bad feeling that they are going to need it before this primary is over.

Tierra's cell phone rings and she grimaces when she sees the caller ID. Then she thinks about sending it to voicemail but decides against it.

"Hi, Austin," she says before her face changes. "What? When?"

Tears form in the corner of her eyes as Victoria and Tyler watch with concern.

"We'll be right there," Tierra says, hanging up and about to burst into tears.

"What is it? What happened?" Tyler asks.

"It's Olivia. She's been in a bad accident and is in the hospital."

"How bad?"

"Doctors aren't sure she's going to make it."

CHAPTER FIFTY-NINE

SENATOR ALICIA STANDISH

Granite State University Democratic Presidential Debate
Durham, New Hampshire

Nothing is more intimidating than a debate. Television cameras beam every word to an audience of millions, magnifying the effect of any mistake. The crowd provides instant positive and negative feedback on your performance, often throwing candidates off their game. Moderators exist to force mistakes for video clips and soundbites more than to ask questions and control the timing of the event. It's a pressure cooker, and Alicia loves it.

"This is a moment in time when we, as Americans, are faced with a critical choice. I am not an outsider. I've been in Washington and experienced firsthand what it has become. An outsider will never bring about the type of change we need most. I am that candidate. I will be that president."

The applause is better than the polite one she received at the rally, but not as enthusiastic as Alicia hoped. Still, she stuck the landing on the opening remarks. Now comes the hard part.

"With the opening statements complete, let's move on," the moderator says. "Senator Standish, tonight's first question is for you. The Burgess campaign has experienced several unfortunate and tragic incidents. Earlier this afternoon, Brian Cooper, your New Hampshire campaign chair, was arrested by the FBI for his involvement. What responsibility does your campaign take for these incidents?"

"None," Alicia says, eliciting groans from the audience. "I set a high standard for the behavior of my staff, and I expect everyone to comply with it. Yes, Brian Cooper was arrested, but his guilt has not been established. Due process will determine his culpability if there is any. If a jury pronounces him guilty, then know that he was operating far beyond what is acceptable in any campaign, and especially mine."

Alicia pauses before pivoting the question to a different subject.

"This primary, and this race for the presidency, must be about the issues that face us. The longer we ignore them, the harder they will be to solve."

"Governor Burgess, these incidents affected your campaign. Would you like to comment?"

"I would. I was prepared to agree with everything the senator just said," he offers, eliciting a surprised reaction from the attendees. "Due process is not only necessary in American society, but it's also critical. It's the foundation of our Republic. And I also agree that this should be an issues-based election. Unfortunately, Senator Standish's actions make her words empty ones."

"That's not true."

"It is, Senator. Let me explain. This was brought to my attention moments before we came on stage."

Luther pulls out a sheet of paper from inside his suit jacket pocket and unfolds it. He puts on his reading glasses and looks over the top of them at the audience moderators.

"The senator sent out a series of tweets before she took the stage tonight from her personal Twitter account. Among boasting about how prepared she was, and for the record, I believe she is, she said something troubling. She tweeted that she was going to 'kick my black ass back to the projects where it belongs.'"

The audience gasps when they hear the tweet's racial overtones. Alicia's mouth hangs open. Why is he making this stuff up?

"I never wrote that, Governor."

"I would hope that you didn't, but this is your blue checked account. I mean, I know there are many fake ones out there for both you and me, but this one is verified."

"I never wrote that."

"I don't know what to say, Senator. I wish you didn't. I never wanted this election to be about race. It's a problem in this country, yes. Racism deserves our attention and our staunchest efforts to eradicate. That's why this hurts me, especially coming from another Democrat."

"I swear to you, Governor, I never wrote that."

It's the third time that she uttered that. What else can she say? She was blindsided, mainly because she didn't write it. She can't imagine anybody she works with doing that, not that they have the password to her account even if the thought occurred to them.

"It's wedged in here between two other tweets. I admit that I'm not savvy on social media, but how could you not have written it?"

"I must have been hacked," she blurts out, desperate for an answer.

"Hacked? Okay," Governor Burgess says calmly, much like a prosecutor examining a witness would. "And the hacker only sent one tweet while you happened to be using Twitter?"

"I can't explain that."

"That's the problem, isn't it, Senator? What should we think? You claim to not have any knowledge about the arsons or the intimidation. I want to trust you, but now you're asking me to believe you were hacked instead of just making a mistake by writing this hateful comment."

"I didn't write it!"

"The American people can't believe anything you say anymore."

Nine simple words can carry immeasurable meaning. Luther's claim had nothing to do with him personally. He stepped into the role of the president. He's speaking for voters across the country, and they will buy into it.

"We need to move on and—"

"No, please, wait, I need to address this," she says, interrupting the moderator. "I would never write something like that. My campaign manager is black, and—"

"Is that because you think she's valuable or because you're guilty over your white privilege?" Luther argues.

"All I have wanted to do is elevate the debate in this country."

"All you have done in New Hampshire is show the nation who you really are and what you're willing to do to win the presidency."

The audience goes ballistic, erupting with cheers for him, jeers for her, and unleashing thunderous applause that the moderators work overtime to squelch. She has lost whatever audience she had won over from her opening statement. She can still recover in this debate, but it's a long shot. Once the second-tier candidates start coming at her to chip away her following, it's going to make for a long night.

CHAPTER SIXTY

CAPITOL BEAT

Granite State University Remote Set
Durham, New Hampshire

Carl grasps his shaking hands, willing them to stop. He's never been this nervous. The anchor of WWDC's flagship news broadcast for years now, he's interviewed celebrities and politicians before. Washington isn't a small television market, but it's not national either. Producers expect tonight's audience to be larger than its usual three million viewers.

"Be calm, Carl. You're fidgeting," the producer says in his earpiece.

He takes a deep breath and thinks calming thoughts. It doesn't work.

"Ten seconds," the floor producer shouts, starting a count that goes silent with him using fingers when it reaches three.

"Good Evening. It is Friday, February 4th, *I* am Carl Brennan in for Wilson Newman and this…is…*Capitol Beat.*

The opening plays, and the producer buries his face in his hands behind the cameras. Carl changed the show's sign-on, despite being explicitly told not to. He was heavy on the "I" like the world revolves around him. Worse, it sounded like he had a stroke pronouncing the word "is."

Carl launches into the latest on what happened to Wilson at the Queen City Mall. He mispronounces two words and calls the man doing the on-site report from the hospital by the wrong name. It's a mistake the reporter is sure to correct when he throws it back to Carl. To add insult to injury, their new shining star flubs the man's name a second time.

Tierra Campos was nervous her first time out as well. Fortunately, she tamped it down quickly and handled the whole broadcast with admirable professionalism. This guy is a travesty wrapped inside a disaster. Despite sharing a mutual understanding with the producers on the direction for the show, the early returns on a side-by-side comparison with Tierra Campos leave no doubt who's the better anchor.

They go to commercial, and the producer searches for something positive to say.

"It's all right, Carl."

"You're damn right it is. I nailed it."

"Uh, yeah. Remember that this is Burgess's first time on the show. Do exactly what we discussed. The questions are on the teleprompter."

Governor Luther Burgess is shown in by an associate producer, from a separate space they set up as a green room. His microphone is adjusted, and some last-second powder applied to his face to eliminate the glare from the lights. When the commercial break is over, the lights come back up.

"We are here now with Luther Burgess, the distinguished governor of the great state of Iowa, and current frontrunner for the Democratic nomination. Thank you for joining us tonight."

"Thank you for having me, Carl. It's Illinois, not Iowa."

"I'm sorry?"

"I'm the governor of Illinois."

"My apologies, sir."

"No worries. I would have been equally proud to have been elected to the office in that state as well," he says, with a beaming smile.

"Uh, that was quite…quite a performance at the debate tonight. What were your thoughts about it?"

"Honestly, I was hoping to see more out of it. Senator Standish was right when she said that we need to be discussing policy. We're facing serious problems in this country. The American people need to hear how each candidate plans on addressing them. Her own words made that impossible."

"Do you believe she wrote that she'd 'kick your black ass back to the projects where it belongs?'"

Burgess frowns. "If she was using Twitter as she often does before taking the stage, then it's hard for me to believe that she didn't write it. It pains me to say that."

"It was a horrible thing for her to say. She should be ashamed of herself."

The producer groans and throws his hands up in the control room. He needs some ibuprofen…or whiskey. Carl's making assumptions without any proof. Does he not know the word "allegedly?"

"It was. I expected more from her."

"Do you think Senator Standish is a racist? Because that comment is about as racist as it gets."

"I don't want to believe that. I've never heard anything like that about Senator Standish. We'll find out in the coming days if I'm wrong, but I'll let America judge."

"Stick to the script, Carl."

Carl glances in the direction of the control room before turning back to the governor. "The other candidates came after you for your Vision 2020 plan."

"Vision 2030. Future, not past."

"Yes, Vision 2030. What are your thoughts on that?"

Luther looks at him like he's a moron. "My thoughts on the vision, or my thoughts about them coming after me?"

"I uh…the vision…and their agreement…disagreement with what you said…or uh, wrote."

"I am leading in the polls in New Hampshire, so I was going to be a target. Criticism of Vision 2030 was expected. I hadn't planned on releasing that document this early, but I'm proud to stand by every word in it."

"You handled their attacks on you admirably."

The executive producer hands his earpiece and mic to an intern from the school that's working with them in the makeshift control room.

"Give this to someone else. I can't watch this anymore."

"Thank you," the governor says, not knowing what to make of the compliment.

"You have a sizable lead that will only grow after Standish imploded tonight. Are you shifting focus to the Democratic primaries in Nevada and South Carolina?" Carl asks, going off-script again to lob another softball.

"I would never disrespect the good people of New Hampshire that way. They take holding the first primary very seriously, much like Iowans do with the first caucus. They deserve my undivided attention until they go to the polls. My volunteers deserve to have me here to celebrate with them if we win."

"When you win, Governor. Would you agree that your lead is almost insurmountable now?"

Governor Burgess looks at his host. This is *Capitol Beat*. Wilson Newman is known as one of the most feared interviewers in America. Did they really bring this guy in to flatter him, or is this a trap he doesn't see coming?

"I don't believe any lead is safe until the ballots are counted."

"You earned a lot more votes tonight. You would have earned mine after that performance. Thank you for joining us on *Capitol Beat*. We'll return from Granite State University, home of the Democratic New Hampshire Primary, after these messages."

"Primary *debate*! Not the primary itself!" the executive producer screams, stomping around behind the cameras after they go to break.

"It's all right, you did great, Carl," Luther says, flashing a bright smile. He shakes his hand as staff take off his mic and escort him off the set.

Carl is nodding his head and grinning as he stares out at the show's cameramen and staff. Not one of them returns his smile. There is bad, horrible, and the affront to journalism that they just witnessed. It should be Carl's first indication that something went wrong. All he can ask himself is what could possibly be the problem?

CHAPTER SIXTY-ONE

SPECIAL AGENT VICTORIA LARSEN

Federal Bureau of Investigation Field Office
Bedford, New Hampshire

3 Days to the New Hampshire Democratic Primary

Pictures never change; only a person's perception of them does. That's why Victoria continues to stare at the printout of the mystery man who put Wilson Newman into a hospital. She scans every detail. No hard evidence exists linking this man to the arsons or the intimidation of kids at local colleges. It's more of a stretch to believe he had anything to do with Dylan Spencer's suicide. Every instinct tells her that he did.

After Tierra and Tyler rushed to the hospital, Seth and Victoria used the digital image provided by Queen City Mall security and ran it through a facial recognition database at their Bedford office. After entering some known parameters, they let the computers do the work and found ways to keep their minds occupied as they waited. It's scary the tools modern law enforcement has available to them. It's after midnight now, and the machine has been chewing on it for hours. She knows this guy is in there.

"I never would have expected mall security cameras to be this good," Seth says, waving a printout of his own.

"The wonders of the digital age. A Ring doorbell has better video quality than my television did in college."

"You think we'll find anything?"

"Yeah, we're going to find something," Victoria says, returning her eyes to the photo.

She checks the caller ID when her phone rings, and she accepts the call, hoping for good news. Shock set in like quick-drying cement when a distraught Tierra informed her that Olivia was in critical condition after an accident on the Everett Turnpike.

"How is Olivia doing?"

"She's out of surgery and resting. Doctors say that the next eight hours are critical."

"I'm so sorry, Tierra. How are you holding up?"

"I'm numb. Austin's here. That's not helping."

"Things are still tense between you two?"

Tierra sighs. "That's an understatement, but we called a temporary truce. I need your help with something. I spoke to the state police. Olivia's car was the only vehicle involved in the accident. There were no witnesses to the crash, even on a busy road. What are the odds of that?"

Victoria closes her eyes. It is suspicious, but it's also likely Tierra is trying to make sense of a tragedy. The mind always wants a reason, and that often leads it to conjure up conspiracies that don't exist. Sometimes, an accident is just an accident.

"Slim, but that doesn't mean anything."

"It's not right, Vic," Tierra continues to argue. "The road wasn't icy. If Olivia were a speed demon, okay, maybe I could see her losing control. That's not her. She drives like a little old lady."

"What do you need me to do?"

"Can you contact the police and make sure that they conduct a proper investigation? I don't want them just passing this off as an accident without being sure."

"Yeah, I think I can help with that," Victoria says, looking at Seth. "I'll be there as soon as we're done here."

"Okay. Thanks. We likely won't learn anything new until morning anyway. How's the search going?"

"Slow. We'll talk soon. Keep your chin up. The last thing Olivia is going to want to see when she wakes up is you looking all depressed."

The women sign off, and Victoria puts her blazer on.

"Uh, oh, Superwoman is putting her cape on," Seth says, not looking up from the monitor.

"I need you to do something for me. Call your friends in the New Hampshire State Police. Have them check every inch of that car for anything suspicious."

"I was planning on doing that anyway. You don't think it was an accident either, do you?"

"Wilson Newman gets pulled down an escalator. Olivia gets into a mysterious auto accident a couple of hours later..."

"Yeah, I don't believe in coincidences either. The question is, why?"

The computer chimes and Seth nearly falls out of his chair. Victoria perks up and moves to stand over his shoulder.

"It's about time."

A link to a Department of Defense personnel file pops up, and he clicks on it. The man who attacked Wilson was ex-military. More curious, his last known address was in Ohio. He's not from New Hampshire or Massachusetts and has no next of kin located here. The little hairs on the back of her neck rise. She stares at the name: Dennis Haskin.

"There's not much here. Haskin did his basic and advanced training as an infantryman at Fort Benning, Georgia. Then he got accepted to OCS."

"He's an officer?"

"He was one. He graduated at the top of his class from Officer Candidate School. He served twelve years, two enlisted, before he resigned his commission as a major and left the military. His postings included stints with the 101st Airborne at Fort Campbell, and with U.S. Army Europe in Wiesbaden, Germany."

"What did he do for them?"

"I don't know. It's redacted. Haskin had a TS/SCI clearance, though."

"Those aren't easy to get," Seth says, pulling his eyes away from the computer to look at her.

"No, they're not," Victoria mumbles under her breath, scanning the file.

Everything about this is wrong. Any clearance above Top Secret provides access to information that may cause grave damage to national security in the event of unauthorized disclosure. Work classified as "special sensitive" requires access to Sensitive Compartmented Information and a TS/SCI clearance. It's not something you can take an online class to get. They dig into your life.

"He lost his clearance. That's why he left the military."

"Does it say why?"

"And make it easy on us?" Seth moans.

Victoria pulls up a chair. "We've got six hours to learn everything there is to know about this guy. Let's get started."

CHAPTER SIXTY-TWO

TIERRA CAMPOS

Southern New Hampshire Hospital (SNHH)
Manchester, New Hampshire

I'm fighting a losing battle with the tears that persist in leaking from my eyes. I dab them away with a tissue, but they reform and continue their relentless march down my cheeks. Olivia didn't deserve this. No matter how many hours I spend at her bedside, my guilt will never be assuaged. There's nothing anybody can say that will convince me what happened was an accident.

I glance up at Tyler, who is seated on the opposite side of the bed. Like most men, he's not a crier. His anguish is written all over his face. Olivia is like a sister to him. He's clinging to the news the doctor delivered that she should regain consciousness today. That's something, at least.

The tension in the room comes from the other side of the *Front Burner* equation. Madison and Jerome haven't said two words to me in the time they've been here. Austin has been curt when we converse at all. It's a whole new level of awkwardness. Our mutual concern for Olivia is the only glue holding us together.

A doctor in the stereotypical white coat comes in and checks her chart. The nurse with him gives a quick rundown on what they've seen over the past few hours.

"How is she?" Austin asks when the nurse finishes.

"Improving. The airbags and seatbelt in Olivia's vehicle saved her life. She suffered a lot of internal injuries, and she's not entirely out of the woods yet, but I'm optimistic that she'll make a full recovery. She's a strong girl."

"Thank you, doctor."

"Of course. Just so I know, have the police determined the cause of the accident?"

"The first report says she was traveling too fast and lost control," Austin says, getting a nod from Madison and Jerome.

"They're still investigating," Tyler says sharply.

The doctor fidgets, sensing the hostility. "I see. I'll be back in a couple of hours to check on her. She's in good hands. The nurses here are excellent."

"Thanks, doc."

"It wasn't an accident," I mumble after he leaves with the nurse.

"There's no evidence of that," Austin counters.

"No, there isn't…yet. It wasn't an accident."

Austin stares hard at me, and I'm happy to return it. The others bounce their eyes between us. They know that this battle was a long time coming. I imagine this was what the Earps and Doc Holliday must have felt like before the gunfight at the O.K. Corral in Tombstone.

"You had better not be blaming me for asking her to come to Nashua."

"I'm not." It was a truthful answer, but my heart wasn't behind it.

"Do you guys have to do this now?" Jerome moans.

"Because I could never have known—"

"I said that I'm not blaming you," I snap.

Austin scoffs. "Tierra Campos, the crime-fighting journalist, is at it again, putting herself in harm's way while others pay the price. First, Tyler at the rally, and now Olivia."

"I don't think you really want to go there, Austin."

"She wasn't responsible for either of those!" Tyler exclaims, shouting over me as he's dragged into this by the boss.

"I could argue otherwise," Madison says, crossing her arms.

"Shut up, Maddie. You can suck up for a promotion later."

Jerome pushes off the wall, ready to come to Madison's defense. That's a sideshow. This is between Austin and me, and he loads his next volley by pointing a finger in my face.

"If you hadn't decided to jump ship and work with *Capitol Beat*—"

I swipe away his hand. "Outside. Now!"

I storm out of the room with Austin right behind me. I turn the corner and spin on my heels, coming nose to nose with him.

"What the hell is your problem?"

"My problem? You're the one in there saying that Olivia's crash wasn't an accident and blaming me!"

"I just said twice that I wasn't blaming you. Can you say the same?"

"Hey, you two!" a nurse says, rounding the corner with an angry gait. "This is a hospital, and we have patients recovering. Kill each other somewhere else."

We move around the corner and down to the lounge area. The mother and her young child there see the anger on our faces and quickly depart.

"Seriously, Austin, what's your problem?"

"None of this would have happened had you not hosted *Capitol Beat*."

"Oh, so because you have a problem with that, you send Ty and Liv up here with me, why? Because they think you're acting like an ass? Then you three stay in a separate hotel out of spite, and this is my fault, how?"

"It's not mine."

"If you want to play the blame game, fine. You were the one who summoned Olivia to Nashua. Not me, and not Tyler. Not the three of us. Just her. Why, exactly? What was so important?"

He doesn't say anything at first. Whatever reason he had, it wasn't a good one. Austin did that out of spite, too. I have no doubt that he sent her on some errand that any one of the three of them could have done.

"This is not my fault," he says, the volume of his voice lower now.

"Are you trying to convince yourself or me? You've treated me like garbage for a week now. That's fine. But if you're angry about Olivia, look in the mirror. You created the circumstances."

"I did no such thing."

"We used to be a team, Austin."

"Yeah, we were. Only I don't know what team you're on now."

"My own now, apparently."

He smirks, and I want to knock it off his face. I don't deal well with condescension.

"Was that ever not the case? It's always been about you."

"Look, if that's what you really believe and don't want me at *Front Burner*, fire me."

He folds his arms. "No way. I won't give you the satisfaction of making your decision easier."

"You're a fool if you think anything about it was ever easy. I'll tell you this, you're making it easier by the minute."

He nods a few times, taking my words in. I don't know if I'm angry at his comment, hurt by it, or both. I was hoping he would just fire me to end the misery. Instead, he's going to be a child and force me to quit. I'm happy to oblige, and hopefully sooner rather than later. This isn't what I signed up for last summer.

"Let me know when you're done visiting Olivia. I don't want to look at you right now," Austin says.

He storms off, and I collapse into a chair. Olivia, Wilson, the feeling that I'm failing Brian Cooper, the people of New Hampshire, and now this…it's more than my already shot nerves can handle. All I can do is cover my face and cry as hard as I can.

CHAPTER SIXTY-THREE

SENATOR ALICIA STANDISH

Standish for President Campaign Office
Nashua, New Hampshire

The staff was dismissed following the interviews with the media after the debate. Some didn't stay that long, opting to resign before Alicia had even made it off the stage. The Lusitania didn't sink as fast as her campaign is going down. When she convenes a meeting with those who are left, it starts with disastrous overnight polls and the reasons.

"Just what are you accusing me of?" Alicia asks, the edge in her voice sharper than a razor.

"I'm not accusing you of anything, Senator," her social media expert Jack says, not backing down as she glares at him.

"It sounds like you are. I didn't type that tweet. I didn't send that tweet. I have never taunted an opponent on social media before."

"None of that matters," Michael says. "People will believe you sent it because it's the simplest explanation."

"Senator, I think what Jack is trying to say is that Governor Burgess was right last night," Angela interjects. "He said that you were tweeting right before you went on stage. Everyone knows that's what you do."

"That's it, exactly," the senator says. "Everyone knows. That means someone wanting to hurt me could have timed it to make it look like I sent it."

"We contacted Twitter to see if there was any irregular activity on the account. They're looking into it," Jack says, not at all enthusiastic about that explanation.

"What about her phone? Could someone hack in and access it?"

"Not likely, Angela, but our IT team is looking at it."

"We changed all our campaign social media passwords. The senator has already changed her personal ones."

"Did you delete the comment, Senator?"

"Yes," she says, feeling slightly lightheaded. She knows that stress is starting to affect her physical wellbeing.

"It doesn't matter," Jack says. "People are putting screenshots of it in their tweets. The hashtag ALICIASTANDOWN has been trending since last night. The comments are brutal. Even Hollywood celebs have gotten in on the act."

"What do we do next?" Alicia asks, not wanting to continue the conversation about that disaster.

She looks around the table and sees defeated faces. Nobody wants to make eye contact with her, much less say anything. They've given up on the campaign, and her.

"New Hampshire is a lost cause, Senator. I suggest we move on to Nevada."

"You and Angela have both told me multiple times that I need to win here."

There's an awkward silence as Michael stares at his hands on the table. Nobody is arguing with him, and silence is consent.

"You won't. Maybe you can salvage the Silver and Palmetto states by making inroads while he isn't there."

Alicia turns to Angela. "You agree with this?"

"Senator, there aren't any good courses of action. Unfortunately, that's the best one."

"You all agree?"

There are slight nods around the table. Alicia leans back. She never thought she would be having a conversation about abandoning New Hampshire. It was unthinkable, even after the arsons.

"I'm not running from Luther Burgess. I will not cede him this state."

"Senator, there is no other way to put this, so I'll say it plainly: if you choose to stay here, you lose the nomination. It's that simple. To keep the slim chance you have alive, we need to pack up and head for Las Vegas. You have a base of support there, and there is a chance to sway the unions into your camp. That's over a hundred thousand people. To win them over in time for the Nevada Primary, you need to leave by tomorrow."

"Are you telling me that I can't win without their endorsement?"

Michael looks up at Angela, who nods. "Senator, it will be hard enough for you to win *with* it."

"I'll let you know my decision. Thank you, all."

The troops leave, including her campaign manager and consultant. She's alone again. The end of the line is in sight, like a bad dream that she's powerless to stop. Only this is the real world, and the end of her primary race won't be in an arena with music, cheering delegates, and thousands of balloons. It is her returning home to Cambridge, humiliated.

CHAPTER SIXTY-FOUR

SPECIAL AGENT VICTORIA LARSEN

Southern New Hampshire Hospital (SNHH)
Manchester, New Hampshire

Victoria and Seth finish getting their hospital visitor passes. It's early, and outside of regular visiting hours, but rarely does anyone at the desk say no to gold badges. Law enforcement spends a lot of time in hospitals. There's mutual respect between them and the medical community.

The pair crosses the lobby and passes the gift shop on the way to the elevators. Victoria catches someone out of the corner of her eye and stops.

"Coffee break?" Seth asks.

"Would you mind getting me one? I need to take care of something before we go upstairs."

"Sure thing."

Victoria walks over to the café, and Seth gets in line. He glances over to see her sit with a man who doesn't look like he's in the mood for company.

"You look like hell," Victoria says after Austin glances up but remains silent.

"It's good seeing you, too."

"Is it? Aren't I on the opposing side of this little battle you're having?"

"It's not like that," he mutters.

"Yes, it is."

Austin shakes his head and scans the surroundings, clearly wishing he were anywhere but here. He finally settles his eyes back onto Victoria.

"You do like being blunt, don't you?"

"Life is too short to spend it skirting around our problems."

"And you think I'm the problem?"

Victoria smirks. "Do you think Tierra is?"

From the moment Victoria set foot in Quantico, she's had little time and even less patience for office drama. The FBI is full of it, but she combats it with an attitude that most of her colleagues and superiors would call "rebellious." She was labeled a maverick because she believes that the job comes first. The posturing that consumes organizations is childish and often counterproductive to its purpose. *Front Burner* is getting destroyed over it.

"I don't know what to think anymore. Things were bad before Olivia's accident. My team is fractured. I don't know what to do about it."

"You know, you guys were larger than life when I first met you. I couldn't have been more impressed with the team you built. That's high praise coming from me, by the way. The FBI and the media…well, we don't mix. You guys were different."

"We are different," Austin says.

"I'm not so sure anymore. If that were true, you wouldn't be bullying a subordinate."

Austin leans back in his chair and lets out a breath. "I see Tierra has been bending your ear."

"We talk. Tierra is more conflicted about the decision facing her than you think. *Capitol Beat* is an incredible opportunity, but *Front Burner* is her home. She loves you guys like family, and yet you ostracized her the first chance you got. The word for that's betrayal, Austin."

"I'm not betraying her."

"Sure, you are. Switch positions. If your roles were reversed, what would you do?"

"Not have considered *Capitol Beat* at all."

He answered that too quickly with a defensive response. Victoria is turning this into an interrogation for a reason. Austin needs some sense talked into him before it's too late. It may already be.

"Bullshit. Stop lying to yourself. You absolutely would have. Every member of your team would be doing the same thing in her shoes. Maybe that's the problem. You're all jealous of her."

"That's not it," Austin sneers.

"Saying the words with an attitude doesn't make them true."

"It went to her head, Vic. Plain and simple. Brockhampton turned her into a celebrity, and now she's acting like one."

"Did it? I haven't spent time with her over the past six months, but I haven't seen a hint of Prima Donna behavior up here. If anything, it's the opposite. Even if I'm wrong and it did, does she deserve to be treated like this?"

"I need to preserve the team."

"You're doing a bang-up job of that so far, aren't you? Yes, knock her down a couple of pegs, so everyone feels better about losing her. That makes a lot of sense."

"Are you really the best person to dress me down?"

The comment stings. Austin was instrumental in applying pressure on the prosecutors in Massachusetts to drop the sham charges filed against her for shooting a man at the riot. She owes him, and this is how she can help repay that debt.

"Probably not, but I'm the one down here trying to fix this before it's irrevocably broken."

"It may be too late for that."

"Take my advice and step back a few paces. Honestly ask yourself if what's going on with Tierra is about her, or if it's about you. I know you don't want to lose her, but you have a shitty way of showing it."

"If you say so."

Victoria ignores the remark. "If you say so" is the male version of "whatever."

"Tierra will either stay or leave *Front Burner*, but it's not her that's tearing your team apart. Deep down, I think you already know that. It'll be you that has to live with it."

Victoria stands and leaves him at the café to think it over. She meets up with Seth, who is patiently waiting with a couple of coffees in the lobby.

"What was that about?"

"Therapy."

"For you or him?"

"At this point, both of us."

Seth punches the floor button on the elevator and the doors close. She doesn't know if she got through to Austin, but she does feel better getting it off her chest. Tierra is one of her few female friends, and Victoria hates seeing her treated like this. Then there's the professional reason for the intervention. She will need Tierra focused if what's in the file Seth is holding is the key to everything that's happened in New Hampshire this week.

CHAPTER SIXTY-FIVE

ANDREW LI

Burgess Temporary Campaign Headquarters
Manchester, New Hampshire

Alicia Standish is on the ropes. Luther landed a few hard punches at the debate last night, starting off with her vicious tweet. It spells the end of her campaign, barring a miracle. The governor has a golden opportunity to snatch a victory that nobody expected. Now he just needs to put her away.

The debate wasn't a problem, but there is no shortage of other challenges facing the campaign. The first is advising the money guys on practical solutions for their finances. Luther Burgess has never been an effective fundraiser. Outside of the late Dylan Spencer, his message is radical and turns off many of the big donors who support the Democratic Party. There was one major reason Vermont Senator Bernie Sanders appealed to small donors to fund his two runs for the presidency: the big kahunas wouldn't cut him a check.

Tons of those same small supporters have found seats under the Burgess campaign tent. The result has been a windfall of cash, especially after the Standish accusations gained traction. Brian Cooper's arrest is sure to have the IT team scrambling to keep the website from crashing and the dollars pouring in.

Campaigns are expensive endeavors. Americans grouse about the money spent on funding campaigns without any realization of how costly it is to do effectively. The small donations, even after a massive influx, cannot match Standish's cash on hand or the war chest of the top Republican challenger. If the governor goes on to secure the nomination this summer, he will be at a substantial financial disadvantage.

The liberal political action committees are ready to throw their weight behind him but haven't committed. The Cooper arrest will be a nudge for some of them, but the support isn't likely to be forthcoming until the polls close on Tuesday, and the winner is announced.

Andrew stands and stretches, needing a break from spreadsheets and pie charts. He grabs his jacket and leaves the hotel, hoping the frigid February New England air will rejuvenate him. He checks his text messages as he walks, reading the pleas for instructions from the advisors who are embedded in various campaign offices. He gets so many of these that he needs two phones to handle them. None are urgent. They can wait for a response.

He tucks the devices back into his pocket, allowing his mind to drift as he meanders aimlessly around the parking lot. After the debate, the media dissected and analyzed every exchange, like judges scoring a gymnastics meet. America doesn't pay much attention to that. They wanted the bottom line, and the pundits decreed their verdicts without the rest of the country knowing how they reached them. It's modern society at its finest.

He has taken a problematic candidate and made him the front runner for the Democratic nomination. He wonders if Angela Mays and Alicia Standish regret choosing Michael Ross over him. Their top advisor's performance has been lackluster thus far. His interview with her campaign was over six months ago, a mere six weeks after she ended her reckless pursuit of the Safe America Act. How time flies.

Brian Cooper is a lot of things, and not many of them good. In that case, he was right. She should have cut a deal with her colleagues and taken the win. Andrew would never be positioned to win the New Hampshire Primary with a man who is barely more conservative than Vladimir Lenin had she chosen that path. It's her loss.

He heads back inside with a single thought occupying his mind: Standish is running out of time. It's late in the fourth quarter, and they have the ball, up by a couple of touchdowns. Only an unforced error could help her, and Isiah can't let his father make one while the rest of this game plays out.

CHAPTER SIXTY-SIX

TIERRA CAMPOS

Southern New Hampshire Hospital (SNHH)
Manchester, New Hampshire

Victoria and Seth arrive in Olivia's room to find Tyler and me at her bedside. We exchange hugs and Ty volunteers to stay with her while she rests. She came around for a few minutes not long after Austin fled with Madison and Jerome. We don't want her to wake up to an empty room.

I explain what happened with Austin on the way to the lounge. Victoria says they saw him downstairs and will fill me in on their conversation later. She has something more pressing to say and hands me a file. I flip through it as she gives me the highlights.

"As good as this is, it's not enough to pin him to the arsons. We need more info."

"Agreed. This is the guy who attacked Wilson for sure. That alone is good enough for a warrant and cause to bring him in for questioning," Seth says.

"Have you asked for one?"

"Not yet."

"Why not?"

"Because I want to know more about this guy," Victoria says.

"What more do you need to know? You have his FBI file and his military records."

Victoria shakes her head. "He had a clearance above Top Secret. A lot of what was in there was redacted. This guy was into some serious stuff. We need to know what."

"It could take the Pentagon months to declassify that," I argue.

The DoD is less than forthcoming with information about their operations, even with the FBI or other government agencies. The kids in the federal government don't share well and never have.

"If they declassify it at all, which they probably won't. That's not what I want. I want to know about *him*," Victoria says, tapping the picture in the file I'm holding.

"I doubt this is the kind of guy who has a Facebook page."

"He doesn't," Seth says. "We already did an Internet and social media search. He has no virtual presence. We need to dig deeper."

Research has never been my strong suit. I can chase things down, but it takes me three times longer than people who are average at it. *Front Burner* hired two top-notch researchers for that reason. Too bad there's a catch.

"There's only one person I know that might be willing to do that for us."

Tyler winces as he walks into the lounge. "Are you sure that's a good idea? She's on Team Austin, and you two are a launch code short of a full nuclear exchange."

"Shouldn't you be in with Olivia?" I ask, angry that he left her.

"The nurse came in to give…she's doing…things that I don't need to see."

Victoria smirks, and Seth grins, putting his hand on Tyler's shoulder.

"I'm with ya, brother."

"Screw it. I'm calling Janey. The worst she can say is no."

The lead *Front Burner* researcher picks up her direct line on the second ring. She's alone in the office since Logan gets a late start most days, especially when Austin is out of town. I use the opportunity to put the phone on speaker and fill her in on what we've learned so far. She takes notes and asks only the occasional question until I finish.

"You want me to do what? More importantly, does Austin know about this? I haven't heard him mention it."

Tyler shakes his head. Victoria and Seth don't react, instead content to let me answer this for myself. They have their own problems to work through.

"No, he doesn't. I need to keep it that way right now."

"Tierra, he'll freak out if I do this for you."

"Then don't tell him."

"I'm not you," Janey says with a smattering of contempt in her tone.

The comment stings. Who knows what Austin has been telling the rest of the team about me? Even if it's close to the truth, it still sounds terrible.

"Okay, I deserved that."

"Janey, it's Ty," he says, jumping into the conversation. "This is bigger than all of us, and you're the best researcher in the business. Austin won't chase this lead despite it being the right thing to do."

"Do you think this relates to Olivia? He told me that you don't think it was an accident."

"I don't know."

"Hi Janey, it's Victoria. It could, but it might not. I'm working with the state police to find the cause. I agree with Tierra's suspicion that foul play was involved. If the New Hampshire police prove us right, this guy is our prime suspect."

This is becoming a team effort, and I appreciate the others coming to my aid in this call. Odds are that Janey would have hung up on me by now.

"He's the guy that attacked Wilson Newman for sure. We need to find him to figure out the rest."

"Why do you think he's linked to anything else?"

"Because this is exactly who Ian and I were searching the database for after the arsons," Victoria says. "He never popped up only because his last address was in Ohio. He could be behind them, or at least a part of the SOF."

"You're all convinced that they don't work for Brian Cooper?"

Tyler shakes his head again. "We need to find them and determine that for sure. A primary election hangs in the balance, Janey."

"Everyone, including the FBI, is looking in the wrong places," Victoria interjects. "We need your help."

Seth and Tyler both grin. I think they both enjoy seeing girl power in action.

"Okay, I'll do it under one condition: Logan can't know. He'll rat me out in a nanosecond."

"My lips are sealed."

"Good. I'll dig into it now and see what I can find. I have some friends at the Pentagon that may be able to help. First, give me all the details you have on this guy."

CHAPTER SIXTY-SEVEN

"S.O.F."

The mood in the house hasn't changed. Trot is playing video games again and counting the minutes until he can head to Logan Airport in Boston for a flight out of the country. Sartre is doing whatever he does on his computer. Marx is reading at a slower pace because he's almost out of novels. After his escapade in the mall, he knows that visiting the local bookstore is a bad idea. It looked like an accident. Even if someone figures out it wasn't, he doesn't think a camera caught a good shot of his face. Regardless, there's no reason to tempt fate.

His burner phone rings and Engels's number pops up on the screen. That's a surprise because he never calls this line. Marx knows that this can't be good news when he answers it.

"Yeah?"

"Hey, brother. Victoria Larsen is up to something."

"I thought you took care of her?" Marx says, now growing concerned.

"I did what I could. The FBI is a massive bureaucracy. Even running someone out for insubordination takes ten times longer than it should. We sidelined her, but she has a badge, and that still makes her a threat."

"That's not good enough, Engels. If she's still poking around up here, then you need to neutralize her."

"I'm working on it," he says, clearly frustrated.

"What do you need me to do?"

"Just watch your back and don't take any more chances. Victoria was in the Bedford office until early this morning. I'm trying to figure out what she was doing and why."

Marx doesn't like the sound of that at all. Sitting at a computer all night means she is on the scent of something. Ordinary people don't surf the net until morning.

"Any thoughts on what she has?"

"No, nothing specific. It could be information about the mall or Trot on the turnpike. It could be something from the arsons or the storage unit. One shred of evidence is all she needs. She's a bloodhound."

Marx curses to himself. Both he and Trot pulled off their missions, but neither was as clean as he would have liked. They were in public areas, and those are always dangerous. The intimidations and arsons were perfect. It must be one of the others.

"Why should I be worried?" he asks, goading Engels, who was quick to declare his superiority to his colleague. "I thought you said she was overrated."

"She is, but it doesn't mean that she's incompetent."

"Will she piece things together in time?"

"I don't see how. Even if she does, nobody at the Bureau is going to listen to her. Larsen doesn't have the support up here to do anything about it. Without significant Bureau resources backing her, she's a lone wolf that you can handle."

"Make sure she doesn't get any help, then."

Marx disconnects the call and checks the living room. Trot and Sartre are oblivious to the conversation and the dangers lurking in the area. He's concerned enough for all of them.

The clock is ticking. He's beginning to think Trot may be right when he insists that it's time to get the hell out of New Hampshire. Victoria Larsen and Tierra Campos have proven before that they are resourceful. They've done all they can. Why stick around if Machiavelli has nothing more for them to do?

CHAPTER SIXTY-EIGHT

SPECIAL AGENT VICTORIA LARSEN

New Hampshire State Police Troop B Barracks
Bedford, New Hampshire

State police barracks all look similar. This one is a dull, nondescript white building not far from the FBI office in Bedford. After checking in with the duty officer, they are immediately shown into the small office of Detective Diego Velez. He stands and moves around his desk to greet them.

"Seth Chambers. How long has it been?"

"Too long. You need to come to Boston more often."

"Cars can drive both ways. New Hampshire is a beautiful state to visit."

"Yeah, in the autumn," Seth mumbles.

"Oh, yeah, as if Boston feels like Florida this time of year," he says with a laugh.

"Diego, do you remember Special Agent Victoria Larsen?"

"From the Manchester arson scene. Without being a sexist, you're not an easy woman to forget, Agent Larsen. What brings you here?"

"You might want to sit back down, Detective," Victoria says. "This might take a while to explain."

She gives him the details of everything they've worked on, starting at the beginning with her suspicions on Dylan Spencer's suicide and ending with the attacks on Olivia and Wilson. He jots down notes and nods a lot as she talks but is content to listen to her briefing until she finishes.

"That's a lot to digest," he says, placing his pen down and leaning back in his chair. "Let's start with the most impactful, no disrespect meant to your friends in the hospital. You're saying that Brian Cooper wasn't behind the arsons?"

"I'm saying that there is enough evidence now to call it into question."

"And you think this Dennis Haskin guy could be the arsonist?"

"We don't know yet," Seth says. "Cooper had a group named the SOF, and this guy and his pals could still be working for him. We need to be sure. Brian Cooper's arrest changed the political dynamic substantially. I don't want to see the good people of this state vote in a primary based on a fraud."

"If we find them, will you help us?" Victoria asks.

"New Hampshire is very protective about its early primary. People around here go nuts for it every four years. They won't like the idea that outsiders are messing with it."

"So that's a yes?"

"Are you kidding? I would be run out of town if I didn't help you. What do you need?"

"For starters, who investigates auto accidents here?"

"The CAR unit."

Victoria and Seth both look at each other. Diego smiles and lets out a little chuckle.

"I get people with that every time. Car, as in C-A-R, the Collision Analysis and Reconstruction Unit. They're the ones who analyze vehicle accident scenes."

"Do you know anybody in that unit?" Seth asks.

"I ought to. They're right down the hall. Let's go talk to them. If there is anything suspicious about Olivia's accident, they'll uncover it."

Victoria is the first out of her chair. If the SOF was behind the attack on Wilson, and Tierra is right, then they could be behind this. Leads, no matter how small, add up. She's hoping she gets enough of them to lead her to their doorstep.

CHAPTER SIXTY-NINE

TIERRA CAMPOS

Autumn Bluff Suites
Manchester, New Hampshire

When Jerome and Madison return for their shift at the hospital, it's our cue to split. Not much was said between us, but at least we got cursory hellos and questions about how Olivia is doing this time. That was something, at least.

Tyler and I jump back into the car and head back to the hotel for showers. We grab a quick bite to eat on the way there and devour it at the kitchen island. He's about to head for the bathroom when Janey calls.

"Hi, Janey. I didn't expect to hear from you so quickly."

"I didn't expect to find anything this fast. The military is tidy about their records. Namely, my friends in the Five-Sided Puzzle Palace wouldn't tell me anything you and Victoria hadn't already learned. Here's an interesting fact, though: your guy was a rising star in the Army."

"How do you know that?"

"They pointed me to some contacts with U.S. Army Europe. It turns out that the command has a robust public affairs office. They have an online weekly magazine that generated tons of articles dating back fifteen years. Your boy came up in a bunch of them while he was stationed there. Most of the images of him are posing with command staff. Check your email."

I do as Janey requests and open the attachments in the message she sent me. Sure enough, he got a lot of mug time with generals and full bird colonels during various multinational field exercises.

"I'm not sure how this helps us," Tyler says as I scroll through them.

"Come on, you guys are supposed to be the smart ones. Look at the U.S. Army Europe flag."

"It's a flaming sword?"

"It's a sword on fire – SOF."

"Whoa, hold on a second, Janey."

Tyler finds a picture and zooms in on the beret the man is wearing. It's blurry, so he opens a browser and does a search for the command and opens a wiki. He scrolls down, and my mouth hangs open when I see the distinctive unit insignia. Written below the emblem of a flaming sword are three words: *Sword of Freedom*.

"Sword of Freedom. SOF. It's written on the unit crest," I mumble.

"Well, that answers that question," Tyler says.

"That sounds better than the sword on fire," Janey says, a hint of disappointment in her voice that she missed that. "I may be able to answer another question for you. You said the hacker told you that Sartre was a socialist?"

"Yeah."

"I found this. Apparently, there was a big problem over there a few years ago. Some active-duty soldiers were actively supporting German Marxist groups."

"I never heard about it," Tyler says.

"It never made the news back here. The Pentagon is good about keeping things like that in-house. Some soldiers formed a group to coordinate their activities. It was shut down after being linked to a couple of violent incidents in major cities. The members of the group were disciplined according to the Uniform Code of Military Justice. Ringleaders were tossed out of the Army with other than honorable discharges."

"Do you know who the leader was?" I ask, wondering where she's going with this.

"Not exactly."

"Tell me they were on social media," Tyler pleads.

"Of course. Every group is. The page was deleted when the group was disbanded, so that was no help. They did have a website. It's long gone, but it was captured by the Wayback Machine Internet Archive."

I did a paper on it for a computer science class in college. The Wayback Machine allows the user to travel "back in time" to see what websites looked like in the past. It's fascinating to see how they've changed in both form and function. Brewster Kahle and Bruce Gilliat cultivated the idea of providing universal access to archived copies of defunct webpages. Over 452 billion pages have been added to the archive since 2001. Theirs was one of them.

"Ugh. They could have used a better web designer," Tyler says, clicking the link Janey provided.

"They spent all the money on the photographer. There are hundreds of images here, but I thought this one would be of paramount interest."

Another email pops into my mailbox, and Tyler clicks the attachment. A picture of four men standing with a flag of a German Marxist group loads. It's a damning piece of evidence.

"Tyler, get this to Victoria as soon as possible, as in right now."

"Will do."

"Thank you, Janey, you came through for us in a big way."

"I'm happy to help. It felt good working with you. Just don't tell anyone that I did."

"Yeah, I understand. I won't."

I hang up with Janey as Tyler prints out a copy of the photograph. I retrieve it from our portable laser printer and stare at it hard.

"I texted the picture to Victoria. Did you read the caption?"

I didn't. I recheck the image. There's a caption below with the names of four soldiers and what must be their group nicknames. Two of them are familiar. The others aren't:

Dennis Haskin (Marx), Tad Healy (Trotsky), Ian Drucker (Engels), and Darko Lukić (Sartre).

CHAPTER SEVENTY

"S.O.F."

Sartre turns up the volume to his headphones to drown out all noise from the outside world. Back in the day, he could always count on Engels to add the drama like oregano to tomato sauce. He was the one who was continually stirring the pot.

Now it's Trot who has taken over that role in the safehouse. Sartre never counted him as a true believer in the cause. He loathed authority and the rigid command structure of the military. He joined their group in Europe only because it was forbidden by their superiors. Doing the wrong thing is in his DNA.

Marx is doing this because he believes in it. Trot thinks it's enough for him to lie on a beach for the rest of his life. It isn't. For Engels, this was about career enhancement as much as it was the cause. Sartre has never been much of a believer in the cause. He agreed to do this mission because he has a side hustle. The money they were making off this endeavor was okay but never worth the risks that they were undertaking.

At this point, he knows the Burgess campaign's computer network better than the techs who installed it do. Remote offices connect to the network via a secure virtual private network connection, while larger state offices have their own dedicated connections. It's an impressive setup for a temporary endeavor.

With so many campaign workers, volunteers, and coordinators needing devices to communicate, it makes the chances of theft or loss high. To reduce the risk, everything is stored in the cloud instead of locally on the computers themselves. All these machines connect back to centralized data stores containing donor information, voter demographics, volunteer lists, press contacts, and all other manner of campaign documents. They are edited locally, but all sync back up to a cloud service.

The constant editing and sharing of information among local, regional, and central campaign planners are necessary for when they go national. The process also provides an opportunity. There is no reason for anyone to think that the attacks on the Burgess campaign won't continue. All he needs to do to turn his unique knowledge into a money-making endeavor is to hijack the network in return for a sizable contribution to his retirement fund.

Ransomware is a form of malware that encrypts a victim's files, much like they did to the video records at the storage unit. Instead of leaving it that way in perpetuity, an attacker demands a ransom from the victim payable in Bitcoin. Once received, they are provided the decryption key to restore access to the data.

Sartre has done this before. Early on, he targeted universities he didn't like because they had smaller, less-skilled IT security teams and did a lot of file sharing, making it easier to penetrate their defenses. He graduated to government agencies, political groups, and law firms because they needed immediate access to their sensitive data files and were willing to pay to keep the compromise quiet.

The Burgess campaign's cloud storage is vulnerable to ransomware attacks because of the sharing and syncing with users' devices. He has already used exploit kits to identify vulnerabilities on their machines and plant the malware on hundreds of systems. Campaigns are notorious for not keeping up to date with patches against vulnerabilities in the operating system. All he needs to do is activate it and allow it to encrypt local files and the cloud storage copy as well.

The best defense they would have is to create cloud backups engineered to quickly recover clean versions of the files before they became infected. Fortunately for Sartre, the IT consulting team brought in didn't employ those measures. It will be a lucrative, high-profile hack, and it was too easy.

Marx wouldn't approve of this at all. He is willing to take the pittance that Machiavelli paid for their services. Sartre has hacked a Twitter account, leaked a critical campaign document, dug up information to intimidate college students, and helped bypass security measures at a storage unit in the name of a cause he couldn't care less about.

The politics and ideological underpinnings of this mission don't interest him. He wants to get paid well for his contribution to making the governor of Illinois president. And he will. If they want socialist redistribution of wealth, let them have it. Nobody will ever find Sartre's money.

Sartre establishes a series of secure connections and makes his way to his favorite chat board. The darknet is a subset of the greater deep web, a large group of unindexed sites that don't return on an Internet search. Not all activities here are nefarious, but the darknet is often used for illegal black-market activities like file sharing and the exchanging of stolen financial and private data. The anonymity it provides from the world is perfect for hackers like Sartre, while still allowing him to boast about his accomplishments to the tight-knit community.

He smiles as he chats back and forth with his peers, most of whom don't believe him. It doesn't matter. They will learn the truth soon enough. Sartre is going to help ensure a candidate wins a primary election in three days, and then he's going to make himself wealthy. If socialist Bernie Sanders can have three houses, why can't he make millions? The chic term for it is champagne socialist, but the hacker prefers to think of himself as a "Neiman Marxist" or "cashmere communist."

He settles into his chair as his peers press him for information. He will give them some. Even if one of them is an FBI agent masquerading as a hacker, nobody can stop him. It will be the greatest of all hacks.

CHAPTER SEVENTY-ONE

SPECIAL AGENT VICTORIA LARSEN

New Hampshire State Police Troop B Barracks
Bedford, New Hampshire

Victoria stares intently at the picture Tierra sent over. She had to sit down when she first opened it on her device and looked at it. Her pride in the ability to judge people's character is shaken. She never saw this coming.

She hasn't known Ian Drucker for that long. He got assigned to work a drug case alongside her last fall, four months after her reinstatement to the Bureau. She regards him as enthusiastic and eager, as most graduates from Quantico are when they get posted at their field office. It turns out that he is more than that.

If this picture is legitimate, how did he ever make it into the FBI? That's an uncomfortable question that the personnel directorate is going to have to answer. He was a member of a violent Marxist group in Germany, and the military knew all about it. That should have come up during a background check and disqualified him.

The hard part is confirming that he's involved. The three of them moved out of Diego's cramped office to a conference area they call the "war room." Victoria is asking a huge favor from Miranda, and it's going to eventually cost her. Now it's a waiting game. She just hopes the technician can come through.

A uniformed state trooper comes in and hands Diego a plain manila folder. The detective opens it, scans the contents, and nods. He thanks the officer, who leaves, and Diego leans back in his chair.

"What is it?" Seth asks.

"There's paint transfer on the front fender and bumper of Olivia's car. Black. According to an eyewitness who came across the accident, they passed a black Dodge Ram truck before reaching the scene. CAR has reclassified the incident as a hit and run."

"Tierra will be thrilled to hear that she's not delusional," Victoria says.

"Thank her for us. If you hadn't brought this to our attention, they never would have caught it. Olivia's car was severely damaged. Black paint blends in well with damage. It wasn't noticeable."

"All right, now what?" Victoria asks. "Do we look for damaged trucks in the area? That could take weeks."

"More like months. This is New Hampshire. There are a lot of pickup trucks up here."

Victoria sighs when her phone rings. She sees Miranda's information on the caller ID and answers with the device on speakerphone so that Seth and Diego can hear the conversation. They're just as shocked as she was that an agent with the Bureau could be involved in this.

"Hey, Miranda."

"Okay, boss lady, I had to cash in some big favors to get this information. You're going to owe some people Red Sox tickets when this is over, and I mean good seats against the Yankees."

Victoria shudders at the cost of that. "Will it be worth it?"

"Oh, yeah. I have access to six months' worth of Agent Drucker's cell phone tracking data. The GPS put him in New Hampshire a few times before the two of you were sent there for the arsons."

"And?"

"He was at the Spencer house the night he died."

Seth and Diego's mouths hang open.

"Are you sure?" Victoria asks.

"I confirmed it. Agent Drucker was pinging off a cell tower located less than a mile from there."

"He was at Dylan Spencer's house the night of his suicide," Seth mumbles in disbelief. "Doing what?"

"If I had to guess, I'd say threatening the family. He didn't drive up on those tracks as a desperate measure to end his life. He had no other choice."

"How would he know?" Diego asks.

"The website link," Victoria concludes. "What if it was the video streamed from the house or something like that? The man on the phone was giving him an ultimatum and had Ian there in case Spencer didn't comply."

The thought of that sends a shiver down her spine. That's cold. If you save your own life, you lose your family and must live with that pain and guilt forever. The only alternative was to do what he did.

"There's more," Miranda says over the speaker. "He was also in Nashua the night of the arsons. The cell tower density is greater there. He was within three hundred meters of Burgess's office."

"Why leave his phone on?" Diego asks. "He had to know it could be tracked. Leaving it powered on is plain stupid."

"He was on duty both of those nights," Victoria mumbles. "It's more suspicious if he doesn't have it with him and powered on when someone tries to reach him."

"You were working with him that night, weren't you?"

Victoria nods, shifting her eyes to Seth. "He was following a couple of suspected dealers and monitoring their activities all night...or was supposed to be."

"He's FBI, Seth. Nobody would ever check his phone any more than we would check the ones of our troopers. There's no reason to ever look."

"Anything else, Miranda?"

"Yup. I checked the incoming and outgoing call log. His phone records mostly contain calls to and from the office or other agents. You know, plain vanilla stuff. He did make one to a number earlier today that I didn't recognize, so I ran the number. It's an untraceable burner phone."

"There's no reason for him to be calling one of those," Seth says.

"We caught a break with that. It was paid for in cash, naturally, but I ran the history of that phone and found it bounced off a cell tower in South Hooksett, New Hampshire. I can narrow it down to about a mile and a half radius."

Victoria and Seth look at the New Hampshire State Police detective. They don't know the area well, but he does.

"It's a suburb of Manchester to the north, and heavily wooded. A chunk of Bear Brook State Park is in the town."

Victoria nods. "You're a genius, Miranda."

"I'll take the compliment, but we're lucky he's an idiot. These guys should have used Twitter to communicate. It's impossible to track a location using it."

"Let us know if you find something else."

"Will do, Superwoman. Go get the scumbags."

Diego gets busy as Victoria terminates the call. Like the old maps that her social studies teachers used to have in their classrooms, he pulls down one of the greater Manchester area and pinpoints the cell tower in marker. Using the legend, he measures out a mile and a half on a string and then uses it to draw a circle from that point.

Victoria and Seth stare at it. There are chunks of wooded areas, but at least it doesn't include the state park. There are also countless small residential neighborhoods, hotels, businesses, and even a university in that range. Their target could be at any one of them or none.

Diego grunts. "Thoughts?"

"They won't be in a public place like the university or a hotel. They'll avoid businesses that have foot traffic. Let's focus on the residential areas and hope for a little luck," Victoria says.

"I can dispatch some units to help, but I'm not sure what we're looking for."

"The truck."

"They might have ditched it," Seth cautions.

"Maybe, but Olivia's crash was made to look like an accident. It was reported that way on the news. I don't think they would get rid of it yet. Diego, have your men change into plain clothes and use their POVs."

"Why personally owned vehicles?"

"Because even unmarked cars can be spotted easily if they're looking for them. I don't want our targets getting spooked by seeing state police vehicles everywhere in town."

"Let's go find them ourselves," Seth says, rising.

"We need to go to the mall first."

"Why? Do you need to get your nails done?" Seth asks with a goofy smile on his face that spares him from getting punched.

"Because if we are going to cruise around residential streets in New Hampshire, I shouldn't look like I walked off the set of NCIS. And you need to develop a sense of style."

Seth looks at her clothing and his. Diego closes his eyes and shakes his head, a grin on his face.

"Okay, good point. You're buying."

CHAPTER SEVENTY-TWO

TIERRA CAMPOS

Southern New Hampshire Hospital (SNHH)
Manchester, New Hampshire

Olivia is awake again. She's still in rough shape, but it's good to see her alert and hear her talking. Nobody has told her about the Sartre lead or how we uncovered the true nature of the SOF. We also avoided mentioning the tension with Austin, although I know she saw right through that.

Needing to stretch my legs, I waited for Olivia to doze off and headed down to the café. I make it to the lobby when my phone vibrates in my pocket. The caller ID reads *THE MATRIX*. Telemarketers spoof caller ID all the time, but they pick something familiar that may get you to pick up. Nobody would call from a fictional computer simulation except one group of people I prefer not talking to.

"Hello?"

"It's DialPirate."

"Great caller ID name. You're living up to your handle," I say, talking over an announcement on the PA system paging a doctor.

"Where are you?" he asks.

"Southern New Hampshire Hospital. The men that Sartre is working with put two of my friends in the hospital."

"You stated that definitively."

"Because it is true."

"I'm sorry to hear that," he says after a long pause. "I have something that might help you find them."

"I'm all ears. Are the others on the line?"

"They don't know I'm talking to you. I want to keep it that way. They would disapprove."

"So why are you?"

"I have my reasons. Let's leave it at that. Sartre posted on the dark web again. He was bragging about a master plan to ransomware a major political campaign. He said it would be a large takedown and net him millions. If they don't comply, he said not only would they not get their files back, he would leak damaging ones to the media."

That gets my attention. There is no shortage of companies or organizations that are susceptible and sensitive to these types of cyberattacks. Political campaigns might be at the top of the list, which is why they spend so much money on cybersecurity. It sounds like it wasn't enough. If true, an attack like that would be devastating to a candidate.

"If he has this plan and knows he could get caught for executing it, why post it?"

"I told you, he's smug. He wants the credit. The easiest way to get it is to announce an attack before it happens."

"Can the FBI stop him?"

"I don't know the target. Ransomware is spread via malware. Even if the feds managed to convince every campaign to shut down their computers and have professionals scan them for threats, you may still not get all the bad code. Sartre must have it set up where he feels they can't stop him."

"Okay, I can alert Victoria, and she'll pass the information on."

"There's more. Hackers need a lot of bandwidth to do what we do. The usage and data transfer speeds are much higher than what an average household uses. I did some digging into area cable companies in New Hampshire."

"Digging?"

"You really don't want more information than that," DialPirate warns.

"Okay, that's true. Why cable companies?"

"Because they cover a large region, their broadband services are easy to procure, and it wouldn't raise eyebrows like having a dedicated circuit installed would."

I nod. "Fair point."

"Eliminating business addresses, I found eighty-two possible spots within a thirty-mile radius of Manchester that fit the criteria."

"Eighty-two? That's a lot."

"A lot of people use streaming video services now. I can try to narrow it down further, but I may miss something. I'm afraid that it is what it is. It might help a little. I'm sorry about your friends. I hope they heal soon."

"Thank you, DialPirate. I appreciate the help."

"You know, the others didn't think you'd be true to your word," he says after another awkward silence. "I bet that you would be."

"Can I ask you something, DP? Have you ever thought that maybe you're playing for the wrong side?"

He doesn't answer the question, not that I expected him to. He didn't have to reach out to me. Something in him wanted to help. I hope he recognizes that he is far better than the digital chaos he causes.

"Good luck, Tierra Del Fuego," he says, using the "Land of Fire" handle Tyler gave me.

I smile as DialPirate hangs up. A moment later, a map pops up on my phone. It's a little creepy that he has access to my device. When this is over, I need to have it scanned for malware. I might have a scintilla of trust in him, but I can't say the same for CyberOreo or AnarchyBooster.

We have assumed that Sartre would need to be local to coordinate his activities with Marx and the others. That isn't necessarily true, but this is what we have. I forward the information to Victoria. Maybe it can help her and Seth track this down. One way or another, the game is going to end soon. I wish we weren't so far behind on the scoreboard.

CHAPTER SEVENTY-THREE

CAPITOL BEAT

Granite State University Remote Set
Durham, New Hampshire

Carl Brennan got a stern talking to during the afternoon planning meeting. The message was reinforced by the executive producer during makeup before the show. The warning was clear: he gets one more shot at this. It was a tough pill for him to swallow, considering he doesn't think he did anything wrong. It was the direction they claim they wanted to take the program. The ratings were huge, so he doesn't see the problem. He wants this job, both professionally and to stick it to that little tart Tierra. He'll play along if it means landing it.

"Good Evening. It is Saturday, February 6th, I am Carl Brennan and this…is…*Capitol Beat*.

The show's opening plays, and the producer rolls his eyes. Despite walking through it with him twice and it being on the teleprompter, Carl forgot to say that he was in for Wilson. It's like talking to a tree. He's left wondering how this guy ever became a news anchor.

After a brief introduction to the broadcast, Carl turns and opens the interview with the frontrunner for the Republican nomination. Fresh off his victory in Iowa, Colin Bradford, the sitting governor of North Carolina, is pulling away in New Hampshire as well. The introduction was polite, but also cold. Anyone watching at home knows that Carl isn't a fan of this governor.

The first questions are perfunctory ones about the current primary race and his win in Iowa. They're conventional fare, and the exchange is dull. Carl senses the boredom with the answers in the room and feels it himself. It's a risk, but one he needs to take. This is anything but inspiring the executives to give him the job. Ironically, he will get this job by doing what Tierra Campos did to get fired from hers: he's going off script again.

"Do you think that you can beat the Democrats in the general election?" Carl asks.

"*Oh, what the hell, Carl!*" the producer says in his ear.

"That didn't take long, did it?" Governor Bradford says, smirking as he leans back in his chair a touch.

"Excuse me?"

"No, there is no excuse for your question. We didn't think it would take long for you to ask a partisan question tonight. We were right."

"There was nothing partisan about it," Carl argues, getting combative at the accusation.

"Yes, there was. 'Do you think that you can beat the Democrats in the general election?' Obviously, we can beat them. Our supporters feel the same way. Why not ask if we think the Democrats can beat us? That's what makes it a partisan question."

"Well, I assure you that it isn't the case."

It wasn't a genuine assurance. Carl had the sincerity of a honey badger killing a rodent.

"Mr. Brennan, we all watched your interview with Governor Burgess. Any average viewer would have thought that you were on his paid staff. The favoritism was astounding."

"Get back to the questions, Carl. Move him off this."

"The Republican contest hasn't been as much of a dogfight as the Democratic side," Carl says, searching for a segue back to the scripted questions.

"Why are you referring to the Democrats again?" Governor Bradford practically shouts, catching Carl off-guard.

"Well, I…"

"You lobbed softball questions to Burgess that a little leaguer could have hit five hundred feet. Not once did you mention the Republicans. That was my third or fourth question, and you've already mentioned our opponents twice."

"We invited you on this program because we thought you would want to discuss what's happening in their primary."

"Really? Because you haven't asked me about their primary yet. And for the record, the troubles they're having are their business. We have our own contest. Why does it feel like you don't care about that?"

"Don't answer that question, Carl."

"We care about delivering unbiased reporting to the American people."

Governor Bradford laughs like that was the most hilarious thing he's ever heard. "Are you kidding me with that? You endorsed Governor Burgess on this set last night."

"I did no such thing," Carl says, his voice rising.

"You said, 'you earned a lot more votes tonight. You would have earned mine after that performance.' If that wasn't an endorsement, what was it? Because it sounded like one to me."

"It was my opinion."

"On a show that you host for millions of Americans. I didn't realize that *Capitol Beat* was in the habit of letting its host give a personal vote of confidence to a politician on air. This show used to be fair to both parties."

"Move off this, now!" the EP screams into Carl's ear.

"Let's move on, Gov—"

"Now this show is another that aligns itself with the left. Republicans have never been treated fairly by the left-wing media. They used to be more subtle about it, but that has been all but abandoned in the modern age. *Capitol Beat* was the one honest broker left. I guess with Wilson Newman out of the picture, even that has changed."

"Maybe if Republicans weren't so out of touch with American voters, it—"

"We have millions of supporters across this great nation."

"In rural areas, maybe, but not in places that matter," Carl says, his frustration spilling out in front of the camera.

The executive producer buries his head in his hands. That was it. He just alienated half of their viewers with one sentence. He checks the dials of the focus group made up of a representative sample from across the ideological spectrum. Meant to give feedback about segments in real-time, they move a knob when they like or dislike something. The Republicans hated the comment universally, joined by some Democrats. Independents were about seventy-thirty.

"Did you just insult half the country, Carl?"

"No, I'm saying what many are: that your policies are out of step with much of America. You're just too blind to see it."

"A strong defense is out of step? Protection of life, belief in the greatness of this country, fostering a strong economy…those are all out of step?"

"*We're cutting to commercial in five seconds, Carl. End this.*"

"I'm sorry, we're out of time, Governor."

"I'm sure you are. So much for giving me equal time with my opponent."

"Thank you for joining us, we'll be back…"

The red light on the camera blinks off, and the lighting on the set dims.

"You're an embarrassment to journalism, Mr. Brennan."

The governor leaves as the EP approaches the anchor desk. He wants to scream, and probably will once this show ends. All he can do is get through the rest of it. The damage is done, and he will have a lot to answer to. At least he had plenty of people in his corner about Carl Brennan being the right choice. There is safety in numbers, and he will need protection when they start hearing from their advertisers. The lost ratings will be catastrophic. He never thought he'd be so happy to welcome Wilson Newman back when he gets discharged.

CHAPTER SEVENTY-FOUR

SPECIAL AGENT VICTORIA LARSEN

Residential Area
South Hooksett, New Hampshire

2 Days to the New Hampshire Democratic Primary

Victoria watches more state police units arrive at the business park off the Londonderry Turnpike. Their lights are off to avoid drawing unnecessary attention. They are a mile and a half from the house, but you can't be too careful in an operation like this.

Another two units park their vehicles. It's an impressive turnout for three o'clock in the morning. Diego has really come through.

"Did you bring enough people?" Seth asks him, watching the legion of state police troopers gearing up in body armor.

"I can call more."

"You do understand sarcasm, right?"

"Do you?" he asks with a smile.

He gathers the team leaders and unrolls a map on the hood of his vehicle. He explains the mission and points out the perimeter they are establishing. Roadblocks are discussed, and he outlines the circumstances under which they will be set. With that part of the briefing done, the assignments are handed out, and the tactical team is assembled for a similar briefing.

"Consider these men armed and extremely dangerous. They have military training and have displayed a high level of coordination in their operations thus far. Don't expect them to go quietly if they see us coming. Questions?"

"Do we have confirmation that they are at the target house?"

"Not yet," Diego admits. "Once the perimeter is established and we are staged closer to the house, we'll look to get that confirmation."

He answers a few more questions before the tactical team moves off to do their pre-execution checks.

"Those guys look like they're ready for combat," Victoria says, impressed.

"Let's hope it doesn't come to that. If anyone escapes into the woods, they'll be impossible to find," Diego says, pointing at the map. "Are you sure this is it, Vic?"

"No, but there were only three spots in all of South Hooksett on the map Tierra's hacker provided. This was the only residence."

"We're basing this entire operation on a cell phone bouncing off a tower and the utility bill provided by a hacker who's probably broken hundreds of laws," Seth says.

"I've conducted operations using worse intel. It's a good spot for a safehouse if it is one. The structure is tucked away on a cul-de-sac, borders a wooded area, has several escape routes once you get off the street, and is rural while still being close to the city."

"These woods are the key. Make sure we seal them off. I don't want to get Lyme disease chasing them through there at oh-dark-thirty in the morning."

"Not that you'll ever find them. Houses ring the entire area, and most of them have sheds or other structures. There are a hundred places to flee to and thousands of places to hide," Seth moans.

Victoria and Seth spend a few moments memorizing the map. The neighbor's house is close to the property line, but the trees separating the yards offer sufficient privacy. The only structures at the target are the main house and a detached garage, so that makes things easier. The big concern is the woods and how to make it to the residence undetected.

"I'll get everyone in place. How do you plan on confirming the targets are there? I know you ain't knocking on the door."

"There will be a black truck in the garage."

At least Victoria hopes it is. There is no reason to believe it wouldn't be. No reports about Olivia's accident have mentioned another vehicle. Abandoning the truck would cause more suspicion than hanging onto it.

Victoria and Seth park the car just south of the T-intersection. The road the house is on is short – only four hundred feet. Despite the short distance, Seth demands he get closer to support her as she recons the house. The FBI agent didn't want to increase the risk of them getting seen by having two people close in. They compromised. Seth will wait in the copse of trees near the neighbor's house and pray they don't have a dog.

The night is still, and despite being as quiet as possible as she moves through the neighbor's front yard, she thinks she sounds like a freight train. Creeping low through the trees that separate the two properties, she sneaks up to the detached garage and waits along the back wall, out of sight from the main house. Content that she hasn't been discovered, she finds the side door and works the knob. It's locked.

She pokes her head up and peers through the window. The one-car garage would be tough to squeeze a sedan through the door without scratching the paint. Only someone with excellent driving skills could back in the big black truck that's parked in there. This must be the place.

There is one surefire way to find out. Victoria can't afford to be wrong about this. The confirmation is worth the risk. At least that's how she justifies it to herself as she breaks the lower pane of glass on the window with her elbow and reaches in to unlock the door.

Victoria lets herself in and closes the door behind her. She only lets a sliver of light escape her fingers covering the front of the flashlight. It's all she needs as she aims it at the bed of the truck and illuminates scrapes and a dent in the rear near the bumper. Bingo. This belongs to the asshole that ran Olivia off the road.

She presses the talk button on her radio. "Target confirmed. Move into position."

"Roger."

Victoria leaves the garage, creeping to the rear of the structure and back to Seth's sightline. She peers around the corner to see if there is any movement inside the house. There isn't. The structure is still.

She can't see much in the inky darkness but can hear the teams moving into their positions in the tree line. Twigs snap, and every noise travels twice as far. It's about as quiet as they are going to be and still move with relative speed. Victoria hopes these guys aren't light sleepers.

Time seems at a standstill. Communications are kept to a minimum. The breach team arrives at the neighbor's house and links up with Seth about fifty feet away from her. A second team reports that they are positioned in the trees facing the front of the house, followed by the two teams in the woods to the north. All she needs to wait for is the west woods team to secure the perimeter around the structure.

A piercing sound rips through the air as bursts of light erupt from the windows of the house. What sounds like a fully automatic machine gun belches fire and lead at the team nearest the road. Rifles engage targets to the north and east. They have every sector of fire covered.

"Man down! Man down!"

"North woods under heavy fire! Shit!"

"We're pinned down!"

Seth moves up to Victoria with the breach team, and they position themselves low along the back wall of the garage.

"This went to hell fast. We need to get in there," he shouts.

"We need to take out the guy in the east window," Victoria screams over the gunfire. "That gives the breach team a clear run to the house."

The men nod. Victoria checks her weapon and feels her body armor. She knows she's wearing it, but the tactile contact provides her some comfort and ease of mind. It will only help protect her. They have heavy weapons. What else could be waiting for them inside that house?

Chaos erupts on the communication channel as men scream into radios. They are taking casualties. Troopers return fire before being forced to take cover. The noise of the gunfire is deafening. This once-quiet neighborhood is now a combat zone.

CHAPTER SEVENTY-FIVE

"S.O.F."

Safehouse
South Hooksett, New Hampshire

The sensors weren't a waste of time after all. When Marx wanted them deployed around the house, Trot complained, not concerned that they would ever be discovered here. That kind of thinking is what gets men like them killed or put in a cage. One of those options would have already happened if the system hadn't been installed.

A rotation was developed that ensured someone is always awake, ready to react if ever alerted. The sensor units are the same inexpensive ones that homeowners use to monitor a driveway, and can be used up to a half-mile away. Eight were placed around the perimeter and in the woods. Seven were tripped by the time they opened fire.

"No, you don't!" Marx shouts as he lets another ten-round burst rip out of his M240B machine gun. The belt-fed beast is a mainstay in U.S. military infantry units, although his weapon came courtesy of the Argentinian Army.

"They're coming through the back! Fifty meters in the tree line!" Trot shouts from one of the bedrooms.

"You have anything, Sartre?"

"There's a small team behind the garage."

Damn. That rules out helping Trotsky. Marx can't cover both the south and east approaches. He looks through his PVS7 night vision goggles. He'd much rather have the PVS14 version, a monocle that leaves one eye with normal vision, but those are harder to obtain and not in the budget.

The men who were closing in on him don't seem to be retreating. They can't survive a protracted siege of the house. Ammunition for the machine gun is limited, and the rifles won't keep them at bay. Marx knows they have one chance to escape, but it needs to be timed perfectly to make it.

Sartre lets out a couple of bursts from his illegally modified AR-15. They can close the distance between the garage and the door to the house in seconds. Once they're inside, the game is over. If they close off the escape route through the woods, they'll be trapped for good.

"Sartre, it's time to go."

"We need to blow it now and make for the truck!" Trot screams.

"They'll have the streets blocked off. We won't get anywhere in the truck!" Marx yells back.

"We ain't going this way, either!"

"Just once will you—"

Sartre's silhouette is exposed in the window a second too long. A single round from a sniper sends him crashing down to the floor.

"Shit. Sartre?"

The hacker is grabbing at his neck, trying in vain to stem the bleeding. Marx pulls out a bandage from his aid kit and readies it. He pulls Sartre's hand from the wound, and blood spurts three feet in the air. He covers the wound with the bandage, knowing it's a lost cause. The bullet severed his carotid artery. He'll bleed out in a matter of seconds.

"Erase…"

"What?"

"Erase the computer," Sartre mumbles.

"We don't have time."

"Do it."

Marx grabs the rifle and opens fire out the window to the east. He does the same thing out the south window that he was manning. It was unaimed fire meant to let them know that he's still here.

He turns his attention back to Sartre, who stares back at him with hollow eyes. Marx curses under his breath. They couldn't hold this house with three men, and they won't have a prayer with two.

"Come on, Trot," Marx says, grabbing the black box from Sartre's desk.

Marx mans the machine gun one last time. He lets loose on full automatic, sending the black-clad men crashing to the ground. How many are hit versus taking cover isn't known. It doesn't matter. This is about escape and survival, not victory.

He drops the weapon and reaches the back door. Trot joins him, and they get ready to move.

"We make for the truck."

"I told you, you won't make it out of there. They secured the garage. We go through the woods and then to the backup vehicle. That's the plan. On three."

He doesn't make it to one. The front door of the house blows open, and two men burst inside. Marx opens fire at them as they enter, hitting one. The breaching team returns fire as he pushes Trot out the door.

Marx taps on Trot's shoulder and shields his eyes. He presses the button on the detonator, and the world around them erupts in light. The explosions aren't deafening, but they are distracting. That was the point.

Movies use explosions as the cause of mass destruction and casualties. They can be used for that effect, but even small, non-lethal ones are disorienting, especially for those wearing night vision. The resulting temporary blindness, light, and smoke are all they need to make it to the tree line.

Marx jumps off first, reaching the halfway point before someone opens fire at him from the north. The bullets aren't close, but the shooter will zero in. Trot wanted nothing to do with this escape plan. He peels off and makes his way around the north side of the house, backtracking towards the garage.

"Idiot," Marx says, reaching the tree line, diving into the thicket.

He stays low to the ground, making use of the remaining fires from the explosions that ring the property. The gasoline is burning off fast, creating the urgency to get deeper into the woods before their attackers' night vision capabilities return. He stands, then immediately collapses to the ground.

"Damn it."

He checks his calf to see the gash in his clothing and the blood oozing from a two-inch laceration. He only got nicked, but the wound will slow him down. He pulls out his remaining bandage and ties it off. It will have to do.

Men begin shouting and firing as a truck engine roars to life. He hears a crash as their Ram pickup accelerates down the driveway. He doesn't wait to see what happens to Trot. He stands and limps off deeper into the woods, away from the house before turning to the south.

After five minutes, he stops and listens. He can hear the distant commotion at the house, but that's it. He allows himself a moment to relax and breathe. He's far from home-free yet, but out of immediate danger. Or so he thinks.

A twig snaps behind him. Then another. His senses go on high alert. Someone followed him into these woods and is hot on his trail.

He sets off again, moving quickly but as quietly as he can. It's no use. Every move makes noise. His pursuer is going to be on him in a matter of minutes.

Marx moves faster now, knowing this is a race to the getaway car. His toe catches a tree root, and he falls to the ground as a shot buzzes over his head. The tree just saved his life. He returns fire from the prone position in the direction he last heard the noise. Nothing is returned.

He stands and continues forward, staying low and darting in a random zig-zag pattern that changes durations and distances. Another branch snaps, much closer this time. He turns and fires, causing a figure to take cover behind a tree. He returns fire, causing Marx to do the same. The two men are exchanging shots when Marx sees an opportunity to end this.

He moves out to the right, finding cover behind another tree while using the first to obscure the man's line of sight to him. The man adjusts his position around the tree to fire at Marx's original hiding place.

"Gotcha," Marx mumbles as he leans out and lines the man up in his sights.

The blow to his shoulder carries him backward before he hears the report of the gun. He falls against the tree, now training his weapon with his one working arm in the direction of the man.

"Drop it," a female voice commands before she materializes next to him with the gold FBI emblazoned on her body armor.

He smirks and shakes his head. He never saw her. She had to have been sixty feet away when she hit him. Marx should have paid more attention to Engel's warnings.

"Agent Larsen, I presume?"

Marx raises his weapon and squeezes the trigger as Victoria fires again into the same shoulder. It hurts even worse the second time. His shot wasn't close. A moment later, he's relieved of his weapon as her friend joins her. Marx sees "Police" printed in block white letters on his body armor. He'd love to stay alive long enough to find out how the state authorities and feds found them.

"Marx, I presume?"

"You know my name. How sweet."

Victoria pulls out a bandage and tries to stop the bleeding as her friend covers him. Everything starts to go numb as he gets colder.

"Who are you working for, Marx?"

"Does it matter?"

"Yeah, it does. Tell me."

"That was one hell of a shot. Not bad for a girl," Marx says with a grin.

"I bet you wish you had just killed him now," Seth says.

"I needed him alive."

She presses harder on the bandage, but it won't do any good. She must have punctured an artery. He's bleeding out, and there is nothing she can do about it. Marx has this strange smile on his face, almost determined to die that way.

"I needed *me* alive," Seth says. "Thanks. He would have had me if not for your sharpshooting skills. I owe you one."

"I knew they would come in handy eventually. You saved me during the Brockhampton riot. I'd say it's even."

He holsters his weapon and searches the pockets on Marx's body armor. He takes the cell phone he finds. Other than spare magazines, there is nothing else on him.

"This could come in handy. Last chance to do the right thing, Marx."

"I already did the right thing."

The radio crackles to life. "Agent Larsen, report."

"We have a suspect down in the woods behind the house."

"Roger. A vehicle breached the perimeter. We were giving chase and lost it. He couldn't have gotten far."

I'll be damned, Marx thinks as the light turns to darkness. Trot made it after all. He hopes the kid fares better than he did. It's the last thought the former soldier will ever have as the light in his eyes extinguishes forever.

CHAPTER SEVENTY-SIX

TIERRA CAMPOS

Autumn Bluff Suites
Manchester, New Hampshire

The passage of time is relative. It flies by when I'm on vacation. A week feels like a day. When I was at WWDC, a workday felt like an eternity. Nothing compares to how slow the minute hand feels like it's moving right now.

Tyler and I sit on the couch of our small suite and watch bad early morning television. I would have taken almost anything marginally entertaining, from reruns of *Three's Company* to a documentary on the Civil War. Whatever this crap is won't get it done. Worse, the other ten channels this hotel offers have nothing better on.

I jump when the phone finally rings. "How did it go?"

"Not great," Victoria says, her voice sounding wounded on the other end. "They had the property ringed with sensors. They knew we were coming and opened fire as we were getting into position. Sartre was killed in the house. Seth and I caught Marx as he was fleeing through the woods. He's dead."

"Were you able to get anything out of him?"

Victoria sighs. "Unfortunately, no. Trotsky jumped into the truck and rammed his way through the perimeter. New Hampshire State Police found it abandoned on the outskirts of Manchester near I-93. He must have either stolen another vehicle or carjacked somebody."

"Now what?" Tyler asks, jumpy like he's itching to do something.

"We're searching for him. We'll find him."

"Victoria, what are you going to do about Engels? He's going to find out about the raid."

"Yeah, I know. Drucker doesn't know how we found the others, and I'm not betting he'll stick around long enough to figure that out. Either way, I have to get the FBI involved in finding him."

It sounded more convincing than it is. Ian is an agent in America's premier investigative organization. There's no telling how much damage he's done or can continue to do before they slap cuffs on him.

"All right, I guess that sounds like a win overall," Tyler says.

"At a steep price. Seven state troopers were wounded in the raid. One of them is Diego."

"What happened?"

"He was coordinating the raid. When it went to shit, he moved up so he could be closer and arrived at the same time Trotsky was fleeing in the truck. They exchanged fire, and his car was rammed."

"My God. Will he be okay?"

"His body armor saved his life, but he still caught a round below his left shoulder above the chest plate. He's getting rushed into surgery now. The good news is that I think all the troopers will make it."

I close my eyes and take a deep breath. Victoria was right; seven wounded was a steep price, and now Victoria has a friend in the hospital. This has become a war of attrition.

"I'm sorry, Vic."

"Yeah, thanks. I'm looking forward to the day when we aren't saying that to each other. There's one more thing. I confirmed the damage on the truck before we moved in. It's how we knew we were in the right place. The damage matches what the state police found on Olivia's Toyota. They caused her accident."

"Are you sure?"

"Positive. I need to go."

"What do you need us to do?" Tyler asks.

I'm hoping she has something for us, but this is a law enforcement matter right now. Victoria is not going to ask us to tag along to apprehend a man who was involved in wounding seven state troopers and countless others. I wish she would, though.

"Nothing, for now. The SOF left behind a lot of evidence. I have an FBI team here from Bedford helping the state police process the house. This is their operation, but I'm going to have them deliver the computers and phones to our Chelsea office for processing. There's no telling what they might be able to get off them."

"What are you going to do?" I ask.

"Find Trotsky."

CHAPTER SEVENTY-SEVEN

ANDREW LI

Eggs on Elm
Manchester, New Hampshire

Andrew forks another helping of eggs into his mouth as Isiah's breakfast remains untouched. He's more caught up in his phone than the bacon, scrambled eggs, and home fries on his plate. Strange since it was his idea to come here.

"Are you going to eat that breakfast or ignore it like an ex-wife?"

"Yeah."

Andrew shakes his head and rips off a corner of his toast. "What's bothering you?"

"Nothing."

"Right. Nothing."

Isiah glances up at his political consultant and tucks his phone into the pocket of his jacket. "I was just checking the news."

"No, you weren't. What's on your mind, Isiah?"

"I've spent years planning this campaign. I honed strategies and studied possible opponents. I gamed how we would respond to the lies told about us and how we would turn them around on those telling them."

"I know. The campaign is incredibly well-coordinated."

"Yeah, yet none of it went as I thought it would."

"That's because you're not the Zoltar machine. You can't predict the future; you can only react to it."

"We've done a lot of that here."

"Yeah, we have. Like Mike Tyson once said, 'everyone has a plan until they get punched in the mouth.' The key to winning is adapting your strategy. You've done that. Because of your efforts, your father is positioned to drive Standish out and coast to the nomination."

"Yeah, I guess," he says, using the fork to kick the eggs around the plate. "'All courses of action are risky, so prudence is not in avoiding danger but calculating risk and acting decisively. Make mistakes of ambition and not mistakes of sloth. Develop the strength to do bold things, not the strength to suffer.'"

"There you go with the quotes again. I haven't had enough coffee for that. Say it plainly."

"It turns out that you were right about Vision 2030."

It's still a thorn in Isiah's side. Andrew was right. The release was news for about two days and was something for the second-tier candidates to focus on at the debates.

That's it. Now, scant attention is paid to it other than mockery from right-wing news channels and the occasional barb from a late-night television host. It's a punchline more than a policy initiative right now. That will have to change.

"This isn't my first rodeo."

"I know it's not. I'm going to need to lean on you in the next races, Andrew. Despite all that's happened, Nevada is still a crapshoot, and South Carolina won't amount to much if we can't get our supporters to turn out."

"I'm here, Isiah, but do me a favor and don't lose sight of this election yet. We are in a great position here, but we haven't won anything yet. Does your father have any events planned for tomorrow or Tuesday?"

"No, he just wants to walk the streets and talk to people."

Andrew grimaces. The man of the people schtick plays well and is in Luther Burgess's wheelhouse, but it's ruthlessly inefficient. He needs to amplify his message so that it makes waves on a national level. Pressing palms makes for a useful five-second video snippet on the evening news but doesn't pack a punch.

"He needs to hold rallies, Isiah. Shaking a hand or two wins a vote or two. We need him to win over thousands."

"I tried telling him that."

"Then try harder."

"Get off my back, will ya? He's the candidate, and what he says goes."

"Unfortunately, that's not how this works. You're still thinking like the dutiful son taking orders from his father. Don't. You are the campaign manager. You run the show."

"Tread carefully, Andrew."

"Or else what? My job is to advise the campaign, and that means advising you. You told me that your father has worked his entire life to be in this position. His dream is to be president. I get it. Now that he's here, he needs to listen to the people who can help him realize that dream. He needs to listen to you."

"It's far more complicated than that, and you know it. 'There is nothing more difficult to take in hand, more perilous to conduct, or more uncertain in its success than to take the lead in the introduction of a new order of things.'"

Andrew wipes the corners of his mouth and sets his napkin down. In the history of bad ideas, having a family member run a national campaign is one of the worst. It's great having someone you can trust at the helm, but the family dynamic is a powerful one and tends to override common sense. Instead of navigating to the desired destination, all too often, you end up hitting the rocks and sinking.

"This isn't the time for your coffee table quote book wisdom."

"It's not that, and I don't care what you think."

"You should. You told me that you needed to lean on me. Well, I need you to lean on your father. There are two more primaries before Super Tuesday, and unless the governor clones himself, he can't be in all those states at once. That means campaigning in all of them while only being in one of them. The time for the meet and greets is over."

"I'm aware of that," Isiah snaps.

"I know you are. Is he? Because in the next couple of weeks, your father needs to figure out how bad he wants this, and you need to find out."

Andrew gets up and drops a ten on the table for a tip. "Pay the bill when you're done playing with your phone."

He heads for the exit, thanking their waitress as he leaves. On the way out, he sneaks a glance at his boss. Sure enough, his nose is buried in his phone again. What the hell is going on?

CHAPTER SEVENTY-EIGHT

SENATOR ALICIA STANDISH

Standish for President Campaign Office
Nashua, New Hampshire

The knock on the door startles Alicia. She left it wide open to provide her staff with easy access to her if there is a problem, but they still knock anyway. The senator might enjoy the interruption to punctuate the boredom if she weren't so damned miserable. She looks up and forces a smile.

"Knock, knock," the man says, leaning in the doorway.

"Come in, Roger. It's awfully early in the morning to see you rapping on my door in Nashua. To what do I owe the pleasure?"

It's surprising to see him here at all. Roger Ackerman is the president's chief of staff and his closest confidant. There is rarely a moment that he isn't at his boss's side, despite overseeing the West Wing whether the commander-in-chief is there or not. Roger is as loyal as an old guard dog. If he's here on his own, it can't be a good sign.

"I see you canceled your rallies scheduled for today."

"Yeah, I can't afford any more fiascos before Tuesday."

"How are you going to make up the ground then?" he asks, sitting in the chair across from the desk.

"That's what they're trying to figure out," Alicia says, nodding toward the front of the office. "It's been a rough week."

"I'm afraid it's about to get worse."

The senator sits up straighter. "That sounds ominous. I'm betting I know what you're going to say next, and the answer is no."

"Senator, you should listen to what I'm about to say with an open mind before deciding."

"Does it involve me dropping out of the race?"

Roger stares at her for a long moment. She holds his gaze.

"Yes," he says, without any emotion.

"Then the answer is no. Thank you for stopping by, Roger. Please give my regards to the president."

"I'm afraid you need to hear me out. You're on life support, Senator. Donations have all dried up. Your campaign is hemorrhaging money, forcing you to cut staff in the Super Tuesday states. If that wasn't bad enough, the media has turned on you, and so have many of your followers. How much longer do you think you'll last? Through Nevada? Maybe South Carolina?"

"Thank you for your astute analysis. Did you read my tarot cards to come up with that last part?"

"No, but you don't need a psychic to tell you that if you lose here, you have no chance to win. That is why you're still in New Hampshire instead of on a plane. I'm sure your staff urged you to get on one."

Alicia lowers her eyes. There is no hiding the painful fact that he's right. The cold, hard truth hurts. She is finished, only she can't face that reality yet.

"It's over for you, Senator. The only question that remains is what you can salvage from it."

She takes a deep breath. "What's your offer?"

"Simple. Drop out before Tuesday's primary and endorse another candidate."

"That's not going to be worth much. I'm damaged goods."

"It's worth more than you think. You have built an incredible machine with capable staff and an impressive donor list. Your infrastructure alone is worth it, and you still have a following that could prove useful in the swing states."

"Gee, thanks, Roger. I'm glad you think that I'm good for something. What do I get in return?"

"A seat at the table. There's room for you in the next administration. If you do this for us, you can have your choice of cabinet positions, including State."

Alicia's eyes flicker. The State Department is alluring because it's high profile and gives any politician more credibility in foreign affairs. It's why Hillary Clinton took the job after losing the nomination to Barack Obama. It burnished an already impressive resume, for as much good as that did her.

"There's no way Luther Burgess is going to give me a position in his administration."

"Who said anything about endorsing Burgess?"

The ominous tone in his voice and weight of his words catch her off guard. He can't possibly be implying what she thinks he is. She waits patiently for an explanation.

"Burgess is a liability. His Vision 2030 plays well with the extremists in the party, but moderates hate it, and we'll get crushed with independent voters. Nominating him would be like handing the presidency to the Republicans on a silver platter."

"And you want me to endorse one of the second-tier candidates to tip the scales?"

"I don't like to think of them like that, but yes. The president wants voters to have a viable option after you leave the race. Burgess wins if he's the default candidate. With your help, one of the others has a shot."

"Which one?"

"Are you accepting the offer?"

The quid pro quo is annoying. Alicia knows the game because she plays it herself. She finds out who the president's personal dark horse candidate is only if she agrees to join the team. He couldn't be bothered to say a word in her defense about the allegations against her campaign. He also didn't have a single kind word to say following the failure of the Safe America Act. Can he be true to his word now, or is getting her to help a middling candidate a ploy to sink her political ambitions forever?

It doesn't even matter. There's a bigger problem. The president is politically powerful, but he isn't God. You can influence voters, but handpicking a replacement rarely works out well.

"You guys didn't learn anything from the 2016 or 2020 races, did you? Burgess may have extreme viewpoints, but his base is large and loyal. You'll ostracize them again. How many more times do you think they'll live with that disappointment?"

"They won't vote for a Republican," he counters.

"They won't vote, period. Turnout is everything in swing districts across the country. We need those to stay blue. You know that."

"You let us worry about that. What is your decision?"

"I will think it over. If you give me an ultimatum and force me to decide now, the answer is no. This is not a decision I will make under duress."

Alicia has been around politics long enough to learn when she has leverage. She has something they want and will extract as much as she can from the deal should she decide to make it. Roger Ackerman knows that, too.

"I understand. I know this isn't easy for you. It wouldn't be for anybody. You have until nine Monday evening. After that we lose the news cycle. I understand that you're going to appear on *Capitol Beat*. It would be the ideal place to make the announcement. Wilson Newman would be first in line to interview you."

"You mean Carl Brennan?"

"My fingers are crossed that Wilson will be out of the hospital and back by then. Good luck with your choice, Alicia."

"Thank you, Roger."

He said all that needed to be said. She appreciates him coming up here to deliver the message in person, even if it wasn't worth the CO_2 emissions for the plane to get here. Some things shouldn't be handled over the phone, especially when it concerns her political future. Still, a call from the president himself would have been appropriate. It's one more thing for her to think about as she chooses which path to follow. It's a course that will determine the rest of her life.

CHAPTER SEVENTY-NINE

"S.O.F."

Interstate 93 Southbound
Stoneham, Massachusetts

Trotsky scans the road out the window. He checks his rearview mirrors for any signs of the police or feds. He even has the sunroof visor open so he can check the skies for helicopters. So far, nothing. If the police are on his trail, they aren't obvious about it.

It wasn't the prettiest getaway. Trotsky had to fight his way off the safehouse's street and then break through the state police perimeter. Once he plowed through that, all he had to do was ditch the cars following him. It wasn't easy, but he managed it before they could call for local backup.

He loved that truck. The painful part of his whole escape was abandoning his beloved pickup — that and dealing with the grating voice of the annoying woman he carjacked.

"You need to let me go," she demands again from the passenger seat.

"I'm not going to hurt you. I just need to get where I'm going."

"Good, because I'm going to kick your ass when we get there."

He stares at the woman illuminated only by the passing overhead streetlights on the highway. Her face is all business. She means it. His gun may be the only thing keeping him from being beaten to death.

"You don't sound scared," he says with a chuckle.

"I've been carjacked before. That dickhead didn't zip-tie my hands together, though."

Trot stares down at the plastic bindings he tied her wrists with. They're still secure, although he doubts that they would deter her from clawing his eyes out the first chance she gets.

"It had to be done. Did you get carjacked here?"

"Chicago. I moved here to get away from that bullshit."

"That didn't work so well, did it."

"Yeah, no shit, Captain Obvious. You in trouble or something?"

Trot rechecks the mirrors. "What gave it away?"

"The stench of fear. Or maybe it's because you smell like you haven't showered in a week. I can't tell which."

Trot clenches his teeth. "You always talk so much?"

"Hey, you carjacked me, remember?"

"You need to shut up now," he says, poking her with the muzzle of his gun for effect. Logan Airport is about an hour's drive from South Hooksett. He has twenty minutes left and won't be able to handle her jabbering the rest of the way there.

"Yeah, that ain't gonna happen. You made me late for work."

"I think your boss will understand once you explain what happened."

"Oh, you do, eh? Trust me, he won't."

Trot looks at his victim. "Why not?"

"He's a bigger asshole than you are," she says, in a matter-of-fact tone.

He grins and rechecks his mirrors. Interstate 93 runs north-south, from its beginning south of Brockton, Massachusetts, to where it merges with I-91 near the U.S.-Canada border. He crosses the interchange with I-95 in Woburn, about a fifteen-minute drive to his destination. So far, nothing. Now is as good a time as any.

He pulls over onto the shoulder. The woman looks at him, surprised.

"What the hell are you doing now?"

"Get out."

"No way. I need this car. I'm not leaving you with it."

"Get out, now, or I shoot you right here."

The woman shakes her head violently. "No way. I worked my ass off to pay for this thing. You're just going to have to shoot me."

Trot doesn't like being challenged. He admires this woman's courage, but that only goes so far.

"Don't tempt me."

She just stares at him. He thinks about the consequences of what he's about to do. It's not smart to show up at an international airport with a body in the front seat. It's a worse idea to leave her on the side of the road. There is one thing he can do.

"Fine," he says, digging through his bag. Trot pulls out a roll of duct tape and rips off a piece.

"What do you think you're doing with that?"

"You're going to shut up one way or another."

"Oh, hell, no."

The woman squirms, but it's a losing battle. He covers her mouth and pulls back onto the highway. She's still screaming at him in muffled tones through the tape as he continues south.

It never should have come to this. Trotsky wonders if Marx was able to slip away. He doubts it. The woods were an obvious escape route that the police would have covered. That's why he opted for this approach, despite the risk.

Under any other circumstances, he would lie low somewhere. The police can't search for him forever. That's what they must be expecting him to do, which is why he's doing the opposite. His passport and ticket are under an alias. There is no way they would suspect he's going to flee the country this soon. They'll be looking for him in all the wrong places.

Trotsky scans the sky again for helicopters and sees none. The odds are long, but he knows he can do this. There is a beach with his name on it waiting for him in the Caribbean. The money in the offshore account no longer needs to be divided up. He can live a long, comfortable life off the grid. He just needs to make it to the plane before he can start living it.

CHAPTER EIGHTY

SPECIAL AGENT VICTORIA LARSEN

Logan Airport Terminal E Parking
Boston, Massachusetts

The 9-1-1 call has been active for over a half-hour. Trotsky should have had his victim throw her phone out the window. For whatever reason, he didn't. It's likely in her purse because she isn't saying anything. The open line makes them easy to track from a distance, and now they know where he's heading.

"That's right, Logan Airport…no, I'm dead serious…I have no idea where. One of the parking garages, probably," Seth says into his phone. "I got fifty New Hampshire State Troopers to conduct an early morning raid with next to no information on their targets. Are you seriously telling me that you can't provide a few units to apprehend…fine, I'll take what I can get."

"Logan is a risky move, assuming he's not lying to us," Victoria says from behind the wheel.

"He thinks he got away and wants to get out of Dodge before we cast a net over New England. Lying low is the safe play. A man who crashes a pickup truck through a perimeter isn't going to pick that route."

Seth answers his phone and outlines the plan for the rest of the drive to the airport. He gives them real-time information as Victoria edges Seth's personal vehicle closer to their target. At least they don't stick out.

"All right, he's heading for Terminal E parking," he says into the phone before turning to Victoria. "Told ya. You owe me dinner."

"Whatever."

"Have two units follow me in. We're fifteen seconds behind the target vehicle. When I say the word, send the unit on the top deck of the garage down, and we'll pen him in."

"Here we go," Victoria says, turning into the garage.

They follow him up to the third deck and watch as he pulls into a spot.

"Third deck," Seth says into his radio. "Target parked and has a hostage. Use extreme caution. Move in!"

It worked better than expected. In Seth's SUV, they were right on top of Trotsky when the unit came screaming around the corner. He moves around the rear of the vehicle quickly, and yanks open the passenger side door. The woman fights him as he reaches for her, finally grabbing her clothing and ripping her out of the car.

Trotsky grabs her by the arm, but she twists and slams him on the forearm with her bound hands. He lunges for her and stops her momentum as she tries to escape, but he doesn't get a good grasp on her when she runs toward the approaching officers. He begins to lift his gun and has second thoughts. Instead of shooting at her, he places his weapon against his right temple.

"Stay back!" he screams, as men bark orders for him to drop the weapon.

"Settle down, Trotsky. You don't want it to end like this, and neither do we," Seth says, his own weapon leveled at the SOF member.

"How do you know that name?"

"We know everything about you, Tad," Victoria says, in a calm voice that's almost eerie for the situation. "It's over."

Trotsky takes stock of his situation, scanning the line of troopers for an escape route. He even looks down over the concrete wall at the ground below. It'd be one hell of a fall if he decides to jump. At a minimum, he'd break both legs. More likely, he'd be dead.

"You can take out his arm, Vic," Seth mumbles. "You're a great shot."

"I could, but it's too risky. I want him alive. He has the answers we need."

Victoria holsters her weapon and takes a step toward him. Seth grabs her arm.

"Are you crazy?"

"Trust me."

She moves ten feet closer before stopping. Trotsky edges toward the railing with his handgun still pressed to his head.

"We're serious. It doesn't have to end this way."

"It looks like it's the only way it'll end," he says, looking around the garage.

"Will you guys please shoot this son of a bitch?" the woman, now ungagged and unbound, barks from behind the troopers.

Victoria stretches her hands out and motions downward.

"Seriously?" the woman asks from behind the line of men and women with their weapons drawn. "Man, you lucky you ain't black. They'd have shot you up already if you were."

"Trotsky, I don't believe you mean that," Victoria says, forcing him to focus on her.

He lets out a laugh and smiles before shaking his head. "Well, it was always a possibility."

"You've had an escape plan for a while, haven't you? Let me guess. You were going to flee overseas. Someplace warm, right?"

"St. Kitts."

"I hear it's really nice there. You were set to go, but Marx wanted to stay. He screwed you over, and here you are. Am I close?"

He doesn't answer, nor does he need to. His eyes let Victoria know that she's on the money with her conclusion. He's only a soldier in their cause—the muscle who executes orders, not the commander who issued them.

"Did you guys work for the Standish Campaign?"

He lets out a derisive laugh. "You guys couldn't be further off-base."

"Who did you work for, then?"

He shakes his head.

"This is your chance, Tad. You have valuable information you can trade for leniency, but the clock is running."

"Not as much as you think."

"Then get your revenge on the man who ruined your plans. You should have been on St. Kitts days ago. He sacrificed you for his mission. Tell us what you know and get some payback."

"You're smooth. Tell me, Miss FBI, then what? I'm rewarded with a long stay in a cage? I don't think so."

Victoria knows that she's losing her chance. His mind is made up. She needs to push harder.

"Don't let it end like this. If you want to have a legacy, it starts right here by telling me who you worked for."

He stares at her, fiddling with the gun held to his temple. Trotsky looks at the officers surrounding them to see if they've moved, which they haven't. He closes his eyes, and when he reopens them, he settles back on Victoria and smiles.

"Burgess. We worked for Luther Burgess."

That's not what Victoria expected him to say. She also can't be sure it's even the truth. There is something about his smile that is off. The good news is that he's cooperating, and that is the first big step toward de-escalation.

"Thank you, Tad. Why don't you put down your gun so we can talk some more?"

"No. That's all you're going to get. I'm not going to a tropical island, but I'm not going to prison, either."

He closes his eyes and takes a deep breath. Victoria draws, hoping she can hit him before he pulls the trigger. She is a split-second too late. The gun fires and Trotsky drops to the ground. Victoria lowers her weapon and hangs her head.

The troopers move in and secure Trotsky's pistol. They begin checking his pockets and find a passport and a slip of paper with what looks like an overseas account number written on it. She can't wait to find out how much these mercenary services cost someone. The going rate for disrupting an election must be high.

"This is all we found. He's clean, otherwise," the trooper informs Seth before moving off. The detective frowns and looks at Victoria.

Victoria reaches into the pocket attached to her body armor and turns off the recording on her cell phone. She'll listen to it later to see if it picked up the conversation.

"We're back to square one unless we find Engels."

"Which we won't unless we give him a reason to come out of the shadows," Victoria says, turning and walking over to the woman who was held hostage moments ago. "Ma'am, did your carjacker have a cell phone on him?"

She gives her a quizzical look. "Yeah, that asshole chucked it out the window on the way here. Who was he?"

"One of the men complicit in the murder of Frederick Lamm."

"He torched those offices?"

"One of them. What's your name, ma'am?"

"Why, am I in trouble or something?"

"No, I need it for some paperwork."

"Oh, I get it. I get jacked, am late for work, and now my name gets stuck in an FBI file. That's how it starts, you know. The next thing is the black helicopters."

Victoria smiles, further annoying the woman. "Nah, nothing like that. I was thinking more along the lines of a commendation from the FBI for assisting us in a dangerous situation with a known terrorist."

Her eyes light up. "You serious?"

"Ma'am, what you did was downright heroic. You deserve to be acknowledged for that. All I ask in return is that you tell us what happened on the way down here. We're trying to understand all we can about this guy."

"He didn't say much other than threaten me. Look, I need to get to work. My boss is gonna hand me my ass as it is."

"Don't worry about that," Victoria says. "I'll set him straight for you. I'm good at stuff like that."

"Trust her when she says that," Seth says.

A trooper comes over and takes the woman's statement. She doesn't know much. Victoria was hoping that Trotsky had kept his cell phone on him, but they're unlikely to ever find it now. Her best hope is that she can convince Fuller to bring Ian in and that Sartre's computer isn't encrypted. Hey, miracles happen.

CHAPTER EIGHTY-ONE

TIERRA CAMPOS

Tranquility Hotel & Suites
Manchester, New Hampshire

I brush past Jerome the moment he opens the door to their suite, and I storm up to a surprised Austin as ice forms on the walls from my colleagues' reception. The cold war between their boss and me is about to get incredibly hot.

"Why aren't you with Olivia?" Austin asks, looking up from his laptop at the kitchen counter.

"Because I'm here instead."

"I explicitly said that I didn't want her left alone. I'm fairly sure even you can handle those basic instructions."

"I didn't want to leave her alone, either. That's why Ty is with her."

Austin shakes his head, going back to his pretend reading. "It shouldn't be necessary to have to stay with her at all."

"You would know," I sneer. I'm done playing this game.

"Did you really come here to—"

"It was an attack, Austin."

"What?" Jerome asks. At least I have everyone's undivided attention now.

"Olivia was hit on purpose."

"How do you know that?" Madison asks with an unmistakable edge to her voice.

I take my time and study each of their faces in silence. It unnerves them. I found out a long time ago that silence is an effective weapon. Conversation is king in our business, and a prolonged period without it is unsettling.

"Because Victoria caught the men who did it," I say, settling back on Austin. He looks unconvinced.

"How do you know?"

"I've been working with her."

Austin grimaces. "Without telling me?"

"I cultivated her as a source like you asked. Don't you remember?"

"It was so long ago, I forgot. I could have convinced Kim Jong Un to defect in less time. Victoria is compromised. You can't take anything she says at face value."

"Yeah, not so much."

I have rehearsed this speech in my head for a while now. I give them the crib notes version of everything we've learned over the past week and how we discovered it. I go into as much detail as I know about the raid in South Hooksett, which isn't much. I finish with the task Victoria has of catching the last two members of the SOF as it really exists.

With one exception, Austin, Madison, and Jerome sit through the recap stone-faced. The only emotion I get out of them is a sadness to their eyes and a hint of remorse when I mention the casualties that the New Hampshire State Police took on the raid. I only hope they have better luck catching the remaining members.

"So, that's what the news was talking about this morning?" Madison asks.

"Yup."

"You reached out to the hackers that doxxed you, and they actually helped track this down?" Jerome asks, following Madison's lead.

"No one was more surprised than I was. Then again, no hacker wants their name printed on the main page of *Front Burner.*"

"Who says I would have published them?" Austin asks.

"They didn't know that. Most people would assume that you're reasonable and easy to work with."

My grin only infuriates Austin further. Nobody outside of our team knows this feud is happening. There was no reason for the hackers to believe I wouldn't have published their names, or, at a minimum, turned over what I had to the FBI Cyber Unit.

"Let me get this straight. You, Tyler, and Victoria put all this together."

"Along with Seth Chambers and Diego Velez."

Austin stands and crosses his arms, using his own silence to his advantage. I wait patiently, with no interest in talking first. I can make this last all day.

"You'll do anything to prove it isn't Brian Cooper," he finally says.

"And you'll do anything to cling to the belief that it is, just like every other news outlet in town."

"We were reporting facts. You know, those pesky things you're ignoring. The FBI arrested Cooper based on the same ones. Unless I missed something."

"I'm after facts, too. Mine are better than theirs."

Austin laughs as he shifts his hands into his pockets. "You're trying to relive Brockhampton, Miss Peabody."

That succeeds in hiking my blood pressure up. I haven't won a Peabody, and there is no guarantee that I will. His jealousy over the possibility of my winning passed ridiculous ten miles ago and is now coming up on insane.

"And that must burn your ass. We had less evidence in Brockhampton, and you still grabbed a shovel and started digging. How can you look at the evidence we've acquired and not at least question your conclusions? The answer is you can't."

"You don't have any solid evidence of anything. You have hearsay and old photos. The SOF Victoria took down could just have easily been working for Brian Cooper. You can't say otherwise. Admit it."

"You used to believe in me, Austin. Six months ago, you'd dedicate every resource we had to find the truth. Now, you're as dismissive and condescending as my old bosses at WWDC News were. For a while there, I thought something internal at *Front Burner* was causing that. It isn't. It's about me."

"You'd like to think so, wouldn't you?"

The comment marks the beginning of an epic stare-down between us. Madison and Jerome have remained quiet throughout the entire exchange, and don't seem eager to inject themselves into the debate now. They watch the both of us, their eyes bouncing back and forth to see who flinches first. Again, I'm determined to outlast him.

"Anything else?" he asks.

"You have summaries of the evidence I collected in this folder," I say, slapping it on the counter. "The first draft of the article I wrote is in the back of the file for your review."

"I think we've already established that isn't necessary. Thank you for the effort. I have a new assignment for you in Nevada to cover the primary there. You leave tomorrow morning."

"I'm not going anywhere. If you don't like it, fire me."

"If I could, I already would have. You're being protected, for now. You're the only writer on the *Front Burner* staff who will have received a prestigious journalism award."

"You had better hope you actually get it," Madison says, acting as if she has any say in my employment status.

"Maddie's right. If you don't, getting rid of you will be easy. Until then, I have to contend with you being the golden child."

"So, you're going to make my life miserable instead? What a class act you are," I sneer, not for a moment trying to hide my contempt and disgust for a man I used to respect.

"I expect you on that plane, Tierra. We can handle things here."

"Yeah, I've seen how you're handling things. Have you done any investigating since you arrived, or are you just taking people at their word like everyone else is? You've gotten lazy, ineffective, and content to regurgitate whatever the party line happens to be. It's a shame."

"Nevada. Tomorrow."

"Since you can't fire me, I can say this with one hundred percent sincerity: go pound sand."

I'm not the scared girl afraid to live life anymore. I wanted to be invisible while hiding in that closet during the shooting in my high school. That didn't stop until last summer. I refuse to be invisible or ignored anymore. If Austin doesn't want me to be a part of his team, that's fine. I'm not going to give him the satisfaction of quitting until I have reason to.

I leave the suite with the same swagger that I entered with. My team hasn't been any help to me, and there is little hope of that changing. I made my pitch to my editor, and he dismissed it. Now I need to find another way to shine a light on the nefarious activities happening in this small but proud state.

CHAPTER EIGHTY-TWO

SPECIAL AGENT VICTORIA LARSEN

Federal Bureau of Investigation Boston Field Office
Chelsea, Massachusetts

Victoria isn't going to wait for permission. What the hell, she isn't welcome here anyway. She enters the outer office and breezes past his distracted admin. Her indifference turns to shock as Victoria reaches the door.

"Agent Larsen, you can't go in there!" she shouts as Victoria pushes open the door and storms in. Lance Fuller looks up from his laptop, the phone cradled in the crook of his neck.

"I'm going to need to call you back," he says, hanging up. "You have some nerve."

"You already knew that."

"I'm sorry, sir. She barged right past me."

Lance looks at his executive assistant with sympathy before glaring at Victoria. "Get the hell out of my office. Now!"

"That can wait. I'm here to inform you that we neutralized the men responsible for the arsons on the Burgess campaign. Two of them were killed at their safehouse in South Hooksett, and a third committed suicide at Logan Airport just over an hour ago. The fourth is still at large."

Lance's jaw hangs open for a moment until he forces it closed. He nods at his admin, who leaves, closing the door behind her. She wants no part of the fireworks she assumes will ignite in there.

"Who authorized you to conduct an operation?"

"Nobody, which is why I didn't conduct it. The New Hampshire State Police did. Seven of them were injured in the raid, two severely. The takedown at Logan was conducted by the Massachusetts State Police. No casualties…well, one if you count the bad guy."

"You mean Seth Chambers did," Lance grumbles.

Victoria grins. Lance may be a bureaucrat, but he isn't an idiot. He can do the math and conclude that anything involving his maverick agent and the state police is bound to include Detective Chambers.

"Tell me you weren't actively involved with either operation."

"I wasn't unless you include killing one of them at the safehouse and trying to talk down the guy who committed suicide."

"Victoria!"

"Yell at me later. We acquired all the evidence we need. Computers, cell phones…everything."

"Where is it?"

"The NERCFL is processing it as we speak. I'll walk you through all of it, but there's a bigger problem that you need to address first. We have taken down three SOF arsonists, but that leaves the fourth and the yet-to-be-identified ringleader."

"Brian Cooper."

"Yeah, I doubt that. We'll debate it later. I know who the fourth member is, but I need your help to get him."

"All right, I'm listening."

That was easier than Victoria expected. She half expected him to call building security and have her dragged out of here. Either Fuller has decided to be reasonable, or he's humoring her.

"Did Ian Drucker have any reason to be in New Hampshire before this investigation began?"

Lance's eyes narrow. "He was working with you. So, no."

Victoria gives a quick nod and pulls out the picture of him with the SOF that Janey found. Lance studies it, his eyes widening before he erects his walls of denial.

"It could be doctored."

"Yeah, I knew you would say that. It's not, by the way, but let's assume it is." She pulls out a small stack of papers stapled in the corner. "These are his Bureau cell phone records placing him in the proximity of the Nashua arson site and Dylan Spencer's house the night of his suicide."

"Wait! Ian left his phone on?"

"I got asked the same question before, so I'll give you the same answer. Why would we ever check it? The short answer is, we wouldn't, and having it off would be more suspicious if I were trying to reach him. Ian goes by the name Engels."

"*Little House on the Prairie?*"

"That's Ingalls. I'm going to forget you asked that question. Frederich Engels was a philosopher. He co-authored the *Communist Manifesto* with Karl Marx. Marx was the man I killed in the woods behind the safehouse."

"In the woods?"

"It's a long story."

Lance studies the papers and the pictures, moving between the cell records and the image. There is no reasonable explanation for either. The Bureau never should have missed his ideological leanings in a background check, and he knows that the photo is the real deal. Victoria watches him struggle to believe it.

"Is *Front Burner* involved in all this?"

"Rogue elements of them are, yes."

"Jesus, Vic. You're working with Campos again?"

"I wouldn't have gotten this far without her. If you want to run me out of the Bureau after this, fine, I won't fight it. I'm telling you that we have an FBI agent involved in a conspiracy to alter the outcome of a primary, and probably change the course of the whole nomination. Ian Drucker is their fourth member, and he's missing."

"Does *Front Burner* know about Ian?"

"They found the picture. Tierra is holding it as a personal favor to me. We need to take him in, and we need to find out who the mastermind is before the polls open."

Lance isn't an idiot and knows what that means. Victoria is using *Front Burner* as leverage, just like she did with Ethan Harrington. He needs to act, or the Bureau will be publicly exposed.

"Does Drucker know that his friends were neutralized?"

"I don't know. Ian had little contact with his teammates according to cell phone records, but we must assume that he does. He's off the grid and not responding to my calls."

"Okay. I'll put out a BOLO for him and get a warrant."

"There's one more thing, sir. Before Trotsky died — that's the third man we caught, at Logan International — he gave us a name when I asked who he was working for."

"What name?"

"Burgess."

Lance leans back and rubs the bridge of his nose with his thumb and index finger. "You're going to turn me into an alcoholic, Agent Larsen. That's one hell of an accusation."

"That's the other reason we're talking. I don't know what to do about it. It could be the truth or a lie. I don't want to wade into those waters and be wrong."

"For once, you made a decision I agree with. Take a walk with me."

Victoria follows her boss past the still-startled admin and out of his office. He may still kick her out of the Bureau, but she's safe for at least another day. The only question left is whether he can help her before the clock runs out on all of them.

CHAPTER EIGHTY-THREE

SENATOR ALICIA STANDISH

Standish for President Campaign Office
Nashua, New Hampshire

These late morning meetings with her advisors have become commonplace since they canceled the remaining rallies in New Hampshire. Her original plan was to crisscross the state today, holding rallies, giving speeches, and meeting with donors. The temperature of the Democrats here hasn't cooled any. Until it does, none of that voter outreach can happen. Alicia assumed the blame for the attacks on the Burgess campaign, and she has been effectively canceled because of it.

Michael and Angela argue about ways to get her out in public without embarrassing exchanges being posted on YouTube and mocked on Twitter. It's a spirited discussion, but she isn't listening to any of it. She has an offer to consider, and the more she hears, the closer she gets to a decision.

"*Capitol Beat* called a half-hour ago," Michael says, drawing Alicia's mind back to the conversation. "They want to have the candidates and senior staff members from the top two campaigns in each party on their primary election eve show."

"Who's hosting?" Angela asks. "Carl Brennan?"

"They didn't say. It sounded more like Wilson Newman would be."

"We should do it."

Michael looks up from his tablet computer. "I already declined."

"Why would you do that?" Angela asks, her eyes wide with surprise.

"Because it's a horrible idea. The questions will all be about Cooper and his SOF at a time when we need people to forget."

"Do you really think that voters will forget just because I don't appear on the most influential political news program in the country?" Alicia asks, speaking for the first time in the conversation.

"It won't be fresh in their heads," Michael argues.

Angela has heard enough. The cauldron of mistrust in her senior political advisor has been simmering on the fire for weeks and just bubbled over.

"Have you turned on the news lately? It's all that the media is talking about. Second, it wasn't your decision to make. You're only an advisor. You don't get to make campaign decisions."

"Someone has to."

Angela bristles at the comment. For a moment, she looks as if she's going to lunge across the table at him.

"Just what are you implying?"

"He's implying that Cooper's SOF stunt was partly your fault," the senator interjects, staring at him.

"I'm not—"

"Yes, you are. You're angry with Angela because this isn't the campaign you signed up for. You thought we had a clear path to the nomination and a legitimate shot at the White House, and you want a seat at the table."

"It's not like that."

"Isn't it? You know the Burgess campaign will be on *Capitol Beat*, as will the two top GOP candidates. By declining, you've forced them to find another campaign to fill the spot. You don't think we deserve to be running second after what happened."

"None of that is true. I've worked with *Capitol Beat* extensively. If Wilson hosts the show, he'll grill all of us. You know what happens then? We lose any chance at salvaging what we have left."

"I'm not afraid of tough questions from Wilson. I know I have much to answer for, and Americans need to hear me atone for what happened. Why would you unilaterally deprive me of that chance?"

Michael leans forward in his seat. Alicia meets the challenge and does the same.

"I'm trying to win."

"So was Brian Cooper. Right now, I'm not sure who was worse, you or him."

Michael recoils. His personal animosity with the former chair of the New Hampshire campaign was palpable. Under no condition will he accept being compared with the man, even by the candidate who signs his paychecks.

"What is that supposed to mean?"

"You've made mistake after mistake since the day I hired you. You're being paid a king's ransom, and all that we have received in return is bad advice."

"I resent that statement."

"I resent having to say it. I needed David Plouffe, and I got Martine Aubry."

Michael gets the reference immediately. Plouffe was Barack Obama's 2008 campaign manager and was credited with the campaign's successful strategy in the presidential primary against then-Senator Hillary Clinton. Aubry was the chief architect of a French law imposed on large businesses that reduced the workweek from thirty-nine to thirty-five hours. It was meant to stem the high unemployment rate plaguing France, but it backfired spectacularly. Eight years later, the country's unemployment numbers had barely moved.

"I don't know what to say to that."

"Don't say anything, just listen. I appreciate your help with this campaign, but your services are no longer required."

"You're firing me?" Michael asks, turning to appeal to the campaign manager. "Angela, we can—"

"You know the way out, Michael."

If he expected her to come to his defense, it was a lousy assumption. He sits in his chair, stunned at the turn of events. Despite his failures to successfully respond to events as they unfolded, he never considered the possibility of being fired. He thought the campaign would fold before that happened.

Stunned and unable to formulate a defense that the two women will find compelling, he collects his things and rises from his chair. "Good luck. You'll need it."

Angela watches him go. To his credit, he doesn't lash out or make a melodramatic exit. Instead, he leaves the two women in the room to sit in silence.

"We're in this together to the end, right?" Angela asks, thinking that she's next.

Alicia offers a weak smile. "I wouldn't have it any other way. Unfortunately, I fear it's closer than we both would like."

"What do you need me to do?"

"Call *Capitol Beat* back. Tell them I fired Michael Ross and that you and I will appear if the slot is still open."

"What if they filled it already?"

"Tell them I have an important announcement to make about the future of the campaign and want to make it on their show."

Angela nods, fully aware of the meeting with the White House chief of staff. She also knows the path to victory for them has been wiped out in an avalanche. Alicia Standish is one of the most cunning politicians she knows. It could be the end for them, but it could also be something far more epic. She's hoping for the latter as she leaves to call the bookers at *Capitol Beat* and offer a mea culpa or two.

CHAPTER EIGHTY-FOUR

SPECIAL AGENT VICTORIA LARSEN

New England Regional Computer Forensics Laboratory
Chelsea, Massachusetts

Victoria walks in with the big kahuna right behind her. Miranda flashes an apprehensive look as they stride toward her. She would have expected Superwoman to walk in with Lex Luthor before accompanying Special Agent-In-Charge Lance Fuller to her desk.

"Oh, boy. This can't be good," Miranda mutters under her breath.

"Hi, Miranda. This is—"

"Lance Fuller. I know. How much trouble am I in?"

"If you're working with her, probably a lot," Lance says, in a semi-jovial tone that the tech didn't expect.

"We're good, Miranda. I need you to walk us through the evidence that the New Hampshire State Police turned over."

"I can do that. I've been working on it from the moment it arrived. It got bumped up to the top of the priority list, so now everyone is."

"I may have had something to do with that," Lance says. "I hear you managed to get access to Ian Drucker's Bureau cell phone records."

Miranda is about to be sick. She knew it would be a risk, but she didn't think Victoria ratting her out was the way she'd get caught.

"Really nice work on that," he continues. "What else do you have for us?"

Victoria grins. Miranda returns it, knowing that they're having a little fun with the somewhat rebellious but overly jittery technician.

"Okay. There's a lot to sort through here, so we started with the easiest. These two guys had the same model of the prepaid cellular phone.

"Which guys?"

"The hacker Sartre and their presumed leader, Marx," Victoria answers.

"Cute names. Very proletariat. Anyway, most of their conversations were SMS messages, and the only numbers in the directory were each other. They never deleted their text messages. That's sloppy tradecraft for military types."

"Overconfidence?" Lance asks. Victoria nods.

"Here are the printouts of their text messages. They were infrequent."

"They match the rough times of the arsons, attack on Wilson Newman, and Olivia's accident," Victoria interjects. "There's one I don't recognize."

"I do. We'll get to that in a minute."

"Classic American novels. Very clever," Lance says, reading the printout.

"There is one name in the directory that doesn't fit: Machiavelli. The texts to him were plain English.

"Who is Machiavelli?" Lance asks.

"He was an Italian Renaissance diplomat, philosopher, and writer best known for *The Prince*. Today's politicians use it as a how-to guide for deception and shady governing… But I'm guessing you knew that," Miranda says, seeing both Victoria and Lance staring at her strangely.

"Who is *this* Machiavelli?" Victoria asks, tapping the printout.

"I don't know. Nobody uses his name."

"Okay, tell me about the code without an incident to match to."

"I'm getting to that. The computer is a goldmine. We're only just starting on it," Miranda says, moving to another desk. "This guy kept everything."

"Why didn't he delete it?"

"There were only three of them in the house and they had four sides to cover. I don't think they could spare him to wipe or encrypt the drives. He was killed as we were moving in."

Lance nods, and Miranda takes that as a cue to continue. "It's a good thing, too. We found this on a notepad."

"What is it?"

"An encryption key."

"Why would he keep it on a notepad?" Victoria asks.

"Simple. A pen and paper can't be hacked. The only access to it was by someone in the house. You're going to love what it unlocked."

Miranda makes a couple of mouse clicks, and a video comes up. Lance and Victoria lean in and study the image. It looks like a gate and nothing more.

"What is this?"

"The storage unit we raided that housed Cooper's SOF goodies. We couldn't access it and thought the folder was corrupted. It turned out it wasn't, just encrypted. I put the key in the lock, digitally speaking, and it worked. We'll start at eleven p.m. for your viewing pleasure."

"That truck looks familiar."

Victoria explains Olivia's accident and how she identified the SOF to Fuller. Miranda purses her lips. The usually smug son of a bitch looks impressed. That's only the second time she's ever heard of that happening. The first was after Victoria presented the damning evidence on the Brockhampton conspiracy in that conference room.

"Hello," Victoria says as she watches the video from a different angle. "They loaded the boxes from an adjacent unit."

"Damn," Fuller says. He had never considered that as a possibility.

"It gets better."

The group watches one of the men breaking into the office and the owner's wife showing up. She leaves, and then they watch the truck pick up the mysterious figure and leave the storage unit property.

"She doesn't know how lucky she was," Victoria muses.

"She said in the interview that the alarm was deactivated when she arrived. Now we know why."

"Did anybody test the campaign's key to their padlock?"

Lance shakes his head slowly. "I don't think so."

"They swapped the original, a perfect copy, knowing we would crack it open when a warrant was served."

"Sloppy."

"Not necessarily. Time was on their side. By the time this went to trial or anybody checked, the primary would be over, and the SOF long gone. It was a simple solution to the problem, and we never thought twice about it. It is actually kind of brilliant."

Lance stands upright and puts his hands in his pockets. He finds a spot on the wall and engages his thousand-yard stare, lost in thought. Victoria is right, they never would have put the pieces together fast enough. The big pieces have all been taken off the board, but the king is still in play.

"That's what I'm worried about. We found fake ballots in that storage unit. What if those are the ones Machiavelli wanted us to find? What if he has something planned to mess with this election?"

"Machiavelli already has messed with it. Someone framed the Standish campaign, and her numbers tanked. If she loses, it changes the trajectory of the primaries and affects the presidential race. What will happen when people realize that it was based on a fraud?"

Fuller lowers his eyes. His head bobs up and down slightly as he processes the information. Victoria watches him, wondering if he is more concerned about preserving the integrity of the American democratic process or the ramifications on his career. She hopes it's the former but concludes that it's probably the latter.

"Agent Larsen, I don't care what you have to do. Mobilize as many agents as you need. Find out who Machiavelli is and who he is working for before the polls open on Tuesday."

CHAPTER EIGHTY-FIVE

TIERRA CAMPOS

Autumn Bluff Suites
Manchester, New Hampshire

Tyler and I sit on the sofa in stunned silence as Victoria and Seth walk us through what her computer nerds have found on Sartre's computer. They still have a long way to go, but none of it is encrypted. Sartre should have known better.

"Sartre was responsible for the hack on the Burgess campaign website and Standish's Twitter account on the night of the debate. They also found an original copy of Vision 2030," Victoria says. "He stole it off one of their systems and leaked it."

"That makes sense," Tyler concludes. "They lose nothing by the release and get to blame the hacking on Standish and Cooper. It's just one more shady thing to pin on them."

"Anything on who they were working for?"

"No, and I don't think they'll find anything, either. The SOF communicated and received instructions using the drafts folder of an email account. Sartre set it up, so that's a dead end. Machiavelli was a code name he used so they wouldn't know his identity if they got caught. He was a shadow. Do you still think it was someone in the Burgess campaign?"

"Yeah, I'm certain of it. I just don't know who."

"Let's start from the beginning," Tyler says, moving to the dry erase board. He loves these things. "The first operation was to take out Dylan Spencer. Why?"

"Rumor has it that he was planning to support Burgess. Maybe deprive him of those financial resources?" I ask.

"Or it was a practice mission," Seth says over the speaker. "Something to get their coordination down."

"Or prove their capabilities to their new boss," Victoria adds. "Whatever it was, they moved on to the intimidations. They threaten the kids and their families with harm if they keep actively supporting Burgess."

"They had to have known those kids would go to the police," Tyler says.

"I think they were counting on it. That story breaks, and then the SOF commit the arsons, leaving the SOF in white paint."

Tyler writes it on the board, caps the marker, and presses it against his lips.

"Then they would have to have known that it would eventually point back to Brian Cooper. How could they? What if they were just leaving their own calling card?"

"It wasn't their M.O., Ty," Victoria argues. "It was the only time. It must have had a higher purpose."

"They were here two months before the primary," I say. "That's plenty of time to gather intelligence. People talk. How hard would it have been to overhear something about Cooper's group in a bar?"

"And the SOF? Whoever would have thought Sword of Freedom?" Seth asks.

"Are you guys really passing this off as a coincidence?"

"No, Tyler, you know better. I think it's more likely they knew about Cooper's group and patterned the name of theirs after it using something they had in common."

"And it worked, Vic. Those three letters led the FBI to the storage unit and what Marx planted there. That led them right to Cooper. It was well-executed."

We all watch Tyler as he makes a couple of notes on the board. There are a few boxes that have no relationship built to them yet. He taps on one of them.

"So, everything up to this point was damn near perfect. Then why attack Wilson Newman and let yourself get caught on video. Why attack Olivia at all for that matter?"

"Fear."

"Victoria is right. It's for the same reason Ian was working to sideline her. We threatened to uncover the operation and needed to be slowed down or stopped altogether."

"You mean it wasn't part of the plan?" Tyler asks.

"Everything up to this point was. I think the SOF did this on their own. I'm not even sure this Machiavelli knew about it. We were poking around, and Marx got nervous. Our Brockhampton reputations preceded us."

"I don't follow," Seth says.

I have so much nervous energy that I need to move around. I pace the center of the room, running through the mental notes I made. This has bothered me since it happened. There is no apparent reason for it. I stop when something dawns on me.

"With Wilson out of the picture, who would people have thought his replacement would be?"

"You. Okay, fine, I get that, but Carl Brennan was scheduled to take the helm."

"Yeah, Ty, but there's no way Marx would have known that. They probably concluded that if I were hosting *Capitol Beat*, I wouldn't be investigating anything with *Front Burner*."

"That makes sense. What was the attack on Olivia, then? A backup plan?"

"Or a message. Or maybe the SOF somehow thought it was me. We may never know."

"This is great, guys, but none of it tells us who Machiavelli is. We need to get the guy pulling all the strings for any of this to matter," Victoria says.

I press my hands together in front of my face. There are no journals to find like there were in Brockhampton. There is no yellow brick road to follow on this one. Everything in my gut tells me it was Burgess or a member of his campaign staff. I just don't know how we can prove it.

"We've talked about this," Tyler says, breaking the silence. "Who had the most to gain if Standish took the fall for these incidents?"

"Luther Burgess, but that isn't evidence, it's an assumption. Other than Trotsky uttering his name, nothing is pointing at him being involved."

"And I wouldn't put too much stock in that," Victoria warns. "He shot himself in the head five seconds later. He easily could have been lying."

"It doesn't mean that he was."

"Then why quietly take out your own campaign contributor and make it look like a suicide? I'm sorry. It's a long leap to get there, guys. I'm not saying he isn't Machiavelli, but I doubt it. The pieces still don't fit. Even if it's Burgess or someone on his staff, we could never prove it in the time we have left."

"Would Engels know, Vic?"

"Maybe. I'll ask when I catch the bastard."

I get up and get a closer look at the whiteboard. There was a lot of planning and coordination. It also took a lot of something else.

"Who paid for the safehouse, Vic?"

"It was a rental," Seth interjects. "Paid in full for six months by an offshore company that's likely a cutout. We'll never know who's behind it."

"Where are you going with this, Tierra?" Victoria asks.

"I'm getting here. Do you know how much money is in that account you pulled from Trotsky?"

"The bank isn't going to hand over that information. Even if we do find out, it will take months. If you're trying to follow the money, it's a lost cause."

"I'm not following it. I'm using it to limit the pool of suspects. Whoever financed this operation has deep pockets. None of this was cheap."

"Okay, that only leaves campaigns, corporations, unions, political action committees, charities, and every wealthy individual in the world."

I usually appreciate Tyler's sarcasm. This is not one of those times.

"How many of those people or groups have a vested interest in destroying Alicia Standish?"

"Who knows? We can start with the Burgess campaign?"

"Campaigns are hard to hide money in. A political action committee, however…"

"It's dark money," Tyler finishes. "Almost untraceable."

"Let's assume that we're even remotely on the right track. How do we prove it?"

I exhale deeply. Victoria isn't going to like this one bit.

"We lay out the evidence in front of America and see if one of them confesses."

"Okay, that's crazy talk," Tyler says.

"How?"

"I have an idea for that," I say, needing to make a phone call. "It probably won't work, but it's worth the try."

CHAPTER EIGHTY-SIX

ANDREW LI

Burgess Temporary Campaign Headquarters
Manchester, New Hampshire

Their polling is way up, both in New Hampshire and nationally. Standish missed her opportunity to stop their momentum in Nevada by pulling up stakes and heading there. Instead, the governor has increased his lead to five points and is pulling away. With so much good news, Andrew can't figure out why their campaign manager has been in a dour mood all day. All he does is check his phones and take the occasional call.

"What is it this time?" Andrew asks, annoyed.

"Nothing."

"I'm sure it's nothing. You've been pissed off at the world all day. Spill."

"That was a booker at *Capitol Beat*. They want us to have another interview with Carl Brennan."

Andrew crinkles his brow. "They're leaving that tool on the air?"

"Apparently."

"Didn't they learn from the last time they had your father on?"

"It won't be just him. They're doing a segment about the entire campaign, so they're talking to the candidates and staff members from the top two Republican and Democratic candidates."

"That could be interesting. We should do it."

"Hasn't Brennan kissed our asses enough?" Isiah moans. He wants no part of this.

"The Standish team is also invited. I don't think he'll be so generous with his praise this time. That's why we need to go."

"Andrew, we're leading in the state. We don't need another interview to win. It can only hurt us."

Andrew closes his eyes. It's like talking to a brick wall sometimes. For someone so smart and well-educated, he doesn't get it.

"Isiah, it's a national audience. We've talked about this."

"It's not your call to make, it's mine. I say we skip it."

"You're right. You're the campaign manager. My job is to advise you and the candidate on how strategies and decisions affect our desired outcome, and I'm strongly advising you to take the interview. You don't want us to be the only campaign absent."

"I don't care."

"What's wrong with you, Isiah? You've been distracted all day, and now you're not thinking things through."

"Just because I disagree with you doesn't mean I didn't consider it. As for being distracted, it's nothing. There's just a lot going on. I'm taking your advice and focusing outside of New Hampshire. Happy?"

"Not really, no. It's a campaign for president of the United States. There's always a lot going on. You've never acted this way before."

"It's nothing, Andrew, drop it. And we're not doing the *Capitol Beat* interview. End of discussion."

"We need to do it, Isiah. The end of the discussion is when you agree with me."

"Agree to what?" Governor Burgess asks while entering the room. Both men fall silent. "Did I interrupt something?"

Both men stare at their shoes while the governor waits. Andrew finally looks at Isiah and then takes the lead in explaining the interview offered to Luther. He listens as both men plead their case. When they finish, he rubs his chin.

"It sounds to me like *Capitol Beat* wants to return to their non-partisan ways."

"That's my point," Isiah interjects. "It can't help us."

"No, but it can hurt us," Andrew argues. "I don't want the Republicans or the Standish campaign to have a full hour of calling us scared."

"We're not scared."

"It will look that way."

Isiah turns to his father. "Pops, this is a bad idea."

"You know, if your mother and I had ever had a second child, this is how I imagined the fights with your sibling," he says with a grin. "What's that quote you like to tell people? 'The more sand has escaped from the hourglass of our life, the clearer we should see through it.' Is that it?"

"Yeah."

"When you offered to run my campaign, I was the proudest man on Earth, not as a candidate, but as a father. I watched you go from diapers to college, and then grow into the man you are today. It's been a great journey and one that I like sharing with the world. I would love to appear on *Capitol Beat* with you next to me."

"Your place is in front of the cameras, not mine. I like standing off to the side."

"You always have. Even in high school, you preferred directing the performance to acting on stage."

Luther leans, reaches out and takes his son's hands in his own. Isiah looks up, and they meet each other's eyes.

"You shouldn't be in the wings anymore, son. You're old enough now to see the game. You know the game. Now it's time for you to go in front of the camera with me and play the game. Book the interview, and we face them together."

"All right. I will."

Luther nods and flashes a smile. "Good. It's settled. Oh, and we'll bring Andrew. He's done a lot for this campaign, and I want that acknowledged. Now, if you'll excuse me, our social media team wants me to do something stupid on Instagram."

"If you don't want me to appear, I'll understand. It could be a good moment with just you and your father."

"Are you advising that?" Isiah asks, scoffing as he crosses the room. "By the way, my father never watched me go from diapers to college. He was never around. First words…first steps…it didn't matter. He even missed my high school graduation. I joined this campaign because it was the only way I could ever get him to notice me. Not because I wanted to."

Isiah pounds the door open and leaves Andrew alone in the room. The admission adds to Andrew's understanding of their complicated relationship. He only hopes that's not the focus tomorrow night.

CHAPTER EIGHTY-SEVEN

TIERRA CAMPOS

Southern New Hampshire Hospital (SNHH)
Manchester, New Hampshire

Wilson is not a man who is content to be chained to a hospital bed. The nurses refused to let him wander around unsupervised, prompting his multiple attempts to do just that. Now they watch him like a hawk. It's stifling for him, and he's lost his sense of humor about it.

My initial call set the wheels in motion, and I arrived early so we could sit and talk. More than anything, the feeling of being back in the game is therapeutic. Wilson should be discharged soon, but time slows to a crawl waiting for that final order to get signed.

"Someone's in a good mood," the executive producer sarcastically pronounces as he enters the room with a couple of associate producers and Carl Brennan following right behind. "This is a strange place for a meeting, though."

"Blame the doctors for not releasing me," Wilson moans.

"You know that we have all sorts of videoconference technology: Zoom, Skype, Microsoft Teams. Please don't tell me that you're too old, and those are only gadgets the kids play with."

"Not at all. I just believe that there's no substitute for the real thing."

"What is she doing here?" Carl asks. It's a question and an accusation.

"It's good to see you too, Carl," I say in the fakest sweet tone I can muster.

"No offense, Tierra."

"Yeah, I'm sure."

"I'm doing fine, thank you for asking," Wilson interjects, proving a point of his own that puts Carl on the defensive. "Tierra is here because she has a proposition, and I thought it'd be best to discuss it as a group. I like the decision to bring the campaigns and their respective staff in on Monday night. For reasons I will explain later, I want Tierra to do the interview."

"What?"

"Carl, I appreciate you filling in for me on such short notice. I think the show needs to go in a different direction for Monday night. I will be back in the chair on Tuesday to cover the primary."

"Are you going to say anything?" he asks the executive producer.

It was a conversation that had to be coming, only the EP didn't have the balls. By any reasonable standard, Carl's performance on the two nights that he filled in was disastrous. I may not be a news media critic, but I am a professional journalist and an avid consumer of the news. I wouldn't watch the show again after what I witnessed.

"I'm afraid I echo Wilson's sentiments. We appreciate you giving us a hand, but a change is needed."

"This is ridiculous! I have already prepped the next two shows. You told me before I came up here that it would be at least five days. It's what the princess here got."

"Your overt sexism aside, we are cutting it short as is our prerogative. You will be compensated for the five days, regardless of whether you are on the air."

Wilson was far more polite than I would have been. I was never a princess at WWDC, and I'm sure as hell not one at *Front Burner*.

"So, that's it? I'm being dismissed? What does she have that I don't?"

"Journalistic integrity, for starters," I mumble.

"Oh, look at me. I'm Tierra Campos. I'm getting a Peabody Award because I'm a school shooting survivor who just stumbled onto a lie in Brockhampton. You think you're so special, don't you?"

"I think you're an entitled egomaniac with a million-dollar smile and two cents worth of talent. You've always thought more of yourself than you should."

"How dare you? I've been the face of WWDC for more than a decade."

"Yes, because Phillip Royce likes to have his ass kissed and you pucker up every time. Everybody there knows the truth, Carl. The news director gave you the job because he likes you, not because others do."

I glance over to see Wilson share his patented "I told you so" look with his EP. Carl showed his true colors, and nobody in this small hospital room liked what they saw. If my former colleague had any chance of landing this job, he just lost it. I think he realizes that, too.

"I don't need to listen to this. You just made an enemy out of me, Tierra."

"Carl, here's some breaking news for you: we were never friends."

"We'll get you a ticket for your flight back to Washington," Wilson says, nodding at one of the producers.

"You haven't heard the last from me, Miss Campos."

"I think everyone has, Carl."

Fresh out of ideas for any comebacks, he storms out of the room. One of the associate producers chases him, ostensibly to make his travel arrangements. Good riddance. The room was starting to smell like cheap cologne.

"That went well," Wilson says, beaming as his executive producer shakes his head.

"He's lucky I didn't say what I wanted to."

"That was you holding back?" the EP asks, offering a slight smile as he shakes his head. "Okay, well, not that I'm sorry to see him go, but I do need to find an anchor for tonight, so let's get on with this. What is this all about?"

Wilson looks at me and nods. I walk him through all of it, much like I did Austin. This time, I'm not being glared at and challenged on my conclusions. When the summary is complete, I give him a rundown of what I want to do. He wears the shock on his face like a Venetian mask.

"You have evidence of all this?" he asks, massaging his temples.

"Some of it. The other parts are conclusions based on assumptions."

"It's a bombshell revelation if she's right," Wilson concludes.

"And a debacle that we can't afford if she isn't."

"I'll take the blame if it goes south."

"That's a nice offer, Wilson, but I don't think we can take that risk."

"I understand your apprehension, but let's look at the stakes," the veteran anchor argues. "First, you need to recapture your viewers, and this will be great television. How many people changed the channel after Carl Brennan's train wreck? How many more did you lose Saturday? This will be a ratings juggernaut that will put *Capitol Beat* back on top."

"More importantly, voters in New Hampshire need this information before they vote on Tuesday," I say, picking up the argument. "There is no better show on television to deliver it to them. America can't find out on Wednesday that someone rigged the game, and regardless of who orchestrated it, that's what's happening here. The outrage will destroy our electoral process. The faith in them has already been shaken to the point of fracture. It's worth the risk."

"Unless you blow it."

"I won't."

"Yeah, Carl Brennan said the same thing."

"He was your choice, not mine," Wilson says, raising his voice. "Tierra is offering you a way out of this mess, and I support her."

The executive producer looks at the others in the room. A couple of them nod, while another one shrugs. They are sold on the idea's merits, if not avid supporters of it. Their silence is good enough. As Josh is fond of saying, "silence is consent."

"All right. I have two conditions: I get to see all the evidence you put together tomorrow before we go on air. It had better be compelling. If I get the feeling during show prep tomorrow that this is a witch hunt, I'll pull the plug, and you'll do the planned interview without question or deviation."

It's a fair offer, at least so far. The producers are assuming massive risk. If this goes bad, I'll be accused of trying to sway a primary election on its eve, and *Capitol Beat* may never recover. Wilson stares intently at me. The ball is in my court.

"Okay."

"Second, I need you to agree to host tonight's show."

"You're running out of excuses to say yes."

I smile, and he returns it. We shake hands, and he offers me a ride to the set down at Granite State University. It's not like Austin can tell me not to. Even if he did, I wouldn't listen. If *Front Burner* wants anything newsworthy from me in New Hampshire, they'll have to tune in.

CHAPTER EIGHTY-EIGHT

SENATOR ALICIA STANDISH

Standish for President Campaign Office
Nashua, New Hampshire

This may be the single hardest thing Alicia has ever done. The last hour has been spent pecking at the keyboard of her laptop and then hitting the backspace button until it all disappears. Everything she types sounds hollow and over-crafted. She isn't saying what she wants and needs to.

"Senator, we really need to sit down and talk about the Nevada events," Angela says, emerging in the doorway.

"Not now, Angela."

"Alicia, you've been distracted ever since Roger Ackerman was here. What did he say?"

"Roger gave me his perception of the truth."

"His or the president's?" Angela asks, frustrated over the lack of a real answer.

"There is no difference, I'm afraid. They share a brain. Let me get through this, Angela. We'll talk when I'm done."

Angela nods and leaves the office. The senator didn't hire her because she's an idiot. Her campaign manager already knows what's going on and just wants to hear the words. First, Alicia needs to finish typing them. She starts again, typing whatever pops into her mind.

A journey begins with a single step. Over a year ago, I took that step when I announced my candidacy for the presidency. Much has happened since that day. The wind cannot always be at your back, driving the ship through the seas. Through the tough times when the currents push against you, and the winds are unfavorable, you must cling to your values and the belief that your ideas are the best ones for the nation.

I still believe that, but life also means pausing to see if you can reach your destination. It is apparent to me that I no longer can, so I must suspend my candidacy in the hopes that a new one can someday rise from its ashes.

Failure is a fickle thing. We strive to avoid it in life, but without failing, we cannot fully realize the joys of success. I take considerable pride in knowing that I have inspired thousands and given them a voice. Ending this campaign is the most difficult of decisions. When anybody commits to a goal, their hope is that it materializes. Sometimes it isn't meant to be. Letting go of that goal, and the dream of realizing it is among the hardest things in life.

I exit this race with my head held high, immensely proud of my campaign staff, and honored at the votes I was able to earn. Knowing I let my supporters down is my biggest regret, and the loss of trust with America is a burden I will continue to shoulder.

My presidential campaign has failed, but the spirit of the ideas it represented is not dead. It is alive and thriving. The voters who subscribe to those ideals will not sit idly on their hands as the election passes them by. They stand ready to serve the candidate that earns their votes, and I will stand with them.

Alicia Marie Standish
United States Senator
Democratic Candidate for President

CHAPTER EIGHTY-NINE

TIERRA CAMPOS

Granite State University Remote Set
Durham, New Hampshire

1 Day to the New Hampshire Democratic Primary

It's been a hectic day. Victoria has divided her time between helping the FBI track down Ian Drucker and ensuring we have all the information we need. Since there is no official case file with the FBI on this, we have free rein to do what we need to. Sort of. She still wants the information handled carefully, and we can't divulge everything. She will have hell to pay for letting us divulge any of this, not that she seems to care.

Olivia is alert and doing much better. I explained why we haven't been there and what has happened since her crash. Despite everything she has been through, she can't wait to see what happens tonight. I can. Every moment we get closer to the broadcast, the butterflies increase the tempo of the waltz they're doing in my abdomen.

"Everything all set?" I ask Tyler, stepping into the makeshift control room installed adjacent to their temporary studio. He set up shop in here with the *Capitol Beat* crew because, outside of her, he knows the plan the best.

"We're ready to take your cues. I can see why you like working with these guys."

Tierra looks at the EP, who grins as he stares over the shoulder of the graphics guy. The engineers and associate producers in the room are top-notch and know it, but don't mind hearing the compliment either.

"Don't inflate their egos," I warn him in a hushed voice.

"I heard that," the EP says. "Do me a favor, Tierra? Whatever happens tonight, please don't go all Carl Brennan on me. My heart can't handle it."

"I couldn't be that bad if I tried," I say with a wink.

I walk over to Victoria, who's pacing nervously behind the cameras. The FBI has been searching all day for Agent Drucker without any luck. Now she feels that he could do something drastic like come here if he feels there is no escape.

"Anything?"

"No, it's quiet," she says. "We're ready for anything, though."

"Do you think he'll show up?"

"No, but I'm not going to gamble with your life or the lives of the top four presidential candidates in case I'm wrong. Are you nervous?"

"I passed nervous an hour ago. Now I'm terrified."

"If it helps, it doesn't show at all."

"Not really. You know, after the Summerville shooting, I spent my life trying to be invisible. I spent most of my career doing human interest stories at WWDC because I was unknown and liked it that way. When I complained about more responsibility and better stories, it was to tell myself that I tried without really wanting it to happen."

"And then you got the Ethan Harrington interview."

I nod. "I'm not invisible anymore, but part of me wishes I were. Wilson would hand me this show in a heartbeat. All I need to do is play the game. Instead, I'm doing this. It's either going to be epic or career suicide."

"Welcome to my world. For what it's worth, journalism is better with you in the limelight. That makes the world better. Whatever happens at that desk, I know you'll do great."

We watch the four candidates, along with their staff, sit in folding chairs opposite each other. One of the associate producers starts giving a pre-broadcast briefing. They will alternate parties, with the two frontrunners going first. After a coin flip, it was determined that the Democrats will bat leadoff. That's good. I would prefer to get this over with quickly.

I walk over to the group off to the side of the anchor desk. A producer introduces me, and handshakes are exchanged. It's the first time I've met any of them, save one. The candidates are warm, except for Senator Standish, who looks like she ate some bad sushi before driving over here. The campaign managers and advisors are also gracious, except for one.

"Why the change in the host?" Isiah Burgess asks. "We were expecting Carl Brennan."

"Carl Brennan was sent home due to creative differences. Tierra graciously agreed to host last night and tonight."

"Thank God," Governor Bradford mumbles. The Republican probably wasn't looking forward to locking horns with Carl again after their last interaction.

"What's the matter? Are you scared, Mr. Burgess?" Kristi Hylton, the charismatic and upcoming mayor of Nashville, Tennessee, asks. She has taken the number two spot on the Republican side but is still a longshot to overtake Bradford.

"Not at all. We had hoped that Wilson would be back for this."

"He wanted to be, Mr. Burgess," I say, smiling. "Unfortunately, his doctors don't care what he wants. They kept him one more night. I think they did it out of spite. He kept trying to interview the nurses."

The group chuckles, all imagining that he was probably doing just that. Wilson is known as a tough cookie in the Beltway. He likes straight answers and hates being babied. Nurses, God bless them, tend to be too nurturing at times.

"I'm happy to see you, Miss Campos. Your reputation precedes you. I'm looking forward to crossing swords with you," his father says, flashing an A-plus smile.

"I don't think it's that kind of interview, sir, but we can always schedule a title fight on another card in the future."

He nods. "I would look forward to that."

The briefing wraps up, and the candidates retreat to separate green rooms to wait for the show to start. I check my watch. With less than fifteen minutes until showtime, my reckoning is coming too quickly.

"Tierra, can I speak to you for a moment?"

I turn to see Senator Standish standing there without her campaign manager.

"Of course, Senator. What can I do for you?"

"This is awkward. I was expecting Carl Brennan as well. For reasons about to be made clear, I would have preferred to have him here."

The comment annoys me more than it offends. "Well, Carl's back in Washington, nursing his wounded pride. I'm what you get. Is that a problem?"

"No. I should have expected it considering… Well, I should get to the point. I don't want to make this known to anyone else, so I'm giving you a heads-up with the hopes that you'll keep it to yourself until the appropriate time."

"That sounds ominous."

"I plan to announce that I'm ending my campaign on your show tonight. That seems fitting, doesn't it?"

I can understand the awkwardness now. Since the failure of the Safe America Act and arrest of her allies in that effort, Senator Standish has held a grudge against me. She thought I torpedoed the bill and wasn't bashful about telling her supporters that in public and in private. Now, it looks like the short antagonistic history between the two of us is about to get longer.

"Is it a done deal?" I ask.

"The announcement goes out right before my segment. My team will make sure your producers get a copy before we start the interview."

I take a deep breath. This is an unexpected development. How can I say what I need to without my divulging anything of substance?

"Far be it from me to tell you how to run your campaign, ma'am, but let me offer a piece of advice: don't do anything until the first set of interviews is over."

"Why not?"

"Because you may have a change of heart."

Alicia studies my face. I'm dead serious about this, and I'm sure she recognizes that.

"Now who sounds ominous?"

"I'm afraid I can't say more. Make a call and hold off alerting the media. If you still want to end the campaign on the second segment, you can announce it yourself, and we'll take it from there."

"You sound convinced that I won't want to."

"You trusted me not to break this news prematurely. Trust me with this now. Good luck, Senator."

I walk over to the anchor desk, not sure if I just did the right thing. I have no time to think about it. Some last-minute powder is applied to my face, and a technician mics me up.

"What was that about?" Tyler asks after I put my earpiece in.

"Don't worry about it."

"The Burgess campaign is being shown to set. Remember to breathe, Tierra."

"Easy for you to say," I mumble as the three men take their seats and get their microphones.

"You look very calm for someone who has only done this a handful of times. Carl Brennan looked like he was about to piss himself when I was here," the governor says.

I force a smile. If he only knew how much of a mess I am. The final sound checks are performed, and the producer announces the one-minute time warning. The moment has finally come. I close my eyes and whisper a short prayer.

CHAPTER NINETY

SPECIAL AGENT VICTORIA LARSEN

Granite State University Remote Set
Durham, New Hampshire

Victoria watches her friend walk over to the assembled group of candidates. She admires Tierra's guts, unsure if she could do what Tierra is about to if the roles were reversed. Right now, she has other concerns.

The FBI has come up empty on their search for Ian. He hasn't returned to his hotel room and hasn't used his cell phone. They are closely watching the roads leading out of New Hampshire. If the man who calls himself "Engels" feels that there is no escape, he might try something drastic.

There is no reason to think that Ian would be bold enough to show up here. Something just makes Victoria believe that four top candidates in the same place are a tempting target for a desperate man. He knows he can't run forever amid a multi-state manhunt underway for him

"Anything?" Victoria asks the agent running communications in the command post. It's his responsibility to check in with the agents on the ground here regularly.

"Negative. Drucker isn't here."

"Damn. All right, keep everyone on their toes."

Victoria is stuffing her walkie back into her pocket when she hears something and turns to see a figure disappear into the corridor. She walks over and listens before drawing her gun and easing the door open. The shadowy figure disappears around a corner.

Adrenalin pumping, she hustles down the corridor, stopping to peer around the corner. The door to one of the meeting rooms in this student center closes. There are multiple ways out of every room here.

"What is he doing?" she mumbles.

The candidates are all in green rooms, but this isn't one of them. Is he hiding out until showtime? Would he dare to execute an assassination on live television? If he were willing to kill a man's wife and children in their home while they slept, he easily could do this.

"Possible target located in the southeast corridor leading away from the set. I need two agents to secure the exits from the room. I'm going in."

"Wait for backup, Agent Larsen."

"Negative. No time."

The agent protests and she turns her radio off. The last thing she needs is the distraction as she enters. She can hear a voice through the door. Ian may have help, although she can't imagine who it would be. She checks the doorknob, quietly pushing down on the handle. The room isn't locked.

She takes a deep breath and rechecks the grip on her weapon. She pushes down on the handle and bursts into the room.

"Freeze! Don't move an inch!"

The startled man drops his phone as he turns toward her in a reflex. She moves her finger to the trigger, her mental cue that there is a threat that needs to be neutralized. When her mind catches up with what her eyes are seeing, she removes the trigger finger and pulls her gun back.

"Jesus, Vic! You scared the shit out of me!" Agent Nishimoto says, with his hands raised to shoulder level.

"Takara? What the hell are you doing here?"

"I have an update on Ian. I came to tell you in person."

Victoria exhales and reaches for her radio, switching it on. "All clear. Return to stations."

"What happened?"

"False alarm," she says.

"You look a little on edge."

"It's been a long couple of days. If you had information, you could have called or walked up to me instead of sneaking around here."

Takara lowers his hands and picks up his cell, wiggling it in front of her. "I was. I got an update just as I was entering the studio and couldn't hear it in the commotion. I was looking for someplace quiet."

Victoria holsters her gun. "And?"

"We moved in on Ian's hotel room. He's gone. His hotel room was cleaned out in a hurry. A car was reported stolen from the parking lot and found abandoned thirty miles away when he switched vehicles. He's not in New Hampshire anymore. He likely isn't even in New England."

Victoria curses under her breath. She should relax knowing that there is no immediate danger, but it also means they are no closer to identifying the mysterious Machiavelli.

"Okay."

"There's one more thing. Ian kept his badge and gun."

"Yeah, that figures. Both of those could come in handy."

"He left his phone, too, but it was smashed to pieces, and the SIM card was missing. It's likely long gone as well."

"What direction was he traveling?"

"West, but who knows at this point? We've expanded the search range."

Victoria frowns. Once news of the takedown hit the air, he packed up and left. He wouldn't be stupid enough to get on a plane, so Logan is out. Trains are also risky. He couldn't have gone too far in a car but has up to an eight-hour head start. Depending on how many times he needed to change vehicles, he could be anywhere in the northeastern United States all the way down to Pennsylvania. It's too much ground to cover.

"What are the next steps?"

"We're going to play catch-up. If we can figure out what Drucker's driving, we can track him."

"Good luck with that," she moans, stroking her hair back.

"I'm sorry, Vic. About everything. I told you after Brockhampton that I wouldn't doubt you again and did. I screwed up."

"Don't worry about it, Agent Nishimoto. I'm getting used to it."

She pats him on the shoulder and leaves the room. Victoria knows that the comment hurt him. She doesn't care. She's tired of worrying about people's egos, feelings, and political standing. Fuller made a choice, and Takara chose to follow him. She will never earn their loyalty. Why should either one of them have hers?

Tierra is in her seat across from the Burgess campaign as Victoria arrives back in the studio. She glances over to see Victoria give her the thumbs down. Her friend nods, knowing the implication. Tierra is the best chance they have of figuring out who Machiavelli is, and she's going to have to do it the hard way.

CHAPTER NINETY-ONE

CAPITOL BEAT

Granite State University Remote Set
Durham, New Hampshire

"Good Evening. It is Monday, February seventh. Live from the beautiful campus of Granite State University in Durham, New Hampshire, I am Tierra Campos in for Wilson Newman and this…is…*Capitol Beat.*

"Thank you for joining us for this special primary eve edition of the show. Tonight, we have the candidates and members of their staff from the four leading campaigns in the race for the presidency. For the Republicans, it's Governor Colin Bradshaw of North Carolina and Nashville, Tennessee Mayor Krysti Hylton. Representing the Democrats are Governor Luther Burgess of Illinois and Senator Alicia Standish of Massachusetts.

"After a coin flip, we will start tonight's show with the Democrat frontrunner, and a man who has emerged from the shadows to be in the driver seat for the nomination. With Governor Burgess are his son and campaign manager Isiah, and senior political consultant Andrew Li. Gentlemen, thank you for joining us this evening."

"It's a pleasure being here."

"*Start slow, Tierra,*" Tyler advises through her earpiece.

"Governor, it has been a wild ride for you over the past month. I don't want to delve into the details about what happened here just yet, but how are you feeling going into tomorrow?"

"*Nice job,*" the EP says. "*Good and steady. You're a natural.*"

"*Shift to Isiah now. You know what to do,*" Tyler adds. Tierra misses the answer completely.

"Let me shift to your son if you don't mind," Tierra says, getting a nod in return. "Isiah, people are saying that the way you've guided Governor Burgess through this turbulent time has been brilliant. You've taken horrible circumstances and turned them to your favor. Some people would say that's almost Machiavellian."

Isiah beams. "Well, *The Prince* was a seminal work in its time."

"You're an admirer of Niccolò Machiavelli?"

"I am. I'm not sure modern society would approve of the methods he employed in the sixteenth century. Those are reserved for Brian Cooper and his SOF."

"*Let that slide, Tierra. Move on,*" Tyler advises.

"What about you, Mister Li? Are you a fan?"

"It's an interesting read for sure, but not applicable to today's governance style. I prefer John Locke."

"I think I agree with that. To Isiah's point, the tactics of the SOF were deplorable. Only we believe that the SOF who conducted the arsons and intimidation up here wasn't Brian Cooper's group."

"Of course they were," Governor Burgess says, sensing trouble.

"No, sir, they weren't. *Capitol Beat* has learned, through an exhaustive investigation by Victoria Larsen of the FBI, that the men had no interaction with Brian Cooper, his Standish Operations Force, or the Standish campaign in general. We know that the men were Army buddies stationed in Europe. SOF, in this case, did not stand for the Standish Operations Forces as the media has been reporting. It stands for Sword of Freedom, the words on the distinctive insignia for U.S. Army Europe."

"That's preposterous," Isiah says, his voice an octave higher. Andrew sits there impassively. I take a mental note of both reactions.

"My son is right, Miss Campos. Brian Cooper arranged this. The FBI found incriminating materials in his storage container."

"Come back to that later," Tyler says.

"Putting up the picture of the group. Focus on Sartre and the video."

"Yes, sir, they did. But that's not the whole story. The picture you see was taken of the four men of the SOF — obtained by *Front Burner* — during their military days. The third one from the left was Darko Lukić. He went by the name Sartre, which was also his hacker handle. He was killed in a raid at their safehouse in South Hooksett, just north of Manchester yesterday morning."

"I don't see how any of this is relevant," Isiah says.

"Please allow me to explain. The FBI sifted through months of video from the storage unit and couldn't determine how the evidence in question found its way in there after the arsons."

"The video was corrupted," Isiah says, getting visibly upset.

"It wasn't corrupted. It was encrypted. Encryption is an ingenious way to ensure it could never be read without destroying it. The FBI and New Hampshire State Police found the key after the raid. The NERCFL — the FBI's computer evidence team — managed to decrypt it. Here's a piece of the video."

"Rolling," the EP says.

Everyone in the studio watches the video roll in silence. There isn't a lot of context that Tierra needs to provide, and what she does can be explained later. They have a lot to get through, and the clock is running. The production team freezes the video and Tierra stares at her guests.

"Cooper must have told them to do it!" Isiah says, earning a disapproving look from his father.

"That may be true, Isiah, but why transfer the phony ballots from another unit? How did it get in there? It doesn't make any sense."

"I appreciate that there are some holes in the case, but why bring this up now, Miss Campos?" the governor asks.

"Go easy, Tierra. Get back to Sartre."

"Because Sartre arranged for Marx to encrypt the files and had the key. The FBI also learned that he was behind the theft of Vision 2030, the hacking of Senator Standish's Twitter account on the night of the debate, and the defacing of your website when you were in Iowa. He also wasn't a particularly good socialist. He was planning a ransomware attack against your campaign, but that's a story for another time."

"Brian Cooper arranged all that."

"Sir, I agree that Sartre was following orders. We also have reason to believe the mastermind behind it worked for your campaign."

It feels like a bomb just went off in the studio. Everyone without advance knowledge of what was about to happen is shocked and dazed, right down to the cameramen. Governor Burgess is the first to recover.

"That's a serious allegation."

"Slander is what it is," Isiah says, clenching his teeth.

"Marx and the cell phone," the EP says, as a picture comes back up on the screen with a circle around Marx.

"It is serious, sir, and not an allegation I make lightly. Let me walk you through it. The man on the right in this picture is Dennis Haskin. He went by the name Marx and was also killed during the raid at the safehouse. His burner phone was recovered and processed by the FBI. This graphic is a recreation of his call record. Isiah, do you recognize the number?"

"No, why would I?" The contempt in his voice is palpable.

"You wouldn't. It's another pre-paid cellular phone. If it's purchased with cash, it's untraceable to an owner. Do you use one?"

"Why would I need to do that?"

Tierra is about to move on to the *coup de grâce* when she notices Andrew's face. He has something to say and is nauseated over it. She tries to do this diplomatically.

"Mr. Li, do you own one?"

"I do. This is mine. We use it for sensitive calls to offices, donors, and key personnel. Isiah has one, too."

"Yes, I have a phone, but I never use it. I don't even have it with me."

Tierra watches Andrew close his eyes. Isiah is lying. All she needs to do is draw it out of him.

"Mr. Li?"

"Isiah, you left this at the office. I thought you might need it, so I brought it along. I didn't think of it until now."

He places the phone on the desk between them — another Holy Grail. Like the Lizzie Schwarzer journals, this could be the key to the whole interview.

"Ring it from your cell," Tyler says, excited.

"Let's see what happens when we dial the number. Andrew, can you read it off the screen?"

"3-1-4-1-0-1-1-9-7-4."

Tierra presses the green phone icon and wait for the longest three seconds of her life. If this phone doesn't ring, it will rank up there with the O.J. Simpson glove in all-time disasters. It's excruciating.

Then the phone sitting on the counter comes to life. Isiah glares at it before reaching over to silence it.

"This doesn't mean anything," Governor Burgess says.

"It does, sir, and you know it. The fourth man in the group is still at large, but the third man was apprehended by the Massachusetts State Police and the FBI trying to flee the country."

"It's a lie."

"His phone was also recovered. These guys didn't delete their messages. They sent coded messages to Marx, who, in turn, sent texts to this number. They coincide with various missions he completed.

"There must be a mistake."

"*Keep going, Tierra.*"

"The first was the supposed suicide of Dylan Spencer. That was a SOF operation. The second and third were the college student intimidations and the arsons at your campaign offices. The final one was the operation to frame Brian Cooper. The SOF was also involved in the attack at the Queen City Mall on Wilson Newman and a vehicular attack on a *Front Burner* employee."

"That doesn't mean—"

"He used the code name 'Machiavelli.'"

"I can't help you."

"You quote him all the time," Andrew says, sheepishly as the meaning of that word hits him.

"I didn't come here to answer your accusations."

"You're not here under subpoena, Isiah. You're free to leave any time you like. However, we're talking about the murders of Frederick Lamm and Dylan Spencer. These arsons, intimidations, and cyberwarfare were all designed to hijack the American election process. If you leave, our viewing audience of three million Americans will wonder why you did."

"*Three and a half, thank you very much,*" the EP says.

"A picture and some phone records? Is that all you have? These men were working for Brian Cooper!" Isiah practically shouts.

"*Hit them with the Marxist angle,*" Tyler says.

"Marx, Engels, Trotsky, and Sartre. The names the SOF used were of four famous philosophers. All of them were socialists. Do you really think they were working for Alicia Standish?"

"Listen to me. I will tell you plainly, right here, right now. I am not Machiavelli."

Isiah's denial is forceful and believable. Tierra has one arrow left in the quiver. This is the make it or break it moment during an interview that will define her career. She takes a deep breath.

"Then your father is."

"What?"

There is still a mountain of information to walk through, but they don't have time on this broadcast. She decides to skip to the most crucial piece.

"The third member of the group — the one you saw on video with Marx — was cornered at Logan International Airport but committed suicide before he could be taken into custody. Before Trotsky died, Special Agent Larsen asked him who he was working for. He gave the FBI and state police on the scene a single name: Burgess."

Tierra glances at the countdown clock. They're only minutes from the break. She needs to go for broke.

"He's a criminal working for Standish trying to blame us!"

"I think we both know that isn't the case, Isiah. If your father arranged this, the question is whether you knew about it."

"This is outrageous, Miss Campos!" the governor bellows.

"How long before the FBI learns that you paid these four men directly from one of your political action committees, Governor?"

"My father didn't arrange this!"

"I understand why you did it, sir. You were down in the polls in the Super Tuesday states and in Nevada and South Carolina. You needed to win in New Hampshire because nobody thought Standish could lose there. You cooked this up—"

"He did no such thing!"

"You needed to plague Senator Standish with scandals long enough to win the state. The killing of a major donor, intimidations, arsons, hacking, framing the campaign manager of your opposition… You found a group of dedicated socialists and put them to work targeting you when it was really designed to hurt her. That was the plan, wasn't it, Governor? And it worked. Standish tanked in the polls. That would give you—"

"No, no, no, my father would never do this!" Isiah practically shouts.

"That would give you a clear path to victory," Tierra finishes, and turns her attention to Isiah. "Your father is brilliant."

"He's not. I'm the architect of this campaign. I'm the brains behind it. My father would be languishing in last place in this race if it weren't for me. Vision 2030 is about equality, environmental responsibility, gender rights, and a system that has deprived too many Americans for too long. It's as much mine as it is his. Everything that has happened has been because of me. I will make him the president of the United States. To realize his dream. I am—"

"You are Machiavelli."

"*Ho-ly shit*," Tyler says into her ear after the words escape her mouth.

The set falls silent. The governor and Andrew both look at Isiah in disbelief. There is an axiom in the television world where dead air is the worst thing that can happen. She broke it. In this case, everyone watching is riveted to their television to see what he'll say next. She's happy to wait a few seconds longer as the tension rises.

"Mr. Burgess?"

"I don't think I should say anything more without an attorney present."

Tierra pushes the prepaid phone to him and leans back in her chair. It wasn't an admission, but it didn't need to be. Every news outlet in the country will be covering this interview. The truth will be out before the polls open. The FBI can sort the rest of this mess out.

"That's probably a good idea, Mr. Burgess. You should call him now. As you see, the FBI is here. We'll see if you still are after this break. We're all going to take a deep breath and be right back with Republican frontrunner Colin Bradford on this special New Hampshire campaign edition of *Capitol Beat.*"

CHAPTER NINETY-TWO

ANDREW LI

Burgess Hotel Suite
Manchester, New Hampshire

Day of the New Hampshire Democratic Primary

Luther just experienced the worst moment of his life. He arrived at Granite State University on top of the world and left campus a ruined man. Sometimes life changes that quickly. Nobody ever expects it until it happens to them.

The car ride back to the hotel was a quiet one. The governor stared out the window at the dark New Hampshire sky as the errant snowflake or two fell to Earth. He's been lost in his thoughts about his only son. Nothing is more damaging to the human psyche than betrayal. It's worse when it's family.

The staff is equally stunned. The clock reads after midnight now. Everyone in the suite is emotionally spent, including Andrew. The governor's entire inner circle is here, hoping to hear words of inspiration from their candidate. Luther doesn't know what to say to them.

"Thank you all for coming over tonight. It's late, so please, go get some rest. I need to speak with Andrew in private."

The staff begins filing out, and the governor's cell phone rings. It must be the fiftieth call he's received, and they all have been left unanswered.

"Is it true? Could Isiah have done this?"

Andrew presses his hands together and stares down at them. "I don't know. He has been acting weird since Iowa. I didn't think much of it until now. I don't know if he was involved or not, but he didn't deny it."

"Why would he do this?" It sounds like the governor is asking God, not his political consultant.

"Isiah knew that you needed New Hampshire to finish off Standish. He was determined to deliver it. He wanted to make you proud of him."

"By setting up the Standish campaign using intimidation and arson? Someone was murdered! What am I supposed to say to that man's family? The same family I embraced only a week ago."

"You tell them the truth. You explain that you had no idea."

"Do you think they'll believe that? Will anyone?"

Andrew falls silent. There has already been so much deception and misinformation in this race. People are numb, and the election is still eight months away. Nobody will dare believe his denials, contrition, or apologies. They will be passed off as political maneuvering because he got caught. Pundits will conclude that campaign managers don't do something so reckless without instructions that come from the candidates themselves. They will call for his head, and the people will join the mob. That's the nature of modern-day America.

"I'm sorry, sir, I just don't know," Andrew says as the governor's cell phone rings again.

"I need to make a statement. I know the staff has been working on one. It's…Why did you give Tierra Campos that phone?"

"I…It was the moment. I didn't know what else to do. I was blindsided."

"Yeah. Apparently, Miss Campos is good at that."

Andrew has been doing this for a long time. He's appeared on hundreds of programs at the regional and national levels. Never was he as scared as he was listening to her spell out the information. She would have made one hell of a prosecutor.

"Have you spoken to Isiah?" Luther asks.

"He's still with the FBI. It will likely be a while."

Isiah Burgess is going to be arrested. If not tonight, eventually.

"Make sure my son has a lawyer once charges are filed. I will pay for his defense under the condition that I never see or speak to him again."

The shocking request rattles Andrew. That is a harsh step for a father to take, even if it's understandable. The complicated relationship Isiah has with his father just got upgraded to toxic.

"Yes, sir."

The governor turns off the television and picks up a copy of Vision 2030. "All this work was for nothing. My entire life's work is all for nothing."

He tosses the copy in the trash, and Andrew stares at it. It's an image that sears into his brain and will become an indelible memory. Lives and families were destroyed tonight in front of a national audience.

"There's still a chance to salvage this," Andrew offers weakly.

"No, there isn't. People will feel betrayed. I know the feeling. Even if I manage to somehow win New Hampshire, there is no chance in Nevada or South Carolina. Even if my son is innocent, the damage is done."

"What do you need me to do?"

"Have my concession speech ready for tomorrow…well, today," Luther says, glancing at the clock. "Prepare the staff for a Wednesday videoconference. I will suspend the campaign then."

"I'm sorry, sir."

"So am I. I'd like to be alone for a while. Turn the lights off on your way out."

Andrew rises, and the two men shake hands. His service to Luther Burgess is over. He does as he's instructed, looking back as the room goes completely dark. Burgess sits alone, motionless on the sofa as his cell phone rings, and the door closes.

CHAPTER NINETY-THREE

SENATOR ALICIA STANDISH

Standish for President Campaign Office
Nashua, New Hampshire

Volunteers flooded Alicia's Nashua campaign office first thing and continued to stream in all morning and into the afternoon. Her campaign went from dead to the hottest ticket in town. Everybody wants to be a part of it, and Angela and the paid staff were quick to enroll them into the get-out-the-vote effort.

Her campaign manager hasn't been this upbeat since their early days in Iowa. Angela is relishing the departure of the black cloud plaguing them for a couple of weeks now. The constant hooting and hollering of the staff as they watch pundits discuss early exit polling on cable news is energizing. The atmosphere is festive, or at least was until thirty seconds ago, when the room suddenly fell dead silent.

Curious as to what's going on, Alicia leaves her office and stops at the main work area. The sight is the last one she expected to see. Brian Cooper stands in the middle of the room with every pair of eyes glued on him. Nobody is saying a word.

"Hello, Senator."

"Brian? Did you come right over here from the prison?"

He scoffs. "I was released days ago. The charges were dropped today. You know, it was nice of you to check in on me…oh, that's right, you couldn't be bothered. You don't notice anything that doesn't directly affect you."

"Why don't we talk in my office?"

"No, I think talking right here is fine. I don't think anything left to be said between us needs to be in private. These people are all working for you. They should hear what I have to say."

Alicia shifts her weight and looks down. She wants to ask him to leave but won't. Before the age of cell phones, she could have had a pair of burly men escort him out. Unfortunately, video is the great equalizer. The clip would circle the world in minutes, and she can't afford to stall her momentum. Besides, Brian has earned the right to have this conversation.

"I know you're angry. You have every right to be. The FBI jumped to conclusions. I was in a bad position, so I jumped to them, too. What would you have done differently if our roles were reversed?"

"I don't blame you for firing me," he says, causing Alicia to perk up a little. "It was the only political move you could make. But here's the problem: you never bothered to ask me if the charges were true. You *assumed* they were."

"What would you have said had I asked?"

"The truth. I told you that I wasn't involved in the beginning, but that wasn't good enough. Truth is subjective, but facts are not. You could have made that determination for yourself had you reached out to me. It was a slap in the face. I dedicated three years of my life working to make you successful. Still, you couldn't be bothered."

"It wasn't like that," Alicia argues.

"Yes, it was. You were angry because you thought I not only was capable of this but actually did it. You hated what it did to you and your campaign. Never once did you consider the impact it was having on me."

"You're right. It's true. I was angry. We've worked so hard to get to this point—"

"I know. I was one of the ones working hard for you."

"You were. And I truly am sorry for that. For everything."

"No, you're not. You're only saying that because you'll win New Hampshire today and probably the nomination in the next few weeks. You should send Tierra Campos a fruit basket or something. She saved your ass last night."

"I don't know what more there is to say," Alicia murmurs.

She meant her apology. If they could ever relive the week, Alicia would still be angry with Brian but would reach out to him. She regrets that and will need to live with the consequences. Brian isn't here for any of that. Whatever he wants, it's not an apology.

"Don't say anything, then. Just listen. I had a lot of time to think this past week and finally figured you out. You have a great many faults, Senator, and lack of trust in anyone is one of them. But that only scratches the surface. Your biggest problem is that you're not doing this for America or to make people's lives better. You're not even doing it for yourself like so many politicians are. No, this campaign is for your parents. Everything you do is about honoring their memory, just like with the Safe America Act. That's the wrong reason to want the job you're running for."

"That's not true," Alicia says through clenched teeth.

"It is true. It's why you always have that old picture of them wherever you go."

"I find strength in wanting to fulfill a promise to them. The picture helps summon that strength. My parents are not the reason I'm running."

"Prove me wrong, then. Why are you? And don't give me the cheesy lines you recite at your campaign speeches. Everyone in this race claims to want to make America a better place. Why are *you* running?"

The force of the question throws her off-guard. She has a canned response, just as Brian said. She's uttered the words hundreds of times, except now. The answer wouldn't be good enough for him. Now she isn't sure it's good enough for her.

"Don't bother answering the question. I won't force you to lie to me and these people again. I once told Tierra Campos that I was a good judge of character. Up until this past week, I believed that to be an absolute truth. Now I know it isn't. Everything I thought I knew about you was wrong."

"I made a mistake, Brian. One that I deeply regret. I want you to forgive me and move past this as my new campaign advisor. Michael Ross was fired. I want you to take his position so that we can rebuild the relationship we once had."

Brian lets out a small laugh and shakes his head in disbelief. "Let me guess. You didn't trust him either, right?"

"It's far more complicated than that. I want you to be Michael's replacement. We're going to win the nomination. I couldn't imagine a better person to help lead me there. It will give us time to make things right. What do you say? Will you rejoin the team?"

He stares at her for a long moment and grins. "Not a chance in hell."

Volunteers and staff grumble to each other before the room returns to dead silence. Brian is wounded and feels abandoned by her. She could use him on the team but figured he would decline. It was worth the shot, as embarrassing as it was.

"I'm not going to be your puppet any longer. My days of being swooned by your slick words and subjugated by your misguided ambition are over. Instead, I'm going to work with anybody and everybody to ensure you never sit in the Oval Office. You're not worthy of the job, and I will spend every breath ensuring that Americans know that."

"That's a little vindictive, isn't it?" Alicia asks.

"Yes."

Brian turns and leaves the office without another word. The staff and volunteers turn to her. There is nothing to say or do other than get back to work. There is a primary to win today. She has the rest of the year to deal with her newest political enemy.

CHAPTER NINETY-FOUR

CAPITOL BEAT

Wilson inhales deeply through his nose and exhales slowly after the producer gives the thirty-second warning. He may have had a decades-long career and be ready for retirement, but if this experience has taught him anything, it's that he may miss it more than he can bear. That's a concern for another time. Right now, he's thrilled to be back in his chair.

"Good evening, it is Tuesday, February eighth. From the stunning campus of Granite State University in Durham, New Hampshire, I am Wilson Newman, and this…is…*Capitol Beat.*"

The opening to the show plays, and it's music to his ears. His live studio audience consisting of a couple of dozen students applauds as the lights come back up.

"Thank you for tuning in to our expanded New Hampshire Primary edition this evening. I'd like to start the show on a personal note. The outpouring of support, love, and prayers I have received over the past few days touches my heart and soul in a way that words can never convey. Thank you so much for all of them.

"The past twenty-four hours may be the most turbulent ever seen in American political history. The fallout from last evening's revelation that Alicia Standish and her campaign were framed for the attacks on her opponent, Governor Luther Burgess of Illinois, has rocked the nation. As New Hampshire residents go to the polls, they have a crucial decision to make with little time to reflect on it.

"The FBI has questioned Isiah Burgess, the governor's son and campaign manager, about his involvement in the scandal now known as 'Machiavelligate.' His failure to deny the allegations against him and the evidence presented by Tierra Campos in an interview on this show last night have confounded voters in this small state.

"To add to the drama is the compelling video evidence of a Marxist group known as the Sword of Freedom. It clearly shows them planting the phony ballots, spray paint, and gasoline cans used in the campaign office arsons a week ago in the Standish campaign's unit. The exculpatory evidence has resulted in charges against Standish New Hampshire campaign chairman Brian Cooper being dropped."

Wilson is still amazed that Tierra and her friend in the FBI managed to put all that together in the time they did. It was incredible investigative work and outstanding reporting. It's also maybe the ballsiest thing he's ever seen a journalist do.

"The result in the exit polling conducted by multiple organizations has been dramatic. The polls have just closed here in New Hampshire, but the result looks to be a decisive victory for Senator Standish, whose campaign was all but finished only twenty-four hours ago.

"Tierra Campos of *Front Burner,* with the cooperation of federal and state law enforcement, has done the nation a great service. She has helped people understand the allegations against Isiah Burgess and the exculpatory evidence absolving Senator Alicia Standish of responsibility. Her article published online this afternoon spelled out the scandal in detail, walking the people of New Hampshire and from across the country through a complex set of circumstances.

"The Campos article was pure journalism. Absent were conjecture, speculation, and opinion. It was a brilliant recount of the facts, leaving Americans, and the good people of New Hampshire, to decide what to do with them. In that respect, it may be more significant than the ones she wrote about Brockhampton last summer.

"To help break down this developing story tonight, we have Lisa Ehler, the attorney general of the United States with us from Washington. We also have spokesmen from the FBI and New Hampshire State Police to provide us law enforcement perspectives, live reports from Southern New Hampshire Hospital on the condition of the wounded troopers, news from both Republican and Democrat campaigns, and from Burgess and Standish voters themselves. We will also host panel discussions on the events that transpired this week, the impact on the primaries looking ahead to Super Tuesday, and what this means for the nation.

"We'll be back with the attorney general on this special broadcast of *Capitol Beat* from Granite State University in New Hampshire after this short break."

TWO WEEKS LATER

CHAPTER NINETY-FIVE

SENATOR ALICIA STANDISH

The big SUV pulls up, and Alicia steps onto the sidewalk. She buttons her wool overcoat as men in suits flank her. The senator and Democratic frontrunner for the presidency is happy to have Secret Service protection now. She's about to walk into the lion's den for this meeting.

Fortunately, she doesn't have to wander in too deep. The receptionist calls Tierra and explains who is visiting. The journalist comes down dressed in jeans and a sweater while carrying her Canada Goose coat. Professional attire is not a thing at *Front Burner*.

"Senator Standish. This is unexpected," Tierra says.

"I apologize for just dropping by. Is this a good time?"

"As good as any."

"You look tan," Alicia says, noticing her darker skin and lighter lines on her temples from the arms of her sunglasses.

"I took some time off not long after New Hampshire. It was needed."

"I'm sure. Please don't say you went to St. Kitts," Alicia says with a smile.

Tierra grins. Despite everything she went through with Austin up in New Hampshire, *Front Burner* asked her to write her articles after all. Unfortunately for them, most of the words she typed were a rehash of what Americans learned on *Capitol Beat*. They missed the scoop that their own employee had.

Like her Brockhampton story, they were widely read. One of the few original parts of the story was what happened to Trotsky at Logan International Airport. The Massachusetts State Police and the FBI, namely Victoria, were gracious in their recount of the event. Trotsky's plans to flee to the U.S. Virgin Islands made it into that story.

"Congratulations on your victory in the Nevada primary."

"Thank you. It was hard-fought."

"Shouldn't you still be campaigning in South Carolina right now?"

"We're heading there later today after I interview a replacement for Michael Ross. Several open positions need to be filled."

Not that the senator needs to campaign down there. The polling advantage has opened to almost double digits since the revelations in New Hampshire and her victory in Nevada. A couple of candidates have already fled the state and are banking on picking off a couple of wins during Super Tuesday. Senator Standish has gone from frontrunner to pariah to presumptive nominee in less than a month. That's one hell of a roller coaster ride.

"I know it's cold out, but you have your coat with you. Are you interested in taking a walk?"

"I was heading out for an early lunch anyway. Lead the way, Senator."

The two women leave the *Front Burner* lobby and turn left down the sidewalk. It's not bitterly cold outside, but the steady breeze does add to the wind chill. Tierra checks behind them to see the Secret Service trailing a few meters away. It's one reason she could never be a top politician.

"I bet you're wondering why I'm here."

"The thought crossed my mind, yes."

"I wanted to thank you for what you did in New Hampshire."

"No need, Senator. I was doing my job," Tierra says.

Now it's Alicia's turn to grin. "We both know that isn't true. Nobody was willing to chase down the truth in that story. The police, the FBI, and the media were all asleep at the wheel. Everyone accepted that it was Brian without question."

"That includes you, Senator."

Tierra didn't level an accusation at her. It was a factual statement, which is why it hurts so bad. She's right, and Alicia knows it. She harbored a lot of distrust of Brian after the failure of the Safe America Act. Worse, Brian struck a nerve with her the other night. Everything he said was right.

"Yes, I'm guilty of it as well. You saved my campaign. I owe you."

"You don't owe me anything. You do owe Brian Cooper an apology."

"I offered one. I'm afraid that he didn't accept it." Tierra doesn't say anything, causing Alicia to look out the corner of her eye. "Have you talked to him?"

"Is that why you're really here? To pump me for information about your former staff?"

"No, it was just a simple question. You're a journalist. Sometimes people ask things without an agenda," Alicia argues.

"Not in this town they don't. To answer it, no, I haven't spoken with Brian."

Alicia stops, causing Tierra to turn. "I detect a little hostility in your voice. Is Washington changing you?"

"I've been working here a while, Senator. I'm already jaded. As for your first observation, you need to understand something. You were the victim of a man who employed all manner of devious measures to gain his father an advantage. Despite that, I'm not convinced that you're the good guy in this."

"Fair enough. You know, I've had to do a lot of soul searching. Do you want to know what I came up with?"

"Are we on or off the record?"

"I don't care. I was running for all the wrong reasons. As you know, my parents both died tragically when I was much younger. Everything I did as a senator and as a candidate for president was for them. It was never about the people."

"And I'm to magically believe that your cause is a noble one now?"

"No. I'm asking you to keep an open mind while I demonstrate it."

"Okay. I will."

Tierra isn't convinced. National politics is a nasty business. The men and women playing at this level don't do it for honorable reasons like the benefit of the people. It's the reason we have the same problems with race, poverty, anti-Semitism, crime, and a host of other issues for generations. This is about power and money, plain and simple. If Tierra has learned anything, it's that the media, including *Front Burner*, are following their lead.

"Let me ask you a question. Do you think I'll win?"

"I'm not a pundit."

"I know, but you are astute. I'm asking your opinion, not the face you put on for the public."

"Too many journalists pretend to be non-partisan when they aren't. They take sides and are unabashed about telling people that their opinion is the one that matters. People listen to them call politics war and one side or the other the enemy. It's dangerous to think that way. People get doxxed, attacked, and destroyed. Answering your question leads to that path."

"What do you want to see in the next election?"

"One based on actual policy, not snarky personal attacks. I don't care who wins or loses. I care that it's for the right reasons. To ensure they are, I'll ask tough questions and demand honest answers. Then I'll let the people decide for themselves."

"Are you staying at *Front Burner*?"

Tierra doesn't answer that either. It's none of Senator Standish's business. Even if it were, she couldn't answer. She hasn't made up her mind yet. Well, yes, she has but hasn't processed the ramifications of the decision.

"You'll find out when everyone else does."

"I understand. For what it's worth, I hope you take the *Capitol Beat* job when Wilson retires. I wish you the best of luck, Tierra."

"Thank you, Senator. To you as well."

* * *

The man checks the LED screen on his camera. He could shoot the moon with the telephoto lens he has on this thing. The picture of Tierra Campos shaking hands with Senator Alicia Standish was precisely what he was looking for. It doesn't matter that most of this conversation looked unfriendly as hell. This is the image that people will see.

The women part company, and he knows today's assignment is complete. He packs up his gear and heads for a coffee shop to warm up. His Southern California upbringing makes this wintry weather inhospitable to him.

He finds a quiet spot in the corner and pulls out his phone. The technophile finds the cheap burner phone annoying to carry, never mind use. Still, he's not getting paid to complain.

"Hey," the voice says when the call connects.

"I should have charged you double for the shot I just got."

"If it's worth it, I'll pay double for it."

That's what he wants to hear. This isn't personal. He couldn't give a damn about Tierra Campos or Alicia Standish. For him, it's business, and cash is its lifeblood. His employer has a far different opinion.

"Get me the image. Do you have anything else?"

"No, not yet. This isn't enough?"

The man on the other end of the line laughs. "No, my friend. This is only the beginning. It will end when I've ruined Tierra Campos."

CHAPTER NINETY-SIX

ANDREW LI

Standish for President National Campaign Headquarters
Washington, D.C.

In comparison to regional offices, a national campaign headquarters is much larger but less frantic. Regional and local offices have a lot of volunteers scurrying around preparing to canvass neighborhoods and call residents as part of the get-out-the-vote campaigns. They can be energetic and hectic.

The national office focuses on fundraising, strategic partnerships, endorsements, and media relations. The staff here are paid and more methodical in their work. If the candidate is the brain of the operation, then the regional offices are the limbs, and this is its beating heart.

"She's ready for you, Mr. Li," the admin announces from the entrance to the waiting area.

Andrew stands and fastens the top button of his suit jacket. It's been two weeks since Luther Burgess folded his campaign. The paid staff scattered to the wind in search of other candidates to latch onto. He only had one in mind. Andrew is hoping this provides him an opportunity to get back to work.

"Andrew, we're pleased to see you. Have a seat," Angela says, gesturing to one of the conference room chairs after he's shown into the conference room.

"Thank you."

"This feels a little like déjà vu."

"It does. You didn't have this office during my first interview, Senator. You also weren't the presumptive nominee of the Democrat Party."

"*Presumptive* being the important word," Alicia says. "I haven't won anything yet, and there is a long road ahead."

Andrew smiles. He interviewed for this job after the Safe America Act cratered, making her bid for the Oval Office far more treacherous. He thought the position was his, but it went to Michael Ross. Andrew went on to secure a job with Luther Burgess, but his heart was always here. He brooded over the loss until he found a way to make it right. He couldn't have planned it any better than he did.

"As I'm sure you already know, we were forced to let Michael Ross go."

"I heard."

"This is the ideal time for you to say, 'I told you so.' You disagreed rather adamantly with the choice if memory serves."

"I did. Out of curiosity, what prompted his departure? If you don't mind me asking."

Angela glances over at Alicia, who folds her hands on the table and smiles. "His advice was less than stellar."

"I'd say."

"Michael's tactics were good for a frontrunner, but not someone in the middle of a battle. It was better to find that out when we did," Angela concludes.

"Whereas you took a devout socialist running way behind in the polls and brought him up to frontrunner status," Senator Standish adds.

"I wish I could take all the credit. Some of that was the…circumstances involved."

"Yes, some of it, but the governor was already on the rise before all that happened. How did you like working for the Burgess campaign?"

"Luther is a good man, but I never subscribed to his ideology. His heart is in the right place, but Vision 2030 flew in the face of reality. Americans would never have embraced it in the numbers he needed to win in the general election."

Angela leans back in her chair. Andrew already knows what she is thinking and has an answer to her next question already prepared.

"You think that he was too extreme?"

"Elections are won in the center. You know as well as I do, Angela. One third will always vote for their respective parties. Get out the vote issues aside, it's the middle third that wins or loses an election. Governor Burgess would have alienated moderates and gotten crushed with independents. If the GOP played their cards right, they would have won in an electoral landslide against him."

"And me? How do you think I would win?"

"Simple. Don't cater to the radicals on the left."

"We need them to show up," Angela argues.

"And they will if Senator Standish positions the race correctly. You need to swoon the middle with policy. The far left will think you're too moderate, so you make this a referendum on your opponent. Their policies will be despised. Make the extreme left vote against them, not necessarily for you. In the meantime, you win over the moderates in the swing states and pick a ball gown for Inauguration Day."

"You want me to make voters choose between the lesser of two evils?"

"In our polarized political climate, the American people have gotten used to that. Everybody has an issue they care about. The problem with most politicians is they try to be everything to everybody. Don't play that game. If someone doesn't like your positions, make your opponent's even less appealing."

"It's not the way I want to win," Alicia says.

Andrew stops for a moment. This is the same path he traveled down the first time he interviewed with these women. It ended in disaster. He's tempted to tell them what they want to hear, but he knows he's right. He's proven it.

"You learned that lesson with the Safe America Act, Senator. Some thought it was too extreme, while others thought it didn't go far enough. You asked me here because you saw what I did with Luther Burgess. He was a far-left socialist who was on track to win the first two races. He embraced every measure in Vision 2030. People like a politician with ideas and convictions, even if they disagree with them. Your ideas need to be centrist to win."

Alicia leans back in her chair. Andrew is right. She was stuck in the middle of the road and hit by traffic in both directions trying to pass her gun control legislation. And Luther may be a lot of things, but indecisive and noncommittal aren't two of them.

"Andrew, did you know what Isiah was up to?" Angela asks.

"No, I had no idea. I've had two weeks to reflect on what happened. It all makes sense in hindsight, but I didn't recognize it at the time."

"Then, you thought Brian Cooper was behind the SOF?"

"I know Brian. He's competitive and likes to win. I thought he either lost control or overplayed his hand."

"In your mind, he was capable of that?"

"Brian was an astute political operative — one of the best in this town. I thought he was taking things too far. The truth is, I never considered any alternatives. In my wildest dreams, I couldn't have imagined Isiah cooking that up."

"You know that he's denying everything."

Andrew grimaces. "I would expect nothing less from an accused man. The truth is, I'm ashamed to have been a part of it. To your earlier point, I thought we were seizing on opportunities. I was turning lemons into lemonade, so to speak. I had no idea that Isiah was orchestrating the whole thing."

The two women share a look with each other. Finally, Angela nods. This is the moment Andrew has been waiting for. It's what he's also been working for.

"Would you accept a position with us if we offered it?" Senator Standish asks.

"This was my first choice for a reason."

"I want you to be the senior political advisor for my campaign. You would report directly to me but would be expected to work closely with Angela. Let me ask you one final question: if you accept the role, what would your first piece of advice to me be?"

"You have the best ideas for America. The failure of the Safe America Act shackled you, but that's no longer the case. Isiah handed you a golden opportunity to erase that unfortunate legacy. Seize it."

"How?"

Andrew smiles. It's been a while since he's had a chance to do that.

"Let's sign a contract, and then I'll tell you."

CHAPTER NINETY-SEVEN

SPECIAL AGENT VICTORIA LARSEN

Senate Hearing Room 216 – Hart Senate Office Building
Washington, D.C.

Room 216 of the Hart Senate Office Building is a small room with a rich history. It has hosted the confirmation hearings of several Supreme Court justices, witnessed members of the 9/11 Commission analyze the deadly terror attacks on the World Trade Center and Pentagon, and is where James Comey testified on Russian interference in the 2016 election. Now it is about to hear from Victoria Larsen.

"I call this hearing to order," the chairman says, rapping his gavel. "Before we begin, I would like to remind our members and witnesses that this is an open hearing. I recognize that what happened in the lead-up to the New Hampshire Democratic Primary is a sensitive issue for politicians and the public. However, this committee was convened to explore how the primary was manipulated, to avoid its future recurrence. To that end, it is critical to ensure public access to credible facts and not have them rely on unsubstantiated media reports."

"If I may have the floor, Mr. Chairman," one of the Democrats says into his microphone.

"No, sir, you may not. You will have your time as was previously agreed."

The ranking minority member doesn't like that answer. There is an adage that the only constants in the world are death and taxes. It isn't true. They forgot partisan politics.

"To our guests in the audience, please accept my heartfelt welcome. The members of this committee appreciate your being here. We also ask that you always observe proper decorum. Disruptions will not be tolerated. I now recognize myself for five minutes for the purpose of an opening statement."

"Mr. Chairman, we object to the public nature of this hearing," the ranking Democrat says.

"You would rather wait until after the election, Senator?"

"This is nothing more than a Republican attempt to smear Democrats in the middle of a primary."

"A political operative attempted to manipulate the voting process that could have altered the outcome of a primary and impact a presidential election. Senator, are you saying that if the roles were reversed, you wouldn't demand hearings?"

"We would search for answers, not use it for political gain," another member of the committee chimes in.

"There is plenty of evidence in the last decade to the contrary. Do you need a reminder of that?"

The room erupts into a combination of murmurs, laughs, and side conversations that Victoria doesn't participate in. She's not here for political theater, despite the politicians' desire to make it that. She has a story to tell, both about what happened in Manchester and the FBI's complete mishandling of the case.

She's not here to settle scores, although that is a likely outcome. Her career is over, having not administratively been taken off suspension for her insubordination. She saved Lance Fuller's hide, and he is still trying to fry her. Good. Two can play that game, only hers will be played in full view of the American public.

"What happened in New Hampshire affected Democrats."

"It was an intrusion in the American political process. The targeted party notwithstanding, it affects all of us. The American people have a right to know what happened."

"Yes, they do, but not to listen to hours of posturing from Republicans looking to capitalize on the unfortunate incident."

"Senator, I have indulged your objections despite you being out of order. We will proceed with the hearing," the chairman says.

"I move to adjourn," one of the other Democrats offers.

Victoria shakes her head. No wonder nothing ever gets done in Washington. They are too busy playing games with each other to accomplish anything useful.

"You don't have the floor to make such a motion, and even if you did, it wouldn't pass. Millions of people are tuning in to this, and we have a distinguished agent with the Federal Bureau of Investigation prepared to testify. Do you really want to waste their time?"

The man looks at the cameras. The answer is yes, he would love to waste their time, but he can't say that.

"I can wait for your answer, Senator, but it won't be forever."

"Mr. Chairman, by all means, please proceed."

"Thank you for your permission, Senator. The committee calls Special Agent Victoria Larsen."

Cameras click, and all eyes in the small room lock onto Victoria as she rises and straightens her jacket. The attention is unnerving. She makes her way down the center aisle to the table as stoically as she can. She takes her seat, immediately reaching for the pitcher of water to pour a glass. Her mouth is parched without speaking a word.

"Special Agent Larsen, I appreciate your appearance before the committee today. I would also like to acknowledge your commitment to learning the truth about what happened in Manchester before the primary. You are a credit to the FBI."

"Thank you, Senator."

He should tell her boss that. Lance Fuller doesn't hold that opinion.

"This committee is looking forward to a candid discussion today. Please feel free to offer your opinions and perspectives without fear of repercussions. Do you understand?"

"Yes, Senator, I do."

"Very well, please rise for the oath."

Witnesses typically take an oath at the discretion of the committee chair during hearings. Like the one used in a court of law, the oath is required during confirmation and investigative hearings. This falls into the latter category.

Victoria came here today resolved to not hold anything back. She will not embellish the truth, but she will not shield others from it. In her mind, Takara and Lance didn't lift a finger to help her. Diego and Seth were the heroes, and one of those men was shot because of it.

America needs to understand that its premier law enforcement agency was working against her. They need to know that it is filled with good men and women who are being handcuffed by a leadership that is more concerned about their positions than justice. It cannot go on this way, and hopefully, this leads to change. Victoria focuses and recites the words she was asked to repeat:

"I solemnly affirm that the evidence that I shall give shall be the truth, the whole truth, and nothing but the truth, so help me God."

CHAPTER NINETY-EIGHT

TIERRA CAMPOS

Front Burner Washington Office
Washington, D.C.

Wow, I have more crap here than I thought I did. I put some more of my personal effects in the second cardboard box. I may need three of them despite only working here for nine months. Where did all this stuff come from?

I didn't expect things to end this way. I suppose nobody ever does. I thought when the day came to leave *Front Burner*, it would be an emotional day filled with tears and surrounded by good friends. Instead, it's just Tyler and Olivia, both of whom look like they're attending a wake. The three of us are joined by Austin. To avoid an inevitable confrontation, they move off when he stands next to my desk.

"Have you ever thought two people could travel such a long road in only a few months?"

"Is that code for something?" I ask, not having the emotional bandwidth to spar with him today. We've done enough of that for two lifetimes.

"No, it's the start of an apology."

"It's usually simpler just to say, 'I'm sorry.'"

"I don't do anything the easy way. You know that."

Those words were the last ones I expected to hear when I walked in today. Things have been frosty enough since I returned from the Caribbean to fade my tan. Apologies are nice, but the rift between us cannot be spanned with one. It makes this awkward. Fortunately, we both get a reprieve.

"Tierra," the managing editor of *Front Burner* says as he approaches us. "Will you join us in the conference room?"

He shares an ice-cold look with Austin. I can only bet what the conversations were like between the two of them. When I wrote the articles following the *Capitol Beat* interview, it was at the request of the managing editor, not Austin. He couldn't have been pleased that the leader of our team allowed them to get scooped when I had the goods all along. This impromptu meeting also might explain his impromptu apology.

I follow the big shot editor into the conference room to find *Front Burner's* leadership team gathered around the table. The last time I was in here with these people, it was a celebration. This looks like a funeral.

"Ladies, gentlemen," I say as I'm offered a seat.

"Tierra, first, we wanted to let you know that you did an outstanding job in Manchester. Your *Front Burner* articles surpassed what you wrote on Brockhampton in terms of readership."

"It's impressive considering the news was broken on television," one of the directors says.

"We spoke to Olivia and Tyler while you were on vacation. We also talked to Austin, Madison, and Jerome. We have an idea of what happened up in New Hampshire and why."

I don't say anything. What can I add? Whatever they were told, I doubt they have the full story. I'm leaving, so there's no need for me to straighten them out. I'm sure they sense that.

"We'll cut to the chase. I know you put in your notice. There isn't a single person at this table that wants to see you go. We want to know what it will take to get you to stay."

"What?"

"We want you to remain at *Front Burner*, Tierra. You may leave anyway, but we are going to fight for you."

"Does this have to do with my possibly winning a Peabody?"

The award still hasn't been given, but the world would be shocked if I didn't get one. I'm prouder of the accomplishment than the accolades, but they mean something in these circles. I may end up with another after what just happened in Manchester. It gives an online news site like *Front Burner* a lot of legitimacy.

"It's nice to have someone on staff with one, but no, it's not the predominant reason," the managing editor says.

"It's about your talent, Tierra. You've been with us a year and broken two of the biggest political stories in a decade. We don't want you reporting for anyone else. Period."

"Name your price. We'll double your salary if that's what it takes to keep you."

That has a nice ring to it. I am already well-compensated, so a raise of that magnitude would be ridiculous. As lovely as it would be, it's not the driving force behind my life.

"It's not about the money. I joined *Front Burner* because I thought they were different. What I learned in Manchester is that it's turning into more of the same."

"Yes, we took our eyes off the ball."

"It's more than that. I could argue that the reporting here was nothing short of journalistic malpractice. I expected more from this group. Much more."

"We understand. It was something we are taking a hard look at. Changes are going to be made to hold ourselves to the standards we set. We want you to be a part of that."

"I appreciate the offer. I know you will be successful. There are a lot of good people working here. Unfortunately, too much has happened for me to be a part of it."

"You're talking about Austin? You know, I've known him for a long time. He's been a value to this group, but his actions regarding you, Tyler, and Olivia were inexcusable. We've talked it over. If you say the word, we'll fire him."

I lean back in my chair, speechless. They're siding with me over him. I never in my dreams would have expected that. Austin Christos helped build this place. Are they that willing to cast him aside?

"Tierra, we're serious about this. I hope this conversation demonstrates that. We want you here. Just name your price. Anything."

* * *

I wasn't back to my desk for ten seconds before Olivia and Tyler scream over to grill me for information. I stare at the boxes. This has become a much harder day than I thought it would be.

"What happened?" Olivia asks.

"They offered me the keys to the castle. Whatever I wanted."

"Damn."

"Wait, you're still packing," Tyler observes.

I smile weakly. It was a joyous moment when Olivia was released from the hospital following her run-in with the SOF. I refuse to call it an accident now. It's what makes this so painful.

"Ty, Olivia, can you give us a minute?" Austin says, reappearing from his office.

"Yeah," he says, walking away. Olivia doesn't say anything.

"What happened in there?"

"Bribery, mostly. They offered to double my salary."

"And you said no?" Austin asks.

"They offered to get rid of you, too," I say, with more hostility in my tone than intended.

"That's because I was wrong."

"It's because you were a jackass. Don't worry, I said no to that as well."

"Why?"

"What good will it do? Whether I stay or go, whether you stay or go, the team is divided. There are no winners and losers here. Everyone loses. It will never be the same, so why try to fight it?"

"I don't agree, Tierra. It's not a lost cause. You should stay. We can help rebuild this together."

"That ship has sailed," I say, putting a lid on one of the boxes.

"Is there anything that I can do to change your mind?"

"Find the DeLorean from *Back to the Future*, go back in time a few months, and not be an asshole."

"I deserved that."

"Let me ask you a question, Austin. I mean, since we're sharing. What did I ever do to deserve that treatment?"

"I've spent the last two weeks asking myself that. It all came back to one thing: you were always drawn to television over written journalism. I knew that when I showed up at Josh's apartment to recruit you. I knew you would eventually leave the team. I didn't think it would be so soon."

"And you responded by pushing me away?"

"I…It was a defense mechanism. I thought it would be easier to lose you if we weren't on good terms."

It's a crazy admission, but an honest one. Austin is wearing it on his face. I thought knowing why he was so horrible to me would help the feeling of betrayal heal. It isn't going to.

"That's stupid," I say.

"I know. At least I know it now."

"You know what, your behavior isn't even the most disturbing part about this. You sold out, Austin. You followed the rest of the media down the same wrong path as if you were being led by the Pied Piper. You didn't ask questions or explore alternatives. You did everything you swore never to."

"I know."

My God, it's like talking to a bookcase. "You know. Great. Was that because of me, or is that the new standard operating procedure around here?"

"Tierra, I've made a hundred mistakes in the past few months. If I could take them all back, I would. Unfortunately, I can't. All I can do is apologize and hope you accept it."

I close the second box and stack it on the first. "I accept it. Good luck to you, Austin. I'm sure I'll see you around."

Tyler makes the "I'll call you" gesture with his hand, and I nod at him and Olivia. I feel bad that they are on their own here, but they could always apply at *Capitol Beat*. I'm sure they would get hired in a heartbeat.

I take the elevator down to the lobby and turn over my identification badge to the girl at the front desk. When I walk out the doors, I leave *Front Burner*. It should have a feeling of finality to it. It doesn't. As I make my way down the sidewalk under the gray Washington sky, I think that this isn't the last time I'll be here.

EPILOGUE

ANDREW LI

The National Mall
Washington, D.C

Andrew sits on a bench along the path running parallel to the Washington Monument reflecting pool, feeling like he's in a political thriller novel. Tourists meander by on their way to the Lincoln Memorial, oblivious to him or how he is about to one day change all their futures.

The man who sits down on the bench next to him is almost caricaturist in his appearance. He looks like a D.C. souvenir shop threw up all over him. Andrew shakes his head as he turns his attention back to the view.

"You went full tourist."

"It helps me blend in," Robespierre says, staring straight ahead. "You don't like it?"

"All you need is a class of eighth-graders to tour around with you to complete the image."

"Who says I don't have one? Where do we stand? Tell me some good news."

"I'm in."

Robespierre chuckles. "You did that the hard way. You could have just waited for Burgess's campaign to collapse or for the establishment Democrats to sabotage him. Instead, you almost handed him a win. That would have been an unmitigated disaster."

"But he didn't win. If I followed your advice, there would be no guarantee that Standish would have hired me. Even if she did, it wouldn't be as her top political advisor. Besides, we learned a lot. We're going to need to apply those lessons moving forward to be successful."

"By 'lessons,' I assume you mean staying away from Victoria Larsen and destroying Tierra Campos."

"Amongst others, yes."

Andrew doesn't bother elaborating. There will be plenty of time for that later. Instead, he continues to enjoy the serenity and bask in the glow of a job well done in New Hampshire. He won't get to enjoy another break like this for a long time.

"It was risky to blame Isiah."

"I had no choice. I knew the feds had linked the SOF to the campaign when I saw the FBI at the *Capitol Beat* interview. I had to act fast."

Andrew didn't plan it that way. He thought that the authorities would uncover the truth organically, but the FBI was slow on the uptake. He counted on the takedown of

Marx and his SOF team days before it occurred. Unfortunately, the feds were so busy trying not to be controversial that they almost caused the whole plan to backfire spectacularly.

Andrew had assumed that it did on the drive to the interview. He needed a patsy after realizing that they had put most of the pieces together. It was always a backup plan, but he didn't expect to need to execute it with Isiah and his father sitting right next to him. Switching the phones was the only part he needed to play. To his surprise and relief, Tierra Campos did the rest.

"Still, on national television?" Robespierre asks, clearly displeased with how that played out.

"Tierra Campos had all the facts. It was impressive that a journalist learned as much as she did in such a brief time when the feds couldn't."

"It must be why Marx tried taking her off the board."

"She's a phenomenal investigator. He must have gotten spooked."

Marx and his team executed his plan to perfection up to that point. He didn't expect the intimidations and arsons to baffle the authorities like they did. These guys were staff pukes in the Army while stationed in Europe. The SOF, as they came to call themselves, weren't Special Forces. They were toy soldiers playing a game that he didn't expect them to have the skills to finish. It's like a *Call of Duty* player seeing real combat. They are vastly different experiences.

Andrew expected them to be sloppy, but they weren't. If they hadn't targeted Wilson Newman and Tierra's *Front Burner* colleague, they probably wouldn't have gotten caught. Instead, he is sitting here while the son of a sitting governor is in a prison cell and taking the blame for the biggest ruse in American political history. The empowering part is that nobody will ever learn the truth.

"What about Isiah? He didn't admit to being Machiavelli during the interview. He only asked for a lawyer because he knew he was being framed. Someone is going to figure that out."

"Are your people in place and ready?" Andrew asks, changing the subject.

"There are a few more pieces to move, but we will be."

"Timing is everything. You've had months to prepare, and the election is only eight months away. Don't screw me now."

"Everything will be ready," Robespierre says, confidently.

"What's next?"

"I go to South Carolina with Standish for the primary. You start the second phase. We both hope that Rasputin does his part and is ready for November."

Andrew gets up and adjusts his coat. Robespierre, in charge of the most critical aspect of this operation, remains seated. He's content to enjoy the view before the sun sets entirely.

"What happens when Isiah starts fighting back? All our asses are on the line. He could ruin everything."

"You do your part. Let me worry about Isiah Burgess. 'The lion cannot protect himself from traps, and the fox cannot defend himself from wolves. One must, therefore, be a fox to recognize traps, and a lion to frighten wolves.'"

"That's cryptic, even for you. Who said it?" the man asks.

Andrew smiles sheepishly. "Machiavelli."

ACKNOWLEDGMENTS

This has been…a year. There is little doubt people will have many nice things to say about 2020 when the final page is written. I am not going to whine about all the lousy things that have happened this year, but I will focus on the good. *Justifiable Deceit* has received multiple awards. It has been great bringing characters like Tierra and Victoria to the world, and I look forward to continuing their journey for the foreseeable future.

This has also been a year of change for me and my wife, Michele, on a personal level. She lost a lot of people close to her in the first half of a year that was already stressful. Through it all, she has shown incredible grit and determination, much like the main characters of this series. Through it all, she has remained steadfast in her support of me, even through this turbulent year.

To my mother Nancy, and my sister Kristina, my brother-in-law Ken, and my nephew Gibson, who can now be found lugging around the three-foot Tyrannosaurus Rex I gave him: your support will always be more appreciated than I could express.

Thank you to Derek Murphy at Creativindie for his insights on the novel during the editing process. I especially appreciate Michael Waitz at Sticks and Stones Editing for a final polish.

JD&J did another fantastic job on this cover. I had only a rudimentary idea of what to do with it and they created something amazing. I couldn't be more thrilled at the job they did.

I shuffled my final thank-you down to the bottom, not out of lack of appreciation, but because it's the final thought I want to leave you with. There are a lot of choices to read. There are a lot of entertainment choices outside of reading. I am honored and humbled that my readers pick up my books. Thank you so much and I hope I can continue to tell you stories for years to come.

ABOUT THE AUTHOR

Mikael Carlson is the award-winning author of *The iCandidate* and the Michael Bennit Series of political dramas. *Devious Measures* is his eleventh novel and the second book in the Tierra Campos series, following the award-winning lead book *Justifiable Deceit.* He is also the author of the political thriller *The Eyes of Others,* among other works.

A retired veteran of the Rhode Island Army National Guard and United States Army paratrooper, he deployed twice in support of military operations during the Global War on Terror. Mikael has served in the field artillery, infantry, and in support of special operations units during his career on active duty at Fort Bragg and in the Army National Guard.

He conducted over fifty airborne operations following the completion of jump school at Fort Benning in 1998. Since then, he has trained with the militaries of countless foreign nations.

Academically, Mikael has earned a Master of Arts in American History and graduated with a B.S. in International Business from Marist College in 1996.

He was raised in New Milford, Connecticut and currently lives in nearby Danbury.